Captain Sedition

book 1

The Death of the Age of Reason

a novel by

K. C. Fusaro

This is a work of fiction. The characters and events portrayed are fictitious, or in the case of historical figures and events, are used fictitiously. Any similarity to real people, living or dead, is unintended by the author.

for Joan, my love

"… the people are entitled to life, liberty, and the means of sustenance, by the Grace of God and without leave of the King."

1774 Declaration by the Worcester County Committee of Correspondence.

Sound familiar?

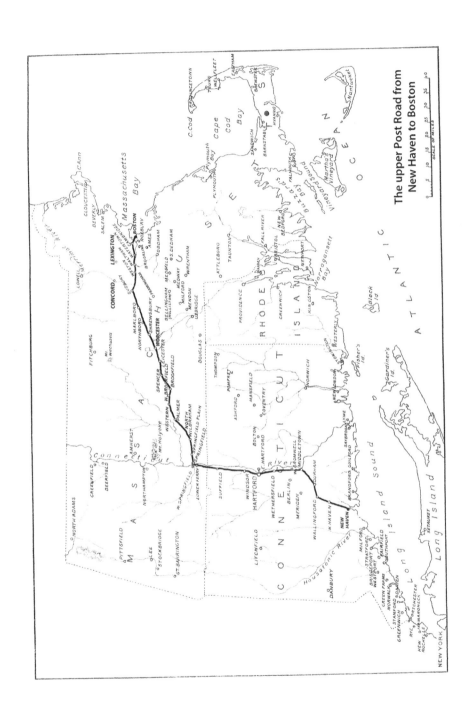

The upper Post Road from
New Haven to Boston

SCALE OF MILES
0   5   10   15   20   25   30   40

1

April, 1774. Marylebone dueling ground, West London.

The Fool wanted to take a blade. It was the only explanation. He'd already been pinked once, a skillfully measured thrust that drew blood but caused no serious hurt. Honor had been satisfied, but the fool refused to quit. If he had any sense he would concede, and thank whatever God he prayed to that his rival had sworn not to hurt him.

Twice.

Once to The Doctor. Once to the woman.

It was her fault.

Everyone thought the duel was over stolen letters of an embarrassing political nature but they were wrong. It was about the woman. She was there watching of course. Lydia Grieves was hardly the type to sit home quietly while two men fought over her. By her own admission it was a scene too precious to resist.

Joethan Wolfe—the fool's adversary—was the least surprised man in England when she came barreling down the road in a hired carriage just as the affair commenced.

After consulting the Fool's Second, Wolfe's Second, a man he knew only superficially but who'd been present when the fool issued his challenge, reported, "Lord Reddy will not cry off. You'll have to gut the little snot." He produced a flask from his purple coat and proffered it.

Wolfe was grateful for the wet. When he handed the flask back, he said, "Young Lord Reddy is about to discover that there is a limit to my patience."

Determined to end the farce, he strode to the mark etched in the dirt and waited for young Lord Reddy to finish guzzling from a bottle. It was a cold morning, but not that cold.

Young Lord Reddy.

The boy was how Wolfe thought of him. Twenty-two years old, Reginald Reddy was five years younger and three inches shorter than Wolfe's six feet. Pampered son of a rich lord, Reddy was no swordsman but he did have dreamy eyes and wavy blond hair that some women admired, and a title and future holdings that all women admired.

But he'd been mad to challenge a grown man to a duel, especially when the choice of weapon was the challenged party's prerogative, and particularly when that party had a well-deserved reputation with a blade. But Reddy had seen fit to demand satisfaction, so here they were.

As Wolfe waited, Lydia absented her carriage and walked to the dueling ground, a scandalous breach of acceptable behavior. But that was lovely Lydia. She wore her disdain for accepted behavior like an ermine cloak. It was one of her many charms but also the cause of much damage to her reputation.

Wolfe moved to urge her back to the carriage but she stopped him with a shake of her head. Instead she went to Reddy and drew him aside. After speaking with the boy, she turned to Wolfe with a disappointed shrug that said, *I tried but he will not listen.*

At least Reddy had sense enough to be frightened when he stepped back to the mark. Wolfe could see it in his eyes. That he wouldn't quit spoke well of his courage, but Wolfe could not admire it. The arrogant shit was set on bloodshed which meant the blood would be on Wolfe's hands.

So be it.

The duel resumed with a clash of steel and as before, Reddy's blade was swept aside in seconds. With Wolfe's blade pressed firmly against his right breast, the young lord backed up—eyes bulging, gulping air like a beached fish—until a small tree stopped him.

"Cry satisfaction now," Wolfe growled.

2

"Joethan, no!" Lydia screamed. Wolfe whipped his head around in alarm, and then pain exploded in his brain.

"How's that for satisfaction?!" Reddy sneered. Wolfe looked down in disbelief at a dagger buried in his side. Against all rules duello, Reddy had stabbed him with a knife. Wolfe noted that the handle of the weapon was finely worked bone, until the cold steel burning red hot inside of him overwhelmed all reason.

He summoned his rapidly waning strength to kill the boy and wipe the smirk off his face, but Reddy jabbed the knife in again and Wolfe's sword was suddenly . . . ponderously . . . heavy.

He puddled like a spent candle.

Reddy stood over him triumphantly as the bystanders converged. Through a rapidly growing haze, Wolfe saw Lydia. He tried to smile up at her through the ocean of pain washing over him, but she wasn't looking. She was fussing over Reddy, ascertaining that he wasn't harmed.

The awful and shocking truth hurt more than the gushing wound in Wolfe's side. *She used me to have the boy*, he thought. *I'm the fool.*

Bloody hell.

2

June 1774. Craven Street near Charing Cross, London

The neat and precise handwriting of the letter in Wolfe's hand, swam before his eyes. Whether it was due to pain, his constant companion, or overpowering despair, he could not say. He shut his eyes and let the letter flutter to the floor.

He hated himself for his despair. Hated himself for moping. Hated himself for hoping. But most of all he hated himself for being a strumpet's tool. Months on and Lydia had never once inquired after his health. He didn't even want the jilt back. What he wanted was the satisfaction of telling her so.

At least that's what he told himself.

And he never stopped wondering if she'd given Reddy the knife and plotted the scream to distract him.

He shifted uneasily in his chair and embraced the darkness in his heart, not for the first time dwelling on events that almost killed him. He was thirty pounds lighter now although he'd started eating solid food again. It turned out that infectious humors were more dangerous than being stabbed. More debilitating in any event. The smell of wound salving vinegar and turpentine had been his eau de cologne for months.

The downstairs door opening and closing disrupted his lassitude. The slow but steady tread climbing the stairs could only be The Doctor.

"Joethan," Benjamin Franklin boomed as he came through the door. The great man was past his sixty-eighth birthday and in spite of a paunch, he still boasted the robust physique of a dedicated swimmer. In his blue suit of finest worsted, The Doctor's vibrant presence was in no way diminished by gray hair that scraggled to his shoulders or spectacles perched on the bridge of his nose.

"You should have joined us at the Grecian," he said.

"Doctor Hewson doesn't want me to tax myself," Wolfe said.

"What does he know?" Franklin snorted facetiously.

Matching The Doctor's flippancy, Wolfe said, "What does the real doctor know?" When Franklin didn't rise to the bait, Wolfe pressed, "Will you deny that your title is but honorary?"

"You must be getting better," Franklin said patiently. "You're nearly your nasty old self. Speaking of, where is the real doctor?"

Wolfe threw a hand toward the back of the house. "Dissecting a body in the garden shed to the delight of the ghouls he calls students."

"Ghouls they may be," said Franklin, "but their practice saved your life. Do you imagine Hewson could have sewn your innards together elsewise?"

"I sometimes wish he hadn't," Wolfe said.

"As do I," The Doctor agreed, but his gray eyes twinkled.

Franklin's slave, Peter, stepped into the room to sullenly pronounce that supper would be served on the hour. When he departed, Franklin said, "What's got his rump in a churn?"

"Being enslaved is my guess," Wolfe said sourly. He was in the mood to resurrect their longstanding argument. Franklin wasn't. He ignored Wolfe's gauntlet and picked up the discarded letter instead. He would have read it but Wolfe plucked it from his hand.

"My father's been taken up for smuggling."

"That's bad luck," The Doctor said.

"Bad luck is what he's known for."

"How much trouble is he in?"

"An old friend insists I come at once. As if I would if even I could."

"You would not help your father if you could?" The incredulity in The Doctor's voice made it clear that he thought such an attitude base. Wolfe

5

wondered if it was because The Doctor had such a poor relationship with his father, or because he had such a poor relationship with his son.

"Race across the ocean to aid the man who sent me away against my will?" Wolfe said. "I think not."

"But if he's in trouble …" The Doctor blustered. Wolfe cut him off.

"'Tis undoubtedly of his own making." Wolfe had little patience when it came to his father, or the memory of him. "For all I know that note is nothing more than a scheme to get me back to America."

"Would that be so terrible?" Franklin said. Wolfe left the question unanswered.

At table that night, The Doctor was uncharacteristically quiet. Middle-aged, statuesque, and proper, Margaret Stevenson, in whose home Franklin and Wolfe resided, asked, "Is something the matter, Benjamin?"

"I'm but preoccupied," The Doctor said, wiping his mouth with great exactitude. Mrs. Stevenson waited for him to elaborate but he didn't. She looked to Wolfe for an explanation but he was as uninformed as she.

Franklin tapped Wolfe lightly on the wrist. "We have a matter to discuss, you and I."

"As you wish," Wolfe said.

Mrs. Stevenson desperately wanted to know what was going on, but The Doctor said, "This is a private matter between Joethan and myself, Margaret." Margaret's eyes bugged in hurt and curiosity but The Doctor wouldn't give over.

After supping, Wolfe followed Franklin to his study on the second floor. By the light of two nub candles, The Doctor ensconced himself behind his little writing desk and gestured for Wolfe to take his usual seat across from him. When Wolfe settled, The Doctor studied him with intelligent gray eyes that missed nothing.

Despite his emaciated appearance, Wolfe's shoulders were still broad, and his striking green eyes were yet those of the cavalier he'd been before the duel. While not, as you might say, handsome, despite the gauntness of his face there was still tenacity in the square chin with the shallow cleft, and toughness in the sturdy nose that had been broken more than once but not disfigured.

The Doctor cleared his throat and said, "I'm quite distressed by your reaction to the letter about your father, Joethan." His statement took Wolfe full aback.

"Why?"

"Because I believe 'tis my fault," said The Doctor. Wolfe was confused.

"My father being arrested is your fault?" The Doctor waved him off impatiently.

"Not that. Your willingness to consign him to his fate with no thought of rendering assistance." Wolfe's confusion was replaced by annoyance.

"I haven't seen the man in fourteen years. Why should I give a bloody damn about him?" The Doctor tapped a sheaf of papers on the desk in front of him.

"These are letters from your father to me. We've been writing back and forth for some years now." Wolfe was too surprised to do more than glare. Unable to meet his gaze, Franklin took off his glasses and rubbed his eyes wearily. "Shortly after you took residence here, I wrote your father to say you were alive and with prospects." Wolfe's green eyes flashed, a sure sign that his ire was growing.

"Why am I just learning this?"

"Because your father desired me not tell you. And I was happy to comply." Franklin sat back in his chair. "You're a womanizing bravo who cares little for his fellow man, Joethan, but I should be bereft were you not here. 'T'would be like losing my William all over again." Tears gathered in The Doctor's eyes. His estrangement from his son William, the great light of his life, always affected him deeply.

When his emotion passed, he said, "Your papa needs your help. As he has oft expressed a desire to see you again, I think perhaps the time is nigh."

Wolfe didn't know what to say. Or think. For eight years, Doctor Franklin had been as a father to him. His best friend. A mentor. It was unlikely Wolfe would refuse him anything within his power to grant. But this? Now? Impossible.

"Even if I wanted to help," Wolfe said, "I can barely walk a block without I'm flagging."

"You must get better," The Doctor said. "And soon."

"Just like that?"

"Just like that. If you will not help your father for his sake, do it in memory of your mother. I have no doubt but it would break Emeline's heart to know her son turned his back on her husband." Wolfe scowled at The Doctor with true malice. Using his mother as a lever was particularly low, even for The Doctor, who could be ruthless in pursuit of an agenda.

"If you will not act for the sake of your family," Franklin said, "I would you do it for me. I've never before begged a favor of you." Wolfe's malice was replaced by disbelief.

"You perjure yourself sir, as well you know," he said indignantly. In response, The Doctor assumed the sad and pathetic countenance of a feeble old man, a stratagem he employed to manipulate people. Usually it worked, but Wolfe knew The Doctor far too well to fall for it.

But The Doctor knew that Wolfe was wise to the ploy and played the card anyway. Which meant what? The Doctor said or did nothing were it not to some end.

"May I read the letters?" Wolfe said.

With exaggerated punctiliousness, Franklin squared the stacked letters and pushed the lot across the desk.

3

The first letter from his father to Franklin was dated more than a year after Wolfe moved in with The Doctor, almost twelve years after Wolfe last wrote to his father. In the intervening time, Wolfe's uncle—his mother's brother, who Wolfe had been sent to live with in England—had written his father to inform him that; Wolfe was kicked out of college, kicked out of his uncle's house, was an incorrigible scoundrel, and would undoubtedly hang. Wolfe knew this because his father talked about it in his first letter to Franklin.

What wasn't mentioned were the mitigating circumstances of Wolfe's behavior; the tyranny and scorn heaped upon him at his uncle's house. The battles forced upon him at college where, as the lone American among snobbish Britons, he'd been the target of relentless bullying.

His father—Pap—responded to Franklin's first letter by saying he was pleased to learn that his son was alive and had come under the influence of such a personage as the great Benjamin Franklin. He also professed great sorrow over the way things shook out with his son, but it was his wife's dying request to send their boy to relations in England, where he might become a proper gentleman. Pap could not go against his wife's dying wish.

Other than burying his wife, Pap wrote, sending his son away was the hardest thing he'd ever done, although not as hard as might have been. The constant threat of being arrested for smuggling, with the possibility of his son being sold into indenture as a consequence, weighed heavily in his decision. The letter closed by asking The Doctor to keep their correspondence secret.

If Joethan were to come home, Pap wanted it to be of his own volition.

A post scriptum referred to a bank draft accompanying the letter; money to pay Wolfe's way if ever he decided to return to America.

That his father sent money was surprising. Wolfe couldn't recall Pap ever having money to give away. Yet it was the conspiracy between The Doctor and his father that humbled him. The correspondence between the men—one or two letters a year for almost seven years—evolved from stiff formality to relaxed amiability.

The main topic of their letters, other than Wolfe, was the political issues affecting the American colonies. It was the type of correspondence Wolfe routinely couriered all over Europe for eminent men, especially The Doctor. The idea that Benjamin Franklin was sharing thoughts with his father, the way he shared thoughts with Kant, Burke and Priestly, was profoundly impressive to Wolfe.

Along the way, The Doctor reported to Pap that Wolfe had no interest in political affairs, which was a matter of great disappointment to both of them. Together they shared a hope that one day Wolfe would spurn London's frivolous amusements and take an interest in the serious events unfolding in America.

Wolfe read and reread letters into the night, and then he lay awake and listened to his brain roil in confusion. Benjamin Franklin was concurrently the most selfish and the most generous man Wolfe had ever known. He loved him as well as ever he'd loved his father—who, it turned out, cared more about his son than ever Wolfe credited.

The next morning, for the first time since the duel, Wolfe was compelled to raid the pantry, his old routine. He was gingerly going about enjoying his plunder when Mrs. Stevenson came in and gasped, "What's happened? You look ghastly." Wolfe chuckled at her concern.

"I slept poorly is all."

"Because of The Doctor?"

"Could there be another reason for a sleepless night in this house?" Wolfe was pleased with his mot but Mrs. Stevenson didn't laugh. She had no sense of humor when it came to The Doctor. She considered Benjamin Franklin's care her responsibility to the world, and treated it as such.

"Whatever is the matter Joethan?" She sat down next to him.

If her concern was anything but genuine, Wolfe would have refused her. Instead he told her what transpired the evening before. He finished by saying, "I have a decision to make."

"You can barely walk. Don't let that old man bully you," she said.

"Do I ever?" Wolfe grinned.

"He bullied you into not hurting the scoundrel who stabbed you," Mrs. Stevenson said grimly. Wolfe's grin disappeared.

"Too true. And I'll admit to being a trifle at sea over what to do." Yet even as he spoke his indecision, he knew it to be untrue. In his heart he'd already decided what must be done, and it wasn't for The Doctor or his father. A man had to live with himself.

Despite his humble origins, or perhaps because of them, Wolfe had a devotion to the idea of personal honor that, according to The Doctor, was beyond what could be considered normal. Or healthy. Abnormal and unhealthy or not, Wolfe would follow the honorable course as he saw it; not the wisest, nor the most practical, nor even the most advantageous.

By Wolfe's reckoning, a son had a duty to his parents. Besides which, if a man did the wrong thing for the right reason, did that make him a bad man? Wolfe had fallen asleep pondering that question and while he had no answer, he'd never been comfortable hating his father. Maybe all he needed was an excuse not to.

He confirmed his intention to himself at the same time he informed Mrs. Stevenson. "I'm for America to do my duty." The information drew a gasp from her.

"Not you too." She withdrew a lace handkerchief from her bodice and dabbed at suddenly watery blue eyes. "This very morning The Doctor said he shall leave England next spring. I shan't see either of you again."

"You'll see me," said Wolfe. "London is my home."

That day he shuffled two blocks to Balin's stable. The essence of horses was tonic to him, but to his dismay, it took a second look to find his sorrel gelding among the half-dozen horses in the paddock. Ordinarily Gascon caught your eye at once due to a noble bearing and intelligent energy. To see him fat and listless enough to blend in with livery stock was heartbreaking.

Five years earlier, Gascon had cost Wolfe every coin in his purse. As Wolfe had been executing various commissions across the continent at the time, every coin in his purse was a considerable sum.

When he finally returned to England, The Doctor excoriated him for being simple enough to squander so much money on a horse—the story of *Jack Spriggins and the Enchanted Bean* being paraphrased liberally and often—but Wolfe never once regretted his decision.

In addition to a naturally even disposition, Gascon was happy to run all day and was not put off his feed by irregular routine, a priceless attribute for a professional courier's transportation. Friends and lovers might be fair-weather, but never his charger.

It was a difficult reunion. Gascon was excited to see him but exceedingly angry with him too—happy but standoffish—until he started sniffing around the wound in Wolfe's side. Perhaps he was drawn to the odor of turpentine and vinegar, but after gently licking at the wound through Wolfe's shirt, Gascon leaned his white splashed muzzle on Wolfe's shoulder in compassion and forgiveness. The gesture did more to restore Wolfe's spirits than all the physic in the world.

Too weak to do much more, Wolfe gave his word to Gascon—and himself—that he would no longer indulge his gloom and bitterness.

When he sat for tea with The Doctor that afternoon, the first thing he said was, "Whom do I need see to obtain a pardon?" The Doctor hid a satisfied smile by devouring a biscuit.

"The question more accurately is, which of His Majesty's ministers be out of funds? You're aware that a pardon will require a considerable purse?" Wolfe nodded.

"As I've oft heard you say, in for a penny, in for a pound. I've braced myself for a gouge but I know of no other way to insure success. Would you not agree?" The Doctor brushed crumbs from his clothes.

"T'would cost less to bribe whom you must in America, but on the whole, I believe your reasoning to be sound."

Wolfe set about recovering his health the next day. Jostling through crowds teeming along the Strand around the vendor's stalls, he was all too aware of his sewn together innards, but he persevered. In a week his daily walk expanded from the Strand down to the Thames and back, and then he did a circuit of both and eventually, another circuit late in the day.

A month on he started to feel more like himself, although the same could not be said of his appearance. His color remained sallow and the circles under his eyes remained dark. He gained back ten pounds before his color started to improve.

A friend long before Wolfe was a patient, Dr. William Hewson—the real doctor—was married to Mrs. Stevenson's daughter Polly, a great favorite of Dr. Franklin's. Many were the times that Hewson, Polly and Wolfe cut up together in company with Polly's mother and The Doctor.

After poking and prodding around the declivity in Wolfe's side, Hewson pronounced his friend fit to start bathing again. The patient was also cleared to resume activities he'd partaken of prior to injury, as long as they didn't include the consumption of alcohol or strenuous physical exertion. To Wolfe's thinking, the latter did not include riding a horse.

That afternoon, Wolfe reveled in a long, hot bath. Mrs. Stevenson's servant woman, Anne, had given him bed baths during his convalescence, but it wasn't the same as having a soak.

When Wolfe was gloriously clean for the first time in months, he took himself off to Balin's and saddled Gascon. As per Dr. Hewson's instructions, he took it easy … for the first few minutes. After that, he and Gascon set about resuming their partnership.

4

"Henry Belasyse, second Earl of Fauconberg, recently ascended to the House of Lords upon the death of his father."

"He's agreed to obtain a pardon?"

"Agreed to receive an offer," The Doctor corrected. "I fear to tell you though; the negotiation starts at three-hundred." Wolfe's stomach sank. Three-hundred pounds represented much of his savings.

"Is there no one else?" Wolfe said. The Doctor shook his head.

"Fauconberg is the most affordable. New man in the club and all that. The alternative is to present a standard petition, although in the case of an American smuggler 'tis not apt to be granted. Your main chance is a sponsored petition by someone the Crown needs in its pocket. Fauconberg is such a man. Mind you, even should all go smooth, I'm told the process could take months."

"To hell with it then," Wolfe said. The Doctor's eyes narrowed.

"A pardon be the only sure way to see your father clear. But of course, the decision is yours. What would you have me tell the Earl?"

"Tell the grasping bastard to bugger himself," Wolfe said. He'd verbalized the choice he knew to be most antithetical to The Doctor's wishes and it produced the desired result. The Doctor nearly choked.

"I will not! I approached him! 'Tis my reputation you trifle with!"

"I knew it!" Wolfe said. "There is no decision to take. You've already struck a deal!" The Doctor shook his finger.

"There is only one sensible course. I presumed you'd take it."

"For three hundred bloody pounds!"

"The purse will work itself out."

"How?"

"I couldn't yet say."

"Then clearly you cannot be sure the purse will work itself out," Wolfe said. The Doctor glared.

"I may be in disgrace with government, Joethan, but I'll thank you to remember I'm still Benjamin Franklin."

The bribe was made and accepted, and then Lord Fauconberg decided a pardon worth three-hundred was surely worth four-hundred. Wolfe's green eyes burned when The Doctor informed him, and again when he handed The Doctor a bank draft for the additional hundred pounds. "Tell that thief to leave the name on the pardon blank," Wolfe said. "'Tis the least he can do for four-hundred bloody pounds."

"Blank?" The Doctor said.

"I have my reasons." But Wolfe didn't say what they were. The resentment he felt—using most of eight years savings to aid his father—was best kept to himself.

Despite the extortion added to the bribe, summer wore on with no sign of the promised document. The King had decamped to the country and his return was dependent on the weather, or so it was said.

As August waned, Wolfe had a fire in his belly to be off. His father's case in all likelihood had already been decided. It didn't take the law degree Wolfe never earned to know that executing a pardon, *posteriori*, would be more difficult than doing it *a priori*.

It was two weeks into September before The Doctor finally handed him a roll of vellum tied with a ferret. Pardon in hand at last, Wolfe let it be known, in the unofficial haunts of government, that he was actively seeking commissions for the American Colonies.

A few days later he received a summons from Lord Dartmouth, one of the most powerful men in government and a regular client prior to Wolfe's injury. That Dartmouth sent for him did much for Wolfe's spirits. He'd feared that the scandal of the duel might drive away his well-heeled clients. A commission from Dartmouth would put an end to that. As the great lords did, so the lesser followed.

William Legge, the Earl of Dartmouth, had a relaxed and friendly visage that belied his great responsibility administering American colonial affairs for the King. In his forties, the Earl of Dartmouth struck one as being tall and soft, and certainly he was physically soft, but he was not a soft man, or sentimental, or forgiving; his evangelical faith saw to that. Everything else was covered by the Earl's steadfast belief in his superiority as a British Peer and an Englishman.

Dartmouth welcomed Wolfe personally into the plush trappings of his private chambers. "I'm happy I see you well," he said, his voice mellifluous and refined, just the right timbre. "I was told you wouldn't live out the spring."

"I'm happy to prove your informants wrong," Wolfe said.

"They shall hear of their error," Dartmouth quipped, only half joking. "I heard Reddy did himself no honor in the affair."

"I spared him twice before he knifed me," Wolfe said. "I intend to seek him out and kill him when I return from my trip."

"And no man will blame you," Dartmouth said. He gestured for Wolfe to take a seat. "At all events, I'm pleased I find you well. You're off to America?"

"I've had word my father is in a bad way," Wolfe said.

"You return to us after?"

"Immediately if not sooner."

"Good. Your services have been missed." Dartmouth sat down. "Now to business. I have private correspondence for Boston. Will your journey accommodate me?" The question had Wolfe smiling broadly.

"With a commission from you milord, I'll be away as soon as I secure passage."

"Excellent," Dartmouth said. "I'll send word when my pages are ready. The matter of a few days, I should think." By the time the interview concluded, Wolfe had a commission that would pay more than his travel expenses, which was as much as a courier on personal business could desire.

The Doctor sweetened the pie a day later by adding a commission of his own, plus another ten pounds, being the amount Wolfe's father entrusted to him for Wolfe's passage home all those years ago.

The Doctor's prediction regarding funds having been somewhat realized, he felt empowered to impart traveling advice to the man who traveled for a living. But that was The Doctor. He always assumed he knew more than everyone else. Usually he did.

"Take your valuables with you," The Doctor said. Wolfe protested that he was returning to London directly upon completing his task, but The Doctor was adamant. "Leave nothing you care about behind."

Wolfe was headstrong and sure that he possessed a superior intellect, but not to the point of dismissing a recommendation from Poor Richard himself, although he was unable to follow The Doctor's advice explicitly. He would be leaving his most prized possession in England.

Reckoning that pasture would see Gascon healthier and happier than Balin's stable, Wolfe boarded the big sorrel at the country estate of a minor peer he occasionally couriered for. It was a bittersweet parting. Wolfe knew he was coming back. Gascon didn't.

The next order of business was a visit to Wright & Gill's on Abchurch street. The stationer was one of Wolfe's favorite shops in London and a great source of additional income. London magazines turned a tidy profit out in the country and on the continent. Wolfe expected to make even more in America.

Mr. Gill, a fit man in his fifties, was a polished and reserved character in a fine white wig. He welcomed Wolfe as the old and valued customer that he was. Being a proper gentleman, Gill didn't ask why he hadn't seen Wolfe for months, a propriety Wolfe was grateful for.

As he toted up the price for multiple copies of *The Ladies Magazine*, *Town & Country Magazine*, *The London Magazine*, and *The Gentlemen's Magazine*, Gill said, "A long trip ahead of you, Mr. Wolfe?"

"I'm off to the colonies, if you can believe it."

"The colonies you say?"

"Boston to be my first port of call," Wolfe said. Gill paused his wrapping.

"I wonder would you mind to deliver a letter for me in Boston. I'm happy to pay."

"I'll accept no money to deliver a letter for you," Wolfe said. He departed with Gill's letter, and at the stationer's insistence, enough free oilskin to enclose all the communications he was to carry across the ocean.

Two days later he was back in Dartmouth's chambers to receive a packet sealed with red wax imprinted with the Earl's personal signet. As the Earl always did in case of mishap, he outlined the gist of his correspondence. "In the coming weeks," he told Wolfe, "Parliament will pass a bill to restrict the importation of arms and powder to the colonies. Governor-General Gage need take steps to secure the Crown's interests before the news is made public. To that end I'm also sending him a regiment of marines and three fourth rates. Have you any questions?"

"Is the information secret?" Wolfe said. The question elicited a chuckle from Dartmouth.

"You know there are no secrets in Whitehall. And you'll do well to remember that in the colonies. Any attachment to government makes you a target for the Boston mob. You needs be wary in that wretched place." Wolfe appreciated the warning but having carried delicate communications through some of the toughest cities in Europe, he wasn't too worried about politically unhappy Americans. Indeed the expectation of getting on with his life, even if it wasn't his own life he was getting on with, imbued him with an uncharacteristic optimism.

The interview concluded with Wolfe being handed a private letter for Governor-General Gage from his banker, a man Lord Dartmouth saw often at his club. A windfall to Wolfe's way of thinking. Good news from a banker was apt make a Governor-General generous.

At Craven Street, Wolfe was greeted with the happy surprise of a farewell dinner. Ostensibly thrown by The Doctor, the feast was in actuality executed by Mrs. Stevenson, her servant Anne, and Franklin's slave, Peter.

Wolfe was gratified that Dr. Hewson and Polly were in attendance. Any dinner that included meat, which The Doctor had long since renounced, was guaranteed to pique his ire. Formal dinners with The Doctor were always more enjoyable if Polly and her husband William were in attendance.

As usual, The Doctor's aggravation began with candles.

Ben Franklin was a frugal man, but when it came to candles, he was an absolute miser. No one really knew why, but anything fancier than a nub candle was sure to set off his thrifty instincts. Wolfe assumed it had something to do with The Doctor's father having been in the candle business, and The Doctor having had to work for him as a boy. Whatever the reason, when Mrs. Stevenson lit her silver candelabras, The Doctor was outraged.

"What can you be thinking, madam?!" he railed. "Your money is literally going up in smoke! You might as well set fire to bank notes as burn so many tapers!" Mrs. Stevenson was quite capable of ignoring The Doctor when it suited her, and it never suited her to compromise the appearance of her table, for anyone, even the great Ben Franklin—which only served to compound The Doctor's frustration.

And then it was time to eat.

As anxious as the unrestrained burning of candles made The Doctor, the presence of meat was worse.

The wonderful pheasant and beef that Mrs. Stevenson provided, at great expense, sparked a diatribe from The Doctor on gastronomic suicide. A diatribe that achieved epic levels of absurdity.

Hewson, Polly and Wolfe spent a delightful time roaring with laughter as The Doctor held forth, and then they egged each other on with their own commentary on what he was saying, half of which went over The Doctor's head, which aggravated him all the more.

Mrs. Stevenson occasionally glared at them but even she cracked when The Doctor began extolling the virtues of simple American roast potatoes, compared to the pretension and tyranny of English meat pies.

It was only afterward that the younger people discussed the possibility that Franklin meant to entertain them all along. One could never be sure. He was a deep cove, was The Doctor.

That night, Wolfe's farewell to William and Polly was no different than any other evening they shared together, the same with Mrs. Stevenson and Anne. Wolfe's trip to America might take longer than his usual jaunts to the continent, but he'd see them again soon enough. Saying farewell to The Doctor was an altogether different matter. It was unknown when or if they might see each other again.

Dr. Franklin and Wolfe shared a bottle of mineral water in The Doctor's rooms before retiring. The Doctor stated his intention of returning to America in the spring.

"I'll be on my way back to England by then," Wolfe said. "I'll wave as our ships pass." The Doctor smiled reflectively.

"I still expect great things of you Joethan."

"As long as you don't measure my great things against your own," said Wolfe.

"That would hardly be fair," The Doctor conceded. "But a new day is coming and opportunities in America will abound. I urge you not to turn your back on them. I also urge you to keep your prick in your britches. America ain't London."

"You should know," Wolfe said, with a smile like a wink. The Doctor harrumphed.

"Which is why I warned you off that doxie Lydia,"

"You did," Wolfe agreed. "I only wish I'd listened to you about her and ignored my promise not to hurt Reddy." The Doctor's shoulders slumped a little and he sighed.

"I was quite wrong to ask that of you. I see that now and humbly beg your forgiveness." Wolfe's jaw dropped in amazement. The Doctor never apologized ... ever. Ignoring the astonishment on Wolfe's face, The Doctor said, "I trust we need never mention the incident again?" Choosing to interpret Wolfe's gob-smacked silence as assent, he changed the subject.

"I know you dislike to be told what to do, especially when it smacks of politics, but you must heed what I tell you now. Wherever you go in America, you must beware the public sensibility. The wrong word in the wrong place is a risk to your life."

"I remind you that I grew up in America," Wolfe said.

"You were a boy in America," The Doctor corrected him. "The things you need know as a man are unknown to a boy. Britons think Americans are unsophisticated yahoos. That ignorance is their vulnerability. Remember that Joethan. Do not underestimate your countrymen." He looked at Wolfe with great fondness. "I believe we'll meet again. I feel it in my bones which is the only reason I can bid you farewell without my heart breaking."

Wolfe hugged The Doctor goodbye with all the emotion he'd been unable to muster for his father so many years earlier.

5

As if to prove Lord Dartmouth's claim, that nothing was secret in Whitehall, the coming ban on American importation of arms and powder was common knowledge by the time Wolfe arrived in Portsmouth. He paid little attention however as a stroke of luck presented in the form of a ship readying to sail for Nova Scotia. Civilian ships bound for North America were scarce this late in the season, and here was the snow *Anna* completing stores.

It turned out that luck was a matter of perspective. Passage on *Anna* would mean cramming into a converted hold with dozens of Scottish emigrants, an abhorrent idea to a man who valued health and hygiene. Wolfe solved the dilemma by signing on as a deckhand. Working his passage saved money but more significantly, as a member of the crew he had a place away from passengers in the fo'c's'le forward.

He had no illusions about the voyage. The North Atlantic was a brutal environment any time of year, oddly however, after months of limited activity, he found the physical challenge of toiling as a deckhand enjoyable. The work was hard and the air was cold, but the cold was mitigated by the work, and the work made the days fly by. Wolfe had grown up on the water and was quite comfortable afloat, capable of far more than hauling sheets. He was a fully accepted member of the crew by the time the passengers started dying.

A snow might be the largest of two-masted ships, but a snow was not a large vessel. Dozens of children shitting and puking in the close proximity of a dank and fetid hold made the spread of sickness inevitable and not unexpected. The first dead child went over the side eight days out, which was not bad, according to Wolfe's shipmates. After the first child expired there were more burials at sea, and not all of them children.

The burly captain of the Anna, Johannes Ochs, had the taciturn confidence of a man who knew his trade well enough to eschew the usual route to Nova Scotia. To avoid the prevailing westerlies of the northern latitudes, the usual route to Canada from England went south to the Canary Islands. From there, taking advantage of the easterly trade winds, the route crossed the Atlantic to the West Indies where a ship could find the always reliable northern current and ride it up the coast of America.

Against usual custom, Ochs charted his course from England to Canada directly west. He claimed the route was viable only in autumn but might be worth two weeks travel if the ship was in luck.

The ship was in luck.

For five weeks Anna enjoyed a splendid crossing with winds out of the north and occasionally the east. And then Anna's luck ran out. Presaged by an ominous wall of black clouds, wind driven snow came howling out of the northeast. The wind steadily increased in ferocity until the hum in the rigging rose in pitch, not by notes, but by octaves, until the tempest was a shrieking demon.

For two days the wind tore white-capped tops off of monstrous gray seas and threw them in Anna's face. The game little ship bobbed, dodged, and shouldered aside the worst of the abuse, but the ill-treatment proved cumulative. On the second night of the storm in profound darkness, the main hatch disintegrated.

The community of Scots settlers below dissolved in panic and chaos as hundreds of gallons of angry, frigid ocean poured into the hold, and continued to pour in with each and every wave that swept Anna's deck. Brutalized by wind and water in the disorienting blackness, Wolfe and his mates fought desperately to fother a sail over the gaping hole into the bowels of the ship.

Wolfe had never been so sure of dying.

He pushed aside his terror, and along with the other sailors, fought the wind as it tried to catch the fothering sail and blow them overboard, if the raging water didn't wash them away first.

Against the odds they succeeded, but they lost three shipmates in the process. No one could say how. The men simply disappeared in the dark and were never seen again. But there was no time to mourn.

At first light, shorthanded and numb with cold, exhausted beyond endurance and not having eaten for fifteen hours, the crew labored to rig a more seaworthy hatch. Every other person was put to work manning pumps and bailing.

Toward mid-day when they were losing the fight and it seemed that no one could expend even one more ounce of energy, a caterwauling joined the shrieking wind and roaring ocean.

In defiance of wind and waves, a sodden and shriveled collection of wool tied himself to the mainmast and began piping for all he was worth. At first the ungovernable squealing was only one more dissonant thread in the cacophony of nature assaulting the ship. But the bellows warmed to their master's resolve and the bagpipes began to organize, to skirl above the relentless onslaught of elements and call the disheartened humans to arms, bleating at them to find the strength to carry on.

And the humans responded. They refused to concede to mother nature for another half of a day, fighting tooth and nail to keep *Anna* afloat. Eventually, mercifully, because even wind and wave have to rest, they gained the upper hand.

In the aftermath of the onslaught, the snow wallowed like a pig, but she swam, and the pumps continued to work. When rays of the sun—like heavenly fingers—finally pierced the shroud of gray sky enveloping the world, every heart dared hope they might yet make landfall.

At noon, Ochs managed to bring the sun to the horizon with his sextant and determine the ship's position for the first time in days. Miraculously, the math said they were hundreds of miles closer to Nova Scotia than before the storm.

Forty-eight days after leaving England, the blessed cry of "Land ho!" came hollering down from the mast head. Later, Cape Breton Island could be seen from the deck as a dark smudge on the horizon.

Anna worked her sluggish way west along the Nova Scotia coast accompanied by the earthy smells wafting from shore. On the fourth day, as the battered ship slipped past the lighthouse guarding the entrance to Halifax harbor, her human cargo lined the rails in barely contained excitement. They looked like cadavers as much as settlers but they'd made it. The achievement glowed on their faces like a visit from the virgin.

The western shore of the Halifax approach was a stunning series of dramatic cliffs crowned with vegetation. To the east were the gently rolling hills of Cornwallis Island. *Anna* swept between them and around Sandwich Point, opening up a view of Citadel Hill beyond. At the sight of an enormous Union Jack flying atop the hill, the crew spontaneously broke into cheers that were joined by the settlers.

Wolfe didn't cheer but the tension coiled inside him was replaced with a lightness he hadn't enjoyed since the storm hit. Hell, it was the second time in half a year that he'd almost died. He was starting to feel like the universe had it out for him.

One of his shipmates, a whip strong man named Alan, clapped him on the back and snorted, "We made it!" but as if he was surprised. Wolfe turned to him and laughed.

"*Anna's* a tough old girl. I knew she'd see us home."

"I'll agree *Anna's* a sturdy ship," Alan said. "But I don't believe you thought we'd make it. That's just the sound of a man lying."

"Yes it is," Wolfe said, smiling broadly.

There was a developed waterfront in Halifax but the density of civilization thinned inland as the terrain rose to the hilltop citadel—which sported a far more grandiose moniker than warranted. The flag flying over the citadel appeared larger than the little bastion.

Due to *Anna's* delicate condition, Ochs sailed past the town docks to bring the ship directly to the royal dockyard north of town for repairs. On his command of, "Let go!" Wolfe helped man the capstan and lower the best bower, his last official act as a member of the crew. His discharge was complete when he went ashore with the last boatload of settlers.

Weeks at sea had the ground pitching and rolling beneath his feet when he landed. His first steps were so wobbly that he laughed out loud. His amusement continued as he took stock of his surroundings.

The royal dockyard, home base of the British North American Squadron, was in a state of high confusion. The settlers were supposed to have disembarked in town. Their appearance at the dockyard was unexpected and overwhelming. The navy was doing their best to deal with the confusion but were ill equipped for the job.

Wolfe shouldered his portmantle, edged around the milling Scots and walked past the blockhouse to the gate. After passing through the fortified stone wall encircling the yard, he set a course for town via the shore road. At the direction of the first man he met, he sought lodgings at Pontack House, a massive three-story building on the waterfront.

By any measure, the Pontack was an impressive establishment. In addition to being the principal inn of the town, housed on the premises at the same time were bakers and butcher's stalls, a slaughterhouse, stables, a ballroom, a kitchen, and that was just the first floor. There was a courtyard in the middle of the place that served as a yard for vehicles, with a stage at one end for theatricals in the summertime.

He hired a comfortable room, took a meal, and slept like the dead all that night and the next day. At dusk the next day, he roused long enough to go downstairs and eat before going back up to sleep. The next morning after a long bath and leisurely breakfast, he went to see about selling some magazines and finding passage to Boston.

Both were surprisingly easy to accomplish. A stationer on the first floor of the Pontach was happy to pay top rate for every publication Wolfe was willing to sell. Wolfe kept a few back because the value of being able to produce a magazine at times was incalculable.

He also made a purchase. The stationer let it be known that he possessed a somewhat clandestine political tract that would undoubtedly be of interest to Bostonians. He wanted a dollar for it. Aware that hard currency was in short supply, Wolfe purchased the tract for shillings.

Finding transport to Boston was likewise as easy. Per the stationer's suggestion, an hour after entering the Crown and Anchor—a smelly waterfront bar—Wolfe secured a berth on the packet ship bound for Boston within a seven night.

He spent the rest of the afternoon listening to sailors disparage a manifesto recently put out by American radicals. British seamen had little patience for the eternal unhappiness of their American countrymen. While Wolfe was at sea, the Americans had really managed to rouse their ire.

In response to London legislation that Americans dubbed, *The Intolerable Acts*, meant to punish Boston for the tea incident, self-appointed representatives of the colonies came together and formed an Association. This *Continental Association* responded to the London legislation with a manifesto restricting the importation, exportation, and consumption of specified goods. A similar ban had put a swift end to the stamp tax ten years earlier. Still, Wolfe found it difficult to believe that a clause in the articles discontinuing the slave trade would ever be carried out, which of course cast every other article of restriction in doubt.

To Wolfe it was a pissing contest and he didn't care who won. By first candle he'd heard more political wrangling than ever he cared to, and returned to his room. There, for the most part, he remained until the packet set sail for Boston.

6

Under piercing blue skies on a brisk December forenoon in 1774—fifteenth year in the reign of His Most Glorious Majesty George III, King of Great Britain and Ireland—His Majesty's Packet *Halifax* fetched the Broad Sound to Boston Harbor on the flood tide. Making six knots under jib and topsail, she soon entered the inner road. With a pennant from the maintop and a gun to leeward, to call attention to the pennant, *Halifax* identified herself.

The object of the packet's communication was said to be the most powerful coastal fort in British America. Situated on the high bluffs of a small island in the channel, Castle William was a beast of stone blockhouse and barracks surrounded by ramparts of bristling cannon. Castle William commanded the entrance to Boston Harbor absolutely.

In response to *Halifax's* declaration, a pennant ran up the fort's flagpole and two thunderous signal guns belched, *permission to proceed*, the barest of formalities. The packet made the trip every three weeks or thereabout, and always with news and letters from home.

Wearing a seaman's wool cap and a double-caped greatcoat of midnight blue, Wolfe stood amidships. From four miles away, through his pocket perspective glass, a score of noble cupolas and spires signaled a substantial American town. Boston was over a hundred and fifty years old by now, and third largest in the colonies, but it was not a large town by European standards.

Occupying a peninsula running south to north, the seat of gravest troubles in British America sprawled over and around three hills which presently glistened under a sheen of new snow.

The tallest hill was crowned by a battery of cannon and a tall wooden mast with a beacon on top that gave the hill its name. At the north end of town, not far from a windmill, another battery was barely visible on the less formidable Copps Hill. Two more batteries could be seen at the southern end of town; one on the waterfront, the other at the top of a long hummock stretching inland from the water as part of the aptly named Fort Hill. Almost a year to the day after a cargo of tea was dumped in the harbor, Boston was an armed camp.

Closed by the Crown in retribution for the tea incident, the port of Boston was hauntingly empty. Nearer to hand a couple of firewood sloops rode high at anchor—empty and outward bound—waiting for wind and tide to shift. The most obvious vessels were two sixty-gun warships of the Royal Navy. Curiously, the two-decker flying an admiral's pennant was surrounded by scores of small open boats like goslings around their mother. Wolfe noted that there was a spring on the admiral's anchor cable. The flagship was prepared to quickly slew a thirty-gun broadside in any direction.

In addition to the big warships, there was a sloop of war and two frigates. Three transports were anchored closer to shore but their yards weren't crossed and they looked as if they hadn't seen the open sea in many a month. One of them flew a quarantine flag.

In fact, the harbor was eerily void of any traffic. No liberty boats or bum boats plied between the squadron and the town, nor was there any sign of the usual ship-to-ship visiting that took place in port. The only things moving in Boston Harbor were buff-bowed dories—locals fishing on the flood tide.

"A capital crossing, I do assure you," Captain-Lieutenant Nunn said, joining Wolfe. Shorter and older than his passenger, Nunn had changed into his best blue uniform instead of the moldy oilskins he'd worn at sea.

"Joy of our landfall," Wolfe said in greeting. He inflected his head ruefully at the empty harbor. "'Tis a might strange though."

"Aye," Nunn agreed. "The first time I saw Boston after embargo was like sailing into a ghost town. The men hate it still. Used to be Boston was a sporting town to rival Spithead. Now you'll be lucky to find a poxed molly willing to entertain a lonely sailorman."

Wolfe pointed at the boats clustered around the flagship. "I have never observed such a deployment as that."

"Those boats belong to the provincials," Nunn said. "Under the very eyes of Admiral Graves, they cannot bribe for use of them. Governor Gage ordered the embargo strictly enforced and so it is. Every ship you see is attached to Government. Even those fishing scows are hired to feed the army."

"The price of goods must be prodigious," Wolfe said.

"A cord of firewood is fifteen shillings," Nunn sniggered. At the shocked expression on Wolfe's face, he nodded that Wolfe had heard right. "Aye. 'Tis madness. But the insurgents prefer the cost high so I say let 'em freeze."

"Why would insurgents prefer high prices?" Wolfe said.

"Makes it easier to recruit," Nunn replied, as if there was no doubt. "When you succor a man's needy family, he's grateful forever. Never mind that them offering relief caused his woe at the first. Boston is the world turned upside down Mister Wolfe."

"Surely it can't be so bad as that," Wolfe said lightly. Nunn raised an eyebrow.

"I hope you'll believe me when I say, when you step ashore, the insurgents will make it their business to know who you are and why you're here." He gazed up at the telltales on the topsail. "Soon's we land I'll shove off for Province House. Hold yourself ready would you join me." Considering that perhaps Nunn wasn't exaggerating the danger in Boston, Wolfe took himself below.

His berth, created out of greasy hanging canvas, was barely large enough to accommodate a hammock and his portmantle. But he was grateful. He had walls and a flap door. Privacy was a luxury aboard a sixty-foot topsail schooner with a thirty-man crew.

He lit a lantern and opened his portmantle. His luggage was a studded, hide-bound wooden cylinder two feet long by sixteen inches in diameter, with leather handles on either end. Three straps with buckles kept it closed, but even when full it was no great weight for a man to carry. More importantly, the slightly arched profile allowed it to ride comfortably over a shoulder or behind a saddle.

An oilskin bag inside the portmantle produced a boxed brace of walnut pocket-pistols and their accouterments. From a small silver flask, Wolfe tapped a pinch of English fine-grain gunpowder into his palm and sniffed it. He also tasted it and rolled it delicately between his fingertips before he judged it reliable.

Loading the pistols was a careful ritual that Wolfe enjoyed. The balls—.56 caliber—with patches, were a tight fit in rifled barrels only five inches long. The powder loads needed to be precise. With precise loads, the well-balanced guns packed a powerful punch that was accurate and lethal up to ten yards. Wolfe set the throat-hole safeties and slipped the guns into pockets in his greatcoat designed to receive them.

Exchanging his wool cap for an expensive beaver-skin, cocked in the Denmark style, he slung a worn leather haversack over his shoulder and reappeared on deck as Halifax closed her destination.

Boston's Long Wharf jutted a third of a mile into Boston Harbor. Lined with warehouses on one side and partway along the other, the wharf could accommodate dozens of vessels, which made it more profound that there wasn't a single ship tied up anywhere. At the end of the wharf, a battery of nine-pounder cannon, manned by bored marines, testified to the way things stood.

Halifax's jib dropped almost before the order was given. With the helm put hard-over, her topsail backed perfectly and she rode the tide onto the wharf as pretty as you please. Marines were there to boom her off, sailors heaved lines, and with much good-natured banter back and forth, the schooner tied up.

Amid the organized chaos on deck, Wolfe took stock of the Boston waterfront. Beyond the bustle around the ship there was little sign of activity. Warehouses and chandleries appeared shuttered. Docks and boatyards were all but deserted.

Drums rattled to life across the water at the South Battery. In response, two companies of Royal Artillery Matrosses, in their distinctive red-plumed leather helms that looked more Roman than modern, poured out of a warehouse and formed up. When the drums changed cadence, the blue-coated artillerists marched off into the town. The drums were still echoing when Lieutenant Nunn and his burly coxswain, Harrison, led the way off the ship.

A strange sense of dislocation embraced Wolfe as he stepped onto American soil for the first time in fourteen years. America was the land of his birth, yet as foreign now as England had been once upon a time. The oddity of the empty wharf only added to the strangeness. Absent the usual cacophony of beasts and men, Long Wharf was unnervingly quiet. Even the gulls were muted.

Nearer the town, a smattering of off-duty Redcoats and Marines, in forage caps and campaign coats, shopped and wrangled at tables in front of two warehouses. The few civilians present were women mostly, soldier's brutes by the look of them. One civilian caught Wolfe's attention.

Loitering in a narrow alley between two warehouses, a middle-aged man in a mechanic's jacket scrutinized the party from *Halifax* closely as they passed. His eyes never wavered when Wolfe met his gaze.

And now they know I'm here, Wolfe thought.

At the shoreline the wharf became King Street, a cobbled thoroughfare lined with austere, two and three-story clapboard and brick houses, and businesses with signs nailed to the wall or swinging overhead. Wolfe's party moved from snow-slicked street onto shoveled brick sidewalk. Contrary to Nunn's warning, the civilians out and about ignored them.

Nunn pointed out a business on the far corner. "That's where Commissioner Robinson cudgeled the knave Otis in sixty-nine." Wolfe nodded but he had no idea what the lieutenant was talking about, except that the British Coffee House wasn't suffering from the current embargo. It lacked an hour till noon and the place was already crowded with Redcoats.

Many of the side streets were narrow and twisting from when they were mere cow paths, but Boston was cleaner and smelled less awful than towns of similar size in England, although that was probably due to the port being closed.

A short walk brought them to a square commanded by a three-story hulk of gray-painted bricks, topped by one of the noble cupolas. Nunn identified it as the Town House, a Government building. Wolfe had already surmised that from the stocks and whipping post outside.

They made a left turn off the square and a few moments later, Wolfe knew they were being followed. A scruffy boy, making a poor job of lingering behind, poked his head around the corner before resuming an aimless meander in their wake. The boy followed them until they crossed the road at a church fronted by a row of sycamore trees and arrived at their destination.

Province House had been home to royal governors for more than fifty years. Set back from the street by an expanse of snow-covered lawn, the three-story, white-brick mansion boasted, perhaps, Boston's most noble cupola: a glass octagonal big enough to house a telescope on a tripod and command a three-hundred-sixty-degree view of the town and environs. A weathervane in the likeness of an Indian shooting an arrow perched atop the cupola.

The property was enclosed by a wrought iron fence terminating at the front gate in a porter lodge, guarded by four grenadiers in bearskin helms. The Corporal of the Guard wasted no time passing *Halifax* through, their arrival having been expected since the signal guns from Castle William were heard.

Nunn led the way along the shoveled walk, up red-stone steps, to a porch surmounted by a pillared balcony with a railing. The Royal Coat of Arms was emblazoned in gilt carving on the facing of the portico.

One of the double front doors opened before Nunn knocked and they were conducted inside. At the foot of a wide Tudor staircase, a gaudily uniformed Redcoat Captain directed Nunn down the hall and Harrison to the servants' quarters, to wait for his officer. Finally, the Captain inquired after Wolfe's business.

Wolfe said, "I have correspondence for Governor-General Gage from Lord Dartmouth." He handed the Captain a calling card.

Joethan Wolfe. Courier. Foreign Commissions Accepted.

Ignoring the card, the Captain said, "You may leave the correspondence with me."

"I place my charge in no man's hand but General Gage," Wolfe said. The Captain shrugged.

"Then you wait."

Directed to a small ante room, Wolfe took off his hat, hung up his coat and poked up the fire. After un-clubbing his shoulder-length brown hair, and combing it out with his fingers, he made comfortable in a ladder-back chair as best he could. He was dozing when Nunn found him but came instantly awake.

"I'm bound for the ship," Nunn said. Wolfe made arrangements to send for his portmantle.

"Now," said Wolfe, "can you point me to an inn or an ordinary?"

"You'll find neither in Boston," Nunn said. "Nor in New England. What you seek is a tavern. Taverns sell spirits as at home, and food, but they let rooms too, and stables like a hostelry or an ordinary. Mind you, they make no distinction 'twixt patrons as you'll find 'twixt inns and ordinaries in England. You never know what cutthroat you might share a bed with here in America." In parting, Nunn said, "You'll want to steer clear of the Green Dragon. That is the very heart of the insurrectionist faction. Your best course might be the Indian Queen."

"Can a man have a hot bath there?" Wolfe said.

"In winter?" Nunn said incredulously. Wolfe stifled a laugh.

"'Tis a custom I'm much attached to."

Nunn shook his head and took his leave. Wolfe settled back to wait.

7

Governor-General Thomas Gage might have been handsome once, but now at fifty-four, the skin of his round face sagged and his soft brown eyes had the sunken look of a harried man. He was big with the heft of middle age, but as if he'd recently lost weight, his uniform coat hung loose, a coat surprisingly unadorned for the highest-ranking British official in North America, and the more elegant for it. There were no epaulets on his scarlet regimentals and the black facings picked out delicately in gold lace were understated, although the buttons were gold and his buff smallclothes were satin.

For his part, Wolfe appeared to Gage a rather capable fellow who could use a shave—with a wardrobe more along the lines of a gentleman than a courier. The hunter-green frock coat was broadcloth, the white shirt and black neck-cloth good linen. Instead of breeches he wore black leather overalls of the kind favored by cavalrymen—so too the high black dragoon boots currently folded below the knee. According to appearances, one might assume there was a bit of the rake in this fellow.

Wolfe produced an oilskin packet from his haversack. Breaking the tar seal with his barlow, he withdrew two letters and handed one to Gage. "Your man at Drummonds deemed this most important, sir." Gage didn't conceal his disappointment.

"My banker?" He dropped the letter on his desk. "Have you nothing from Whitehall?" He spoke with the refined lilt of the English aristocracy but there was raw urgency in the question. Wolfe held out a second letter.

"From Lord Dartmouth."

Gage fairly snatched it from him.

As Gage read the letter from Dartmouth, Wolfe gazed out the window at snow-shrouded gardens behind the house and inwardly cursed. He'd hoped, even expected, that the letter from Gage's banker would increase his tip. That no longer seemed a reasonable expectation, and was proof that, to Wolfe at least, Boston was upside down. In his experience, Generals abroad were always more concerned with letters from bankers than orders from Horse Guards.

Gage slapped his desk in satisfaction. Locking gazes with Wolfe, he said, "Did Dartmouth entrust you with the contents of this letter?"

"Aye, General. The official order should arrive soon."

"He says I'm to have reinforcements."

"A small fleet. Three fourth-rates and a regiment of marines."

"One regiment? Is that all?" Gage's voice was sharp.

"I cannot say that is all, only what I know," Wolfe said.

"How long ago did they sail? What was the weather coming across?"

Wolfe could not say. The fleet would take the usual southern route across the Atlantic and the weather up north might not signify.

"You've done good service for your king," Gage said. "I thank you for it." He came around his desk and handed Wolfe five gold sovereigns, two more than Wolfe's best hope. Generals were not known for their largesse. Wolfe thanked Gage for his extravagance. The General nodded.

"A drink with you?"

"I'd be grateful for a wet," Wolfe said. The General grunted and poured two glasses from a decanter on the sideboard.

"I don't have much use for the French but their brandy will serve on a cold day." He handed Wolfe a glass and proposed, "The King."

"The King," Wolfe echoed. They downed the brandy and Gage refilled their glasses.

"Tell me, Mister Wolfe. What is the mood in London?"

"My sense is of impatience with the provincials," Wolfe said carefully. Gage gave him a tight smile.

"Don't you mean impatience with me?" Wolfe met the general's tight smile with his own.

"There are some who say that." Gage nodded.

"They think I should just clear the rebels out and be done with it. T'would be laughable were it not so perilous. I've three thousand redcoats to subdue a population can muster thirty thousand armed men."

"Would they really make so bold as to defy the King with arms?" Wolfe said. Gage snorted.

"They most assuredly will if their leaders order it. Hancock, he's the purse, is the richest man in the colony but he don't get his hands dirty. He finances Adams and his bullies for that. And to keep his warehouses safe from Adams' mob. At present there are pending in the courts some four or five hundred indictments against Hancock for smuggling. You can see why he has an interest in defying Government. But Adams . . ." Gage shook his head. "Adams is the devil. Which is confoundedly difficult to believe. The man's failed at everything he's ever done and that includes running a thriving brewery into bankruptcy. Failing as a brewer in Boston, Mister Wolfe, is like failing as a collier in Newcastle." Wolfe chuckled. Gage grinned at his own wit and nodded. "Precisely. And after the brewery failed, friends got him a job as tax collector so he could feed his family, and the scoundrel embezzled eight thousand pounds! And the people love him!"

"This is the man who leads the rebels?" Wolfe said.

"Sam Adams," Gage affirmed. "While he's a rather poor excuse for a man, he is undoubtedly a first-rate conspirator. Has a genius for sedition, you might say." The general gazed into his brandy. "When you return to England Mister Wolfe, you have my encouragement to assure every man you know that nothing less than a campaign will stem the rise of democratic despotism here in Massachusetts."

"When I left London, sending an army to America was not a popular idea," Wolfe said. Gage nodded, frowned, and drank off his glass.

"I have no doubt but you're right." He poured himself another drink. "What brings you to Boston? Surely 'twas not to deliver the post?"

"No sir. I've come to discover the whereabouts of my father. I've had no word of him for some time."

"Here in Boston?"

"To the south. On Long Island." Mention of Long Island sparked Gage's interest.

"Where on the Island? I had my headquarters in New York before coming to this blasted place."

"Setauket," Wolfe said. "In Brookhaven."

"Brookhaven," Gage said. "Good country that. Good hunting." The General sighed. "There's nothing left to hunt around Boston, even out in the country. Hasn't been for many years, I'm told." Wolfe smiled sympathetically.

"I wonder, sir. This time of year, with the port closed, might you suggest the best way of getting to Long Island?" Gage considered the question.

"I'll tell you what. Come back tomorrow afternoon. You can carry correspondence for me and I'll arrange to get you aboard one of His Majesty's ships. Will that serve?" Wolfe flashed a broad smile.

"That is most handsome of you, sir." Gage nodded.

A knock at the door preceded the Captain who ushered Wolfe in. Gage put down his drink and smiled tiredly. "Yes?"

"The admiral's man is here, sir."

"Very well. Send him in. And summon the staff. Soon as I've done with the navy, we've work to do. There's news from London."

Wolfe slipped out of Province House under scudding change-of-weather clouds. The boy who'd been following him was still on the job though, huddled in the doorway of the church across the street.

Tough little bugger, Wolfe thought. He called the boy over but got no reaction. "Don't make me come get you," he called. The waif trudged over but would have stayed at fleeing distance if Wolfe didn't suddenly close on him and grab his arm. The boy tried to wriggle free but he was caught.

"I dihn't do nothing," he whined from under a snot-crusted scarf. Wolfe peered down into a flushed face and runny nose.

"Why are you following me?" The boy's blue eyes fell and he mumbled something until Wolfe gave him a shake. "Speak up or I'll have the hide off you."

"I report on wheah yah goes s'all." The nasal twang of a thick Boston accent and the frozen rapidity of the boy's speech took Wolfe a long moment to decipher.

"Report to whom?" he finally said. The boy looked at him scornfully.

"You wouldn't know who they was."

"Don't suppose I would," Wolfe admitted. "You're a proper little rebel, are you?"

"If you hurt me theah's 'em'll hurt you."

"I don't make a habit of hurting boys. What's your name?"

"Christophah Mahlow."

"After the playwright?"

"Who?"

"You don't know Marlow the playwright?"

"Nevah heard of 'im. Mighten' you let off now?" Wolfe relinquished his grip.

"Where is the London Bookstore?"

Christopher wiped his runny nose with a sleeve. "You passed it."

"Show me and make it simple for both of us," Wolfe said.

Grasping the advantage of such an arrangement, Christopher Marlow set a course back toward the middle of town. This time, Wolfe followed him.

8

The London Bookstore resided nearly in the shadow of the Town House. Pane windows opaqued by steam promised warmth within. Wolfe opened the door and held it for his guide. "Might as well wait where it's warm." As Christopher ducked under his arm, Wolfe said, "Can you read?"

"I'm nigh on eleven," came the insulted reply. Wolfe grinned to himself.

"Wait by the fire. I'll be finished directly." Christopher scuttled happily over to the corner fireplace next to a large but conspicuously unused tea set on a sideboard.

Yellow pine display tables occupied much of the floor space in the bookstore although the current stock of pamphlets and broadsides was thin. Bookshelves occupied two walls. One wall was devoted to stationery and Chapman ledgers of various types. In the back, behind a polished-plank counter, a door led to the bindery from which a large, overweight man appeared.

Two inches taller than Wolfe, the man was every bit of two-hundred-fifty pounds. Shaggy blond hair, loosely clubbed, framed his blue eyes in a pale face proportional to his girth. A worn leather work apron struggled to cover his vast middle, but Wolfe had misjudged the physique. The man was fat but there was brawn underneath.

"Henry Knox, proprietah," the big man said. His speech was as difficult to decipher as Christopher's. Upon reading the card Wolfe handed him, Knox said, "Whitha come thee, Mister Wolfe?"

"London by way of Halifax this forenoon," Wolfe said. Knox's pale eyebrows shot up.

"What news, man? What news from London?"

"The public clamors for Government to quell the Massachusetts insurrection by any means," Wolfe said cheerfully. Knox was visibly shocked.

"But commerce is choked!" he sputtered. "What of the merchants? They support our cause!" Wolfe shook his head.

"Not as you suppose. Commerce concedes to resentment when loyal citizens are attacked by mobs and courts are taken over by farmers. Such acts revile everyone." Knox was flustered.

"Come, sir. Everyone?"

"From the meanest to the better sort." Wolfe handed the bookseller a letter. "From Mister Gill."

"Anxious for arrears no doubt." Knox gestured to the empty store with a left hand conspicuously wrapped in a handkerchief. "Used to be The London was quite the ton for soldiers and gentlefolk." Wolfe looked around the empty shop.

"What happened?"

"A ban on goods from the mother country," Knox said. Wolfe dug into his haversack.

"I have a publication that may interest you. 'Tis entitled Remarks on American Affairs, by Mister Day of the Nova Scotia Assembly."

Examining the treatise, Knox said, "I know of Mister Day. Alas I don't have much to offah." Wolfe smiled. He'd been dealing with shop keepers using the same line for years.

"The tract examines the different levels of society in the colonies and supposes by what they are influenced. He also calls for an end to royal oppression and a provincial bill of rights."

"Sounds rathah sensible," Knox said.

"But," said Wolfe, "he also urges expansion of special privilege for royal appointees and chosen landholders. 'Tis quite a pudding."

"How much do yah want fah it?"

"Very few were struck and for the eyes of powerful men only. I doubt there's another in Boston." The look on the bookseller's face told Wolfe he was right. "I'll take four dollars and that almost not worth the trouble." Knox laughed derisively.

"Four dollah! Why not twenty? Don't you know our port is closed?"

Wolfe took back the treatise and laid it on the counter. He handed Knox a thick packet. "This is for Doctor Joseph Warren. Doctor Franklin said it should find its way through you."

"I'll see he receives it," Knox said. "Are you acquainted with Doctor Franklin?"

"For many years," Wolfe said. Knox studied Wolfe's impassive face. "Are you entrusted with any news that mayhaps, Franklin didn't write down?"

Wolfe went with his first impulse which was to have a little fun at the big man's expense. With an air of complete nonchalance, he said, "I suppose The Doctor would mention that a small British fleet is en route. In addition to Marines, they carry Orders in Council banning the importation of arms and powder to America. They will also seek to secure all stores already in the colonies." Knox's eyes bugged out. Excusing himself, he disappeared into the back. Moments later he was engaged in muffled conversation with someone.

As the minutes dragged on, Wolfe went nosing among the books. He found what he was looking for as raised voices erupted from the bindery.

A stocky man of middling height and dark complexion came stomping out of the back, buttoning his mechanic's jacket. "It's sedition Knox!" he yelled back into the bindery. "I'm taking my business elsewhere!" Stuffing a wool cap down over thick dark hair, the man winked at Christopher and departed.

Knox came out of the bindery a moment later, muttering, "Forbear, forbear," but Wolfe was having none of it. He scooped up the treatise to put it away but Knox stayed his hand. "Four dollahs is robbery but you leave me no choice. I'll have the tract." Wolfe put the book he'd selected on the counter.

"I'll have this."

"I'll subtract the cost," Knox said. Wolfe shook his head.

"The price for the tract is now four dollars and the book." Knox's eyes narrowed to angry slits. Wolfe cocked his head and said nothing. Eventually the bookseller lost hope that the price would come down.

"You are a shahp!" he snapped, and retreated into the bindery. He came back with a stack of paper bills and certificates that had Wolfe laughing.

"A moment ago, you accused me of being a sharp. Now you think me a fool. Payment in metal, Mister Knox. I shan't be long in Boston and will not accept local scrip." With another put-upon sigh, Knox disappeared. This time he returned with a handful of coins that he slapped on the counter. "Devil burn thee for thievery!" he said.

Wolfe didn't take it personally. "Fair's fair and I dare say you've friends to share the cost." As he tucked the coins away, Wolfe said, "I wonder can you commend a tavern where a man might bathe?" Knox squinted in disbelief.

"In wintah?"

"This very night if I can manage it."

Knox thought for a moment. "Missus Davis has a tub in summah."

"A bawdy house?" Wolfe said. Knox shrugged.

"Do you know where Missus Davis lives?" Wolfe called to Christopher. The boy nodded and got up. Wolfe said to Knox, "By my guide's able direction, I take my leave."

Lamplighters were at work as Wolfe followed Christopher back past Province House and beyond. "Can I hire you to take a message for my things?" Wolfe said.

"Not to the whahf," Christopher said. "I dasn't." Wolfe handed him the book he'd taken off Knox.

"Some works of your namesake." Christopher handed the book back.

"I shan't take a message to the whahf."

"One has naught to do with the other. Look." Wolfe opened the book to the title page and angled it so the dying rays of the sun illuminated the author's name. Christopher's name. "Should you learn the plays and verse well enough," said Wolfe, "you might convince people you wrote the book." Christopher was unsure if he was being made sport of until Wolfe laughed, then he reacted angrily.

"Mayhaps I will write a book someday."

"About that fellow in the bookstore perhaps?" Wolfe said.

"Who?" Christopher said, playing dumb. Wolfe chuckled.

"The fellow who winked at you, of course." Christopher tried to deny it but Wolfe said, "No use denying 'til you're better at disguising. I saw him wink and you hide a smile. Shoddy work, that." Embarrassed to be caught out professionally, Christopher hung his head.

"What's his name?" Wolfe said.

"Revere." Christopher was saved further discomfit by a curious gonging, joined moments later by a hand bell. "C'mon!" the boy said, "there's Tories out!" He tucked the book under his arm and started running.

Wolfe followed him around a corner onto an unlit street fronted by a ropewalk for a block. In addition to the tar stench that lingered over all ropewalks, on the other side of the fence enclosing the walk, a man was beating a sheet of copper with a ladle.

At the end of the block, five or six men surrounded a two-horse sleigh. Christopher sprinted ahead but Wolfe declined to keep up. The snowy road was too slick for his riding boots.

As he drew closer, he identified the men around the sleigh as ropewalkers, waterfront types who worked at twisting hemp into the miles of rope used to rig ships.

Christopher returned bubbling with excitement. "It's Commodore Loring! A mandamus! One ah tha biggest Tories in town! They'll tah and feathah him sure!"

"I'll see every man-jack o' you hang!" Loring was an angry old squire in a brown day wig and old-fashioned cocked hat and carriage coat. From inside the sleigh he brandished a two-barrel coach gun. Next to him, a black man in a fur hat had a pistol the size of a small cannon, although the situation was a stalemate. One of the ropewalkers had the sleigh's team of matched grays by the reins and thus controlled the situation, but none of his friends were anxious to press matters and get shot.

Coaxed into existence by a man hidden from Wolfe by the sleigh, a fire burst to life on the side of the road. The grays reacted, dragging the ropewalker holding them almost off his feet.

Blocks away a large bell began to toll.

A ropewalker ran up and placed a cauldron in the roadside fire.

Wolfe stepped forward and inserted himself into the group of men gathered behind the sleigh. "Pardon me gentlemen," he said. "I'm seeking Missus Davis' Tavern?" The ropewalkers turned as one and Wolfe shrugged. "Forgive my interruption."

"They'll be eno' tah for two directly," one of the men said threateningly. His grizzled scowl revealed shockingly rotted black teeth. Wolfe ignored the man's threat and posed a question, but as if the answer was inconsequential.

"So you mean to tar and feather these men. For what crime, I wonder?"

"For the crime of serving my king and country faithfully!" Loring growled from the sleigh. "As will I always! I'll shoot the first man that moves against me! Who's it to be?"

"I believe he means it," Wolfe said to the man with the bad teeth. The man glared back. "As I see you're engaged," said Wolfe, "I'll endeavor to find my own way." He knuckled his Denmark politely and edged around the crowd. Christopher was nowhere to be seen as he walked down the street until the dark swallowed him.

It was not in Joethan Wolfe to turn away when trouble presented. As he adjusted his black neck cloth to cover his white face, it occurred to him that intruding on an armed confrontation in Boston was reckless to the point of insanity. But he really hadn't cared for the snaggle-toothed bugger's attitude.

More men ran up the street, shouting and laughing as if on their way to a raree show.

The man holding the horses had his back to Wolfe. He was extremely surprised when Wolfe thrust a pistol against his ear and said quietly, "Don't move or I'll blow your brains out." Snatching the reins out of the man's hand, he slipped astride the near horse, whipped both horses with the ends of the reins and cried, "Ha!"

The nervous team leapt forward. The sleigh lurched sideways and then whiplashed straight ahead as the horses found purchase on the snowy road.

"You got 'em!" the black man yelled from the sleigh. Wolfe was well aware of it, but riding postilion wasn't the problem. Not knowing where he was going was the problem. He trusted the horses to know, a powerful, well-trained team.

The Commodore's carriage gun roared as they pounded into the dark, until a sudden turn down a narrow lane almost whipped the sleigh into a line of trees. Wolfe was caught off guard but the clumsiness of the heavy vehicle saved it. Coming out of the turn he reined in the team and straitened their line, restoring a more measured pace.

A torch burned up ahead. Without hesitation, the team turned into a driveway and came to a heaving, quivering stop in a stable yard lit by torches.

9

Wolfe jumped down and was quickly joined by Commodore Loring. "Well done, man!" Loring said. "Good and well done!" He grabbed Wolfe's hand and shook it. "Joshua Loring in your debt. You were in the nick, I tell you. In the nick! Come up to the house. I must see to our defenses at once."

After ordering the driver, Cuffee, to set pickets and make sure they knew their duty, Loring set off for the house. Limping at a brisk pace, he was unaware or uncaring that he'd lost his hat and wig. His shaved head steamed in the night air. "Got the bastards good," he said.

"Killed?" said Wolfe. Loring shook his head.

"Swan shot. Won't do to start the war just yet."

Two torches lit a path leading to the back of a large clapboard house. The cellar door flew open as they approached and a woman's voice called, "Are you whole, Mister Loring?"

"Quite well, Missus Loring. Is Captain Brown here?"

"You've lost your wig."

"And damned glad that is all!"

They followed Mrs. Loring through a basement divided into amply stocked cold stalls. As they climbed a flight of stone stairs, lit by an ancient ship lanthorn, Loring asked again, "Is Captain Brown here?" When Mrs. Loring did not respond at once, he barked, "Blast it woman, 'tis urgent!"

"He's upstairs."

"Get him. There's mischief afoot."

When they reached the main floor, Mrs. Loring fled. The Commodore pointed Wolfe to a door. "You'll find fire and drink in there. I'll join you direct I secure the house." Wolfe was about to protest that he could be of service but Loring saved him the trouble. "Out in the country I should not like to say, but here in Boston His Majesty yet rules. Though I'll wager a company of Redcoats will curse his name and mine tonight."

Wolfe found himself alone in a carpeted room with a large map of New England on the wall and a heavy mahogany desk. A fire and two upholstered wing chairs were complemented by a small table spread with cheese, cold ham, bread, and mustard. He found a ball-belly pitcher of Madeira and poured a glass, then he helped himself to some food.

The house came astir as he ate, many feet coming and going. He was studying Loring's map, wiping his mouth with his handkerchief, when Mrs. Loring swept in. Exuding a charming intelligence, her gown of red silk and gold brocade shimmered in the firelight.

"Is it true you rescued the Commodore from certain abuse?" she said. Her eyes were deep-ocean blue, her hair thick honey gathered up and held in place by an aromatic sprig of pine. About the same age as Wolfe, her petite nose was subservient to a sensual mouth and mischievous dimples in her cheeks, especially when she smiled. A delicate cameo dangling from a black choker drew attention to a lush bosom. In fact, the word luscious crossed Wolfe's mind. He reckoned Loring a lucky man.

In answer to Mrs. Loring's question, he said, "I think the ruffians were in more danger than he was." Mrs. Loring chuckled, an enchanting sound, lowered her eyes and curtsied.

"Elizabeth Loring. I give you joy of your triumph. The Commodore is not easily impressed yet so have you done." Wolfe made a leg.

"Joethan Wolfe at your service."

"Did you happen upon the assault by chance, Mister Wolfe?"

"I was on my way to a tavern, that I yet must find by and by." He poured Madeira into the glass she held out.

"A tavern down by the ropewalk?" she said.

"A Missus Davis' place."

Mrs. Loring covered a snicker gracefully with a fan that magically appeared. "I see. Missus Davis. Of course," she said.

"Am I to understand that Missus Davis sells women's time?" Wolfe said dryly. Mrs. Loring chuckled.

"Hers is the most infamous brothel in Boston."

"Does Missus Davis even have a bathing tub?" said Wolfe.

"I'm sure I don't know," Mrs. Loring said, perhaps less affronted than she portrayed. "Where are your things, Mister Wolfe?"

"My portmantle is yet aboard the packet." He was about to elaborate when the Commodore limped in, a weathered, heavyset man with bushy gray brows, piercing blue eyes and large jowls.

"I see you've met my daughter-in-law," he said. "If you would be so good as to name yourself, I should be right happy to shake your hand again." Wolfe was glad he'd acted. He liked Commodore Loring right off. When he finished introducing himself, Loring patted him on the arm and admitted, "I didn't think t'would turn out well back there."

"'T'was I said going home were foolish," Mrs. Loring chimed in. The Commodore responded quickly, as one used to going tit for tat with a strong woman.

"'Tis a most unappealing trait of your sex, Elizabeth, to say I warned thee."

"'Tis more unappealing that men do not listen," his daughter-in-law said.

"Is this not your home?" Wolfe asked the Commodore.

"Since the Faction forced me from my farm in Roxbury 'tis," he said. "I snuck out there today for the first time in months." Mrs. Loring handed her father-in-law a glass of Madeira.

"Joshua can manage things quite well at the farm, Papa," she said.

Loring turned to Wolfe. "If she really believed that, you may be sure I should worry less. In the event, you'll have to stay here tonight and for as long as you must. Won't do for you to be seen in town. The Faction will want revenge." Loring raised his glass and smiled broadly. "Your fine health, sir!"

When they had drunk, Loring said, "If I may make so bold, what are your plans Mister Wolfe? You are lately from London?"

"Am I so identifiable?" Wolfe chuckled. Mrs. Loring chuckled back.

"An active gentleman with a London accent and a swagger? I should say."

The Commodore sighed, "Leave the man alone, Bets." But Mrs. Loring would not be denied.

"Who is the bon ton in London this season Mister Wolfe? What is the new fashion? Speak to me of anything but the troubles and I shall be grateful beyond measure." She would have continued but her father-in-law held up a hand.

"I'll thank you to retire now, Elizabeth. We men need talk. You'll have Mister Wolfe all day tomorrow. He'll not be going anywhere." Wolfe started to disagree but Loring cut him off. "When she blows out o' the nor' east like this, ain't no one goin' nowhere. Depend upon it."

"Be warned," Mrs. Loring said to Wolfe, "I'm a desperate-bored woman." She curtsied and would have retired but Wolfe bade her wait. He retrieved his haversack and handed her a *Ladies Magazine* that she accepted with unbridled delight.

Watching her sweep out of the room, Loring said, "She's too smart and pretty by half."

"Your son is a fortunate man," said Wolfe.

"Madeira?" At Wolfe's nod, Loring refilled their glasses and indicated Wolfe's haversack. "I see you are a courier. A rather capable one, as I know. Are you in the employ of Government?"

"I accept a ministerial commission upon occasion," Wolfe said. "But if you wouldn't mind Commodore, I heard someone call you a mandamus tonight. I've been wondering what that means ever since."

"I'm a mandamus councilor for the Province of Massachusetts Bay." When Wolfe still didn't know what that meant, Loring explained, "Some months ago, to combat the obstruction of insurrectionists on the Governor's Council, the King suspended the right of town councils in this province to elect their own representatives to the Governor's Council. By a writ of mandamus, Gage appointed his own councilors to take their place. Thirty-six were appointed but only ten of us have taken the oath and not resigned. Of course, we've had to flee our homes. Out in the country they have their own councils now as if they rule themselves."

"So 'tis open rebellion?"

"And will undoubtedly end in bloodshed." Loring waved Wolfe to a wingchair as he retrieved an elaborately carved pipe from the mantel. He lit it with a straw kept there for the purpose, and when the pipe was drawing satisfactorily, said, "The farcical thing is, I generally agree with the Sons of Violence and they know it." At Wolfe's quizzical look, he explained, "Sons of Violence is what I call those who flatter themselves Sons of Liberty. What most folk call the Faction. But as I say, their grievances are mine."

"Yet you support the king," Wolfe observed. Loring smiled wanly.

"I've always eaten the king's bread and I always will. I commanded a royal fleet in the French war. Got part o' my leg shot off. I'll not stain my honor for men that will swing at the end of a rope in the twelvemonth." He was warming to his subject.

"The Faction terrorize the town as Sam Adams decrees and rely upon Tommy Gage's good nature to spare them Government's wrath. They don't know it yet but Gage will act soon if only to preserve discipline in the ranks."

"The men are disaffected?"

"'Tis a wonder we yet have a garrison. Rum is cheap and the Faction promise land to any Redcoat that goes over the wall. Everyone imagines Gage erected works across Boston Neck to keep the country folk out, but really, it's to keep his Redcoats in. Is there any news you can share?"

Wolfe told him about the Orders in Council, which only served to deflate the Commodore further. He sighed deeply. "That news troubles you?" Wolfe said. Loring frowned.

"The timing is poor. The ban shouldn't have been issued until there was an army capable of enforcing it. Now the Faction have time to hide what arms they have and obtain what they don't. Both defeat our purpose."

"Yet denying arms and powder to the enemy can't be all bad," Wolfe said. Loring's visage sagged.

"The thought of my neighbors as enemies is rather troubling of itself Mister Wolfe. And I grant you the ban is long overdue." The sound of an approaching drum intruded and Loring got up. "That'll be Brown and the Fifty-Second. Care to meet an overweening captain?"

Fires were lit around the periphery of the property. From a front window, Wolfe and Loring watched the light company of the 52nd Regiment of Foot deploy around the yard. It was a thin company, perhaps thirty men, but they'd be glad for the fires. The clear skies of morning had given over to spitting sleet.

It wasn't long before a knock came at the front door and Loring welcomed in a British officer shrouded in a blue camlet cloak. Captain William Brown was of a size and age with Wolfe—watery brown eyes, a prominent nose, a tic in the muscle at the back of his cheek, and an overwhelming countenance of British hauteur.

Despite the weather, Brown's white wig was perfect, as were his scarlet-and-buff regimentals. Tucking a black Cocked Hat with a single strip of white lace under his arm, Captain Brown bowed in a most studied fashion.

"The Fifty-Second is here, Commodore. I've posted guards."

"No need," Loring said. "I've pickets out who know the roads. We'll have word of any approach. Your men may use the barn."

"That is generous," Brown sniffed, "but I mean to use the weather to toughen the company."

"You know best," Loring said without conviction. He offered to have a room prepared for the Captain. Brown made noises about sharing his men's hardship, but he accepted soon enough.

They adjourned to the parlor, a comfortable room with a large fireplace dressed in oak, and French paper on the walls. Loring poured brandy and at Brown's urging, related the sleigh incident in detail. Mrs. Loring arrived before the climax, greeted Brown with a modest curtsy, and poured herself a drink.

Brown's focus shifted to her in a most unsettling way. Awkward under his gaze, she moved to the other side of her father-in-law. Loring was not unaware but he continued his tale. He was relating Wolfe's entrance into the drama when Mrs. Loring interrupted.

"What would you have done if the man had not let go the team, Mister Wolfe?" Wolfe smiled.

"I'm happy to say we'll never know."

"Was you loaded ball?" Captain Brown asked. When Wolfe affirmed that he was, Brown's face grew stormy. "That was damned rash," he said too sharply. "You might have started a war." Loring came to Wolfe's defense.

"If there's to be war, captain, I'm glad to have it start by saving my skin as any other man's." The rebuke was mild but raising his glass pointedly, Loring demanded apology from Brown by toasting, "To Mister Wolfe." In the circumstance, Brown could not but honor the salute.

The Commodore finished his drink and put his glass down. "By your leave, gentlemen, I shall retire. Elizabeth, will you . . ."

"I'll see to it," Mrs. Loring said. Loring grunted his thanks, patted Wolfe warmly on the arm and limped out. Brown helped himself to another drink.

"I did not like to say in front of the Commodore, but I do hope the villains that threatened him turn up tonight." Mrs. Loring looked at him aghast.

"I'll thank you to keep such thoughts to yourself, Captain. I have a babe in the house."

Brown was crushed. "I only meant I desire to teach the blackguards a lesson."

"I know what you meant," Mrs. Loring said. "But you tempt fate. Foolishly." Only the crackling and hissing of the fire was audible until Wolfe broke the awkward silence.

"With the port closed, how do goods come into Boston?" he said. Mrs. Loring smiled at him, grateful for the change of subject.

"Everything by water comes through the ports of Marblehead and Salem. The rest comes overland but it's a wretchedly slow business. The irony is, closing Boston harbor has minted more insurgents than its discouraged."

"Boston reaps what it sowed," Captain Brown scowled. "And the situation shan't improve 'til Gage treats insurgents with as much firmness as he treats his own men. You may be sure things would change if we hung some of the rabble."

Thoroughly tired of Brown's influence, Wolfe finished his drink. "With your permission Missus Loring, I too shall retire." Mrs. Loring pouted.

"Do all heroes to bed before nine of the clock? I had a notion that Londoners live by candlelight." Wolfe smiled at her warmly.

"We do. Much to the dismay of a particular friend of mine, I can tell you. He reckons the cost of candles burned in London a national scandal."

"Never!" Mrs. Loring said. "I adore the world by candlelight."

Wolfe knew why. Candlelight rendered Mrs. Loring the most desirable of creatures.

She led the way upstairs with a whale-oil lamp, to a small bedroom in the back of the house where the ceiling sloped beneath the plunge of the roof. Gesturing to a bed draped with heavy quilts, she said, "'Tis plain enough but you'll find it cozy and dry, which I expect matters most."

"You have it just right," Wolfe said.

Mrs. Loring tucked up a strand of hair fallen across her eyes and smiled wearily. "Sleep well, Mr. Wolfe. And know that you have my esteem for protecting someone I'm quite fond of."

10

Wolfe awoke after sunrise to the howl of wind. A quick look out the window confirmed the Commodore's prediction. Snow was blowing hard and thick out of the northeast. As he donned his jacket and tied his neck cloth, he knew he wouldn't be retrieving his portmantle today.

Breakfast was robust in the British style: oatmeal, smoked fish, fresh bread, spreads of apple butter and honey, kidneys, sausage. The absence of Captain Brown was also congenial. The Captain was currently overseeing his men as they chased windblown tents and got organized to move into the barn.

"Most of those men are so froze they'll be useless for days," the Commodore said. He was perfectly content in a blue satin banyan that matched the soft cap covering his shaved head. "The Captain means to drag some of them with him to deliver a report I've written about yesterday's incident. I told him it'll wait 'til weather-break but he calculates delivery in a snowstorm an act worthy of notice. He's nothing if not ambitious, is Captain Brown, but he's no officer I could love." The Commodore relaxed. "Rest assured my report puts you in a flattering light, Mister Wolfe."

Wolfe nodded his thanks. Upon request to send a note to headquarters along with the Commodore's report, he was provided pen, ink and paper. Loring's heavy brows furrowed in unrestrained curiosity as Wolfe scribbled regrets for breaking his appointment with General Gage. It was certain that no ship would be sailing today and Wolfe wouldn't presume to take up the General's time unnecessarily.

As Wolfe sanded the note, Loring said, "I see you have friends in high places."

"Hardly," Wolfe chuckled. "The general offered me a ride to New York on a King's ship. I merely mean to take him up on it."

"Where in New York?" Mrs. Loring was fashionably undressed, sans farthingales. Her simple white gown with its yellow petticoat and stomacher lent a cheerful air to a dreary day.

"Long Island," Wolfe said in response to her question. "Where I was born."

"We are countrymen!" Mrs. Loring beamed at him. "My people are Lloyds. I drew my first breath in Queens Village. I knew there was something between us. Are you glad to come home?"

"I find America strange," said Wolfe. "I never imagined the cry of liberty meant the liberty to attack respectable people in the street."

"My very point to the Faction," Loring said. "Liberty without rule of law is but tyranny of the strongest gang."

"That may be," said Mrs. Loring. "But the importance of yesterday is you were accosted right here in Boston, Papa. What is to come when decent people can't travel the streets of a garrison town?"

An adolescent serving girl came in and whispered to Mrs. Loring. She excused herself and followed the girl out. When they were gone, The Commodore said, "What of you, Mister Wolfe? The King is in need of resourceful men."

"You may be sure I will do my duty," Wolfe said. "But for now, I need discover if my father yet lives." They were interrupted by the front door slamming hard enough to shudder the house, Captain Brown having misjudged the strength of the wind.

The captain was having a difficult morning. His perfectly coiffed wig was bedraggled, his cocked hat laden with snow. He stalled as he received Loring's report, no doubt hoping that Mrs. Loring would appear. It wasn't until he departed that she swept in however, swaddling her son in the crook of her arm.

"Is he gone?"

The Commodore gave Wolfe an exasperated look. "As if she weren't the one who invited him here in the first instance."

"I thought he would be good company," Mrs. Loring said. The Commodore harrumphed.

"An easy mark is what you thought. How much money have you taken off the Captain at cards?"

"A gentleman would never ask such a question," Mrs. Loring pouted. The Commodore looked at Wolfe, as men will, when women are being women, but Mrs. Loring ignored him. "Mister Wolfe is mine now as you promised," she said.

"Don't play at cards with her," Loring said to Wolfe. "She will take your money."

Mrs. Loring smiled sweetly at Wolfe, took his arm and led him away; through a newly constructed hallway that served to connect the house to the kitchen and scullery in the backyard—warm and aromatic from baking bread.

On the other side of the room from the ovens and hearth, a half hogshead filled with steaming water danced in the lantern light. To Wolfe's astonishment, his portmantle sat on the ground next to it.

"Your bath awaits," Mrs. Loring said triumphantly.

"You're a woman to be reckoned with," Wolfe said. She laughed girlishly.

"I have drawn you a bath, Mister Wolfe. You may call me Elizabeth. Or Betsy as my friends do. And with your permission, I shall call you Joethan."

"My friends call me Joeth," Wolfe said.

"Hop in while 'tis yet hot!" Mrs. Loring pulled a sheet folded over a clothesline across the room for privacy. From the other side, she said, "Do you have a change of clothes?" When he replied in the affirmative, she said, "Leave the ones you wear and I'll have them washed."

Wolfe stripped down and rummaged through his portmantle for a chunk of soap and a small comb. As hot bathwater seeped into his bones, he breathed a sigh of relief before commencing the arduous task of ridding himself of lice. He hated lice but they were unavoidable aboard ship, so he scrubbed, and combed, and groomed like an ape until he was reasonably certain he was vermin free.

Sitting back afterward, he relaxed for the first time in America. Idly he felt around the scar below his ribs on the right side. Even underwater it was yet yellow and puckered, but it hadn't wept in two months and a feeling of vulnerability no longer consumed his consciousness. Sighing contentedly, he drifted to the sound of the wind as it frequently rattled the windows.

Presenting himself in the parlor later, he was clean-shaven and dressed as stylish as any man in London—buff breaches, white silk hose, leather pumps with silver buckles, white linen shirt and a pale-blue waistcoat embroidered with a subtle floral design.

Betsy looked up from reading *The Ladies Magazine* and favored him with a dimpled smile. "You positively shine." The admiration in her voice may in some measure have derived from his appearance being due to her efforts.

"There is nothing quite so pleasant as a hot bath in winter," Wolfe said. "And clean clothes. You have my gratitude." He handed her two Spanish dollars. "I'd be grateful if you'd share these among them that labored on my behalf." Betsy was impressed by the gesture. Pocketing the coins, she requested he pour them warm cider from a pitcher by the hearth, that they might celebrate the servants' good fortune.

"You have a son?" Wolfe said, as he poured the cider.

"My Johnny, yes."

"Does he have brothers or sisters?"

"My daughter Lizzy is at the farm with her father and Grandam." Wolfe handed over a glass and took a seat on the divan beside her.

"Are they not in danger?"

"The villains would never harm our family. Most folk are deeply attached to The Commodore. He's loaned money to some."

"Yet they drove him out," Wolfe said. Betsy nodded but not in concession.

"They may be exceedingly ungrateful but they will not harm our family."

"They would have hurt the Commodore yesterday," Wolfe said.

"Those men were not our neighbors."

"Is The Commodore married?"

"Quite married," Betsy laughed. "We rely upon my mother-in-law's presence at the farm for protection. Her brothers are with the Faction." Somewhat ruefully, she added, "And she refuses to leave affairs solely in the hands of her son, my husband, who is a perfectly capable man." She said the last as if perhaps her husband was not perfectly capable. Corralling some loose curls with a finger, she tucked them into her upswept hair.

"What of you, Joeth? What brings you home?" He told her he was come to find his father but she didn't believe him. "I'll wager there's a woman involved," she said. Wolfe laughed.

"With a bachelor of a certain age, one could almost always assume there's a woman involved."

"I'll have the truth of it before you leave," she said. Wolfe grinned.

"A particular friend influenced my return, if you would know." Betsy's eyes narrowed.

"That's the second time you've mentioned your particular friend. What is his name that we might refer to him precisely?"

"Benjamin," said Wolfe. "But as he's quite older, I refer to him by his title, which is Doctor. Doctor Franklin is what most know him by."

"Benjamin Franklin?" Betsy said. Wolfe nodded. Betsy said, "Your particular friend is the most famous American in the world?" Wolfe considered for a moment.

"I suppose he is. I never thought of it like that."

"Never thought of it," Betsy gushed. "How precious. How did you meet the great man?" Her fulsome reaction didn't come as a surprise. Wolfe had witnessed it many times before. He'd even exploited it upon occasion. He gave Betsy his usual answer.

"When I was a boy and not long in England, The Doctor took note of me as a fellow American. Later when I left school and might have gone destitute, he gave me a place in the world." Betsy was thrilled.

"How very fortunate for you. What is he like?" Again, Wolfe's answer was rote.

"He likes to play the rustic but in truth he's more calculating and aware than any of the important men. His great gift is a fondness for living that is quite contagious. A magnetism as Mesmer might say."

"What don't you like about him?" Betsy said. It was a question Wolfe did not often get.

"For a man so outwardly pleasant, The Doctor can be a right Tartar when crossed. And on any given day he's more manipulating than Machiavelli."

"That's what I like to know," Betsy giggled, "the true measure of a man." Then she was serious. "After the affair of Mister Hutchinson's letters, I presume Doctor Franklin is wholly a creature of the Faction."

"I was there the day they humiliated him in the Privy Council," Wolfe said.

"Were you?!" Betsy's face was curious repulsion as if he'd mentioned seeing Hulga the bearded lady. "I don't think Doctor Franklin was right to make those letters public," she said. "Yet if Parliament did as Governor Hutchinson suggested, we might never have met, you and I."

"True," said Wolfe. "But for how long can Government suppress a population on the other side of the ocean against its will?"

Betsy regarded him sternly. "Do you always see both sides?"

With a cocky smile, Wolfe said, "We live in an age of reason. To not consider both sides would be unreasonable. N`est-ce pas?" He was pleased when Betsy crinkled her nose in mock distaste.

The long-case floor clock chimed one.

"Already?" Betsy stood up. "I must make certain The Commodore's dinner is ready at two as it has been all the years of his life." She gave a shallow curtsy. "Shouldn't like to be flogged, you know."

The Commodore was in high spirits as they sat to dinner. "How I longed for mutton," he said happily.

"Can mutton not be had in town?" said Wolfe. Loring shook his head.

"The Sons of Violence have banned the slaughter of sheep, deeming wool more important than meat. 'Tis a sorry state of affairs when a man can't enjoy mutton of his own farm, but that's what some call freedom these days."

Dinner was more elaborate than breakfast, and Wolfe liked a saddle of mutton as much as the next man. Conversation was confined to the cordial until the serving girl cleared the table and Loring passed around a bottle of port. "The King," he said, raising his glass.

When the toast was drunk, Betsy said to Wolfe, "You mentioned that you were present at the conclusion of the affair of Governor Hutchinson's letters.

May I impose upon you to tell us about it?"

"What's this about Hutchinson?" Loring said.

"Joethan was with Doctor Franklin when he appeared before the Privy Council," Betsy said. Loring looked closely at Wolfe and arched his eyebrows expectantly.

"Well?"

Wolfe poured himself a fresh glass of port. "I must first remark that the disclosure of Governor Hutchinson's letters was a perfect example of Doctor Franklin being too clever for his own purpose. It was a scheme, you see. The entire affair was a failed diplomatic tactic."

"Unless designed to enflame the Massachusetts populace against Government!" Loring sputtered. "In that regard 'twere a flaming success!" Wolfe burst out laughing and couldn't stop. The harder he tried, the worse it got.

When his eyes were wet and his giggles more sporadic, Wolfe finally managed to say, "You may be sure I will tell The Doctor *that* the next time we meet!" As he wiped his eyes, he said, "Let me assure you, Commodore, Doctor Franklin's aim was precisely opposite of the effect you stated. As Governor Hutchinson's letters showed him to be the author of policies most inimical to Massachusetts, The Doctor reckoned if they were made public, and Parliament withdrew the policies, the ire of the people would deflect to Hutchinson and faith would be restored in the King."

"He's mad!" Loring rasped. "Franklin's been too long at court! The time for political subtlety passed long ago. What Hutchinson's letters did was call for abridgement of American liberties and punishment for the Sons of Violence, two things apt to make matters worse! When Franklin gave those letters to the Faction, private letters, I remind you, he imperiled the life and property of every loyal Briton in this colony." Wolfe nodded.

"I have no doubt but you're right. Yet I do assure you, Doctor Franklin was the most surprised man in England when the council condemned him for the affair." Wolfe's laughter started bubbling over again. "For the life of him he couldn't understand why they didn't appreciate . . ." and then he was laughing uncontrollably again.

When he regained his composure he apologized, explaining that although the incident occurred a year ago, he had never laughed about it until this very instant. "I had a hand in events you see, and the way they treated The Doctor, well, there was naught amusing at the time."

"What role did you play?" said Betsy. Wolfe shook his head.

"I'm afraid I can't speak to that."

"'Course he can't," Loring said. Wolfe ignored Betsy's pout and continued.

"On the twenty-ninth day of January last, as the official representative for the Province of Massachusetts Bay, Doctor Franklin presented a formal petition to remove Thomas Hutchinson as Governor of the Massachusetts Colony. The Pit, as they call the Privy Chamber in Whitehall, was full, and with many famous names as you might expect. General Gage was there on leave from America. Lord North. Edmund Burke. Charles Fox. It was in all respects the political event of the season."

"I've oft wondered why they call it the Pit," Betsy said. Loring bristled.

"Will you let him get on with it!"

"Generations ago 'twas the site of a famous cockfighting pit," Wolfe said to Betsy. She stuck her tongue out at her father-in-law.

"You must remember," Wolfe said, "Doctor Franklin had only recently come forth as the man responsible for making the letters known, and only because a duel was to be fought over accusations regarding their theft."

"All of Massachusetts followed the proceedings closely," Betsy said.

"In the event," said Wolfe, "it was overwhelmingly decided by the Privy Council, with many harsh words for the people of Boston, I may add, to reject the petition for Hutchinson's removal. It was then that Solicitor-General Wedderburn laid into The Doctor about the letters. With the gallery cheering him on, Wedderburn publicly called Doctor Franklin a thief, and accused him of insurrection and treason. The Doctor, near seventy years old, mind, remained on his feet for more than an hour and took it like a hero, never once offering a word in his defense." Wolfe didn't mention the steel in The Doctor's carriage as the taunts and jeers of the gallery washed over him, or the deep hurt in his eyes.

"The Doctor said 'twere the most important service he ere rendered his country, and perhaps it was. Yet in all the years I've known him, that were the first time he appeared old to me. And as you know, he was dismissed postmaster for the colonies soon after. What you may not know is, many and more he once thought friends now shun him." Wolfe drank off his port and placed the glass upside down on the table. "And that is what transpired in the Privy Council, January last."

"Well," Loring commented in the ensuing silence, "better Franklin a fool than a traitor."

Wolfe tried not to glare at the Commodore as he said, "I do assure you, sir. Doctor Franklin may be an optimist, but he is never, ever a fool.

11

Wolfe spent the rest of the day reading back copies of the Boston Gazette. The "dung barge," Loring called it. He said he read it to keep track of what nonsense the Faction was currently peddling.

The astonishing degree of vitriol aimed at Government in the pages of the Gazette startled Wolfe. In one instance, as a means of efficiently combating smallpox—a disease that ravaged Americans in numbers unheard of in Europe—inoculations for the poor at a hospital in Gloucester were to be paid for by the local community. A certain faction, deeming free inoculations for the poor to be unfair taxation on the rest, burned the hospital to the ground. There was no report of the perpetrators being punished or even sought after.

From Wolfe's perspective, the words freedom and liberty were used so often in the Gazette that they ceased to have meaning. Every action taken by the Crown or its representatives was proclaimed an affront to the rights of free Englishmen. Banner headlines trumpeting the danger of American enslavement appeared in every issue. Invariably in the same paper however, advertisements offered rewards for the return of runaway slaves and indentures, an irony apparently lost on the publisher.

Reports on the closing of Boston Harbor were equally one-sided; full of indignation at the trampling of English liberties, but with no acknowledgment of the criminal activity prompting the bill's enactment. Wolfe soon grasped that what Bostonians called their English liberties, didn't exist in England, or anywhere else for that matter. The Crown had come to the same conclusion the previous spring, and after shutting down the Port of Boston, issued a series of decrees.

Henceforth, Americans accused of crimes against the Crown would be sent to England for trial, a strike directly at the Faction. In Massachusetts, for fear of reprisal, a jury would never convict a Liberty Man. In England they would hang.

The so-called Murder Act was a variation of the same. It decreed that Crown officials accused of killing a provincial would be tried in England.

Gage's mandamus appointments—part of the Massachusetts Government Act, another of the decrees—was an abridgment of American rights that Governor Hutchinson called for, as was the direct royal appointment of judges and justices of the peace, positions that had always been elected in America. It was easy to understand why Americans were irate over the changes, but if elected judges and justices wouldn't, or couldn't, enforce the law, what was to be done?

Indeed, the American prohibition of British goods—the articles put forth by the *Continental Association*—required Americans to enforce the prohibitions by oppressing and punishing their neighbors more than the Crown ever did; whether their neighbors agreed with the Articles or not, or even accepted the right of extra-legal representatives to enact such a document.

One of the Articles banned most forms of entertainment including horse racing, cockfighting, and theater. It was said that gambling and amusements were dissipations of American wealth at a time when they shouldn't be squandered. To Wolfe it smacked of Puritanism. He marveled that the reach of the restrictive sect had spread so well in the colonies. In England the authors of such a proposal would be drawn and quartered by national consensus.

The Quebec Act was Government's decree incorporating recently conquered French Canada into the British Empire. In addition to ceding the *Habitants* their traditional lands in the Ohio country, land coveted by rich American speculators, including Franklin, the Quebec Act allowed the French to openly practice their Catholic religion. In British America, hatred of the Scarlet Whore, as the Catholic Church was called, was perhaps the only thing that Loyalists and Liberty Men agreed upon. According to the Gazette, allowing the French to openly practice Catholicism was nothing less than a plot to instate popery throughout America. Wolfe couldn't imagine even simpletons believing such nonsense, yet he knew that they would if it was printed in the newspaper.

The Quartering Act—requiring private Americans to house Ministerial Troops upon the mere command of a British Officer—was particularly odious to Bostonians, and Wolfe sympathized with them. The edict was outrageous. It was almost as if government was trying to provoke Americans.

One of the few voices of reason he came upon was in a different publication, by a Crown supporter signing his letter "Massachusettensis." According to Massachusettensis, an imperfect government—which he readily conceded the British Government was—would always be a pretense for libel by those seeking to undermine the government, especially free men with the right to speak out. True or not, by calling the government 'tyrant and oppressor' loud enough, a portion of the public will come to believe that the government is tyrannical and oppressive. Once the seed of sedition is planted, and some people act accordingly, the government must react, thus rendering the accusations of the libelers self-fulfilling.

Wolfe thought the analysis astute, especially the closing which pointed out that throughout history, the aftermath of rebellion always resulted in greater tyranny and oppression; either by the state seeking to punish rebels, or a new government seeking to purge its enemies.

Wolfe dozed off in front of the fire with a sense that New England was a rather grim and intolerant place, ready to erupt in self-righteous bloodshed.

In defiance of The Commodore's warnings, after a light supper, Wolfe indulged Betsy and sat to cards. They played *All-Fours*, Betsy's game. Despite her fearsome reputation, she was no match for Wolfe. He'd spent too much time in the gaming clubs of London to be distracted by a flirty woman with good cleavage. He considered throwing her a few tricks as she grew more agitated, but in good conscious he could not. He respected her. As upset as she was at losing, he was pretty sure she'd be angrier if she thought he'd lost on purpose.

After pocketing three of Betsy's shillings, Wolfe needed a stretch. She insisted on coming with and they walked out together. The evening was beautiful in its way. Heavy clouds backlit by a waning moon, the wind all but ceased, the snow reduced to gentle flurries of large flakes.

Near a pit fire at the edge of the property, blinded somewhat by flames, they didn't notice a dark figure approaching until Cuffee stomped up in snow shoes. "Jess checking the pickets," he said.

"Shan't they freeze in this weather?" Betsy asked.

"Never worry, missus. They's warm enough. Still got to see 'bout the harbor road though. You may wish to steah cleah of the barn. Some o' the soldiers is drunk." Knuckling his fur hat, he set off toward the waterfront.

As Betsy let the casually falling snow tickle her face, a snatch of muffled laughter came from the barn. "They despise us, you know," she said.

"Redcoats?" Wolfe clarified. She nodded.

"America may be British but 'tis not their country and no mistake. Most Boston families live better than their own in England and they resent it. For as every Britoner, they presume themselves superior to every American, which, as you may expect, does not endear them to any American, loyal or no. Those soldiers who cannot be bribed to sell their arms or desert, utterly detest us." She curtsied gracefully in summation, an endearing picture in her hooded red cloak and Wolfe clapped softly in appreciation.

"Did he but hear you, Doctor Franklin would be in love with you."

Betsy beamed under the compliment.

As they returned to the house, she slipped and clung to his arm for support, the feeling of which remained with him until he fell asleep.

12

A team of oxen pulling a plow was breaking out the snowy road when Wolfe came downstairs the next morning. One of Loring's house servants went out with a pitcher to slake the plowman's thirst. Another servant led a pair of oxen from Loring's barn and helped the plowman add them to his team. When they were hitched, the plowman continued down the road where more oxen would be added at the next house, and any oxen that were tired, put up in that neighbor's barn.

At breakfast it struck Wolfe again that Loring the younger was a lucky man. While seeing to it that the table was not wanting, Betsy bustled about with her son comfortably settled on her hip, softly singing "*Sally of the Alley*," a song Wolfe's mother used to sing.

Of all the days within the week, I dearly love but one day
That's the day that comes between, Saturday and Monday
For then I'm dressed in all my best to walk abroad with Sally
She's the darling of my heart, my Sally of the Alley

Captain Brown appeared at noon with an invitation for Wolfe and Commodore Loring to dine with General Gage on the morrow. Much to everyone's surprise, Brown then excused himself. Loring inquired if everything was all right.

"Sedition is like the ravening bite of a mad dog," Brown said. "It must be put down at once or the madness will spread. You'll be happy to know I have orders to see there is no further disturbance from the ropewalk."

That afternoon, Betsy demanded that Wolfe give her an opportunity to recoup her losses and reputation at cards. Unfortunately for her, before the first hand was dealt, they were interrupted. A man at the door sought audience with Commodore Loring and Mr. Wolfe.

Dr. Warren was received in Loring's study, and despite Wolfe's disinterest in colonial affairs, even he knew that Joseph Warren was one of the leading lights of the Boston Sons of Liberty.

A handsome and fastidiously fashionable man of middling height, Warren's traditional black physician's coat was of fine wool in the latest fashion from London. The ruffles at his wrists were lace, his small clothes and stockings of fine black satin and white silk respectively. His eyes were brown and intelligent, his manner disarming. Six- or seven-years Wolfe's senior, Warren carried signs of success around the waist and in his open and friendly face, but there was nothing complacent about him.

Warren opened the encounter by making a fuss over the attack on the Commodore. Double rows of blond curls above Warren's ears—earlocks—shook as he expressed his concern until Loring roared, "They were your creatures!" But Warren wouldn't hear it.

"I'd not see you harmed for the world," he told the Commodore. "Truth be told, I spend more time keeping Liberty Men from causing trouble than I do scheming against Government." Loring looked doubtful.

"I've known you boy and man, Joseph. You've something on your mind so out with it."

Warren frowned. "As you wish. I've come to warn out your guest. Mister Wolfe, I believe is his name." Warren and Wolfe exchanged nods.

"What nonsense is this?" Loring blustered softly.

"I'm warning Mister Wolfe out of town," said Warren. "In exchange for which, he shall go unmolested and be allowed safe passage out of town. Provided he departs as soon as the roads are passable."

"That old law hasn't been enforced in years," Loring scoffed.

"Precisely!" Warren was proud of it. "I had to improvise. Those who don't wish to hang Mister Wolfe desire to provide him a suit of tar and feathers and run him out of town on a rail."

Loring laid his best scowl on Warren. "You would threaten a guest under mine own roof?"

"I'm trying to avoid bloodshed," Warren said. "I was told Mister Wolfe is leaving soon anyway. I had to give the radicals something. Letting them chase him away harms no one and preserves the peace. A clever bargain if I do say."

The Commodore would have argued but Wolfe said, "I'll be gone in a few days, Doctor Warren. If that complies with your order, we are agreed."

"We do our utmost to keep the radicals in check," Warren said regretfully, "but they grow bold as country folk." As if to bring matters to a happy conclusion, he put his right hand over his heart and bowed his head.

Raising his head, his mien changed. "I now consider that I have performed my official duty," he said. "Forgive me Commodore, but I wonder if I might have a private word with Mister Wolfe?" It took Loring a moment to realize that Warren wanted him to leave.

On his way out the door, Loring said to Wolfe, sotto voce, "Know you that Joseph Warren should've been a lawyer before a doctor."

When it was just the two of them, Warren said, "You've instigated some trouble, Mister Wolfe, but I'm grateful. T'would be tragic were the Commodore harmed. Yet I'm confused. Your . . ." He paused for the right word. "Your ... honesty, regarding certain facts, has probably done a great service to America by now. Doctor Franklin speaks of you with the utmost esteem, indeed his letter holds me responsible for your safety. Yet your actions might have started a war. We have only the weather to thank that events did not escalate, by the way."

"Captain Brown of the Fifty-Second Foot would've been most happy to oblige such an escalation," Wolfe said pointedly. When Warren didn't react, he said, "Pray what do you mean, 'done great service to America?'"

"The information you provided," Warren said. Wolfe cocked his head.

"I've said nothing secret to anyone in America."

Warren smiled patiently. "Come, Mister Wolfe. Let us not bandy words." When Wolfe didn't respond, Warren sighed. "All right then. By warning of the Orders in Council, you've done all liberty loving Americans a great service." Wolfe was struck by the inherent injustice of Warren's premise.

"So, for having done a great service, I'm threatened and ordered out of town. Strange reward that."

"These are strange times," Warren said. "Consider that the gulf between Commodore Loring and the Sons of Liberty is not whether American protests are justified, but how to fight the injustice."

"And for that he was to be tarred and feathered?" Wolfe didn't hide the disdain in his voice. "Doctor Franklin once famously said, wars bring scars. Do you consider that the Commodore might be against war because he's fought in one before?"

"The times do not allow for such distinctions," Warren said, but there was no glib in him. "Justice is the first victim of idle men and cheap rum, Mister Wolfe, both of which we have an abundance of in Boston." He gestured that he should like to sit near the fire. When they were seated, he said, "You must realize that your current situation presents a rare opportunity to render assistance to your country."

"Does it indeed?" Wolfe said skeptically. He marveled at Warren's audacity but there was no guile in the man. "I'm a courier, Doctor Warren, not a spy."

"Yet you gave valuable information to a complete stranger."

"News known publicly in Portsmouth before I sailed," Wolfe said. Warren gave an indulgent smile.

"I'll wager you were paid to deliver the news to Gage." Wolfe swallowed the first response that rose to his lips.

"The Commodore was right about one thing," he said, "there is the distinct whiff of the Esquire about you Doctor." Warren laughed. Wolfe smiled thinly. "I appreciate that you're doing what you see as your duty, but I'll thank you to know I don't see it as mine. You'd be wrong to consider me for any scheme Doctor Franklin may have suggested. "Despite our friendship, we're not always of similar mind." Warren started to reply but Wolfe talked over him.

"With all due respect, there is nothing for us to discuss. I have no intent of taking sides in your quarrel. I merely helped a man being set upon in the street. I'm passing through your town. That is all. I can't make myself plainer." He stood up. "I would you respect my wishes and tell any others."

"I shall," Warren said, rising also. "But the time draws nigh when you'll have to take sides if you remain in America, Mister Wolfe, and not just here in Boston."

"That may be," said Wolfe. "But until then I have personal business to attend."

"Then I hope if we meet again it will be as friends," said Warren. Wolfe shook the hand he extended.

"I should hate to see it otherwise," Wolfe said, and he meant it. He liked the man.

13

Captain Brown had nothing to show for his day's adventure when he returned to Loring's. The workers had decamped prior to his arrival at the ropewalk. Discovering Wolfe and Betsy playing cards did nothing to quell his distemper. Quickly downing a number of brandies, he decided to put Wolfe—whom he considered an interloper and an inferior—in his place.

"I don't suppose you are familiar with the art of fence, Mister Wolfe?" he said arrogantly. Tired of Brown's condescension, Wolfe paused mid-deal.

"I've been known to cross blades but I haven't a sword," he lied. His sword was in his portmantle. He just wanted to shut Brown up. Unfortunately, in front of Mrs. Loring, Brown wouldn't back off.

"I'm sure we can find you a sword," he said.

Loring's stable was tight and well found, but even with the doors shut it was cold. The combined respiration of Redcoats and Loring stable hands, anticipating entertainment, clouded the eaves.

Brown and Wolfe stripped down to waistcoats to spar in the corridor between stalls. They were armed with short swords of the type carried by officers and gentlemen. Wolfe's was a loaner from The Commodore. Simple and unadorned, it was in fact a finely balanced weapon with a walnut grip and a blood gutter the length of its Toledo steel blade. A sword made for work, not show.

The combatants saluted each other and commenced sparring. As was custom, they moved through the classic evolutions of attack, parry and riposte, a somewhat stately exercise more akin to dance than sport, which was fine with Wolfe. He could feel every minute of the months since he'd last flashed a blade. As his muscles warmed however, the core strength acquired from years of swordplay came to the fore. Ten minutes of mundane but steady work had both men glistening with sweat and in need of a break.

"I see you are trained," Brown commented, blotting his brow with the neck cloth he'd removed.

"I'm rusty," Wolfe said. "But grateful for the exercise."

"Shall I take that to mean you wouldn't care to make our session more interesting?"

Wolfe tried to gauge the purpose of the challenge. The captain wasn't good enough to be sure of beating him. His style was brawny in the fashion of the army but his footwork was clumsy and unsure, unless he'd been baiting a trap. Wolfe decided to know the truth of it. "What did you have in mind?"

"Three touches?"

"The purse?"

Brown smiled arrogantly. "What do you say to a shilling a touch?" Wolfe smiled back. The captain wasn't so sure.

"A dollar a touch would be more interesting," Wolfe said. "The Commodore to judge?" The trace of a scowl crossed Brown's face but he bowed his head stiffly.

"As you say."

"A touch is 'twixt waist and neck," Loring pronounced. "Blood is a touch for the bleeder. Retreat beyond the boundary is a touch." He glared at the contestants until they nodded.

Taking his charge seriously, Loring paced out boundaries and scored furrows with the heel of his boot in the hard, hay strewn dirt floor. Not content, he rearranged the spectators so they were out of the combatant's direct line of sight, which wasn't easy. A few civilians and almost a company of Redcoats were milling around betting furiously with one another. Only when all was to his satisfaction did Loring call Brown and Wolfe to the mark.

Wolfe almost lost the first touch when the Commodore shouted, "Commence!" and Brown lunged with far greater reach than he'd displayed earlier. Only a desperate garde by Wolfe kept the Captain from scoring. As it was, Brown's blade slashed across Wolfe's right forearm. To Wolfe's disgust, the sleeve on his shirt was ripped and blood from the cut on his arm would ruin the rest. To the jeers and taunts of the attending redcoats, Loring tied Wolfe's neck cloth around the wound.

"We can forgo the match if you're too injured to continue," Brown said. "Of course, the purse would be forfeit."

"I'll continue," said Wolfe.

"As you've drawn blood that's a touch for Mister Wolfe," Loring said to Brown.

"Only a body or head bleeder counts against!" Brown snapped. "'T'ain't my fault he got cut!"

Wolfe nodded to the Commodore. "He's right. That shouldn't count against."

"As you wish," Loring said.

Brown and Wolfe resumed their places. This time when the Commodore barked, "Commence!" Brown miscalculated. Counting on the surprise of repetition, he lunged again, but Wolfe was ready. He'd been victimized the first time because such a rash attack was foolhardy. If it failed, the attacker was left open. Wolfe easily knocked the Captain's blade down and finished with his point inches from Brown's chest.

"Touch!" cried the commodore. The few spectators betting on Wolfe pounded the stalls and hooted.

We'll have no more of that nonsense, thought Wolfe.

The third round assumed a more satisfying aspect. The rhythmic clash of steel was interrupted only by an occasional frenzied exchange as Brown struggled to counter Wolfe, who was taking it somewhat easy on the Captain. In the end, Brown was betrayed by his footwork.

Under stomping boots, the mud-trampled straw had become slick. Backing up as Wolfe pressed the attack, Brown slid enough to dip his blade. Wolfe needed less of an opening to beat a better swordsman.

Loring called the touch and ordered a pause. The combatants were panting hard. Brown quenched his thirst from a canteen of rum. Wolfe guzzled beer from a skin that Cuffee provided.

"That's enough," the black man said, taking back the skin. "It'll slow you down. I got purse on you."

"You've naught to fear on that score," Wolfe said.

Loring called the men back. "The score is Mister Wolfe two. Captain Brown nil."

"We're aware the way things stand," Brown said curtly.

The bout resumed with the Captain throwing caution to the wind and attempting to beat Wolfe's blade down with brute force. In a different circumstance Wolfe would have countered such a tactic rather easily, but his arm strength was waning and the Captain managed to prick his shoulder hard enough for the spectators to catch their collective breaths. Loring called the touch but Brown smugly kept his blade hard against Wolfe's shoulder, until Wolfe slapped it aside with his blade.

When they toed the mark for the next round, there was bad blood in the air.

"A moment." Wolfe stepped away to examine the blood-soaked neck-cloth around his arm. The cut was deeper than he thought, and then it occurred to him that he hadn't once thought about the puckered wound in his side. When he stepped back up to the mark, the sword was in his left hand and he felt unbeatable. Brown misread his demeanor and smirked.

"Really Mister Wolfe, there is no dishonor in conceding."

"I concede nothing," Wolfe said. "Maestro Angelo is quite insistent that his students handle a blade with either hand." Brown blanched. "Angelo?"

"You've heard of him?" Wolfe said innocently. He was sure that Brown knew Angelo was the premiere fencing master in London. Cuffee didn't know it though. Wolfe could see it in the slave's face. He was worried that Wolfe had changed from righty to lefty. Wolfe winked at him.

Brown was cautious when they started back in, probing more than engaging, uncomfortable facing a cock-hander. Wolfe was content not to press matters. He was enjoying himself. He felt strong and he was the better swordsman with either arm. Only fatigue would lose him the day and he was sure that Captain Brown wouldn't maintain his composure long enough for that.

He was right. Brown suddenly attacked furiously, resolved to gain the touch with brute force again or drive Wolfe out of bounds. Wolfe parried the captain's strokes easily but let it seem as if he was being overwhelmed. He let himself be bullied all the way to the back line, then stepped aside and let Brown's ferocious but empty finishing lunge carry him clumsily out of bounds. Wolfe gave him a swat on the bum with the flat of his sword for good luck.

"Boundary!" Loring yelled with a satisfied grin. "Match to Mister Wolfe!"

"Bleedin' ass wipe!" shouted a redcoat who'd lost a wager. Brown spun on the man and pointed his sword.

"Inspection! Ten minutes!" Brown's men scrambled to organize their gear. Brown was seething as he turned back to Wolfe, but he brought his emotions under control. "I trust you'll accept my mark until I can return to my quarters."

"You know where I'll be," Wolfe said.

"Let us get that arm tended to." Loring draped Wolfe's greatcoat over Wolfe's shoulders and led the way from the stable. Outside, Cuffee was collecting money from a soldier. When he saw Wolfe, he grinned broadly and gave a little salute.

Loring took the sword from Wolfe and dunked the grip in the snow, leaving a trail of blood. "'T'ain't much to look at but she saw me safe through the wars."

"'Tis a fine sword," Wolfe said. "Don't let anyone tell you elsewise. 'Tis light and well balanced. T'were a pleasure to use it and I thank you for the privilege." His words pleased the Commodore.

"I thought Brown'd piss hisself when you said you trained with Angelo. Is it true?"

"True enough," Wolfe snickered. "T'were but a handful of times however." Loring laughed.

"True enough indeed."

Betsy's concern over Wolfe's wound was gratifying and pragmatic. She unwrapped the neck cloth, examined the cut, and with some well-chosen words regarding the amusements of men, led him to the scullery. A middle-aged black woman was kneading bread.

"Mister Wolfe needs ligatures, Amelia. Would you mind?" Amelia wiped her hands on a stained apron tucked into her belt and gestured for Wolfe to approach.

"Come to me here by the fire." Examining the cut, she said, "Grab yon rum, 'Lizbeth." When Betsy handed her the jug, Amelia laughed. "For him." Handing the jug to Wolfe, she said, "Drink. An' keep your arm up." To Betsy she said, "Clean his arm whilst I get my things."

Betsy helped Wolfe pull his shirt off. Examining the blood-stained fabric with her fingers, she said, "A pity 'tis ruined. Good linen costs dear these days."

"My fault." Wolfe said. "I was bloody careless." Betsy ignored his profanity. She'd noticed the evil scar below his ribs. She traced the contours with her finger.

"Was this carelessness as well?"

"That," said Wolfe, pausing to take a pull on the rum, "is Doctor Franklin's fault." Betsy's eyes went wide.

"One of his experiments?" Wolfe gagged on a mouthful of rum. He managed to keep it down but was left gasping and snorting in laughter. Betsy cried, "Am I so silly?" and would have flounced away, but Wolfe caught her hand and refused to let go.

"You're not silly," he said. "You're lovely. Were you not married, I'd court you myself, and that after taking a blade for my last such attentions." His confession mollified her somewhat. She smiled smugly.

"I knew there was a woman."

Wolfe resumed drinking but kept hold her hand. She rested the other on his naked shoulder, boldly intimate for a married woman. "What was her name?" Betsy said softly. He didn't answer. She would have pressed him but instead pulled away and fussed with his shirt as Amelia returned.

Wolfe was glad for the interruption. His thoughts were turning lascivious. "Let us get on with it," he said to Amelia.

"An' I got to wax the thread, don't I?" Amelia grumbled. As Betsy cleaned the blood-stained skin around the cut, Amelia drew five short pieces of thread through soft wax near the flame of a candle. After dipping her fingers in nut oil, she slicked the waxed threads, passing the last one expertly through the eye of a needle. Taking the rum from Wolfe, she took a big swig for herself.

"Ready?" she said. At Wolfe's nod, she pushed the needle through the edge flaps of the cut and told Betsy to press the skin together so she could knot the first ligature. After five more large, but well made, stitches, she pronounced the job done. "Don't need a plaster lest you want one," she said.

"That won't be necessary," said Wolfe. "My thanks. And you also, madam." He turned to Betsy. She stopped stroking his bicep and lowered her eyes demurely. Amelia laughed, revealing molasses ravaged teeth.

"Take a piece o'shirt and make a bandage, 'Lizbeth."

Wolfe smelled pine in Betsy's hair as she bandaged the sutures. She was aware of his scent too. Amelia was aware of the two of them together. Cocking her head, she said to Betsy, "Is that your son I hear cryin'?"

14

Captain Brown did not appear the next day to escort Loring and Wolfe to Gage's headquarters. A lieutenant led the eight Redcoats who trotted behind Loring's sleigh for the journey. With the sun out at last, the glare off the melting snow was dazzling.

They arrived at Province House through a back gate in the stable yard. As Cuffee brought the sleigh to a stop, a three-pounder cannon behind the house barked.

"Signal gun," Loring said. "Something's afoot." The report of a cannon on Beacon Hill and another from Castle William out in the harbor seemed to confirm his estimation.

General Gage and a mud-spattered man were studying a map when his guests were ushered in. "I'm afraid I shall have to beg off our engagement," Gage said at once. "It seems there's to be an attack. Probably has been an attack, I should say, on Fort William and Mary up in Portsmouth. Mister Barnsdall here," Gage nodded at his companion, "says four or five hundred insurgents were preparing to move on the fort when he left yesterday. The mischief has probably been done but I mean to show the colors."

"Can't the fort hold out?" Loring said. Gage shook his head.

"'Tis manned by an invalid corp. But one officer and six men barely fit to serve."

"The war starts in Portsmouth of all places," Loring muttered in disbelief. Gage didn't disagree.

"It seems Mister Revere informed the insurgents of an impending ban on arms and powder. I assume they mean to possess the stores in the fort."

"How could he know that?" Loring said.

"How should I know!" Gage snapped in frustration. "The damned insurgents have my orders before our men on Copp's Hill do!" He was embarrassed by his outburst and turned away to stare out the window. Wolfe felt his stomach turn sour at the same time.

'*Done great service,*' Warren had said.

"There's a goodly store of powder up there," Gage said to the window. "I must do something." After a deep controlled sigh, his shoulders squared into a posture befitting the royal governor. He was composed when he turned back to the room. "Admiral Graves will be here shortly. I must prepare a plan."

"Of course," Loring said. "What of Revere? Will you arrest the rascal?" Gage struggled to control his emotions.

"As far as I know he's done nothing illegal. Unless it's proved he incited the attack."

"Nothing illegal?" Loring glared. "He's at the very …"

"I'll hear no more," Gage cut him off. "If I break the law to prosecute insurgents it serves their purpose. I will act only to promote the Crown's advantage and none other. Good day, Commodore." Loring wasn't pleased, but years of service discipline were ingrained. He made a stiff bow and withdrew. Gage stopped Wolfe at the door.

"I haven't forgotten you, Mister Wolfe. My plans include sending a message to New York at once. I shall also send a note to the Port Collector at New Haven. That will be your best bet for Long Island, I think. You could go all the way to New York of course, but it's another fifty miles to Brookhaven. New Haven's just across the Long Island Sound. I would know your preference before I write my cover."

"New Haven, sir. By your leave."

"You should know that New Haven Town is not friendly to Government. They may not look kindly upon a ministerial messenger."

"Would I be apt to suffer tar and feathers?" Wolfe said.

"Does that worry you?" Gage said.

"It didn't before I came to Boston," Wolfe chuckled. Gage didn't chuckle.

"I would have your answer."

"I accept," Wolfe said. Gage was pleased.

"I shouldn't wonder if you receive word to take ship this very day. That was a smart piece of work you did, by the way. Saving Loring. We drank your health three times three." Wolfe accepted the compliment with a nod.

"Thank you General. And the best of luck to you." Gage smiled anemically.

"It's come to civil war, Mister Wolfe. Heaven help us all."

Loring sulked when they left Province House. He was cross with Gage and angry that his sacred dinner hour of two o'clock was compromised. When he finally broke his silence, he said, "That bastard Revere should have been arrested long ago."

"Why?" said Wolfe.

"He's a troublemaker for the Sons of Violence," Loring growled. He didn't speak again until the sleigh pulled into his stable yard, then—as one who doesn't want to, but must—he said, "I don't suppose you told Warren something t'other day?" Wolfe was glad that he could say he did not.

The possibility that war had broken out lent a somber mood to a late dinner. Betsy rocked her boy in her arms and debated whether to flee Boston and join her daughter and husband in Roxbury. The Commodore disabused her of the notion, saying, "You'll be safer in town. T'would make more sense for them to join us here."

A brief discussion regarding the nature of Wolfe's departure followed. He was of a mind to slip down backstreets with one of Loring's men as a guide, an idea Loring also summarily dismissed.

"You'll go in the open and with a force the Faction defy at their peril. There's more here than getting you to the wharf. Lest there be any doubt, people must see that His Majesty controls this town." Wolfe's reaction caused him to add hastily, "And of course, going in the open has the advantage of being the safest course for you." Wolfe shook his head at the Commodore's weak attempt to mitigate his previous comment. Interpreting Wolfe's reaction perfectly, Loring said testily, "We're at war, Mister Wolfe. A little boldness if you please." Wolfe laughed aloud.

"You forget, sir. Doctor Franklin is the puppeteer of the age. I know when I'm being dangled." Loring harrumphed and blustered denials but they were half-hearted.

At first candle, two Redcoat Officers delivered a note requiring Wolfe to repair at once aboard *HMS Rose* at the Long Wharf. Included was a packet from General Gage to the Port Collector at New Haven. Loring took charge of Wolfe's departure and went to put all in motion.

Betsy was emotional. Sniffling dolefully, she said, "I know 'tis silly but I feel as if I'm a losing a great friend. I was looking forward to celebrating Christmastide together."

"And winning your money back," Wolfe said lightly.

"That too," she said, trying to smile. Wolfe raised up her chin. He desperately wanted to kiss the plump lips of the dimpled smile. She wanted him to, he was sure of it, but she was married.

Bloody hell.

He took her in his arms and intimately kissed her good-bye.

Torches cast shadows of activity across the snow in the stable yard; Cuffee adjusting the horses' harness, a half company of the 52nd Foot dressing their lines. Calmly overseeing it all was The Commodore.

"Should be ready in a trice," he said. "Your pistols charged?" Wolfe patted his greatcoat. "Warren's word is good," Loring said, "but that don't mean some fool won't make trouble. My two-barrel's in the sleigh, loaded pellet and ball. Fresh charged by my own hand. You can trust she'll spark."

The same lieutenant who led the escort earlier in the day bellowed, "Charge firelocks!" Wolfe noted an eagerness in the Redcoats as they loaded their muskets. The lieutenant barked, "Fix bayonets!" and the 52nd mounted their bayonets with a satisfying metallic shiver.

Cuffee signaled that he was ready and Loring turned to Wolfe and extended his hand. "Godspeed, Mister Wolfe. You've a place at my fire always."

Fifteen Redcoats trailed the sleigh out of the yard. Immediately upon gaining the main road, a bell began to peal. It was quickly joined by others.

Wolfe checked the priming in the Commodore's carriage gun and made sure the flints were tight in the dog-heads.

Summoned by the bells, people came out of their houses to witness Wolfe's departure. From the gliding sleigh they were but fleeting forms in the darkness. They said and did nothing, yet their very silence and inaction were intimidating, punctuated as it was by tolling bells.

Streetlamps were lit in the vicinity of Province House and the number of people lining the road swelled. Now Wolfe could see them bundled against the cold, dutifully silent, warm respiration lingering in clouds over their heads.

The fence around Province House was lit by small bonfires. A regiment of Grenadiers with fixed bayonets stood formation in the yard, their red uniforms like blood on the snow, as intimidating in their ready silence as the people lining the road.

The sleigh slowed to a walk when they reached Town House Square, and mercifully, the insistent clanging of bells ceased. In the aftermath, the unnatural quiet of hundreds of silent onlookers was eerie. The only sounds to be heard were the thud of hooves on packed snow, creaking and jangling harness, and the muffled tread of the men of the 52nd.

In the yellow light of streetlamps—at a walk—Wolfe could make out faces staring at him as if he was an animal in a menagerie. On impulse, he doffed his Denmark as a hero might in a parade. First to one side, then the other. He received glares and insulting finger salutes in reply, but not a word was uttered against him.

At the end of King Street, the sleigh passed through a company of Royal Marines and whispered onto the Long Wharf. Drawing to a stop, Cuffee turned to Wolfe with a relieved grin and said, "Nothin' to it."

"Aye. Never a doubt," Wolfe said drily. He handed Cuffee the carriage gun and a Spanish dollar. "Sorry for the inconvenience." Cuffee knuckled his forehead with the dollar in thanks.

Wolfe shouldered his portmantle and found the lieutenant leading the escort. "Captain Brown owes me two dollars," he said. "I would he stand you and your men to a firkin of rum with that money. Will you be so good as to relay my wishes?" The lieutenant happily promised that he would.

Far down the wharf, a frigate was completing stores by the light of lanterns in the rigging. Wolfe moved to the bottom of the gangplank and named himself to the adolescent midshipman who had the watch.

"Been expecting you, sir," the youngster said. He called to the ship, "Pipes!" A sailor bundled in a watch coat and wool cap appeared at the top of the gangway. "This is Mister Wolfe," the Midshipman called. "Show him to Mister Welky's old berth." Pipes knuckled his brow to the boy.

As Wolfe strode up the gangplank, Pipes said, "Welcome aboard, Mister Wolfe."

15

Captain James Wallace was a rarity in the Royal Navy, having been a scholar at the Royal Academy before entering the service. In his forties now, Wallace was a confident if not tyrannical commander, although his crew liked him well enough. They had faith that the driven man would make them a fortune in prize money when war broke out.

"I'm to put you ashore in New Haven," Wallace said.

"New Haven is what I was told," Wolfe agreed. He'd been summoned to the captain's cabin shortly before noon. Despite *HMS Rose's* relatively diminutive size—five hundred tons, twenty-eight, nine pounder cannons— her great cabin was as handsome as any first-rate of a hundred guns, albeit on a smaller scale.

Wallace was seated at his desk pouring liquor into a steaming mug of coffee. The Rose had warped out on the ebb tide and he'd been on deck all night. Tired and preoccupied, he commented offhandedly, "New Haven's a town that aught burn. My orders say you're to deliver correspondence for General Gage. Be this a Royal Commission?" Wolfe grabbed an overhead beam as the ship took an awkward swell.

"General Gage needs a letter delivered. I'm Long Island bound. There is nothing more subtle than that. All I require is to get ashore at New Haven."

When Wolfe offered nothing further, Wallace said, "I see you are not at liberty to discuss matters so I won't waste your time nor mine. Our passage will be tedious enough. Here in New England a nor'easter is always repaid with a westerly. We'll beat all the way up Long Island Sound is my prediction."

Captain Wallace was too right. When *Rose* made her westing beyond Nantucket, she found herself beating up the Sound into the teeth of a northwest wind and the confused chop of gray seas. With plenty of time on his hands, Wolfe set about opening Gage's letter.

Like all travelers, couriers were at jeopardy to some degree, although highwaymen were not typically anxious to take them on—most couriers being armed and rarely with enough purse to warrant the risk. Intrigue, however, was another matter entirely.

Wolfe had been targeted once; the unwitting bearer of information a certain party would do anything to stop. Wolfe barely escaped with his life. After that he delivered nothing blind, not even for Dr. Franklin. Especially for Dr. Franklin. The Doctor was always sending correspondence that could land Wolfe in trouble but assuring him it was naught but innocuous musings on the weather. Wolfe never delivered anything for The Doctor without reading it first.

Gage's correspondence to New Haven informed His Majesty's Customs Agent of the ban on powder and arms, and ordered him to supply an inventory of such stores currently residing in the town. Wolfe wasn't thrilled to know he was carrying a letter that could get him tarred and feathered, but at least he knew. Fore-knowledge afforded some protection.

The difficult part of examining a letter was resealing it. Gage used the official seal of the Province of Massachusetts, an engraving far too intricate to reproduce.

Wolfe took a roll of lumpy leather from his portmantle. Untied, it unrolled to expose a half-dozen pockets containing the tools of his trade. A cylinder of wax divided into sections of different colors yielded a red and black which would mix to a brown such as Gage used.

From another pouch he removed a collection of letter-slugs like those of a printing press. The slug he chose snapped into the end of a small wooden handle designed to receive it. After heating the brown wax, Wolfe substituted a fancy G for the Massachusetts seal. Upon inspection, he was satisfied that only a suspicious eye familiar with Gage's personal seal would find anything amiss.

He took his meals with the ship's officers as a guest of the wardroom. They were a decent lot, for the little he saw of them. Mostly they slept or were on deck in the fatigue-inducing cold. To stay out of the way, and stay warm, Wolfe spent his days in the caboose, reading aloud to the cook. He'd found the wardroom's copy of *Fanny Hill*, and the cook, Walters, a salty gimp with a pigtail as long as his back, was glad for the amusement.

As a schoolboy, Wolfe and his mates reveled in *Fanny Hill*. The *HMS Rose* copy of the book looked as though it had seen a generation of officers through lonely nights at sea. To the illiterate Walters, having it read to him was as good as a bawdy show in Covent Garden.

On the second day of their westing, Wolfe was invited to dine with the captain. He was seated next to Mr. Bunder, a flaccid surgeon in a ragged wig whom Wolfe knew from the wardroom. Across from him was the midshipman who'd been on duty when he boarded, Mr. O'Brien. Wolfe had also met Folkes, the short and rat-like purser. Others at the table were Lauper, a king-and-country captain of marines, and Savage Gardner, the ship's sailing master.

Fresh from port with full larders, Wallace laid a worthy table. Conversation was polite and correct as the company enjoyed a fine meal. After dinner however, when the cloth was pulled and the bottle had gone around the table a few times, the polite tone changed.

"Americans grow rich because they act as rivals to British trade," Wallace said. He belabored his belief by pointing out that Americans paid less duty on goods than their British counterparts, yet cited taxes as an excuse for insurrection.

When he was well in his cups, Captain Wallace shed all restraint and bitterly castigated Government's leniency toward the treasonous American dogs. "But that is all about to change," he said dramatically. As his subordinates leaned in, Wallace said, "After we deliver dispatches to New York, Rose shall resume station in Newport. Unlike our previous postings on that station however, our orders are to actively seek out and punish any and all transgressions against the Crown. In short, gentlemen, we are to be unleashed to hound the damned rebels at last. Let's see how brazen the toothless bastards are when they've a proper English hunter on their arse!" His officers pounded their glasses on the table in approbation. Wolfe leaned over to Mr. Bunder.

"Does the captain mean anything in particular when he names the rebels toothless, or is it merely an expression?" Bunder nodded as if the question was quite to be expected.

"He is indeed being particular. I dare say you noticed the teeth of the people in Boston. You can always tell a Yankee by their teeth."

"Their teeth?"

"Aye. Their rotted teeth," Bunder said, as if it was a well-known fact. "From the molasses. In addition to drinking morbid amounts of rum, they put molasses in everything they eat. Turns their teeth to mush."

A man who liked holding court, Wallace opined his distaste for Americans long into the next watch. Before he was finished, he openly confessed a desire to put every town in Massachusetts to the torch until the smell of burned timber overwhelmed the stench of treason. Wolfe stumbled back to his berth knowing that Captain Wallace of the Royal Navy hated Americans as much as Betsy Loring's Redcoats did.

There was a sea change when he roused shortly after sunup the next day. The air wasn't as raw and during the night the wind had shifted out of the west to a little east of north. *Rose* was no longer beating into a headwind. She was making eight knots and the confused motion of the ship had been usurped by an eager rhythmic surge.

Wolfe poked his head above deck then instinctively ducked at the discharge of a cannon.

"Good shot, Mister Jonnson!" Wallace was using a speaking trumpet from the quarter deck to communicate with his lanky first lieutenant, forward firing the bow chaser. Lieutenant Jonnson doffed his hat to acknowledge the captain's approval.

"Put one more alongside!" Wallace called amiably. "If they don't heave-to I shall luff and give them a broadside!" Jonnson waved that he understood. Wallace called down to the waist, "Clear for action, Mr. Herbert!" The starboard gun crews cast off their tackle and loaded their nine pounders.

Wolfe found an open spot on the larboard foredeck and took out his pocket glass. The object of the frigate's activity was a half-mile ahead, a twenty-foot open boat with a stubby mast and threadbare gray sail. She was steering directly before the wind, a sensible maneuver, before the wind being a poor point of sail for a square rigger like *Rose*, but in this instance it didn't matter. Even with the wind dead aft, the frigate was a greyhound chasing a turtle.

An eight-gallon keg went over the side of the fleeing boat—a firkin—followed by more firkins. The smugglers were trying to lighten their load, for smugglers they must be.

The bow chaser boomed again and Wolfe saw the ball splash into a wave alongside the little boat. With Long Island yet many miles distant, the smugglers had no hope of escape, yet they were determined to try. In a last effort to eke every bit of speed from their ponderously heeling craft, they hiked out on the windward gunwale as far as they dared.

Wallace was delighted, and determined to have a little fun. He called forward, "House your gun, Mister Jonnson!" Aiming his speaking trumpet at the gun deck, he called, "Run out your guns, Mister Herbert! Wait for my order when we luff!"

The frigate's starboard broadside ran out with a rumble.

Wallace's next orders were spoken quietly to the sailing master, Gardner. A moment later the bosun's whistle shrilled, the mizzen gaff sail flew down and the helm was put hard over. *Rose* fell off the wind with a *whoooosh* from the bow wave and presented her starboard broadside to the fleeing smugglers.

Wallace raised his speaking trumpet and waited for the ship to settle before giving the order to fire. In that instant, the fleeing boat's sail sheeted down in surrender. Wallace cursed in annoyance and Wolfe thought he might give the order to fire anyway, but he called for Pipes to launch the cutter instead.

The daring smugglers proved to be two young men, little more than boys really. One would be a sturdy fellow when full grown; the other was slight, with fair hair and blue eyes.

Wallace was waiting when they stepped timidly aboard *Rose* amidships. Rather than lay into them however, much to their surprise, the British

Captain smiled kindly and welcomed them aboard.

"Do you know why I says welcome?" Wallace purred. Crew members watching the exchange sniggered until Wallace held up a hand for silence. "Do you know why I welcome you aboard, lads?" he said again. Neither of the boys spoke so Wallace pressed on like a jolly uncle. "I welcome you aboard because His Majesty needs good lads to serve his ships, and here you are!" The fair-haired boy protested at once.

"We'll not serve in a king's ..." He never finished his sentence because Mr. Leopold, the boatswain, cuffed him hard on the side of the head. Wallace looked on happily as the boy hit the deck like a sack of oats.

"Two prime hands," Wallace gloated. "Prime hands! That little fellow looks like a top man, wouldn't you say Mister Leopold?" Leopold grinned.

"Aye, sir. First rate top man."

"I'll read them in directly," Wallace said. He turned to the first lieutenant. "Mister Jonnson, soon as the contraband and the cutter are aboard, we'll have a little target practice on the boy's boat. Then we'll make all sail for New Haven."

Wolfe stepped forward and spoke before he could censor himself. "Beg pardon, Captain, but you can't press these boys. They . . ." His voice trailed off as he realized he'd made a grievous error. The convivial background hum of the crew ceased. Wallace's face morphed into misshapen purple anger.

"You presume to tell me what I cannot do aboard my ship?!" He spat as if tasting shit. "Are you lunatic?" His voice rose in timbre with his outrage. "Gage's orders be damned! I'll press you and give you a dozen at the grate by God!" As the threats in his brain went too fast for his mouth to attend, Mr. Leopold shoved Wolfe aft.

"Get thee below before he do as he say," Leopold hissed.

Wolfe fled below into the dark little booth that was his cabin. He was vibrating with anger, unused to being at the mercy of another man's whim; but well knowing that aboard his own ship, Wallace was the closest thing to God as existed in the English-speaking world.

Wolfe cursed himself long and hard for speaking up. In the first place because nothing he might have said would've made a damn bit of difference, and especially because he could trace most of the trouble in his life to speaking up when he should have shut up.

Long after the smuggler's boat was sunk by a broadside, and well past the serving out of the holy grog ration at eight bells, Wolfe lay in his hammock staring at the deck beams above. As the hours stretched on, the utter dread, of being pressed into the British Navy, grew inside of him like cancer.

16

Late in the afternoon, Mr. Leopold came to fetch him, and the bile in Wolfe's stomach churned to a head.

"You're a lucky one," the boatswain said.

"I'm to be put ashore?" Wolfe dared hope.

"Myself I'm sorry to see thee leave," said Leopold. "Most of us wagered the captain would press you. As it appears he ain't, you're a very unpopular man just now."

Wolfe didn't care what the crew's opinion of him was. That he wasn't going to be pressed into the Royal Navy was the only thing that mattered. In the hours he'd spent worrying, he had to confront the idea that his current life was less than it might be. He had a comfortable life, quite adequate, but upon reflection he discovered that adequate was not a description of his life that he could take pride in. Something needed to change and it wasn't joining the Royal Navy.

"The boys' names is Phipps and Leary," Mr. Leopold whispered. "From New London." He thrust a slip of paper into Wolfe's hand. Wolfe's surprise was written all over his face and Leopold responded to it. "Their people should know they ain't dead s'all I'm saying. Can you see to it?" Wolfe said that he would.

Rose hove-to off the mouth of New Haven Harbor. Captain Wallace was not on deck as Wolfe made his way to the main chains, but in an act of solidarity with their captain, crewmen previously friendly turned their backs on him. The crew of the launch ignored him too. They pushed off and went to work as if he wasn't there, eight oars dipping and sweeping in professional unison.

Away from the olfactory-numbing odors of the ship, Long Island Sound filled Wolfe's senses so familiarly that the years fell away in an instant. As Wolfe knew, and Dr. Franklin could prove, every body of water had its own essence. According to The Doctor, essence depended on depth, salinity and a dozen other variables. By Wolfe's lights, the thing that set the Sound apart was that it was the body of water he was weaned on.

Wolfe recognized New Haven harbor perfectly. As a boy he'd sailed there dozens of times with his father, besides which, the two massive rock formations looming inland beyond the town were unforgettable. Especially the western formation which rose seven hundred feet over the surrounding country and was twice the height of the eastern one.

The town nestled below thick woods carpeting the hilly distance between the rock formations. Flanked on either side by a river, New Haven Town stumbled down to the harbor in a hodgepodge of structures; some shake and some clapboard, but many more than Wolfe remembered. Fourteen years of change in America was far more dramatic than in London.

An hour before dusk the harbor was quiet but not desolate. The dozen or so brigs and sloops at moorings and dockside were well found and shipshape.

At the end of the harbor, the Port Collector's residence was a two-story clapboard warehouse with windows at one corner on the second floor. A central interior chimney poked from the peaked roof and the whole was made larger by a coat of whitewash. The cutter discharged Wolfe at the dock and departed without comment or farewell.

As Wolfe took his bearings, an old man with a pronounced limp emerged from the customs warehouse. As he drew close it could be seen that he had once suffered a terrible accident. His left eye socket was empty and a wispy gray beard did little to hide the flattened and lopsided aspect of his face. It was hard for Wolfe not to stare.

"State your bishnessh," the man said with an odd whistle.

"Is the commissioner to work?"

"Dependsh on who'sh ashkin.'"

"My name is Wolfe, the man who just stepped ashore from a king's ship, as you know." The mangled man was unapologetic.

"Can't be too careful theesh daysh."

"I need speak the collector," Wolfe said. "If you would lead the way, I should be grateful." The mangled man bowed awkwardly.

"Elijah Cumminsh at your shervice, milord." Wolfe ignored the inherent sarcasm in the man's use of the honorific, 'milord,' and followed him inside. The bottom floor of the customs warehouse was empty but for a few lonely chests and a little stack of barrels. "We got tea if you like," Cummins said. "You're a Briton, you like tea,"

"I'm American," Wolfe said. The mangled man stopped before the stairs to the upper floor and glared.

"You don't shound American."

"Yet I am," said Wolfe.

"You come off the Roshe. I know her cutter well enough. Only got to shee a boat onesh an' I knowsh it. Where you shail from?"

"Boston."

"What they doin' 'bout mattersh in Boshton? Whatsh the newsh?"

Wolfe sighed. "There is to be war."

Cummins's one eye looked at Wolfe as if he was an idiot. "O' courshe they'sh gonna be. What'sh the king doin' 'bout it?"

"A small fleet is en-route to reinforce Gage. May we go now?"

"We need a proper army ish what we need."

"How long have you worked here?" Wolfe said. Cummins smiled a grimace.

"Shince you wash shucking your mama's teat."

"And what happened to you?" Wolfe said.

"What do you mean?" Cummins asked. Wolfe laughed.

"Well-practiced, Mister Cummins. Well-practiced indeed." Cummins cocked his head and cackled.

"Frenschman shtove my head in wish the butt of a mushket in fifty-eight," he said. Wolfe shook his head sadly and patted the mangled man's shoulder.

"Did the Frenchman hit you because you kept him waiting instead of showing him to the collector's office?" It took a moment for Cummins to grasp Wolfe's jibe, but when he did—as one who appreciates well-made repartee even at his own expense—he cackled again. Still chuckling oddly in his throat, he led Wolfe upstairs.

The office had a Franklin-type coal stove in the fireplace and corner windows overlooking the waterfront. Sitting behind a desk that looked far too big, Lawrence Debins, in a white wig and plain blue business clothes, appeared in all ways official except that he was a cherubic, pink-faced youngster in his teens.

The young man poured wine and explained that he was filling in for the Port Collector who felt it necessary to remove out of town. In any event, Debbins explained, the local Liberty Faction rendered the collector's job irrelevant. Americans did as they would. The Port Collector had no way to call them to account. New Haven was a Faction town and no one doubted it. He, Debins, was more in the way of a caretaker keeping an eye on the place.

"Perchance you have a document stating you are the acting Port Collector?" Wolfe said. It was probably not the first time Debins encountered the problem because he readily produced a parchment from his desk. Scanning the young man's bona fides, Wolfe commented, "I wonder that being commissioner is not as dangerous for you as your predecessor?" Debins took umbrage.

"Who says? Being bachelor was a chief consideration in my appointment. I'm here to make my name but I assure you 'tis not without risk." Wolfe handed back the document.

"Did you take an oath to king and country?"

"As you would expect."

"Do you yet honor that oath?" Wolfe said. Debins finally got angry—pinker.

"I know I appear young, Mister Wolfe, but that is no reason to insult me. Another such and I'll bid you good day."

"I mean no offense," Wolfe said. "I trust you'll understand that I have to be sure." He handed over Gage's letter and named who it was from. Debins' ire morphed into alarm.

"Has something happened in Boston? The insurgents went mad 'round here last time and 'twere but a false alarm."

"Boston was calm when I left," Wolfe said. Before Debins could launch into more questions, Wolfe said, "I need hire a reliable man to take me across the Sound. Can you suggest someone?" Debins laid Gage's letter on his desk.

"There's boats back and forth all the time but they're no friends to Government." Wolfe sighed and Debins caught his frustration. "Cummins will know a reliable man. You can stay here while you wait. I welcome the company."

"But you have Cummins for company," Wolfe said, straight-faced.

Just as straight-faced, Debins said, "Cummins. Yes. He's quite a comfort." Wolfe's laughter dissipated any lingering resentment on Debins's part.

The acting commissioner summoned Cummins and informed him that Wolfe would be staying overnight. Then he asked him about hiring a boat. "But an older captain," Debins said. "They're all thieves but given a choice, the young ones incline to piracy of any stripe." Cummins said he'd get back to them presently.

When Cummins was gone, Wolfe said, "I suppose you'll tell me he's not so mad as he appears." Debins frowned.

"Never. With that face of his, how could he not be mad?"

"Then as you might expect," Wolfe commented dryly, "I'm not sure I prefer to have a madman handle my travel arrangements." Debins giggled and snorted like a boy.

"Elijah is quite up to pointing out a likely boat and captain," he said. "He's known this waterfront all his life. And when all is said, he is loyal to the Crown."

Candles were lit and Debins and Wolfe were well into their third bottle of wine when Cummins brought out fish stew and a loaf of bread. The timing was auspicious. Debins had just finished explaining that Cummins's injuries were not sustained in the late wars with the French, as might be construed from his description, but by a French trading partner when they were both blind drunk one night.

On the heels of Debins' narrative, Cummins joined them at table. He sat across from Wolfe, where Wolfe couldn't avoid looking at him as they ate, a somewhat trying exercise whereby Cummins's lopsided face leaked bits of food from his deformed mouth. It was a trial Debins had undergone once upon a time and he watched Wolfe's initiation with barely suppressed hilarity.

"Where you want to go?" Cummins grunted. Wolfe tried to ignore the goo dribbling from the corner of Cummins' mouth.

"Brookhaven."

"What'sh your bushinesh there?" A glop of half-chewed fish spewed from Cummins's mouth and landed on the table. Wolfe stared at it wordlessly, mesmerized by the utter repugnance of it.

"What'sh your bushinesh?" Cummins said again, ejaculating another half-masticated glop. Wolfe dropped his spoon noisily into his bowl.

"Do you want to earn a few coppers and hire me a boat or shall I find someone else?" Cummins was contrite.

"Where in Brookhaven? Old Mansh? Drowned Meadow?"

"Setauket."

"I know jusht the man if he'sh shtill in town. 'Twill take hard money, but."

"I'm willing to pay fair but I won't be gouged," Wolfe said. Cummins looked the worst sort of pirate in the candlelight.

"And he desires to go soon as may," Debins said.

"You runnin' from shompun?" Cummins said. Wolfe shook his head wearily.

"I am to manage some affairs here in America then return home to London, Mister Cummins. Where, I may say, one does not face an inquisition everywhere they go."

Debins was without sympathy. "'Tis the nature of New Englanders to pry," the young man said. "Goes back to their ancestors. Zealots as you know. Puritans hiding from king's men, afraid of witches. You cannot live a stranger among them. They will not tolerate it."

"If I live among them I will surely take that into consideration," Wolfe said. "But as my people fled New England to get away from New Englanders, I think it most unlikely."

The next day Cummins told Wolfe he'd found his man. For two dollars Wolfe could join a planned voyage in four or five days. For six dollars they'd take him on the ebb tomorrow night.

"Will they think me rich at that rate?" Wolfe said. "Will they kill me to steal my supposed riches?"

"If you got six dollarsh hard money you are rish in theesh parsh. But if he shay he will, my man will put you ashore on the Island."

"Then make it so please," Wolfe said.

"You musht firsht meet the captain," said Cummins. "If he shay all a tanto, my man'll take you." Debins saw that Wolfe didn't understand what Cummins was talking about.

"You have to be approved by a captain of militia," Debins explained. "'Tis his permission you seek. If he gives leave, any boat may take you."

"Yeah or nay?" Cummins said impatiently. Wolfe asked him to proceed.

After dark, Wolfe followed the mangled man's lantern down the low street to a little warehouse on the waterfront. Cummins knocked lightly at the door and stood aside.

Militia Captain Arnold was a little shorter than Wolfe and older by four or five years. His complexion was dark, his nose strong and unrepentant. His thick black hair was constrained in a tight queue but his dominating physical presence was piercing, ice-gray eyes.

"Cummins says you desire to get to Long Island," Arnold said.

"I was told to see you if I wish to hire a boat."

"We don't like strangers going back and forth," Arnold said. He led the way over to a woodstove. When they both had a cup of coffee, he said, "You wish to go to Long Island. I wish to know why came you here on a ministerial ship." Wolfe handed over a slip of paper.

"Those are the names of two New London boys pressed aboard the frigate Rose. I said I'd get word to their people." Arnold glanced at the names.

"I'll see to it. How came you to be aboard the Rose, Mr. Wolfe?"

Wolfe told him of Gage's favor but not about the letter he carried to Debins. He told what he knew as the latest word from London and about the fleet being due, but not about the attack on Fort William and Mary. He said he was on the way to aid his father, taken up for smuggling.

"Would I know him?" Arnold said.

Confident that Arnold would at least know the name, Wolfe said, "Captain Nick." Everyone on the Sound knew Pap—whose real name was Nicholas—as Captain Nick. The name 'Nick' for a smuggler was too droll to go unremarked.

"Didn't know Nick had a son," Arnold said. "He was taken up some time ago, or so I heard. Haven't seen him so I suspect it be true."

"Do you know what became of him?" Wolfe said. Arnold shook his head.

"But that is not rare. Men are condemned and disappear. Bargains are struck and they reappear. Do you have people on Long Island?" Wolfe nodded.

"Have I your permission to return?"

"I have no objection. Tell Cummins the wind blows free in America. That is the signal." Seeing Wolfe's amusement, Arnold shrugged. "I'll not apologize for making an old man feel important."

17

Debins kept Wolfe laughing all the next day by pointing out ministerial activities that were anti-Government in their effect, and provincial activities inimical to their supposedly cherished freedoms. To Debins it was miraculous that war hadn't broken out long ago, not that either side would win, mind you.

That night found Wolfe in a warehouse jutting over the water such that the whaleboat *Polly*, rocking at moorings inside, could go about her business unseen. Six sailors lounged on the indoor dock smoking clay pipes by the light of a candle. Most were young. Two were dark skinned.

The crew was bored and restless by the time the warehouse door was kicked violently open. A large man with the haunch of a sheep slung across his shoulders edged sideways through the door. Sweating under the load, he went straight to the boat and laid his burden gently in the bow. Turning to the men he said, "Get aboard you lubbers. The wind's out o' the north. We'll break our fast in Setauket."

The crew extinguished the candle and scrambled aboard the boat. Before he took his place at the tiller, the captain squinted at Wolfe in the pitch dark. "Did they say liberty's crown don't tarnish or some such?" he asked. Wolfe chuckled.

"The wind blows free in America." The Captain sighed.

"Embarrassing is what that is, but I s'pose you wouldn't know to make it up." Turning to the crew he gave the order to shove off.

Far enough out in the harbor to pick up the offshore breeze, the crew of the *Polly* shipped oars and stepped a sixteen-foot mast. In addition to the modest mainsail, they rigged a small spritsail. When finished, the two sheets powered the thirty-foot craft at a respectable five knots.

With the wind fair, *Polly* fetched middle ground at slack tide. By the time the north shore of Long Island loomed in the false dawn, the flood tide was starting to run and they picked up another knot of speed. Wolfe had drifted off a few times on the way across but now he was wide awake. Returning to his childhood home was suddenly real. He found himself nervous and excited.

The island unveiled slowly in the heavy morning dew. Gaping black holes in the darkness became salt hay fields, stands of pine trees, and laurel, crowding along the bluffs and down to the shore. Winter came late to Long Island and there were still drabs of color in the oak, maple and hickory trees, and solitary houses, like apparitions.

The sun peeked over the horizon and the men in the boat began to materialize out of the dark in their fur hats and oilskins. Wolfe sat in the stern sheets by the captain, who had the tiller.

When the shoreline lay only a few miles distant, Wolfe thought, *one long reach sees us home.* At the same time, one of the bow oarsmen sang out, "We might got trouble!"

Behind Wolfe, ten miles to the northwest, a frigate was tearing along under all normal sail. Wolfe identified her as the *Rose* at once. She must have done her duty in New York and spared no time to dally, for here she was on the starboard tack, every sail drawing perfectly. A noble sight in the first rays of dawn.

"I'm glad we ain't got no contraband," the *Polly's* Captain said to his crew.

"Three days ago, that ship pressed two boys from New London," Wolfe said. "I believe 't'would be a grave mistake to let them stop us." *Certainly for me*, Wolfe thought.

"Devil take their press!" the Captain said. He swiveled around to Wolfe with a laugh. "I'll be buggered if ..." he stopped cold in astonishment. "Joeth?"

Wolfe blinked in wonder. "Cal?"

Rose fired a gun to get *Polly's* attention. A moment later a pennant ran up and unfurled from her foremast. The starboard bow oarsman had the best view. "They's ordering us to heave to!" he called.

"Did he fire on the boys?" Cal asked Wolfe.

"Never hesitated."

"I don't believe we will heave-to," Cal said to his crew. To prove it, he hardened up to the wind. *Polly* picked up speed at once and spray came over the bow for the first time. Wolfe had the impression that the crew was glad of it, enjoyed being chased, for now they were being chased. *Rose* changed course and started flashing out every sail she could think of to close the distance.

The whaleboat maintained a south-by-west course to bring them straight into Setauket. *Rose* sailed south by east to intercept but would soon be limited by shoals. The frigate's draft was deeper than the whaleboat's and they daren't pursue too far inshore, not with the wind out of the north.

The high bluff of Mount Misery Point lay a half mile south. Stretching west below the point was Drowned Meadow, a vast expanse of mudflats disappearing under the incoming tide. The inlet beyond looked perfectly safe but as every local knew, the flats were impassable lest you knew the bars and shoals intimately, provided they hadn't shifted in the last storm.

A spit of barrier beach stabbed into the mudflats from the west and marked the actual entrance to Setauket Harbor, west of Drowned Meadow. Sharp Point, as the rocky beach was known, extended a mile from the mainland promontory of Old Field Point, and protected the coves and bays that made up Setauket Harbor.

Rose fired a ranging shot from her bow chaser. At the end of its trajectory the ball skipped like a stone but was still short when *Polly* ducked behind Sharp Point.

The wind died in the lee of the beach and Cal's crew dropped the sails. Soon they were rowing strong to the west away from the flats. The backed topsails of *Rose* were perfectly visible a half-mile the other side of Sharp Point.

Concentrating on finding the sweet spot of the incoming tide, Cal said, "What's she doing?"

"They's launchin'," Bow Oar said.

"Launchin'?" Cal said in disbelief. "The bastards are launchin'?"

"They's puttin' a boat in the water. The falls is working!"

"Pull you lubbers!" Cal bawled.

Polly drove forward with greater purpose.

Setauket Harbor lay to the south beyond a bottleneck of channel that widened out below. Atop the raised height of Little Neck—the right-hand, or west side of the bottleneck—St. George's Manor kept vigil, a large two-story house that was far less imposing than Wolfe's memory had it.

They churned past the bottleneck to bypass Setauket Harbor and were just starting a southern turn on the far side of Little Neck, when *Rose's* launch came around Sharp Point.

"They're inside," Wolfe said to Cal's back.

"What the devil's got into jack tar?" Cal said.

Polly ran the quarter mile of narrows between Little Neck and Old Field neck and then they were into Old Field Bay. Rocky pasture and acres of salt hay slipped by on either side.

Wolfe kept expecting Cal to put ashore and ditch the boat but they kept to the middle of the bay for the entirety of its length. They were making for the finger at the southern end, a narrow channel extending into woods.

Rose's launch entered the bay but was lost to sight when *Polly* slipped down the finger. Cal's men were laboring now, sweating profusely and breathing hard. The additional oars of *Rose's* launch would prove fatal if the chase went much longer, but it couldn't go much longer. The bottom of the finger was fast approaching.

Wolfe realized they were making for the Crunchers.

Twice a day the tide ran inland through the woods for some two hundred yards before petering out in the tidal marshes of a mill stream from the interior. In their youth, Wolfe and Cal often swam the tide in for fun, or rode the mill stream out, but it was too shallow for a boat, and the rocks at the entrance of the race, the 'Crunchers,' were too close together to pass anything approaching the six-foot beam of a whaleboat.

"Ready up oars," Cal ordered the crew.

Wolfe rationalized that something must have changed, but he braced himself when Cal yelled, "Up oars!"

The whaleboat surged through the rocks with a foot to spare on either side. At the look on Wolfe's face, Cal laughed fit to pee himself. Wolfe laughed too. Sheepishly.

One of the Crunchers had been moved, the race deepened.

In the woods, Cal pulled the boat over next to hard ground and dropped off a crewman named Kinney. "Puttin' a rock back 'twixt the Crunchers," Cal said quietly to Wolfe.

Two men used their oars to pole the whaleboat through the woods into a mucky little tributary hidden by six-foot rushes. The barely visible transoms of two other boats were already pulled up in the cattails.

Kinney returned before the crew finished battening down the boat.

"And another provincial boat disappears mysterious-like," he said theatrically.

Wolfe handed Cal six Spanish dollars. Cal gave each of the bow oarsmen two dollars to pay off their respective watches. He handed two dollars back to Wolfe, saying, "Your money's no good with me."

Wolfe accepted back the coins and examined the best friend he'd ever had in the world.

18

Caleb had grown into a big, strapping man. A week's growth of dark beard blended into long brown hair curling down from beneath his fur hat. Under a sheepskin coat he wore a leather jerkin over a rough sweater. Heavy twill trousers tucked into oilskin boots completed his costume.

"Damn if you don't look the bloody Viking," Wolfe said. Cal struck a pose.

"I am a Viking. A Raider of the Devil's Belt!" Wolfe grinned stupidly. The Devil's Belt was an old-time sailor's name for Long Island Sound. 'Raiders of the Devil's Belt' was what Wolfe and Cal called themselves as boys.

Cal clapped Wolfe on the shoulder. "I hardly dare think you're here. I figured you'd be back years ago but when you didn't come, I figured you weren't comin'."

"Came soon as could," Wolfe said. He pointed at the mutton haunch in the boat. "What're we to do with that?"

"Get it up to Austin's tavern."

"Austin who?"

"Roe. He bought Strong's old place down the harbor. You'll see."

Wolfe stepped into the boat. "Got a rope?" They trussed the haunch to an oar and set off on a path through the woods, circling around the grist mill.

In the lead, with the end of an oar over one shoulder and his portmantle over the other, Wolfe was taking great pleasure in the lingering scent of bayberry, the smell of his youth. The memory was interrupted by Cal snickering loudly. Without turning around, Wolfe said, "What?"

"You sound like a Englishman!" Cal said, highly amused. Wolfe grunted.

"I am an Englishman. So are you. And I'll thank you not to talk behind my back."

Cal laughed, same as he used to.

The path split and Wolfe started down the left fork toward the harbor. He was pulled up short by Cal yanking on the oar. "We can't go down there with the sun up." It took a second for Wolfe to grasp why.

"You're not supposed to slaughter sheep?"

"Can't be seen goin' 'gainst the Articles."

"I like the ban on wagering," Wolfe said. Cal snorted in disgust.

"There's a brilliant stroke against the King."

"So you do as you please," said Wolfe.

"As we must," Cal said. "We do as we must."

The report of a cannon sent birds squawking angrily through the woods. "Recall gun from the frigate," Cal said observationally.

A family Cal knew had a cold crib dug into a hillock in the woods. After stashing the haunch, they avoided the village and made their way across stubble fields composted with late cabbage that stank in the mild temperature.

"What do you know about Pap?" said Wolfe.

"That why you're here?"

"Pru sent a letter said he were taken up. What do they do with smugglers these days?"

"He weren't taken up for smuggling," Cal said. "'T'were sedition." Wolfe stopped in his tracks.

"Sedition?"

"Pamphlets. He were an insurrectionist, Joeth." Wolfe shook his head in disbelief. Smuggling was one thing, treason another.

"It's a damn good thing I have a pardon then, yeah?" Wolfe said. Cal's jaw dropped.

"A real one?"

"Signed by King bloody George."

They passed through a copse of trees and out onto the North Road, the main east-west track that roughly followed the shoreline of northern Long Island. Cal gestured for Wolfe to be quiet. The cedar-shaked general store, run by his cousin Joseph, was fifty yards ahead. They snuck past because Cal didn't want to stop at his parent's house, and if Joe saw him, he'd mention it to Cal's parents, and then Cal would never hear the end of it.

The area around Setauket harbor was not much changed since Wolfe's youth. Two small mills, a blacksmith, a boatyard, and a half-dozen houses. Among them was Austin Roe's tavern.

The last time Wolfe saw Roe's Tavern it was a modest, two-story saltbox house belonging to the Strong family. At some point, a simple addition of four rooms had been added to the north side. Later someone attached a two-story house with gables onto the south side. Now the structure had three roofs of differing heights and direction yet somehow it all looked harmonious. Roe's Tavern was a place any man might be proud of.

Across Setauket harbor, golden morning light warmed the salt hay marshes and oak trees of Little Neck, backdrop to a score of fishing boats riding peacefully at moorings. To the west, the road wound past Caleb's cousin's place and disappeared up the hill as it always had.

South across the road from Austin's, the muddy training ground was also the same, as was the smell of wood fire mingled with salt air and damp leaves. Wolfe drank it all in with a sense of bitter nostalgia. After many long years purging Setauket from his heart, it was part of him again in an instant.

No lamps were yet lit in the taproom of the Tavern. It took a moment for eyes to adjust. A black man dressed in homespun looked up from stoking the fire and said, "Mornin,' Mister Brewster."

"Is master to home?" Cal whispered loudly.

"Out back," the black man said.

To Wolfe, Cal said, "This here's Scipio." To Scipio he said, "This here's Joeth Wolferd, a old friend." Scipio bowed. He was short and sturdy with the flat nose and blue-black skin of the natural-born African.

A young woman transporting a baby on her hip strode purposefully into the room. Cal's presence brought her up in surprise. "What you doin' back so soon?" she said. Cal swept off his fur hat.

"Allow me to name my particular friend, Joethan Wolferd. Joeth, I have the honor to present Katherine Roe. Austin's wife."

Kate Roe's skirt and apron were baby-stained and worn. Her dark hair was stuffed under a sooty cap. Still sporting the weight gain from her child, she would be as wide as tall someday, but right now she was a cheerful and healthy young mother. Wolfe made an abbreviated leg.

"Your servant madam."

"I am yours," Kate curtsied. "You men must be hungry. I'll have Scipio bring something." To Cal she said, "Does this mean you didn't get my mutton? Tell me you found my mutton?"

"Have I ever failed you?" Cal said. Kate looked at him askance. "Once," Cal said. "One damn time. An' me riskin' everything!"

"Where is it?" Kate said.

"I put it in Everett's cold crib. Couldn't come to the harbor. We was chased by a bleedin' frigate."

"So that was the commotion. Is Kinney with you?"

"Course."

"He best think twice 'bout going home. Peg's ready to knock him on the head."

"When ain't she?" Cal snorted. "Where's your old man?"

"Feeding the livestock with Justus." The babe on Katy's hip started squalling. Retreating into the back, she called, "Help yourself to beer. I got chores 'fore Missus Lund rings for breakfast."

Cal drew two pots of beer from a keg behind the bar cage and joined Wolfe at a trestle table near the fireplace. "So where are they holding my old man?" Wolfe said. "What's the word on his whereabouts?" Cal's countenance sagged.

"I don't know how to tell you, Joeth." He paused to slug down his pot of beer. When he was done, he wiped his mouth with a sleeve and looked Wolfe in the eye. "He was to be branded and sent to the Indies … he was killed trying to escape, Joeth." Wolfe felt the air go out of him as he sighed deeply. "I'm sorry to have to tell you." Cal said. Wolfe nodded but he was fixated on the reality that all the effort, time and money he'd expended was for naught.

Then he felt bad because he should've been mourning his father, but his father's death was abstract. The memory of him was more impression than remembered fact. There was a great deal about his father that Wolfe didn't know, and would never know, he realized.

Cal retrieved a bottle of rum from the bar and handed it to his old friend. After taking a long, long pull, Wolfe was unsure if the moisture in his eyes was from sorrow or spirits. Knuckling tears away, he said, "Where'd they bury him?"

"Huntington, I reckon," Cal said. "That's where it happened anywise." After a couple more swigs of rum, Wolfe made a decision not to discuss his father anymore.

"So how is Pru?" he said. Pru was short for Prudence Jayne Forester, third of their childhood triumvirate and never was a girl more inappropriately named. It was her letter that set the last six months of his life in motion. Thinking of her in Cal's presence made Wolfe smile. She probably had four babes by now. "How's Pru?" he said again. "Her brother yet by?" Pru's brother Charles was five years older and an arrogant bully in their youth.

"He's a right piece of work, he is," Cal said. "She ain't married, you know." That surprised Wolfe. When last he saw Pru, she'd been a wild twelve-year-old with a face tanned by the sun. Mostly he remembered her big brown eyes.

"Never married or lost a husband?" Wolfe said.

"Never married. Word is there was one fella but Charles ran 'im off. What'd she say in the letter?"

"Pap's been taken up. He needs you. 'Tis serious."

Cal nodded. "T'were serious eno'. No one wants any part of sedition just now."

"I take it my mother's people did nothing?" Wolfe said. Cal snorted, and that was all that need be said about that. When Wolfe's well-to-do mother eloped with a smuggler, her family cut her off as if she was dead. Thirteen years later not one appeared at her actual funeral.

Scipio interrupted with food. Wolfe was surprised that news of his father's death did nothing to dull his appetite. Further conversation was put on hold as he and Cal dug into heaping trenchers of eel cooked just the way Wolfe remembered, and ham and eggs, and a loaf of fresh bread.

They were wiping the trenchers clean with the last of the bread when Austin Roe came in with his brother Justus. Three years younger than Wolfe, Austin was short and slight with dark eyes and a complexion to match. His bearing was quick and active like all the Roes except Justus, who was ten years older, bigger, and somewhat slow.

Austin and Wolfe greeted each other as the childhood acquaintances they'd been. Justus, who used to hang back in the presence of others, was equally happy to see Wolfe.

"Sorry ' bout Captain Nick," Austin said right off. Justus echoed his brother precisely. Wolfe thanked them for their regrets and changed the subject.

"A fine place you've made for yourself," he said. Austin looked around proudly.

"Kind of you to say it."

"A wife and a new babe," Wolfe added with a big smile, "glad to see someone in Setauket turned out respectable."

"Respectability's for Tories," Cal said. Justus guffawed, a sound Wolfe remembered perfectly.

"How fare you Justus?"

"Tol'able. Got a possum."

"And you better not let Katy see it in the house again," Austin said. To Wolfe, he said, "I have a room if you need one. Let you have it on the cheap."

"Done," said Wolfe.

Kate summoned Austin from the hallway. As he was leaving he said, "We'll talk later. I expect the whole village'll want to hear 'bout your adventures in London." Wolfe caught Austin's sleeve.

"If you don't mind, I prefer that my presence go unremarked." Austin's face showed his disappointment.

"As you wish. Of course."

When they were alone again, Cal looked at his old friend sourly. "He offers you a room on the cheap and you tell him to keep mum. Where's the fair in that?"

"I'll be answering questions from every man in Setauket," Wolfe said.

"And he'll be pouring for 'em!"

Wolfe stuck out his chin. "I'll pay him full for the room but I want private." Cal knew the stubborn thrust of Wolfe's chin well enough not to push the issue.

"S'pose you tell me what's goin' on in Boston. You came from there, yeah?"

For the next few hours, as the taproom filled and emptied around them, they got drunk together for the first time. When it got dark they retrieved the mutton, giggling like schoolboys, and brought it to the tavern. Afterward, Cal staggered off to meet his crew for the run back to Connecticut. Wolfe passed out in one of Austin's rooms.

19

Wolfe took to the North Road going east the next morning, at sixes and sevens over what to do next. Cal said Pap was to have been branded and transported. Wolfe had been prepared for that. He'd half expected his journey to end up in the Islands, what with the amount of time that had passed. But his plans had never gone further. News of his father's death changed nothing; yet changed everything.

Reflexively he left the road and walked northeast through a wood of cedar, hickory and pine. A small wood now as it turned out. Many trees of his youth had been cleared for a two-story farmhouse, a barn, a couple of cribs and a sty.

At the edge of the cleared acres of the farm, he stopped to watch the sandbars of Drowned Meadow disappear under the incoming tide. It was an entertainment he'd shared with his parents hundreds of times. The memory of it struck him hard. He was surprised at how hard.

Where the meadow sloped down to the shore, he entered a wooded hollow and lost sight of the water. The path was wider and more pronounced than he recalled, and there were other paths he did not recollect at all, but at last he caught sight of his boyhood home.

His memory of the shake-and-shingle saltbox he grew up in had nothing in common with the tiny house he looked at now. The little barn was there too, though just barely. It had always canted west, now it had a decided list.

The smell of a morning fire. Someone was home. He'd been told that Qua lived there, a Setalcot Indian who'd sailed with Pap long before Wolfe came along. Qua must be near seventy by now. He'd been Wolfe's favorite uncle although he wasn't a blood relation. He'd just been closer to Pap than any other man. Wolfe hadn't had any contact with him since leaving America. Qua never did get his letters.

An unseen dog barked, summoning a thin old man wrapped in a trade blanket from the house. "Is you lost, friend?" the old man called. Wolfe stepped down the path into the open. The old man squinted but it wasn't until Wolfe was ten feet away that a ragged smile lit his face. "Well, well, well," he clucked. The voice was dry and brittle but as familiar to Wolfe as his own. "Kettle a-boil," Qua said, as if he'd seen Wolfe yesterday instead of fourteen years ago.

The old Indian's long hair was gray and his wrinkles were pronounced. As Wolfe followed him inside, he winced to see the toll age had taken on a man he once idolized.

One of the most important memories of Wolfe's youth was being forty feet up a mast with Qua during a brutal gale at sea. He could still conjure the picture of his uncle, supernaturally lit by frequent bursts of lightning, his waist-length, black hair whipping sideways in wind-driven rain, as they battled heavy canvas for their lives. The determination Wolfe witnessed and shared that day informed his destiny. Afterward he was not the same as before.

It was dim inside the little house, warm and a little smoky—low ceilings saw to that—but largely the place was unchanged. There were fishing and game traps his mother would have never tolerated inside but the furniture was the same, although his mother would have choked at the abuse her pine floors had suffered.

Wolfe hung his coat on the door peg he used as a boy. A strange feeling.

Qua poured coffee. "Got tea," he said. "Prefer coffee. Wi' rum, course. You?"

"Coffee, if you please." Wolfe accepted a bowl of coffee while gazing around the house. He was not unmoved. Silhouettes of his mother and father still hung over the fireplace, it was they who drew most of his attention.

Qua bade him sit. Wolfe made comfortable in his father's chair. It was obvious that Qua used his mother's. The upholstered wing chairs had been his parents' pride and joy and were still comfortable, although the fabric was getting threadbare.

Qua took two battered clay pipes off the mantel and offered one to Wolfe. When they were puffing away, the old Indian said, "You heard 'bout Pap?"

"That he was killed trying to escape?" said Wolfe. Qua nodded sadly.

"He allus said he'd take the north channel if he had to. Kept his word." In Qua and Pap's world, the north channel meant escape or die trying. Wolfe hadn't heard the expression in fourteen years, but he'd known the phrase as a boy. Qua once told him it came from an old shipmate. He wouldn't say more than that though, and his father wouldn't speak of it at all. Said it was just an expression.

"Want to see Nick's letter?" Qua said. At Wolfe's nod, he retrieved a folded letter from a box on top of the mantle. Laying a gnarled hand on Wolfe's shoulder, he said, "Makes my heart glad to see you all growed up Joeth." Wolfe was touched.

"We're the only family we have now," he said, as he unfolded the letter.

"Would you mind reading out?" said Qua. "I ain't heard it but once."

Wolfe let his eyes adjust to his father's close handwriting before reading aloud. "*Qua. I'm in it this time. Sedition is the charge and they mean to warn others by my fate. They offer something if I name names but I have to live with myself so that ain't in it. The thought is they shall brand me for transport but I'll take the north channel ere that happens. The ship is gone but I have hope the crew may yet go free. Even if they press the boys 'tis better than slavery in the Islands. You know where I stand on matters so let us have no regrets. Fare thee well, old friend. I'll see you on the next voyage.*"

Qua handed Wolfe a newspaper from the previous September. A report of the recent fatal occurrence at Huntington. The story was unambiguous and succinct. Liberty Men attacked Royal Marines, to free convicts awaiting transport. Most of the prisoners escaped but two were killed in the melee, one being Captain Nicholas Wolferd, recently convicted of sedition. *If his remains go unclaimed, he shalt be buried in ye potter's field at ye public expense.*

Wolfe handed the paper back to Qua and they smoked in silence. After a while, Qua said, "Where you stayin'? This be your house and there's plenty room." A pleasant wave of emotion swept over Wolfe.

"Thankee. I'll take you up on that. My purse grows light. I spent most of what I had laid-by on a pardon." He went to his coat and brought back the oilskin-wrapped vellum. Unrolled on the table, the pardon was a beautifully executed document, rendered mystical by the power it might have wielded, by the unmistakable George R signature at the bottom. They gazed at it together.

"You left the name open. Good." Qua meant the name to whom the pardon was issued. The comment elicited a chuckle from Wolfe. For one summer in his youth, debate raged throughout Setauket; was it better to have the name filled in on a pardon or left blank? A man on the south shore had been hung on a technicality. The name he was arrested under, Cowboy Ned, was not the same as Edward Currant, to whom the pardon was issued. Everyone knew it was the same man but as he was a well-known thief, no one complained when the magistrate nullified the pardon and hung him.

The debate that ensued afterward was absurd even to Wolfe's eleven-year-old mind. It wasn't as if pardons were commonplace or petitioners able to choose the form of the pardon, yet inexplicably, for one long summer, the question was argued vociferously. Qua and Pap came down on the side of never filling in the name if you could help it. At the least, an empty name made the document valuable for resale.

Wolfe's mother had been of the belief that he would be best served who never needed a pardon.

"Nick had shit luck with everything 'cept your ma," Qua said. Wolfe shrugged in agreement. His father did have shit luck. Everyone knew it.

After putting the pardon away, he moved about the room remembering. He touched the walls, the furniture, studied a burn mark in the floor and recalled how it came to be there. When he was full, he moved outdoors for air.

Fifty feet from the house near a pine tree overlooking the water, a large white stone marked his mother's grave. Wolfe was not religious but he was not immune to the currents of time nor the whims of fate either. His mother's memorial stone looked lonely. He thought of Pap lying in Huntington and felt a deep sadness.

When he returned to the house, Qua said, "There's something Nick would want you to have."

Pap's tomahawk was somewhat renowned among his friends, it being known he'd put more than one man in the grave with it. Wolfe had forgotten about the weapon until Qua handed it to him, and then Wolfe realized it was probably the one thing of his father's he would most like to have. On Long Island a tomahawk was as a sword in London. It marked a man, especially a seagoing man who might call upon it for survival at any moment.

Pap's hatchet, as he always called it, was unremarkable in design, but the head of Sheffield steel attached to a hickory handle was perfectly balanced, length to weight, and wondrously light in the hand. It was undoubtedly a great thrower. Wolfe was supremely pleased with the legacy, but Qua wasn't done. With obvious enjoyment, he poured out the contents of a good-sized, cinched leather bag on the table.

Wolfe had never considered that someday there might be an inheritance from Pap, but here was a few thousand in coin of every denomination. Portuguese Joes and silver crusados. British guineas and sovereigns. Spanish dollars. Dutch silver dollars. Two score of gold buttons, gold chains, pearls. Wolfe's mind raced with what the hoard meant but eventually his better nature prevailed.

"You must keep this for yourself," he said. "'Twill see you fair the rest of your days, Qua." His uncle patted him on the shoulder the way he did when Wolfe was a boy.

"I got plenty Joeth. This am Pap's. He always meant you to have it. I'll leave you mine too, now you're here. No one else I'd rather have it 'cept Missy, and maybe a taste for Goody Mavis. That'd put horns on her old man for once and all!" He took a moment to relish the thought and make a decision. "Five dollars to Goody Mavis to get the town waggin' one last time," he said. "Will you do it?"

"It shall be done," Wolfe promised with a laugh. "But why didn't Pap use this for his trial?" Qua waved at the booty dismissively.

"T'were politics and scheming done Nick in. Government here ain't cowed by Liberty Men like up in Boston. But they do fear spread of the freedom religion."

"It's to be a religious war, then?" Wolfe joked. To his happiness, Qua still appreciated his humor.

"Providence be called upon so regular," Qua said, "'tis a wonder Jehovah ain't come already." His joviality faded. "'Tis a religious war, Joeth. Same one the Puritans fought against the King a hundred years ago in England. They're just gettin' back to it now the Catholic French ain't around to distract. You best be wary of it. A King's man can be reasoned with or bribed. At worst there be the King's justice. A Puritan or Congregationer, or whatever they call theyselves now, is a zealot. Beware of zealots Joeth, for they don't care unto their own destruction. As for justice, I heard what's in them Articles the rebel Congress put out. Telling men they can't eat their own animals be tyranny worse than any King George ever conjured." Qua leaned across the table.

"When I'm gone, I want you to have what's mine. Hear? You give Goody Mavis five dollars and share out the rest with Missy. Promise?"

"I'll do as you wish," Wolfe said. "You have my word." Qua reached out and patted Wolfe's hand.

"You recall the hidey hole you made for your secrets?"

"The hollow tree?" said Wolfe. Qua nodded solemnly.

"You'll find mine there when the time come. You take half and give Missy half." It was very important to him and made Wolfe uncomfortable.

"Of course I'll do as you ask, and I thank you. But you'll probably outlive me." Qua disagreed.

"Dark days a comin' Joeth. I can smell 'em clear 's a hurricano. Nick was happy to see 'em come but he had the freedom religion almost as bad as Missy." Wolfe was about to ask who Missy was when the unseen dog outside barked. Qua wasn't surprised.

"That'll be her," he said. "Thought you was she. Ask her in."

20

A woman was tying a small horse to the stable fence. She was dressed much like Cal, in oilskin boots and a wool coat, although layers of skirts flared below the coat. Thick tangles of auburn hair tumbled from under the flaps of her sheepskin hood. When she saw Wolfe, she instinctively put the horse between them and bristled.

"Who are you sir, to stand in Qua's dooryard so bold?"

"He is my uncle. Are you Missy?" The woman's mouth dropped open. Wolfe saw a hundred thoughts flash across her face as she realized who he was. He already knew who she was.

"So it's Missy now?" he said. Prudence Forester started to laugh and then stopped abruptly.

"Where've you been? You're too late!" She almost sobbed the last.

"It's worse than you know," Wolfe croaked, his voice suddenly leaving him. Pru came close, put a mittened hand on his arm and looked into his eyes. Hers were deep brown with flecks of gold.

"Where have you been?" Her voice was soft but conveyed a dozen different emotions, each one clear to Wolfe.

"Arranging a pardon," he said softly.

"That what you mean by worse?" she said. Wolfe nodded. She patted his arm. "I must get something." She went back to the horse and retrieved a jar from her saddlebag.

On the way into the house, Wolfe said, "Missy?"

"Mistress Forester."

Inside the little house, a warm scene was made poignant by Wolfe's presence and the glaring absence of his father.

"Dare you believe he's home?" Qua asked Pru with a happy grin.

"I told you he'd come," Pru said, as if there was never a doubt. "He was allus late as a boy if you recall."

"Missy, Missy, Missy," Wolfe sighed loudly. Pru looked at him in exaggerated distress.

"Only Qua and Pap have leave to address me as Missy. You do not." Wolfe laughed at her. She tried to scowl at him but was too happy. "Very well, Percy," she said, teasing out his middle name in the degrading way she used to when they were children. When Wolfe roared with laughter, her eyes welled in happiness, and sadness. It was more than a year since the little house resounded with men's laughter.

Pru handed Qua the jar. "Leave this by the fire. I'll rub it on when I return." To Wolfe, she said, "It's good you're here. You can help me. Put on Pap's sheepie lest you ruin your fancy coat." To Wolfe's distraction, she then began removing her skirts, although underneath she wore overalls. When she noticed his attention, she misconstrued masculine interest for moral disapproval. "Do you expect me to ruin French petticoats gathering seaweed?" she said.

"I'm wondering why you're gathering seaweed at all. Where are your slaves?"

"Charles took them away to the south shore," she said tersely.

"You used to swear you would never own slaves," Wolfe recalled. Pru's back stiffened.

"Only Charles can free my father's slaves and that he will never do."

Wolfe let the subject drop.

They retrieved a harness from the barn and led the horse down to the beach. "You used to hate gathering seaweed. Remember?" Pru said. Wolfe was amazed that she recalled such a thing, and she was right. One of his responsibilities growing up had been to collect seaweed to trade as fertilizer to farmers for produce. He'd hated it.

A small, two-wheeled cart was drawn up just inside the woods at the shoreline. They hitched the horse to it, took the driftwood pitchfork from the flatbed and got to work. The high-tide mark was a line of mounded seaweed with an occasional clump of mussels tangled within. No one had collected off this stretch of beach recently and the cart was soon full. When they were done tying the load down with a well-worn skin, Pru said, "Thankee, neighbor. 'Tis quicker done with two."

"And a horse," Wolfe said. "I wouldn't have hated harvesting the beach if I had a horse." Pru smiled an enchanting smile that Wolfe didn't recall and wouldn't have forgotten.

Back at the house, Qua had shellfish stew waiting with corn dodgers to sop it up and a mug of beer to wash it down. When they were sated, Pru sat Qua on a stool in front of the fire and peeled off the old man's shirt. Thick ringlets of auburn hair fell across her eyes as she massaged the now viscous balm into Qua's scarred back.

The French ancestry of the Foresters was obvious in Pru—big dark eyes, full red lips, high cheekbones. She was lithe but not without feminine plush, as Wolfe could tell. Her blouse did little to obscure the sway of her breasts as she worked. Engrossed in her task, she was unaware that her childhood playmate found her uncommonly alluring.

Qua basked in the glow of his rub as Pru donned her skirts. When she departed with the horse and cart in tow, Wolfe kept company with her out to the road, where their paths must diverge.

Taking her leave, Pru curtsied gracefully as she used to when they practiced at school. "Will you do me the honor of attending Christmas dinner at my house tomorrow with Qua?" she said. Wolfe doffed his Denmark and bowed to her in best London fashion.

"I would be most delighted," he said. Pru was impressed.

"You make a fine leg, Mister Wolferd. I don't know what else they taught you in London but you do make a pretty leg."

"In London that's half the battle," Wolfe said.

"And the other half?"

"Whom you know, of course."

"Of course," Pru laughed.

As she led the horse and cart up a path on the inland side of the road, she began to sing a ditty about a bonnie lad, a blue ribbon, and the Josephus fair. It came to him how much Pru loved to sing when they were children. He didn't remember her voice from back then but he thought it quite lovely now.

21

He made his regrets to Austin Roe that evening, easing the innkeeper's disappointment with a big tip. Afterward, Austin was very understanding of Wolfe's desire for solitude in the wake of his father's death.

At the beginning of his career as a courier, it seemed to Wolfe a fine thing to be the center of attention wherever he went; to eat and drink freely in exchange for sharing news that he might share with any man over a beer. The minor celebrity a courier enjoyed was also an easy way to attract the favors of local women. He preferred anonymity when he traveled now. As he walked to his old house the next morning, he felt free for the first time in many months.

Once again the unseen watchdog announced his arrival. Qua came out and called a gray-muzzled mongrel from hiding. "This be Bait," he said, fondly petting the dog.

"He looks like bait," said Wolfe. Qua held the door open and followed Wolfe inside.

It took no time to move the traps out to the barn and settle in. Qua had long ago taken Wolfe's tiny room for his own, so his parents' room fell to Wolfe. He wondered how it would feel to sleep there, especially after exploring his mother's blanket chest. It looked as if it hadn't been disturbed since the day she died. Sadly, the clothes folded carefully as she left them were mildewed and rotting. Wolfe put them back and closed the chest.

When the sun was directly overhead the next day, he and Qua followed a split-rail fence along acres of pasture and orchard belonging to the Jayne family. Their route turned east on the road in front of the Jaynes' two-story shaked house, until they took a wide rutted path to the southeast. Half a mile through bramble wood interspersed with fields and a meadow brought them to Forester Hall.

Wolfe remembered Pru as being well off, but Forester Hall had never looked so grand. A wing had been added to the manor house, as had a covered portico and shuttered windows. There were more outbuildings too, including another barn, and tenant crofts.

While on a grand scale Forester Hall was impressive, Wolfe saw signs of neglect when he got close. The wellhead needed mending. Shingles were missing off the roof. A paddock fence was falling apart.

A girl in her mid-teens opened the door at his knock. She was cute the way girls are when trying to act grown-up, and cute in appearance too—red hair, freckles. Her good country linen gown draped a figure well along to womanhood, but she was still a girl. She curtseyed formally.

"Good day, Master Qua. And you must be Mister Wolferd," she said. Wolfe bowed. "Your humble servant, miss." She met his gaze and giggled involuntarily. He smiled back at her. "Is your mistress to home?"

"She's within. If you'll follow me." The girl led the way to the dining room where she carefully filled two glasses from a silver punch bowl, giggled and scurried out.

Pru made her appearance soon after, and if her intent was to dazzle, she succeeded. Her hair was scandalously loose, tumbling down around her face and shoulders wantonly. Her gown of brown velvet, picked out with delicate vines of silk yellow flowers, moved with her luxuriously. A brown velvet choker accentuated her aristocratic neck. She wore no linen over her décolletage, but there was no undo plumping of the bosom as was popular in London either. Wolfe approved. Pru needed no enhancement. Her physical charms were obvious to any man with eyes.

"You look lovely," he said in admiration. "How is it you are yet spinster?" Qua glared at him. Pru changed the subject.

"Did Molly acquit herself well with you?"

"Is that the girl?" Wolfe said. Pru sighed.

"She didn't offer her name?"

"Everything else was proper," Wolfe said. "Most genteel."

"I'm trying to teach her manners," Pru said.

"An indenture?"

"We have no paper 'twixt. There are two others living here that you'll meet presently. We're a little family of orphaned women. And there are tenants to help with the farm."

"What about your brother?" Wolfe said. Pru sighed as if he'd mentioned something distasteful.

"We're legally bound by my father's will until I marry or he dies. Do you remember how he used to be?" At Wolfe's nod, she said grimly, "The boy is but more in the man. And thereby hangs the reason for my spinsterhood, if you must know. I cannot marry lest Charles approve and he will only approve someone who agrees to give him this farm as a dowry. So he can sell it, the scoundrel! Thus am I likely to be spinster all my days. As long as I live here unmarried, he cannot sell the farm nor throw me out." She raised her glass in mock salute and drank off her punch. "Now what about you?" she said. "Are you home for good?"

Wolfe held out his glass to be refilled. "In the immediate future I purpose to claim my father's body and bring him home from Huntington." Pru and Qua were immediately in favor.

"The ground's hard but," Qua said. Wolfe nodded.

"Aye. But not yet froze. I'll hire a man if I must."

"I allus knew you were a good lad," Pru said.

"I need hire a wagon," said Wolfe. Pru said she had one.

"When do you reckon to go?"

"Soon as I obtain a letter of introduction."

Qua abruptly left the room. Pru leaned close to Wolfe and confided, "Celia's in for it now. She's our cook and Qua assumes she's grateful for whatever attention he bestows. Usually she's not."

"And he rebukes me for my manners," said Wolfe.

Pru took his arm and led him to the parlor, decorated everywhere with mistletoe in celebration of the season. Without warning, she threw her arms around him and kissed him on the mouth. When he responded in kind, she broke off and danced away, teasing, "A kiss is but the requirement of Christmas mistletoe!"

Wolfe didn't argue but he knew when a kiss was a kiss.

The Forester parlor was made handsome by hip-raised paneling, Persian carpet, and beautifully rendered flowers painted on the plaster walls in lieu of paper. A tilt table for cards sat folded against one wall. A clavier claimed the far corner. In the center of the room, upholstered chairs orbited a two-sided divan from which you could face the fire, or as Pru bade Wolfe, sit facing tall windows with a view of the drive up to the house.

Sitting down beside him, she said, "I can arrange a letter of introduction. I know just who to see."

"How long do you think it to take?" said Wolfe.

"Tomorrow if he's to home. Mayhaps I'll accompany you."

"Done." Wolfe clinked her glass with his own. They sat together quietly and basked in the warmth of the fire and the proximity of an old friend. An inner feeling of contentment washed over Wolfe and he reached for Pru's hand. She gave it willingly and leaned into his shoulder.

The long-case parlor clock struck three before Molly summoned them to dinner. As they took their seats, Wolfe was introduced to Charity, a rotund middle-aged woman in a cheerful red Osnaburg dress and white linen cap. She'd found refuge at Forester Hall when her husband died and she was evicted from her home.

Qua brought out a saddle of mutton on a pewter platter followed by Celia, an old woman in drab homespun. Her heavy lappet cap looked older than she was. As Qua commenced expertly carving under her watchful scowl, Wolfe laughed. When Pru sought the reason for his amusement, he said, "Since arriving in America all I've heard about is the embargo on slaughtering sheep. The reason I laugh is that everywhere I go, mutton is on the table." Pru reacted as though he'd slapped her.

"I'll have you know we observe the Articles in this house. That mutton was slaughtered before and brought out especially for Christmas." She was hurt and occupied herself filling bowls of onion soup from a silver tureen.

"I meant no disrespect," Wolfe said. "My amusement was observing the relationship between reality and rhetoric." Pru handed him a bowl of soup.

"Observe something else, if you please."

In addition to mutton there was ham, oysters, eel, succotash, bread pudding, mincemeat pies and a frothy hot custard posset for desert. Yet dinner was a dull affair wherein Setauket gossip was the main topic. Most of the conversation was led by Charity, ebullient and well informed about local scandals involving people Wolfe didn't know or had long forgotten. He smiled, laughed and drank, but he couldn't wait for the meal to come to an end.

Qua drank steadily too, and occasionally winked lewdly at Celia, much to her dismay. Celia was what crude men termed a thornback—an unattractive woman well past her prime. In addition to, or perhaps because of, her lack of physical beauty, Celia had a profoundly gloomy countenance. In Wolfe's presence she didn't speak much but when she did, it was with the reproach of a Congregationalist at an Anglican Christmas feast. Wolfe wondered why a Congregationalist would reside in an Anglican household at all, let alone break bread at Christmas. Congregationalists abhorred Christmas.

Everything about Celia was a little odd. Her redeeming feature, as he tried to understand Qua's attraction, was a massive bosom and the near certainty that other men weren't beating a path to her door. Wolfe didn't think that enough, even for a man of Qua's advanced years.

As dinner dragged on, Wolfe was struck by how vastly his circumstance had changed in the course of a year. In mostly Anglican England, Christmas and its attendant season were celebrated for no less than two weeks. There were rounds of parties and balls, illuminations, fireworks. It was perhaps the cheeriest time of year in England. Looking around the table he felt supremely out of place.

Except for Pru. She shone, and would in any company.

After dinner they removed to the parlor where Pru played the clavier for everyone to sing along. They started with *The Old Hundredth*, the hundredth psalm set to music, which even Celia couldn't find fault with. This was followed by more psalms common to Anglicans and Congregationalists, but when Pru launched into a rousing version of *Joy to the World*, Celia retired.

The bawdy songs were played when the hour grew late, culminating in Charity's rendition of *My Dog and I*, a filthy double-entendre ditty that Molly sang lustily along with, unaware that the dog in question was a euphemism for a man's appendage. Wolfe and Pru laughed themselves silly.

The final song of the evening was Molly's, and Wolfe thought a more dramatic rendition of *The Downfall of Piracy* would be hard to imagine. He knew the song well, the lyrics being one of Doctor Franklin's first published works and very dear to his heart. He wished The Doctor could have heard Molly sing about Blackbeard's demise. He would have loved it, especially the end when Molly became particularly dramatic.

"Maynard boarded him," she recited, "and to it they fell with sword and pistol too. They had courage and did show it, killing the pirate crew. Teach and Maynard on the quarter, fought it out most manfully, until Maynard's sword did cut Teach shorter, and losing his head, there … he … did … die."

After Charity and Molly went to bed, Pru covered Qua in a blanket as he snored soundly in front of the fireplace, then she and Wolfe retired to the library.

22

Pru's library was the main source of reading material for Wolfe as a boy. He whistled softly when he saw how large the book collection had grown.

"My chief vice," Pru confessed.

"Then we yet have that in common," Wolfe said. They opened a bottle of port, and after toasting the memory of Wolfe's father, talked about books. Wolfe was surprised that Pru was as well-read as he. Better-read.

Later they dove into current affairs and Wolfe mentioned the incident at Fort William and Mary. He finished by saying, "I believe the day of reckoning is not far off."

"Which is why you must stay by," said Pru. "America is where those who love you, need you." Wolfe chuckled at her pronouncement. Or perhaps in embarrassment.

"I would you know there are people in London who love me," he said.

"You have a woman!" Pru gasped. "Why didn't you say so?" Wolfe didn't correct her at once. Instead he remarked upon the reasons it would be impossible to move his life across the ocean. Only when Pru demanded to know about the woman did he confess that no such person existed.

A year ago he'd have said otherwise, and been wrong.

They established that Pru was ardently of the Liberty Faction, in opposition to her brother Charles, and his friends, who were for the King. Pru also declared that Wolfe was a traitor if he didn't stay and fight for America. "You would run away from the biggest adventure of the age?" she taunted. "I don't recall you were craven as a boy." Her efforts to convince him to stay in America twisted down every emotional alley she could think of, but unlike their youth, Wolfe would not be convinced.

He was highly amused however.

They communicated easily as if no time had passed, lingering together long after the candles burned down. When they were leaving the library, inebriated, Wolfe collected the kiss she'd cut short earlier and this time she didn't break off ... until the rising hunger between them demanded advance or retreat. They retreated, but with the certain knowledge that the issue was not settled.

The next morning, they sat for breakfast quite late by country standards. Afterward, Pru, Qua and Wolfe walked out with two of the late Mr. Forester's fowling pieces. Pru's dog, Whitey—a herder that was no birder but might serve to flush—excitedly led the way.

But Whitey didn't have to flush. Below a swale in the meadow, four fat geese grazed in swampy ground. Wolfe handed a gun to Qua but his uncle declined to shoot. "I have old man's eyes," he said. Wolfe vowed to take enough for both of them and was true to his word.

By the time they walked back, he'd bagged two geese and a rabbit. Celia paused from splitting kindling to accept the bounty with a ragged smile. She didn't seem to mind when Qua bussed her on the cheek and squeezed her bosom in farewell.

Wolfe and Pru met on Setauket green the next day. To his surprise, she brought him to the parsonage of the Presbyterian Meeting House. On the rare occasions Wolfe attended church as a child, it was at the Caroline Church, the same Church of England service that Pru attended, a stone's throw from the Presbyterians.

Pru introduced him to the Reverend Tallmadge. Tallmadge remembered Wolfe as a boy, a memory Wolfe did not share. The Reverend was a taciturn man of fifty. Despite a sober and weary countenance, he emanated a kindly spirit that superseded any visual impression one might take away. He'd barely known Pap but was glad to provide the service asked of him.

"This is to my friend Reverend Prime in Huntington," Tallmadge said as he wrote a letter of introduction. "I have attested that you are the son of the late Nicholas Wolferd, Joethan, and that it would be a Christian kindness to release your father's bones unto you. "That should be enough. I cannot imagine Ebenezer will raise an objection. I didn't know your father well but he gave his all in the cause of liberty. 'Tis little enough he be allowed to spend eternity with a beloved wife."

The Reverend's quiet words made an impact on Wolfe. He was touched that a man of obvious quality like Tallmadge respected the actions of his father, actions Wolfe didn't much appreciate. That the Reverend was a Liberty Man also impressed. He was clearly no wild-eyed radical.

On the green afterward, Pru said, "We should go to Huntington tomorrow before the weather turns." Wolfe agreed, pleased that Pru's time sensibility was the same as his own.

As they walked home, he said, "What is the difference between Presbyterians and Congregationalists?" It took Pru some moments to formulate an answer.

"I don't believe there is a difference theologically," she said. "The way I understand it, governance separates. A council decides doctrine for Presbyterians instead of each individual minister deciding for himself as Congregationalists do. Both are strict although Presbyterians have lighter hearts." She smiled her wonderful smile. "But not as light as us Church of England!"

The next morning was gray and windy when Wolfe arrived at Pru's. He was greeted by Molly bounding off the porch lugging one of Mr. Forester's fowling pieces. A powder horn and shot bag banged against her knees. Running for the pasture, she yelled over her shoulder, "Might be we have a thief!"

Wolfe caught her up, took the gun, horn and bag, and had her lead the way. Beyond a fence in the upper pasture, a path through laurel bushes and raspberry stickers led to a grove of scattered oak trees. After following the trail for another ten minutes, they found Pru lurking behind some bushes, intently studying something.

The something she was studying was a scrawny boy about the same age as Molly. He was sitting with his legs splayed out in a little hollow on the other side of the bushes, plucking a chicken. His clothes were ratty and torn seaman's slops, but he wasn't a seaman. A far too large brown wig covered his head.

Pru whispered for Wolfe to remain where he was before she pushed through the bushes. The boy didn't notice her at once. When he did, he dropped the bird, and his head, in abject defeat. Pru waited for him to say or do something but eventually it was she who broke the silence.

"When was the last time you ate?"

"Two days by," came the muffled reply.

"Were you going to eat that raw?"

The boy raised up his head. "I ate worse."

Wolfe recognized the boy's accent at once. He was from the London streets. Near St. Giles, Wolfe would have bet The Doctor if they were together. They often bet on inane things.

Wolfe stepped through the bushes and said, "For what crime were you transported?"

The boy gaped at the stylish Londoner suddenly appearing in the provincial woods. With his last shred of defiance, he said, "Nicked two yards lace. Took fourteen 'stead o' the gag."

"He means he took fourteen years indenture rather than hang for stealing," Wolfe said to Pru. She scowled back in dismay.

"I know what he said, Joethan. I'm not an idiot." A snicker returned her attention to the boy.

"How old are you?"

"Sixteen." He was small and undernourished for his age.

"If you go back to England and are caught, they can hang you," Pru said.

"Rather 'ang than be a bugger boy," the thief said.

"Did you hurt someone?" Wolfe said. The boy's defiance crumbled.

"Doubt I 'urt him. Hit 'im wiv a pail, I did, but his Dutch skull were thick as a bleedin' choppin' block. If he ever claps 'ands on me I'll wish I kilt 'im, I know that."

"What's your name?" Pru said.

"Ady Baker."

Pru made a decision. "Come along, Ady Baker. We'll roast that capon and figure out what to do with you." The boy looked around for an escape route but Wolfe's glower warned him not to try.

Ady fell in step with Molly as they trudged back to the barn. Wolfe and Pru walked behind. "What am I to do with him?" Pru said quietly.

"Assuming he told the truth, how likely is he to be caught?" said Wolfe.

"If the pederast is unmindful of reputation, very likely. How like is he to be caught in London?"

"But a matter of time," Wolfe said confidently. "The men who control the streets keep very good notice of who comes and goes. Convicts and indentures that return are soon under their control. Should they not do as bid, they are turned in for reward. If they do as bid, they are inevitably taken up."

"How do you know so much about it?" said Pru.

"I spent a few years living on the London streets," Wolfe said.

Pru wanted to know more but she said, "So there is yet hope for Mister Baker?" Wolfe looked into her sparkling eyes and shrugged.

"Depends on what it is you hope for."

Celia was appalled that Pru invited Ady back to the house. She refused to cook for a thief so Pru cooked the chicken herself. Ady ate it all and more, slowing only when Celia appeared brandishing a large knife and promising to use it on him if he even thought about stealing from them again. And especially if he came within ten feet of Molly.

As Pru escorted Celia, the avenging Puritan, away, Ady looked fearfully at Wolfe and said, "She 'ave a slate loose?"

"You best watch yourself around that woman," Wolfe said. "Her particular friend is a red Indian." There was nothing Londoners feared more than savage red Indians. Ady Baker was no different. He looked at Molly to see if Wolfe was lying. She gave the young man a reassuring smile.

"Mister Qua is a Indian and they say he were a pirate, but he's very nice." Ady blanched.

Pru rejoined Wolfe with an idea. "Ady can stay with you and Qua." The stricken look on Wolfe's face slowed her not a wit. "Here he might be remarked upon by any number of people. No one will see him at your place. Qua and Pap allus had a younker or two on the boat after you left."

"I'll be in Huntington," was the first objection Wolfe thought of. Pru ignored him.

"Molly's too young to be around Ady, and he a city boy no less. If he stays here there'll be trouble." Wolfe could not disagree and he scowled at her. Pru smiled back smugly. "I'm glad you can be reasoned with. That is promising."

Later on, Wolfe walked home with Ady wondering what Qua's reaction would be. Barely home two days and he was bringing someone to live with them. Ady however, was all but skipping down the road.

"What are you so gay about?" Wolfe said. Ady grinned from ear to ear.

"H'ain't hungry. H'ain't on a boat. And I h'ain't got a Dutch bastard trying to bugger me."

"Did you leave family in England?" Wolfe said.

"No one I miss," Ady said.

"Well, the man you will soon meet is my family," Wolfe said. "My uncle. If you dishonor him in any way, we're done. You savvy?" Ady stopped grinning and looked Wolfe in the eye.

"I'll tip it double 'fore I cause your folk trouble, Mister Wolfe. So help me Davey."

Wolfe extended his hand and Ady awkwardly shook it. "Get used to it," Wolfe said. "They shake hands incessantly here in the colonies. And learn to talk provincial like. To blend in, yeah? You're on the dodge now."

Bait's sharp barks brought Qua from the barn. Ady's eyes bugged out as the old Indian walked up and took his measure. Examination complete, Qua turned to Wolfe and said in wonder, "Barely home and already picked up a stray." Wolfe had kept all kinds of critters when he was a boy, even aboard ship. His uncle was one of the few people on earth who knew that and it made Wolfe feel good.

"Where'd you find this 'un?" Qua said. Wolfe clapped Ady on the shoulder.

"Master Baker is on the run from a Dutch buggerer who bought his paper. Pru thought it best he lay-up here while she figures out what to do with him." Qua took new interest in Ady.

"Stick his nob in you, did he?"

"I 'it 'im wiv a pail and run off before," Ady said.

"A pail," Qua mused. "You should'a used a knife and cut off his pecker. Tend the details and you'll nay go wrong." Ady's jaw dropped. Qua said, "You like rum? You look like you could use a dram." Ady Baker was in a daze as he followed Qua to the house.

"If he give trouble, you but let me know," Wolfe called after them.

Qua rasped back over his shoulder, "I got a knife. He give trouble, I'll cut *his* pecker off."

Wolfe snorted in amusement. Ady Baker's education was about to begin.

23

When Wolfe arrived at Pru's the next morning, she had a good-looking mare hitched to a light flatbed wagon with a bench seat. After Wolfe settled his haversack next to a hamper of food and Pru's necessaries, she firmly denied his expectation of driving and they set off for Huntington.

On another unseasonably mild day, the North Road was firm and fast and Pru's mare was strong and happy to go. Wolfe didn't recall the road being as wide or as busy when he was a boy, but he was getting used to the idea that not much was as he remembered.

They stopped twice to rest and water the horse, the second time just outside the little village of Cow Harbor, where bovines grazed in open fields next to the water. While they snacked on mutton, bread and cheese, and washed it down with beer, Pru swapped her sheepie coat for a red cloak not unlike Elizabeth Loring's. She caught Wolfe staring at her and once again misread his scrutiny.

"Makes it easier to bargain," she said defensively. Wolfe found her discomfort at being admired very appealing. He'd spent too much time with a woman utterly bored by compliments.

"I would give you the shop but you asked," he said. "You're a comely woman, Prudence." His words made her self-conscious and she sought to cover it.

"And if I flutter my lashes as The Ladies Magazine says I must, does it make me more fetching?" She demonstrated in a comical fashion that drew a laugh from Wolfe.

"Then the illusion be quite destroyed," he said.

But the illusion of Pru's eyes sparkling gold never went away.

She sang softly over the last few miles which Wolfe found quite satisfactory. Her song selection was good, her pitch was true, and her timbre was pleasing. She ceased singing when they crested a hill and Huntington Village lay spread out below, clustered at the end of a harbor.

The Presbyterian Meeting House was easily found on the way into the village. It was a twin to the one in Setauket, both having been built according to the Duke of York's Laws. The Huntington parsonage however, was more impressive than the one in Setauket.

Reverend Prime answered Wolfe's knock himself, and Wolfe thought he might be older than Qua. Dressed in sober black like Reverend Tallmadge, Prime exuded none of that man's calm. Prime's countenance was one of severity and wrath reinforced by a permanently flushed face.

The Reverend brought his visitors into a library boasting more than a hundred volumes, a substantial number of books in one place on Long Island. The envy with which Pru and Wolfe eyed the collection was to Prime's satisfaction. "I was librarian of a club in town for years," he said. "When the club ended there was no call to remove the books, so I'm happy to act as caretaker. You're welcome to examine them."

Wolfe and Pru combed the bookshelves to see what treasures they held. "You'll find no fiction," Prime called as he read Tallmadge's letter. "I don't hold with fiction." When he was done reading, he called Wolfe over. "Of course, you may claim the body." Prime folded his spectacles into a pocket. "Sadly, we could afford your father no more than a pauper's funeral. Rest assured he was given all the proper rites. I'll have Thomas show you where he lies."

When Prime had gone out, Pru put her hand on Wolfe's arm. "Are you all right?"

"Perfectly fit," he said calmly.

The Reverend returned with Thomas, a large, hairy man who bore the imprint of the mentally feeble, a lucky brute who'd found a legal station to exploit his outsized physique.

Wolfe expected Pru to go to the village and do her business while he reclaimed his father, but she insisted on coming with. They trailed along together as Thomas grabbed two shovels from a shed and shrugged off Wolfe's help to drag a two-wheeled cart up to the burial ground.

At the back of the property beyond a brush fence delineating the church cemetery from the potter's field, two graves were still mounded. Wordlessly, Thomas began to dig. Wolfe grabbed the other shovel and joined him. Together they soon reached the body.

Pap had been buried in a shroud. Not even a cheap pine coffin in a land of pine trees.

Wolfe waved Thomas away and lifted the body out of the grave himself. His father, who seemed so large and present in life, was small and light in death. Echoing Wolfe's thoughts, Pru said, "He seems so small." She looked away as Wolfe unwrapped the shroud.

It wasn't Pap. It was a man roughly the same age but in no way to be mistaken for Pap.

"It's not him," Wolfe said.

"You're sure?" Pru said, dabbing at her eyes. Wolfe cocked his head in disbelief. "Well it must be t'other," she said.

To Thomas, Wolfe said, "He must be in the other grave. We should put this one back, yeah?"

In the second grave, the corpse was again wrapped in a cheap shroud but this time it looked to be the correct size. Pru turned away as Wolfe lifted the shroud away from the face. It was a black man. An *R* burnt into his cheek said he'd been a runaway slave at some point.

Wolfe swore and turned to Thomas. "I seek a man killed in the escape last August. Captain Wolferd. Do you understand?" Thomas nodded.

"That be them. The two what was kilt." Wolfe stared at the grave digger until he was uncomfortable. "The 'scape," Thomas said. "Some got away. Those two din't."

"Have you dug any other pauper graves since last summer?" Wolfe said. Thomas shrugged.

"Those the two kilt tryin' t'scape. If it ain't who you have in mind, I can't help more. Them's who I buried from the fracas. I don't 'member names lest I know 'em but that be them."

They reburied the second man and went and found Reverend Prime. The Reverend didn't know what to say but he insisted that Thomas was not mistaken in the location of the graves. He retrieved a Chapman book that showed Nicholas Wolferd being interred with another man by the name of Hughson.

Looking for answers, Wolfe pressed Prime until the Reverend seized upon royal officials as the culprits. They gave him the names and bodies. If he didn't know the men, how was he to know the names were incorrect? That was not his responsibility. He performed the rites as duty required. Thomas buried them.

Wolfe asked for the name of someone in the village with a Government connection. Someone who might be able to help him sort things out. Prime hemmed and hawed but was thoroughly unhelpful. "A name," Wolfe beseeched the old preacher. "Give me but a name." Prime said many things but nothing actually useful. Finally, Wolfe's frustration boiled over and he said, "Reverend Tallmadge esteems you highly, Reverend Prime, but thus far I could not say why."

Manifesting a tight-lipped scowl that would strike Wolfe dead—if only the great Jehovah would cooperate—Prime said, "Call on Thomas Reeve. Might be he knows the connection you seek, for clearly I do not. Good day to you."

24

"Something's amiss," Wolfe said when they were back in the wagon.

"I dare say. They lost Pap's body," Pru said. Wolfe shook his head.

"I don't believe it."

"What then?"

"I haven't a notion. But if those were the two men killed in the escape, what happened to Pap? Prime knows something. He's old but not feeble. He's playing at something."

"Perhaps we shouldn't trust him," Pru said. Wolfe expelled some of his frustration with a scornful laugh.

"Indeed."

They drove into the village, perhaps a hundred houses built out around a green that had long ago ceased to function as a grazing area. There weren't many storefronts, most folks conducting business out of their house or an outbuilding on their property. Pru steered the chair onto a path around the back of a small cedar-shake house. Behind the house she pulled up to a slant-roofed workshop with two small windows and a chimney. A crude sign proclaimed it an apothecary.

Handing the reins to Wolfe, Pru said, "Leave this to me."

A bell tinkled as she stepped inside the little workshop. She was greeted by the thick aroma of herbs hanging in the rafters. Behind a crude counter, a slight man in a frazzled brown wig was playing with the innards of a watch. His leather apron bore the stains of every decoction he'd ever boiled.

"A good day to you, Master Higgs," Pru said warmly. Higgs gave her a shy smile.

"And to you, Madam Forester. This is an unexpected pleasure. I trust your journey was uneventful?"

"Quite so, quite so," Pru said. "There was much traffic, but."

"So have I heard," Higgs said. "Some say the whole country is on the move though I have not seen it for myself." He set aside the watch. "How may I be of service?"

Pru produced two jars of cow balm and put them on the counter. "I believe leeches and fever bark would be fair. I'll pay for a bottle of calamine." She gave Higgs her most disarming smile. "And two dozen of peppermints if you have them." Higgs melted. Pulling three leeches from a delft jar with a pair of tongs, he put them in a leather bag she handed him.

"You must feed them every three or four weeks when it gets warm, mind."

"I've had some live for years," Pru said proudly. "A question, Master Higgs. What do you know of Thomas Reeve? Be he a King's man? A town official?"

"Oh my, no. Never. Mister Reeve is decidedly not a King's man. Why do you ask?"

Pru lowered her voice. "Were you called to examine the two men killed in the escape last August?" Higgs finished wrapping a strip of cinchona bark in a piece of parchment and handed it over.

"Remember, Quinquina condaminiae works best when mixed with wine. The wine strengthens the effect. And you can use the parchment for poultice." In answer to Pru's question, he said, "I did not examine those men. Government sought to keep the affair very hush. They was quite red-faced you know. Most of the prisoners escaped. Two of 'em died, but that wasn't bad, considering. Thomas Reeve may well be one who helped them escape but I don't know that."

Pru emerged from the shop a short time later and reported what she'd learned.

"Thomas Reeve, then," Wolfe said. Pru looked at him doubtfully.

"Is that wise? You asked Prime for someone connected to Government.

He gave you the name of a Liberty Man."

"'Tis a name and we've nothing else."

Reeve's house was on a small plot west of town. A man chopping wood in the dooryard ceased working when they pulled up. He looked like any other small farmer in a homespun coat and flop hat, except he'd suffered a nasty bout with the pox in his past.

"Is you lost?" he said.

"Not if you be Thomas Reeve," said Wolfe.

"I'm Thomas Reeve. Who's askin'?" Wolfe introduced himself and Pru.

"Reverend Prime thought you might be able to help me," he said. "Regarding the escape last summer."

"I wadn't there," Reeve said.

"The Reverend said you might know something that could help me locate my father's remains."

"I don't know what he's talkin' 'bout. Or you." Reeve's glare dared Wolfe to suggest otherwise.

"Perhaps I should explain," Wolfe said calmly. "My father was one of the men killed in the escape. I've come to bring his bones back to Setauket. The graves in the churchyard do not contain his remains so I'm trying to discover what happened to them. If you have no knowledge of the affair, is there someone you know who might? Prime gave me your name particularly." Reeve looked back darkly.

"I don't know 'bout any o' that and if you put it 'round I do, you'll deserve what you get. Prime thinks to punish me but he got another think coming. I'll thank you to be gone now. I got work to do."

In a voice dripping with sarcasm, Pru said, "Thankee ever so much for your Christian kindness!" Reeve wheeled around with sharp words on the tip of his tongue, but he didn't say them. He'd been conditioned to honor ladies of the better sort since birth. He might be a Liberty Man but he was by no means free.

"I don't like to be unfriendly to folk I got no quarrel with," he said grudgingly. "But strangers askin' questions ain't a clever enterprise these days. I'll just say, lest you don't know, you'd be smart not to talk about that escape too much. I can't say precisely why cause I don't know. And neither does anyone else. But I do know one thing."

"What's that?" Pru said, as she was meant to.

"T'ain't gold buys such silence," Reeve said.

As they led the horse and wagon back to the village, Wolfe and Pru debated what to do next. During a lull in conversation, Pru looked at Wolfe oddly. "I wonder is it your clothes. Now I study it, you're the very picture of a raving Tory, what with your Denmark skyscraper and French greatcoat."

"Prussian, if you please."

"You look like one of Charles's friends," Pru said. "No wonder no one trusts us."

"Trust us to what end?" Wolfe said in exasperation. "I'm trying to recover the body of a dead man. I can't help it if I don't present as a drab."

"There's more to it than that," Pru said. Wolfe sighed deeply.

"That's what I said."

On the outskirts of the village, a black man in a good woolen coat and mathematical cocked hat emerged from the gate around a two-story clapboard house. Wolfe hailed him.

"Who lives there?"

"That would be my master, Mister Titus," the slave said deferentially.

"What does Mister Titus do that he has such a fine home? Is he a King's man by chance?" Wolfe said. The slave looked at the ground nervously.

"He be a squire," the slave said, keeping his eyes down.

"I need see your man at once," said Wolfe.

25

Lawyer Eliphar Titus was shorter and older than Wolfe, with a handsomely craggy face and a sun-bleached, blond queue tied with a black ribbon. Upon learning that Wolfe was in the way of needing a lawyer, he brazenly proclaimed that he was the best lawyer in Huntington.

"But are you for the liberty faction or the King?" Wolfe said. Titus was wary.

"Depends on who asks and why."

"I need know if you will act on my behalf impartially, for I am of neither party." Wolfe explained the situation.

"Are you in funds?" said Titus.

"I can pay fair," Wolfe assured him. Titus smiled.

"Then I'm your man. T'would be interesting to find out what happened that night. No one seems to know, which is never the case in this village. I'm not privy to the agenda of Liberty Men, and am no great friend to Government, but something is amiss. Bodies that don't match their names is not a usual occurrence in these parts."

"One body doesn't match. I can't speak to the other," Wolfe said.

"An official record will be lodged in Coram by now," Titus said. "I can send a rider and have it copied. 'Twill take all of the morrow and more, but. Do you have lodgings?" Wolfe shook his head.

"This all just happened."

"You'd be welcome to stay here," Titus said. "I regret that I must charge a small fee, but you'll find my house more comfortable than a tavern and it shan't cost half as dear. Is that acceptable?"

"Quite," said Wolfe. Titus held out his hand and they shook.

"I'll have Cato see to your needs whilst I arrange for a rider."

After stabling Pru's mare, they settled into the half-empty house. Titus was a widower of some years, with no children, siblings or in-laws. It was just him, the slave Cato, and a slave couple, Lyrica and Henry. Pru conjectured that Titus was as glad for their company as their business.

Lawyer Titus returned after dark and invited them to sup. When they were sharing hot beans, bread, and small beer by the light of two candles and the fireplace, Titus related a few tidbits he'd learned. "Most interesting is that the escape was not the work of Liberty Men as most people assume. Not Huntington Liberty Men anywise. Guess is 'twere boatmen."

"Boatmen?" said Wolfe.

"Smugglers," Pru said. "Like Pap."

"It makes sense," Titus said. "The local Liberty Men were as disgraced as the Redcoats. That may be why Mister Reeve was put out. 'Tis said there were not any locals involved at all. The prisoners were kept in a barn under guard of Royal Marines. The barn was attacked by night, a few shots were fired and the prisoners ran off. Two men were killed but none of the marines was seriously harmed. Makes you wonder how hard they fought."

"'T'would be interesting to know what ships lay by that day," said Wolfe. Titus agreed.

"As it happens, I have connections all over the harbor. I'll look into it tomorrow."

"What about Reverend Prime?" said Wolfe. Titus shrugged.

"'Tis hard to believe he weren't involved. At least in burying the wrong man. He's no fool despite evidence to the contrary."

"As you say," Pru chuckled.

"The public record will have the names and descriptions of the condemned," Titus said. "That should tell us who they count dead, escaped or transported. We'll learn something. Royal clerks are great ones for records. I don't like to give false hope but I begin to smell a flimflam. Would your father be apt to take part in a charade to escape?" Wolfe and Pru looked at each other and laughed.

"'Tis what he would do especially," Pru said. Titus bobbed his head happily.

"I do dote on a conspiracy. I miss lawyering. I do."

"How's that?" said Wolfe.

"I don't get many cases," Titus said. "Not enough to live on anywise. Folk around here barely get by. Victualing ships provides my living and it be a good living, but I miss lawyering."

"Why don't you move where they need more lawyers?" Pru said. Titus shrugged.

"I like living here." He raised his glass. "To Captain Wolferd's escape."

After they drank the toast, Pru said, "Who will you declare for when the time comes, Mister Titus?"

"Please call me Eli."

"Who will you declare for when the time comes, Eli?" Pru said. The lawyer hesitated, perhaps worried that the wrong answer would put the pretty stranger off.

"I suppose I shall stand with my neighbors," he said at last. "But I dread what is to come. I fear it will be terrible." Before the gloom of his words could settle, he added, "So gather ye rosebuds while ye may, isn't that what the poet says?" He held out a pitcher to refill his guest's glasses.

"Robert Herrick," Wolfe said, in reference to Titus's poet. "To the Virgins, to Make Much of Time."

"A particular favorite of mine," Titus said. "Gather ye rosebuds while ye may, old time is still a-flying; and this same flower that smiles today, tomorrow will be dying."

"I'll grant you 'tis prettily spun," Pru commented dryly. "But I believe Herrick is referring to all people, not just virgins."

"'Tis what makes Herrick scathing," Eli agreed. "Everyone be virgin in some aspect." His comment prompted a deep discussion of poetry and literature that went long into the evening.

The next day, with Eli gone off to the waterfront, Pru and Wolfe drove out to the farm where the escape took place. As Wolfe handed Pru down from the wagon, a woman, who looked older than her years, came out of the rambling farmhouse. Mrs. Hicks—she named herself—wore a heavy linen cap and a flower-print shawl over a frayed homespun dress.

After Wolfe made introductions, he said, "We seek the farm where the prisoners escaped last August." Mrs. Hicks squinted at him.

"Why would you do that?"

"My father was one of them that was killed," Wolfe said. "I seek his body that I might bring him home to rest beside my Mother."

"Those that died am up the churchyard in the potter's field. We buried no one here." She turned to go inside but Wolfe stopped her.

"Someone else is buried in my father's grave at the churchyard. I'm trying to find out what happened to his body." Mrs. Hicks scrutinized Wolfe more closely. Deciding that the matter would not attend quickly, she invited the strangers inside.

Two massive logs in a big stone hearth heated the rustic parlor amply. A lazy old hound came over and sniffed the visitors halfheartedly before laying back down on a braided rug. When they were all settled in rough-hewn chairs near the fire, Wolfe explained the situation. Mrs. Hicks was intrigued by his story but surprisingly, knew little about the escape.

"T'was after midnight you see, and no moon. We was asleep and heard shots and then it were over. Later they drug one of the soldiers, marines I mean, in here."

"Was he bad hurt?" Pru said. Mrs. Hicks shook her head.

"Not really. And one other man was cut. And there was two prisoners killed. They was in the barn."

"Did you see them?" said Wolfe.

"I wrapped 'em up," Mrs. Hicks said.

"What did the dead men look like?"

"One was a slave. Had a brand anyways. T'other was a white man."

"And there were no others?" Wolfe said. Mrs. Hicks shook her head.

"Just the two. 'Tis a wonder any were hurt. The officers was gone off and the soldiers was drinking all day."

"Where did the officers go?" said Pru.

"Reverend Prime gave a dinner to thank them for their service. And he sent two kegs o' rum out here to the farm for the men."

"That was generous of him," Pru said. Mrs. Hicks nodded.

"Yes it were, an 'generous' ain't a word oft associated with Ebenezer Prime. Not to mention he's a well-known Liberty Man. I ain't sayin' nothing, but a certain Reverend was curiously connected to the business."

"So 't was Liberty Men staged the attack?" said Wolfe.

"I don't know," Mrs. Hicks said. "But Liberty Men would'a burnt the barn or done some mischief to warn us off. They did neither."

"Did you see the prisoners?" said Pru. Mrs. Hicks shook her head.

"Only the two what died. I don't like to see 'em. I feel sorry for 'em even though most are the worst sort."

"Why do they come to Huntington?" said Wolfe.

"The Redcoats pick up prisoners at the east end of the island and march west collecting more along the way. When they get to York City they hang 'em or ship 'em off to the spice islands."

"Do you know if one of the prisoners was Nicholas Wolferd?" Wolfe said.

"That your pa?" Mrs. Hicks said. Wolfe nodded.

"I have a pardon for him."

Mrs. Hicks's jaw fell open. Pru chuckled at the woman's reaction. "'Tis rather like a novel, is it not?"

"I never read a novel," Mrs. Hicks said. "But maybe I ought." To Wolfe, she said, "They brought him from a ship after the others come in. "I din't see him. I don't like to see the prisoners. My boys saw 'em. The Redcoats drum them in and my boys dearly favor a drum. I recall they said the sedition man looked like a pirate."

"That's him," Pru said. Wolfe leaned in.

"You're sure none of the other prisoners was killed or buried elsewhere?"

"Don't know 'bout after," said Mrs. Hicks. "But only two died here and they's buried up the churchyard."

"What about the three prisoners who didn't escape?" said Wolfe. "Do you know if Wolferd was among them?"

"Couldn't say," Mrs. Hicks admitted. "My boys might know." She retired from the room to blow a shrill one-note horn out the back door. Wolfe smiled when he recognized the traditional staccato foxhunt signal to return to the stable.

Mrs. Hicks came back in, followed by a bright-eyed boy with dark unruly hair, happy to get away from chores for a while. Wolfe asked the boy if the Sedition Captain had been one of those who escaped. The boy looked to his mother for a cue. Nodding at Wolfe, Mrs. Hicks said, "That man be his son. He desires to know if his pa got away. If you ain't sure, you say so."

"He got away," the boy told Wolfe. "I know sure he didn't march on with the marines. And he wadn't one o' the dead ones. I seen 'em." The boy was proud of that. His mother's scowl warned him not to be.

"Do you recall what my father was wearing?" Wolfe asked the boy.

"Had a beard," the boy said at once. "An' a sea captain's coat of blue, and sea boots." Wolfe fished a shilling out of his pocket and gave it to the boy with thanks. The boy showed the coin triumphantly to his mother. With a smile for his glee, she held out a hand.

"I'll keep it for you. Now get thee back afore Pa get pissy. And don't let me catch you boasting to your brother. Might just as well been him Pa sent down." The boy nodded but his happiness was undimmed as he tore back out to the barn.

Wolfe and Pru departed soon after. Back in the wagon, Pru gave in to her happiness and hugged him tight. "Nick is alive! Qua will be so happy!" Wolfe was touched by her happiness but he was also very unsettled. He hadn't failed after all. Pap was alive. The pardon residing in his coat could yet give Pap back his life.

If Wolfe could find him.

In Wolfe's estimation, the only person who could provide further answers was Reverend Prime. They found him at the parsonage and he was not surprised to see them. Nor happy about it. "I've done what I can to aid you," he said. "I can do no more."

When Wolfe replied, Pru saw in him an intimidating presence born of cold anger, feral green eyes, and a palpable intensity that Joethan hadn't possessed when they were young.

"I know my father escaped," Wolfe said to the Reverend calmly, but there was menace in the calm. "And I know you had something to do with it. I thank you for that but now I need find him. I'm not religious such that it would constrain me from getting answers, Reverend. And I'm not a man to be trifled with twice. Please believe me." Pru believed him. Prime glowered.

"You threaten me?"

"How you take it is up to you," Wolfe said. "You're a well-known Liberty Man. Who was my father smuggling pamphlets to? He was captured in Huntington. Like as not, someone here was involved. I shouldn't wonder was it you." The quiet accusation yielded a big reaction. Prime's face grew red and Wolfe thought the old man might go apoplectic. Instead, Prime pulled a large handkerchief from his sleeve and had a coughing fit into it.

Eventually, after blowing his nose, spitting into the linen and cramming it back up his sleeve, Prime fixed Wolfe with a malevolent glare. "You will kill me with your questions," he growled. "You say your father is alive? Rejoice! If he is counted dead, rejoice again for none shall think to look for him. Now go home and leave me alone!"

26

"The old black coat may be right." Titus was standing by the fireplace in what he called his study, although there were no books other than the four volumes of Blackstone's *Commentaries on the Laws of England* any reputable lawyer was expected to own. He looked the proper esquire however. He'd changed into an expensive maroon jacket and gray satin smallclothes. The silver buckles on his breeches matched those on his calfskin shoes.

"Prime all but said Nick would be home again," Pru said for the third time.

"I heard you," Wolfe said for the second time. "But I don't believe Pap will come home. Great care has gone into making the world think him dead." As an afterthought, he said, "If the war comes, who knows if he'll ever see Setauket again." Titus agreed.

"I said I was unsuccessful today, yet I did learn something. There are those who have an opinion of what occurred but will not express it, even to surmise as people do. I make no doubt 'tis fear of reprisal and not likely to change."

"Might be Caleb can help," Pru said, but Wolfe shook his head.

"He didn't know a few days ago. Qua doesn't know. You didn't know. Pains were taken to keep Setauket out of it."

"All that remains is to examine the official version of events," Titus said. He looked ruefully at his guests. "When you're gone this house will seem so empty. You remind me how solitary my life has become."

"Take a ride out and visit me," Pru said. Titus locked her eyes with his, smiled broadly and bowed his head as if to say that he would take her up on her offer. Wolfe was oblivious to the interplay.

"Was it outside Liberty Men staged the attack or boatmen?" he said.

"Boatmen are Liberty Men," Pru said. "Have you considered that Pap may be more important than we credit?"

"Assuming the escape was for his benefit and not a lucky coincidence," Titus said. Wolfe laughed.

"'Tis well known that my father is particularly unlucky. There is no chance he was at the right place and time accidentally."

Pru frowned, "You are harsh, Joethan."

"But am I wrong?" he said. She didn't answer.

"Where would he be apt to go?" Titus said. Pru answered.

"The war's coming to Boston. I doubt he'll be far away."

"Boston," Wolfe muttered disgustedly.

"Boston is the most exciting city in the colonies right now," Pru chided him.

"Boston is but a town," said Wolfe, "and bent on its own destruction at present"

"That bad?" said Titus. Wolfe laughed.

"The Redcoats hate Americans. The Liberty Faction hate the Redcoats and the Tories. The Tories hate the Redcoats and the Liberty Faction, and they all hate Gage. I wouldn't even know where to look for Pap in Boston. Well, I might, but I wouldn't want to. They asked me to leave when I was there." Pru's eyes grew wide.

"You were asked to leave? The town asked you to be gone?" Wolfe had little choice but to recount what occurred. When he finished, her eyes sparkled. "I could go to Boston with you, Joeth. Doctor Warren would help us. You should write him."

"I will," said Wolfe.

"I'll go with you," Pru said again. Wolfe couldn't pretend not to hear her again.

"Let's see what Warren says before making a decision."

"I know diplomatic when I hear it," Pru said bitterly. "Do consider. I long to see Boston." Wolfe cocked his head.

"You have some romantical notion in your head. Boston is but a powder keg with a lit match."

"Yet I want to see for myself. Imagine that. A woman."

"You can abandon the farm so easily?"

"Now's the time if I'm to go. We'll be planting twelve weeks hence. I can bring a load of supplies. They'd welcome us."

"They'd tar and feather me," Wolfe said. "No thank you."

Titus's rider returned late the next day under a gray and roiled sky. The copied documents made it clear that facts had been altered. Captain Nicholas Wolferd, convicted of sedition, was listed unequivocally as dead and buried in Prime's churchyard. The dead slave, Preston by name, was also listed as dead.

Wolfe tried not to think about the body taking his father's place in the grave, but it bothered him. Had the man deserved his fate? It was ghastly to think he might be some unlucky chicken thief arbitrarily chosen to die so Pap might go free.

Titus put on a handsome feast to celebrate the resurrection of Nicholas Wolferd. It was a spirited little dinner party punctuated by clusters of musket fire from the nearby green in celebration of New Year's Eve.

The evening was well along when shouting erupted outside. Cato came in to report a group of mummers demanding to address the lord of the house. Titus put down his glass of wine and sighed. "I suppose I must toss them a few coins or they'll destroy my gate."

Wolfe and Pru went with him to witness the traditional foolery directed by commoners toward the better sort on New Year's Eve. As he opened the door, Titus said, "Let us hope their verse is more clever than the usual misrule."

Four men in animal masks stood in the yard, loudly singing a bawdy ditty. Their leader waved them quiet after a rousing chorus. With a florid bow, he addressed Titus, "My lord esquire. We come to bid you joy of the eve, in hope you have spare coin up your sleeve. We don't ask for much so have you no fear, and we'll drink to your health throughout the new year!" Titus turned his head to Pru and Wolfe and rolled his eyes.

"Rather thin gruel that," he said to the lead mummer. "But I'm game." He tossed some coins out to the men. The lead mummer protested—came right up to the door.

"Can you not spare a wet for your countrymen?"

"I'll have my man bring you a couple of bottles," Titus said. "I bid you a prosperous new year." He was closing the door and calling on Cato to give the mummers a couple of bottles, when the door crashed back into his face and the lead mummer was shoving his way inside.

Wolfe leaped forward and blasted the mummer with a fist to the side of the head. The man staggered and collapsed in the entryway but as Wolfe seized his coat to heave him outside, a cocked pistol was thrust in his face.

"Leave off mate or you're a dead 'un."

The mummers crowded inside with drawn pistols and helped their wobbly mate to stand up. Through a handkerchief he was using to staunch the blood pouring from is nose, Titus demanded, "What the devil are you playing at? What do you want?" The mummer who'd been struck pointed at Wolfe.

"That son of a bitch." With his mask off, he was ruddy from a life in the sun, almost handsome but for rum-ravaged teeth. "You're coming wi' us," he said to Wolfe.

"Without an introduction?" Wolfe said sarcastically.

"Cap'n Roedale. *Sweet Nancy* out of Fairfield," Roedale sneered. "The man you'll wish you'd never met."

"Boatmen," Pru whispered to Wolfe. To Roedale, she said, "There's no need for trouble, Captain. We're leaving tomorrow."

"He's leaving tonight," Roedale said. Pru was undaunted.

"Why? We share your cause. We'll be gone tomorrow."

"Clap a hatch on it," Roedale said. "You," he said to Wolfe. "Collect your things. If you try to play the gallant, these two shall bear the recourse."

"No need for that," Wolfe said curtly. When he'd gone to get his haversack—accompanied by two men—Pru looked Roedale in the eye.

"You're from Fairfield, are you? You must know Caleb Brewster. Captain Brewster who has the *Polly*?" Roedale stayed mum but Pru could tell he knew

Caleb and pressed on. "I promise you, Captain. The man you're taking away is Nicholas Wolferd's son. If you harm him, you will surely answer to his father, not to mention Caleb Brewster who is his lifelong friend. Personally, I should not like to have either blood-mad at me." She was still glowering when Wolfe returned.

"May I have a word with Miss Forester?" he said.

"Like to be your last," Roedale growled.

Wolfe led Pru to the other side of the room but she spoke before he could. "They're from Fairfield. Mayhaps they'll bring you there. Look for Cal." Wolfe nodded mechanically as he sorted out what he wanted to say to her. "These men know Cal," Pru persisted.

"I'll keep that in mind when they throw me overboard in the middle of the Sound," Wolfe said impatiently. Her worst fear spoken aloud, Pru quieted—and Wolfe felt guilty. As scared as he was, she was worse.

"Forgive me," he said. He took up her hand and kissed it, then he leaned in close and whispered, "If they kill me, I would you get word to Doctor Franklin. Will you do that for me?" Pru's lower lip started quivering the way it used to just before she started blubbering when they were children. "Will you do that for me?" Wolfe said again. Pru bit her lip and nodded. Wolfe said, "If I survive, I'll get a note to you soon as may."

"Time to shove off!" Roedale barked.

Pru hugged Wolfe to her and whispered fiercely, "You swim home if you have to, Joethan!" Roedale barked again and Wolfe broke off the hug with a deep sigh. Pru smelled of lilacs and wood smoke. Roedale and his men smelled of poor hygiene and low tide.

Maintaining their disguises, the boatmen walked Wolfe unhurriedly through knots of drunken revelers on Huntington green. Beyond the light of the last bonfire, they dropped pretense and hustled for a mile or so to a place known as Long Swamps. With no moon and an overcast sky, all was dark shadow and darker obstruction. Wolfe relied on the man in front to find his way.

When they reached the shore, a whaleboat loomed darker in the inky night. Four men waited aboard. Before Wolfe got in, he said to Rodale, "I have a request."

"Jolly good for you," Roedale said snidely. Wolfe ignored him.

"If you mean to throw me overboard, I'd rather die here then drown out there, if 'tis all the same with you." The men around them stopped what they were doing to listen. Roedale sighed.

"If you don't start trouble, I spect you'll see t'other side." Wolfe sensed that something had changed.

"Is it possible you will unite me with my father?" he said.

"Until the woman spoke up, I din't think Nick had a son," Roedale said. "I know him ten years an' never heard he had one. Or wife even. We figured you was puttin' it 'round you was his son cause you 's working for the Crown. You look like you work for the Crown."

Loud enough for the crew to hear, Wolfe said, "I was sent to England fourteen years ago at my mother's dying wish. "I came home when I had word my father was in trouble. When I arrived in America I was told he was dead and buried in Prime's churchyard, only to find he is not. Now I may find myself trading fates with him. 'Tis a strange turn of events and no lie."

The crew hung on every word.

"Do you know Qua?" Wolfe said. Roedale didn't answer but Wolfe could see that he did. The other men knew Qua too, of him at least. "Qua is my uncle," said Wolfe. The men whispered to each other and Wolfe apprehended that Qua held, perhaps, greater weight with them than did his father.

He settled in the narrow stern sheets next to Roedale and said quietly to the crew, "If you played a part in Captain Wolferd's escape, you have my gratitude and admiration, gentlemen. 'Twere a flash affair entirely."

There was nothing so well received by boatmen as a handsome compliment, handsomely paid. All the men of *Sweet Nancy* afterward agreed, it was as fine a compliment as could be paid, for clearly the man was a gentleman with an appreciation of the more licentious side of things—not a right prig, as you might say. They were also in agreement that it was as genteel a kidnapping as one could ask for. Every man but doing his duty. They also spoke of the good hard pull across the Sound and how genial the gent had been to entertain them with gossip from London; especially the ridiculous heights of women's hairstyles and particularly, the scandal of a new corset that offered up the apples of men's desire as if on a tray! Oh, he was a right fine gent to be sure.

At sunup they put the gent ashore on a deserted stretch of rocky beach in Connecticut. Before they parted, one of the men gave back Wolfe's haversack, but it was light. His mates came to the rescue by pressuring the man to return Wolfe's pocket pistols.

"The Post Road is but a short walk inland," Roedale said. "Westward brings you to Fairfield and hence to York City and Long Island. Should you return there I trust you'll not tarry in Huntington. It need be known there are penalties for mucking about in other men's business."

"Where do I find my father?" Wolfe said. The crew of the whaleboat looked away. The answer to that question was the captain's responsibility and no other.

"You shan't be far wrong if you go to Boston," Roedale said carefully. "If you was to ask after the Sedition Captain from Setauket at the Green Dragon say, or any other liberty house, I 'spect someone'll know something."

"Or like as not try to kill me," Wolfe said.

"Or kill you," Roedale agreed jovially. "There's a tavern east o' here on the Post Road. My regrets but folks must know we keep our word."

"I quite understand," Wolfe said. "Though in the matter of a son looking for his father's body, I believe an allowance might be made." Roedale shrugged.

"Not if that 'llowance is apt to put men's lives in the hands of a stranger. Even one calling himself Wolferd."

"I yield the point," said Wolfe. "But I would you mark, I don't call myself Wolferd. My name is Joethan Wolfe. It was changed when I went to England and as it is what I'm used to, I intend to keep it." He stuck out his hand and Roedale shook, to find his hand held prisoner in a crushing grip that surprised him.

With a feral smile, Wolfe said, "I wonder was my father well when last you saw him?" Roedale grinned his rotten-toothed grin and with the aid of his other hand, pried free from Wolfe's grasp.

"He weren't unhappy, I can tell you that." Roedale winked and moved to rejoin his men in the boat, but then he stopped and turned back. "A proposition occurs to me. You're in liberty country now, won't find many who openly declare for the King. I wonder would you trade toppers? I quite admire your Denmark and the road might be easier if you appeared less the Government man."

Wolfe would have told the boatman to bugger himself if he hadn't meant to replace his Denmark when he got home to London. As it was, his practical nature asserted itself. The Denmark was a city hat, a heavy topper, especially on a long trip in rain or snow. In Europe a Denmark might ease the way among the better sort, here in the colonies a big cocked hat was impractical and even notably pretentious. It had been a mistake to wear his Denmark to America.

Roedale took possession of the hat happily, although it was too big. Wolfe consoled himself that the captain's sheepie hood was more practical for a man traipsing around the colonies on foot. And he still had his wool cap tucked away in the big pocket inside his greatcoat.

"I'll tell you one thing," Roedale said, brushing lightly at a smudge on the Denmark. "If I was on the run trying to get to Boston, I'd take the inland Post Road at New Haven. T'other way follows the coast where a swift ship might overtake me in a day." With a quick nod, he donned his new topper and shoved off.

27

Wolfe found the Post Road and soon the tavern. It was yet early and being Sunday, nearly six hours passed before the tavern keeper and his family returned from church. Fortunately the barn was sound and when Wolfe awoke from a deep cold sleep, the tavern keeper wasn't vindictive enough to start trouble or religiously zealous enough to turn down business.

Being the Sabbath from sundown Saturday until sundown Sunday, there was no one abroad. Spared the usual interrogation of a stranger, Wolfe ate and enjoyed a fire privately as he considered his next move. Despite the emotional turmoil his kidnapping imposed, he'd come away well enough. He had money and was armed. The difficulty was deciding what to do next.

Boston seemed a bad idea, weeks away. Yet with Pap alive, Wolfe's life wouldn't be his own until his commission—self-imposed or not—was successfully concluded. He could remain outside Boston and send word in to Warren, or maybe he'd find Pap before he got to Boston. Or perhaps he should hire a boat to take him back to Setauket and write Warren from there. Whichever he decided, New Haven seemed the place to start.

He set off shank's mare the next morning. Despite the constant pain in his ankles, inflicted by boots designed for riding, he kept a good pace. Occasionally he shared the road with local travelers for a mile or two, but mostly he was left to his own thoughts. Frequently his thoughts turned to Setauket and Pru.

Pru of the golden eyes and clear heart. In only a few days they'd made a deep connection, perhaps because they'd been children together and shared a commonality of reference, or perhaps because their intercourse was unobstructed by the rigors of London society. But that was rational analysis, rarely the equal of irrational emotion. When Wolfe limped into Milford, Pru had spent much of the day with him.

Milford had only one church steeple but the houses were handsome and prosperous looking. The town was situated for prosperity. In addition to a sheltered harbor, there were sawmills and gristmills clustered along a river where it tumbled over cascades of man-made dams.

He passed the night in a tavern on the east side of town, using the pain in his ankles to beg off all but the most obligatory niceties. Thankfully he didn't have to share a bed with a stranger.

The next day, after wrapping his ankles in soft leather bought from the tavern keeper, he arrived in New Haven at noon—limped up to the Port Collector's warehouse. A very surprised Elijah Cummins answered his knock.

"Din't shpect to shee you again," the maimed man cackled. Wolfe laughed right back.

"Nor I, you, Mister Cummins. Is Debins here?"

"Mr. Debinsh not here."

"When's he due back?"

"Cout'ent shay."

"Do you know if Caleb Brewster is in town?"

"Brewshter? Nah. He ain't here mush. He be a Fairfield man."

"What about Captain Arnold?"

"An't you jusht full o' queshtions."

"Who does that remind you of?" Wolfe said. To his great amusement, Cummins looked at him blankly. "Captain Arnold?" Wolfe said.

Arnold was aboard a neat little trading sloop. Garbed like a deckhand in a watch coat and wool cap, he invited Wolfe into the master's cabin. His cabin. It was his ship. When they each had a mug of coffee, Wolfe said, "I need get a note to Setauket. I thought you might lend some guidance."

"Too bad about your father," said Arnold.

"You knew?" said Wolfe. Arnold grunted.

"I knew."

"That he was killed?" Wolfe clarified.

"I thought it best you heard the news from kin."

"Only he's not dead," Wolfe said. Arnold was genuinely surprised, and thoroughly delighted when Wolfe recounted what transpired since last they met.

"Word was Cap'n Nick paid his debt to nature in Huntington," Arnold said. Wolfe nodded.

"He is dead officially. By and large t'were a rather slick affair. But just now I need get word of my whereabouts and intentions to a friend."

"Who is your friend?"

"Prudence Forester in Setauket."

"Any relation to Charles Forester?"

"His sister."

"Forester is a well-known King's man," said Arnold. Wolfe nodded.

"I've heard. His sister is not. I would she know I'm alive. You can read the letter." Arnold waved him to the chair behind his desk.

"What is it you intend, if I may ask?"

"To place a pardon in my father's hand was the reason for my journey to America," Wolfe said as he wrote. "I have yet to accomplish that." Arnold handed Wolfe a sander.

"'Tis well you're undaunted. Your task will not be easy." Wolfe sanded the letter and held it out for Arnold to read. He declined.

"Have you any thought where I might seek word of my father?" Wolfe said. Arnold's brow furrowed.

"I don't know you Mister Wolfe, so I won't pretend to trust you with anything of a private nature. I would also caution you. The penalty for asking the wrong question in the wrong place can be most severe."

"The very reason I ask you now," Wolfe said. Arnold gazed out the cabin windows. When he turned back, he fixed Wolfe with his striking gray eyes.

"You should consider joining up with a wagon bringing supplies to Boston. Must be one or two pass north most weeks."

"Wagon would take three times longer than a horse," Wolfe reflected.

"Aye. But wagons stop at common places," Arnold said. Wolfe took his meaning at once.

"Where would I find such a wagon?"

"They stage on the other side of the bridge." Arnold gestured to the north and laughed. "A hostelry run by a man named Bragg. Use my name and perhaps he won't rob you. And that'll be sixpence for the letter."

***

Sprawled across a few cleared acres, Bragg's place was paddocks, stables, barrels, scraps of rusting iron and the scattered bones of old wagons. The inn side of the concern was a tavern with a crude dormitory, luxury being neither expected nor furnished.

With the weather clear, the place was busy. Most of the traffic was carts and drays, but one wagon, a Pennsylvania freighter, easily dwarfed every vehicle in the yard. A massive twenty-five feet long and eight feet wide, the blue-painted body was shaped like the hull of a boat. The transom of the wagon—held in place by chains—folded down to become a ramp for loading. A once-white canopy, now weathered to tawny, stretched over bowed ribs of oak.

The wheels of the freighter were painted red, the two in back as tall as Wolfe and a foot wide. The front wheels were shorter and thinner to improve the turning radius. A jack, water buckets, feed trough and tools slung from the sides. A grease bucket and spare wheel were chained beneath. It was said that a Pennsylvania freighter could haul six tons. Upon examination, Wolfe was inclined to believe it.

He found Bragg—a short plug of smelly middle-age—and supplied Arnold's introduction along with a flimsy story of wanting to help the people of Boston. Bragg didn't care what Wolfe's story was, but he did know what was what. There were two wagons Boston bound, one of them being the freighter which was owned by the Widow van Roos, and she making her third trip since last summer.

Bragg pointed Wolfe to a paddock where two men contemplated oxen feeding at a trough. One of the men hanging on the paddock rail was a black fellow shorter than Wolfe but stout as a hogshead. The other man was a woman.

The Widow van Roos wore leather leggings and a beaver-fur coat and hat like an over-mountain man, yet presented as undeniably female. Older than Wolfe but not yet old, jeweled bobs on her ears matched haunting pale-blue eyes in a face burnished gold from the sun. Two yellow braids hung half way down her back. An upturned nose gave her a snobbish, yet mischievous air at the same time. If Cal looked a Viking, she could be his spear wife.

Wolfe gave her the same story he'd given Bragg and she laughed at him. Taken aback, he said, "Is it impossible a man should wish to help his suffering countrymen?"

"When he sounds like a Briton and wears a ten-guinea coat it is." She spoke with the unmistakable accent of the New York Dutch, but her English was educated and refined. She was no commoner.

"Is the reason I wish to go to Boston of utmost concern?" Wolfe said.

"Are you on the run?" she asked. The notion that his father might have traveled in company with this very wagon popped into Wolfe's head.

"I'm looking for someone," he said. The widow's eyes grew hard.

"If it be a slave you seek, you'd not be welcome with us."

"I seek a dead man and no slave."

"And if you find this dead man before we reach Boston?"

"Then I'll reconsider my circumstance," Wolfe said. "I'm volunteering, not indenturing."

The widow turned to the black man. "What say you, Sam?" Sam looked Wolfe over.

"Does you know cattle?" His voice was a soft, rumbling baritone.

"I'm good with beasts although my inclination is horses," Wolfe said. Sam grunted.

"Don't see as you got a blastin' iron. Can you handle one?"

"Well as anyone. And I am armed. But I thought this was liberty country." The widow snorted but not in amusement.

"There be cutthroats aplenty on our road," she said.

"I can certainly help with that," Wolfe said, but she was unconvinced. She pulled Sam aside for a quiet conversation then came back to Wolfe.

"I mean to leave on the morrow. I don't expect you'll last, but as I have no one else you may join us."

"You don't have to flatter me," Wolfe said. She ignored his jibe.

"This is my rig," she said firmly. "I'm boss." She pulled off a beaver-fur mitten and proffered her hand as a man would. Her pale-blue eyes bored into him. "What I say goes."

Meeting her gaze, Wolfe said, "Fair enough." He shook her hand.

The Widow said, "You may address me as Mevrouw van Roos."

"Madam van Roos it shall be," said Wolfe.

"Mevrouw' will suffice," the Widow said.

"Yes, Madam."

28

Wolfe's volunteer servitude began at dusk. The widow's main concern was that someone always be on watch. He was assigned first shift and didn't play proud when she offered a blanket to help with the cold.

"You said you were armed," she reminded him. Wolfe showed her his pocket pistols, at which she smiled in amusement. "I've bigger if you're inclined," she said.

"What kind of threat are we talking about?" asked Wolfe. "Some poor yahoos trying to steal a sack of oats?" Although she was only five or six years older, Madam Roos regarded him as if he was a child.

"I worry about Loyalists. Kin of a man who's been tarred and feathered perhaps. Men who'd like nothing better than to burn a freighter of supplies bound for Boston rebels. We usually travel in train as there's safety in numbers, but this time it's to be just us and one other." After giving Wolfe a few seconds to reconsider, she said, "Are you in mind of a bigger gun?"

"I suppose I am," Wolfe said. She motioned for him to follow her over to a wooden box attached to the exterior of the freighter. Inside were two finished cases. The smaller case, made of cherry wood with a felt interior, contained a smooth bore horse pistol, a well-made gun with a butt that would serve as a formidable weapon when reversed.

Nesting in the other case was a half-musket with a swollen mouth—a lethal scattergun that could be loaded with virtually anything, and rather easily on horseback or atop a coach.

Picking it up with delight, Wolfe said, "Bugger me if it ain't a blunderbuss." The widow ignored his vulgarity but corrected his nomenclature.

"Donderbus," she said, her pronunciation decidedly Dutch. Wolfe smiled.

"Donderbus, yes. I've heard it called so before."

"From donder, which is thunder and bus which is pipe," the Widow said. Wolfe ran a well-trained eye over the gun.

"Donderbus makes me think of a story used to frighten children in Flanders. A story of scarred-faced men that roam the countryside."

"Deelgelaat mensen," Madam said. "Shard-faced men, not scarred-faced men. And there are as many stories about them as clever storytellers can invent."

"The story I heard," said Wolfe, "was of a farmer breaking dishes for ammunition to protect his family from an evil gang of banditti." Mevrouw van Roos giggled. The first outward sign of femininity Wolfe had seen from her.

"Ya," she said. "The farmer shoots the men and they run away but the dish shards so ravage their faces they are forever known and hunted. They live in the woods like animals, waiting to pounce on misbehaving children."

"Aye, that's the tale," Wolfe said, at the precise moment he discovered that the donderbus was nonfunctional. The barrel was fouled with a concretion of solidified nitrate and rusted bird shot, as if doused in water when loaded and never cleaned. "This gun has been treated scandalously," he said. The widow crossed her arms.

"I'll say to you as I've said to others. If you clean it, you may use it."

Wolfe decided to give it a try. After taking the gun into the darkness where he could pee on it in private—urine being good to break down solidified gunpowder—he went to work. By the light of a torch, with pick, worm, metal brush and uncharacteristic patience, he brought the weapon back to life. When Sam relieved him hours later, he had an eye-headache from squinting in bad light, but he was looking forward to shooting the donderbus the next day.

Despite the freighter being somewhat empty, it was surprisingly warm inside. Suspended by chains from one of the canopy struts, a covered Dutch oven filled with hot embers threw an admirable amount of heat. Wolfe rearranged a few sacks of corn to make a bed and drew his blanket close. The next thing he knew, he was being shaken awake.

Yoking up oxen was easier than harnessing horses. The rig was simple, and expensive beasts like the widow's had paired yokes carved specifically for the tandems that shared them. Her three-pair were matched for weight and height, and were more docile and better trained than most horses.

With a quiet word from Sam to, "Walk on," the oxen stepped off.

Unaffiliated other than by destination, the wagon accompanying them— pulled by a pair of oxen—was a farm hauler of the type Wolfe was familiar with from his youth. Twelve feet long and four-feet wide, like the freighter, the wagon had no seat or footboard. Also like the freighter, the back wheels were bigger than the front. Unlike the freighter, there was no canopy and it was full. A heavy canvass tarp over the bed protected the load.

The man whose wagon it was, a skinny, dour fellow with an enormous head, was introduced as Israel Grange. Grange wore drab brown homespun head to toe. A worn black preaching hat was his only nod to sartorial finery. Under his hat, salt and pepper hair scraggled to his shoulders. Informed by his conservative appearance, and obvious disapproval of everything about the freighter, when out of earshot, the widow referred to Grange as "the Puritan."

Wolfe shadowed Sam at the head of the team. The drover kept up a steady stream of conversation, mostly imparting the various quirks and personalities of the oxen. They might have been his children, the way he spoke of them, but Wolfe respected the attitude entirely. He felt the same way about Gascon.

According to Sam, in Pennsylvania colony, where they were common, freighters were usually pulled by strings of horses decked out with bells and fancy headdresses. On the narrow roads of New York and New England— where freighters were rarely seen—the big wagons were apt to be pulled by cattle without decoration, the mere sight of the massive vehicles being notable enough. For a goad, Sam carried a five-foot-long, heavily etched stick. Wolfe asked why he didn't use a switch like most drovers.

"This here stick am better protection than a sword," Sam said. Wolfe smiled amiably.

"I doubt that."

"You got a sword I'll prove it," Sam rumbled.

The route north passed beneath East Rock and on into the valley of the Quinnipiac, where winter meadows stretched west to the river that gave the valley its name. The road was poor but as Sam explained, "This way we only has to cross the river but once."

On a long stretch of road in flat country, where no vestige of civilization could be seen, Madam gave her approval to test the donderbus. Wolfe estimated the charge required for a handful of pellets and with Madam, Sam and Grange looking on, he held the gun away from his body and fired. The donderbus shot as it ought and as the barrel didn't blow up, Wolfe considered his restoration a success. The widow seemed almost as pleased by the result as he was.

He'd gone light on powder with the first shot in case the barrel contained hidden flaws. Now he reloaded with the appropriate amount of powder for pellet and ball. This time when he pulled the trigger, the donderbus kicked like an angry horse and belched a two-foot tongue of flame from the barrel. As the echoing report died away and the thick gray powder smoke dissipated, Wolfe grinned to himself and thought, *now that be a thunder-pipe*. He pitied anyone he ever had to use it against.

With the road in surprisingly good shape, they arrived midmorning at the village of North Farms. While New Haven boasted Yale College and an established gentry, North Farms was a place of farmers, yeomen and laborers. In addition to mills that turned out bricks by the ton, there were active docks and a shipyard along the river.

Before they entered the town, Madam sought out Wolfe. "I would you not talk to anyone," she said. "I fear they may think I'm harboring a Redcoat deserter or spy. Which, for all I know, is what you are."

"I won't admit to either," Wolfe said glibly. Madam didn't so much as crack a smile.

There wasn't much activity as the freighter drew up outside a tavern on the North Farms green, but as if by magic, a small crowd soon gathered. Wolfe assumed they were drawn by the novelty of the freighter but he was wrong. They'd come to thank the Waggoneers for their efforts on behalf of the people of Boston. People much like themselves, they imagined, brethren in the cause of liberty.

The widow conferred with the tavern keeper, Mr. Andrews, a short energetic fellow, then she went inside and shared news with any who cared to listen. Wolfe and Sam watered and fed the oxen at a drop-down trough on the side of the freighter. When the beasts were content, they ducked inside to grab a bite themselves. The widow joined them at table but sent Wolfe out to keep an eye on the freighter.

As he sat outside and listened to his stomach grumble, Wolfe pondered his hunger and the stern woman who'd imposed it. He thought she was a hard case but upon reflection, he softened his estimation. Madam Roos was no different than any teamster running a rig, except she was a woman, of course. Perhaps the fault lay with himself, but further analysis was interrupted. Two men brought bundles of pre-hackled flax up out of the cellar of the tavern to donate to the people of Boston.

Wolfe dropped the rear ramp of the freighter and loaded the flax. Only about sixty pounds were added to the load, but if every village along the way contributed as much, the freighter would be full long before Boston.

When he finished loading the flax, Wolfe asked tavernkeeper Andrews for a word in private. Trying to approximate an American accent—or at least minimize the London in his voice—he named his father by all his various titles and asked if Andrews might remember him.

"He has green eyes and a dented chin like me, but older of course," Wolfe said. "I'm told by those who saw him last that he had a beard, and appeared as what some might say, a pirate." Andrews chuckled jovially.

"A pirate or highwayman describes half the creatures that travel this road. Regretfully I do not recall your particular man. All I know is if you do good works, he that watches over us all will reward you."

Shortly after, a woman appeared with a bowl of stew, bread, and a pot of beer. Wolfe accepted the donation to his appetite as reward enough for now.

29

The road north shadowed the river through the vast marshes that surrounded it, until the Quinnipiac Valley opened out onto the New Haven plain. Here they gained the Post Road proper, a roadway dozens of yards wide in places and sandy enough that twice the freighter got stuck. Madam van Roos took control of the team when that happened, so that Sam and Wolfe could heave on the sunken wheel.

By weaving back and forth across the road, Sam eventually found the firm track and the oxen settled into an easy, steady gait. By midafternoon they were climbing a ridgeline east of the plain, and before dusk, rolling into Carrington's on the outskirts of Wallingford Town. There the scene in North Farms was replayed by the light of torches and whale oil lamps.

Carrington's was asleep by the time Wolfe ended his watch, offering no chance to question anyone. It was of no consequence. His ankles were raw from his boots and he was exhausted.

They departed the next morning before the sun was over the north-south ridgeline of the Wallingford Mountains—mountains only by virtue of rising above lowlands. Still, the first few hours were a pull uphill through thickly wooded slopes interrupted occasionally by denuded acres where timber had been harvested for high pasture.

The branch of a tree lying in the road inspired Wolfe. He jogged ahead and removed it but afterward kept an eye on the edge of the woods. Eventually he found what he was looking for in the limb of a fallen chestnut tree.

As he whittled away at the branch with his barlow, Wolfe fell under the spell of the oxen's unwavering pace, Sam's rumbling voice and the rhythmic creak of the freighter, which was not unlike that of a ship. The morning passed as a pleasant stroll, or would have if Wolfe's ankles weren't being destroyed by his boots.

Coming down off the ridge, Wolfe helped Sam install lock chains on the back wheels of the freighter, so the heavy wagon wouldn't push the oxen downhill too fast and injure them. The freighter skittered down the slope safely but with the rear wheels unable to turn, descent was clumsy and slow.

Back on level ground, they passed through an expanse of swamp, and so into the village of Durham, little more than a collection of scattered houses and one small church. The tavern, proclaimed by a gilded ball hanging outside, was a simple two-story house. A large barn with an extensively fenced yard implied that there was traffic on occasion but at present the place looked deserted.

Madam returned from inside with two loaves of bread and a troubled look on her face. "We'll leave soon as the beasts are happy," she said. Wolfe saw a glance pass between her and Sam.

"Is everything all right?" he said.

"I would you not ask after your dead man here."

Later as they set out, Madam came to him again. "I would you trail behind and fire a warning shot if we're followed."

"What's acting?" said Wolfe.

"We'll speak of it later," Madam said curtly.

Wolfe plucked the donderbus from the back of the freighter and shambled along behind as the freighter rumbled away. At a massive rock affording a commanding view of the surrounding country, he sat down to keep an eye on the road.

Whittling at his stick, he wondered what the cause for the widow's concern was. He gave up soon enough. No doubt it had to do with the factionalism abroad in the country. What in particular he couldn't begin to guess and so he relaxed and enjoyed the weather. It was another mild day. He remembered January being far more severe in his youth.

The road behind stayed empty and in due course, he ambled along. By midafternoon the country was flat fields between hay and grass, which offered unobstructed views in all directions. Seeing no advantage to be had by trailing, he broke into a comfortable lope and caught up with the Puritan.

All but ignoring his oxen, Grange marched behind his rig loudly singing a psalm which infused his dour aspect with a radiant happiness. As Wolfe fell in step, the lanky man nodded but kept on singing. When the hymn finally came to an end, Wolfe said, "You have a fine voice, Mister Grange." Grange smiled at him with more vanity than fellowship.

"'Tis the Lord's gift to me," Grange said. "I am never so joyous as when I can repay his kindness in psalmody. Would you care to join me in, *My Days Have Been So Wondrously Free?*"

"I'm not familiar with that one," Wolfe said. "In truth I'm not much in the way of religion at all." The light in Grange's eyes went out.

"I mourn to hear you say it. For God's love will never fill your heart, Mister Wolfe." Wolfe smiled warmly.

"Right you may be, Mr. Grange. Yet many times have I felt my heart so full that I thought it must burst. So you see, even if what you feel for God is greater than any joy I will ever know, I am content." Before Grange could respond, Wolfe walked on and caught up with Madam, walking ahead of the freighter.

He reported all clear and she thanked him. "Mind telling me what's acting?" Wolfe said.

"A Tory house in Durham was torched by a mob yesterday," she said. "Mister Swathel feared if my wagon was seen at his place, Tories might take revenge upon him. Or us."

"You should have told me," Wolfe said. When she didn't reply, he said, "I would've known better what to look out for." Madam studied his face and found no reproach.

"Forgive me," she said at last. "I don't trust anyone but Sam. I was afraid you might think our journey not worth the risk and as you know, I've no one else just now."

"I'm not easily discouraged," said Wolfe. "And I'll thank you to consider our interests mutual as long as we share the road. 'Tis my skin as well as your own." For a moment he thought she'd argue but instead she nodded.

"Of course."

"We're agreed?" Wolfe said. Madam nodded. They plodded along in silence after that until Wolfe observed, "It would seem that Connecticut is not the bastion of liberty minded folk I was led to believe." Madam didn't reply and he thought she was ignoring him. Some minutes later, he realized she'd been considering her response.

"I've found that where a man stands politically depends upon his station or religion. The most warlike insurrectionists are in the country because that's where the meaner sort outnumber the better sort. And because the only thing Puritans hate more than the Scarlet Whore, is paying taxes to keep Anglican clergy landed, clothed and fed. The very clergy that cast them out of England, as you probably know. In large towns like Middletown, where we'll spend the night, the factions are more evenly divided as you would expect."

"Why would I expect that?" Wolfe said. She replied as if the answer was obvious.

"There are more rich men in large towns and rich men are Church of England most likely. You may be sure they and the people who rely on them for a living will fight to preserve their place." She nodded at the stick in his hand. "What is it you've been carving?" He showed her the branch.

"Sam assures me his stick is more protection than a sword. I mean to learn the truth of it."

Madam gave him a rueful smile. "I believe you'll regret it but I wish you joy of the lesson." In response to her implied dismissal, Wolfe fell back and joined Sam. The drover nodded at Wolfe's stick.

"You mean to try me with that?"

Wolfe held up the stick. "It'll serve for a sword." Sam gave a low chuckle.

"Don't hold it 'gainst me if I hurt you."

They trudged along silently for a bit, Wolfe admiring the sway of the widow's hips up ahead. "Tell me about Mevrouw van Roos," he said. "What happened to her husband?"

"Nigh on six-year dead," Sam said.

"Alone ever since?"

"'Cept me an' some others who work her place."

"Will she not take another husband?" Wolfe said. Sam snorted.

"Why? You got a notion?"

"Not me," Wolfe laughed. "But she's not unattractive and hardly old. I should think someone would be interested." Sam shrugged.

"I don't say men ain't tried. Mister van Roos were from a family what they call Patroons. When he died, men paid court to her from all over. His people even tried to marry her to a nephew so's to keep the plantation in the family, but she were havin' none of it. Told 'em if they gave her a bowery on the property for her own, they could have the rest and no tussle. And that's what they done."

The information gave Wolfe a deeper respect for the widow. Patroons were the Dutch land barons of New York. Some of their estates still stretched for miles along the Hudson River, although perhaps not the sixteen miles deeded in the original grants.

"She gave up a fortune then?" Wolfe said.

"Freedom an't cheap," said Sam.

"Children?"

Sam shook his head. "Wilhemina were Mister Roos' third wife. He were nigh on fifty when they wed."

"Wilhemina?" Wolfe said. Sam sighed.

"Don't go saying I told her name. She don't like folks knowin' her Christian name lest she tell 'em herself."

The road to Middletown banked sharply left as it followed the great bend in the Connecticut River. Although the familiar features of any port town were to be seen—forests of masts along the waterfront, warehouses and maritime industry lining the streets down to the water—the number of negros working those streets was unusual to Wolfe. He didn't recall slave gangs as a boy. In the north anyway.

Middletown was a genteel settlement with stately trees arching over the road and columned houses with roomy porticoes and large gardens.

And slaves.

After passing a handsome church, the freighter pulled into Bigalow's Tavern and Madam went inside. A few minutes later, a ten-year-old boy came out and competently expedited getting the oxen settled. With an hour of daylight left, Sam tapped Wolfe on the shoulder with his staff.

"Might as well get this over with," the drover said. Wolfe grinned.

"Might as."

30

They squared off in the stable yard with only the boy and a slave man as witnesses, and it wasn't as unequal a match as Wolfe expected. Having never faced a quarterstaff, Wolfe expected to best Sam rather easily. Instead he discovered that in the right hands, a staff was every bit the weapon Sam claimed. Wolfe was hard pressed to defend himself, let alone press an attack.

Sam's intent was to whack Wolfe enough times to convince him that his boast was true, but that was not to be either. Wolfe was quicker and more accomplished with a sword—or stick—than anyone Sam had faced before. Their initial flurries yielded neither an advantage and they stepped back eyeing each other and sucking air.

"You're a regular Little John with that staff," Wolfe said respectfully. Sam looked at Wolfe quizzically.

"Who?"

"Little John," said Wolfe. "You know. Robin Hood's accomplice."

"Never heard of 'im," Sam said.

"Outlaws," Wolfe explained, neatly parrying a head shot from Sam's stick. His own thrust to Sam's chest was knocked aside and he had to lunge back to avoid a blow from the other end of Sam's staff. They separated and circled each other warily.

"Robin and Little John robbed the rich and gave the loot to the poor," Wolfe said.

"Do tell." Sam bayoneted his staff at Wolfe's midsection. Wolfe parried inside out, spun past and delivered a clean whack to Sam's back. Had his branch been a blade it would have ended the contest at once—the first advantage either had gained. Wolfe grinned. Sam frowned in annoyance.

Spinning his staff in one hand like a baton, Sam said, "What this Little John got to do with me?" Wolfe knew he had yet to see the drover's full effort and knew it was coming.

"Robin Hood was the finest archer in England," Wolfe said. "Little John was a demon with a quarterstaff. When they met they fought with staffs and Little John knocked Robin into a river."

"As will I, you!" Sam attacked, feinting and striking with both ends of his staff. Wolfe could do naught but retreat and parry until one of Sam's blows caught him flush on the shin. As he yowled in pain and hopped around, Sam stepped back with a satisfied grin.

"If I'd a put my all into it, your leg'd be broke. Had enough?" Wolfe rubbed his shin gingerly and eyed the drover.

"I'd say that makes us even."

"Why don't we jest leave it there?" Sam said. The look on Wolfe's face said that he didn't want to leave it there. "All right then," Sam said. A heartbeat later, he went for the coup de grâce with a nasty body poke. Wolfe was ready and parried, then he slid his sword stick down the staff hard into Sam's callused and meaty left hand. Sam almost dropped his staff as he barked in pain and twisted away.

"If that had been a sword," Wolfe said, "you'd have no fingers to hold your staff."

Sam examined his tender digits and swore. "You an't half bad with that stick."

Someone clapping drew their attention. A couple of blue-uniformed men in black cocked hats were watching. One man was clapping. "I thought he had you," the man called.

"He did," Wolfe called back. The man laughed and waved before entering the tavern with his friend. Madam was watching too.

"Come eat," she called.

"You all right?" Wolfe said as he and Sam went inside. Sam allowed that his hand didn't feel too good. Wolfe tried to cheer him up, saying, "My shin will be purple tomorrow."

An hour after Wolfe began his watch, the soldier who'd clapped at the sparring session came outside and offered him a pot of beer and a pipe. "Mind if I join you?" He was in his early thirties, wiry, with a high forehead, curly brown hair and an aquiline nose. When they were both puffing away on a pipe, he stuck out his hand and said, "Return Meigs."

Shaking the man's hand, Wolfe said, "Return is an unusual name."

"First time I've heard that," Meigs said dryly. When Wolfe stopped laughing, Meigs explained that his grandmother had second thoughts after rejecting his grandfather's proposal of marriage and bade him return. "And that is why my father is Return Meigs and so am I. Friends call me John."

"Well, John," Wolfe said, "I'm wondering what uniform it is you wear." Meigs' blue jacket with white turnbacks, white smallclothes, white gaiters and a black cocked hat was as professional as any in the British army. Meigs exhaled a cloud of smoke.

"I'm a captain of Connecticut Militia."

"I didn't know militia were so well turned out," Wolfe said. Meigs gave a wry smile.

"We're not all tag-rag and bobtail."

"Well, you look a proper soldier," Wolfe said. Meigs was unsure if he'd just been slighted.

"We might not drill so well as the Bloodybacks but my men'll outshoot 'em."

"But will they stand when the Redcoats shoot back?" Wolfe said. "That is the important question."

"You a soldier?"

"Not I," Wolfe chuckled. "But I gambled and drank with enough of them in London to know what they think of Americans. They insist it don't matter how you aim but whether you can deliver three rounds in a minute when bullets fly. Can your militia do that?"

"I believe we'll find out ere long," Meigs said. "You're American?"

"Born and weaned. I was sent to England as a boy."

"Guess it took. You sound like a Britoner."

"First time I've heard that," Wolfe said. Meigs laughed. Wolfe held up his pipe. "This tobacco is good."

"Tobacco's a big crop 'round here." Meigs drew the sword from the scabbard at his hip and held it out. "You handled your stick rather handsomely. I have to carry this damned thing but know little how to use it. I'd be grateful for any advice you might share."

Meigs' blade was a somewhat handsome small sword but as soon as Wolfe had it in hand, he felt something amiss. It was light in the hilt, meaning the tang had probably been shaved too small by an inept cutler, the pommel stuffed with something to fill the space. Wolfe used the ramrod of the donderbus to tap the blade lightly and listen. The sound was dull and flat. Next, he tried to flex the blade but it was rigid. Finally, after taking a few practice cuts, he handed the sword back to Meigs.

"This blade will get you killed," Wolfe said. "'Tis made of inferior steel. You cross swords in anger with this blade and it will break." Meigs eyed the weapon in his hand with disgust. He was so crestfallen that Wolfe offered to show him some maneuvers."

By the light of torches in the yard, he taught Meigs the fundamental concepts and techniques of swordplay, and exercises that would build up the muscles needed to execute them. When they finished, Meigs said he owed Wolfe a debt. Willing to collect at once, Wolfe asked, "Do you know the man who keeps this tavern?"

"Tim's been ailing," Meigs said. "His wife Lizzy runs the place."

Wolfe told Meigs about his search and asked if Meigs would question Mrs. Bigalow on his behalf. The militia captain undertook the mission and wasn't long gone.

Handing Wolfe a fresh pot of beer, Meigs reported, "A man his friends made sport of as Captain Sedition were here. But he wasn't bearded. He was clean shaved with a dimple in his chin." Wolfe rubbed the shallow cleft in his own chin and elicited a smirk from Meigs. "Sound like your da to me," he said.

"Did she know where he was bound?" Wolfe said. Meigs shook his head.

"But one of the men he was with was from Boston."

31

At dawn, after taking on nearly five hundred pounds of garlic, onions, firewood, and tobacco—which Wolfe helped himself to a good supply—the freighter crossed a swampy meadow and entered what was known as the upper house of Middletown, where the better sort lived. They passed through without stopping.

On another mild day, Grange began singing shortly after sunrise and continued a steady program of somber hymns all the way through the parish of Stepney, another scattered collection of houses strung out along the river. Mercifully—to those in the freighter—he ceased singing when they neared Wethersfield.

The road into Wethersfield was lined by handsome houses set back behind fences of rail and picket. The Christopher Wren–like spire of a church poked above bare trees. To Wolfe it was as a bit of England transported. Quite unexpectedly, he experienced a wave of homesickness that had him questioning what he was doing in America. In New England. In the middle of nowhere.

His duty, he told himself. He was doing his duty. And then he put one foot ahead of the other and trudged on.

They left Wethersfield and passed on to the Hartford Road. Thereafter the villages and hamlets were thick. The next was Worthington Parish, a village Madam was familiar with. After she pointed a few things out, Wolfe asked how she knew the area so well.

"Hollanders settled here first," she said. "This was our country before the English seized it. Those who lived here under out laws and our ways had to accept English rule or leave." She spoke unemotionally but in the flash of her pale-blue eyes, Wolfe thought he caught a glimpse of her motivation for freighting to Boston.

"My husband has relations all through this country," she said.

"Will you stop and see them?" Wolfe asked. She chuckled sourly.

"Not by choice. They haven't any use for me since my husband died. And I never had any use for them. They are slave owners and King's men."

"Are most Hollanders royalists?" Wolfe said. She smiled a little sadly.

"Hollanders are of commerce, first and always, Mister Wolfe. There is a jest among us that the reason for our tolerance of other religions is because our true religion is money. As rebellions tend to disrupt commerce, I fear you will find very few Hollanders among insurrectionists."

Worthington's Dutch roots were evident. Older homes with gable roofs were unlike their newer, gambrel roofed English neighbors. Some people on the street had pale-blue eyes to rival Madam's.

As they passed through Worthington, the Widow ducked down an alley and disappeared. She didn't reappear until they were once again on the Hartford Road. She rejoined by handing Sam a sack of dough balls cooked in hot oil. *Oliebollen* she named them. Sam grabbed a handful and passed the sack to Wolfe. Almost as delicious as they smelled, the *oliebollen* were all but gone by the time Madam noticed, snatched back the sack and scolded Sam and Wolfe like naughty boys.

To the accompaniment of Israel Grange's pious psalmody, the wagons rumbled past mounted overseers driving slaves maintaining irrigation ditches in the fields alongside the road.

"Do you think the men with whips are with the Liberty Faction?" Wolfe cracked. Sam didn't laugh. Madam turned a weary eye on Grange.

"Let us put some road between us and the Puritan. I'll grant he has a good voice but would it hurt to sing plain song now and again?"

Sam hupped the oxen and soon Grange's singing came only in snatches.

After scouting both sides of the road all morning, Wolfe found a likely limb of seasoned hickory. He'd been impressed by the effectiveness of Sam's staff and resolved to learn how to use one. When he showed the limb to the drover, all he got was a grunt, but enough of a grunt to affirm that the branch would serve. Wolfe studied the limb and imagined how he'd shape it. His attention only faltered when an insistent clamor erupted from up ahead.

A roly-poly man swaddled in a massive bear-fur coat was leading a horse. The beast was weighed down with panniers from which all manner of goods clanged and clashed together with every step. When he drew close, the man called cheerily, "Well met, fellow travelers. Might be you're in need of a tinker."

"What news in Hartford?" Madam said. The news was that the tinker, Horatio, was returning from a disappointing trip. The great valley to the north was in poor circumstance. There was no hard money to be found and everyone was hoarding in expectation of hostilities. He also gave an account of the attack on Fort William and Mary, the incident Wolfe first heard about in Gage's office.

Wolfe had heard different versions of the fall of the fort everywhere the freighter went. There were colorful twists to each version of the story but the commonality was that the fort had been taken, powder and shot removed, the perpetrators escaped. No one had been bad hurt, no one had been arrested and war hadn't broken out. A remarkable outcome, all things considered.

Madam van Roos told Horatio about the Tory being burned out in Durham. "Odds bodkins!" the tinker swore. "That's a game not worth the candle!"

Wolfe asked Horatio if he had any knives. He was shown a wide-ranging collection. Most were inferior but there was an English trade knife that would suit. For what he considered practically nothing, Wolfe purchased the knife, a horn cup, and a broken-in leather strap with a buckle. When tinker and customer parted, each felt their journey had taken on a more satisfactory aspect.

Wolfe spent the rest of the transit to Hartford adapting his new strap to fit the empty slings on the donderbus. By the time the freighter left the Post Road to skirt Hartford to the west, the gun hung comfortably from his shoulder as if it always had.

In midafternoon they were on bad road in thick forest with no trace of civilization. For no apparent reason, graded road suddenly manifested. Not long after, just above the trees, the blades of a windmill could be seen, and then the far-off beat of trip hammers could be heard. Shortly after that, the unmistakable tang of forges and furnaces was in the air.

The freighter emerged abruptly from the forest on the outskirts of an ironworks built on a tributary of the Tunxis River. Minus intervening forest, the percussion of trip hammers was chest thumping, the roar of the massive furnace pervasive.

In addition to the windmill and furnace, the plantation boasted a foundry, a charcoal house and forges. Driven by water from the river via man-made sluices, half a dozen waterwheels provided power. Mountains of logs were everywhere. A dozen tarp-covered flatboats were pulled out along the riverbank.

A short distance from the ironworks, in the middle of the plantation, lay the infrastructure required for such an undertaking. Barns with labyrinths of paddocks and coops faced one side of an acre of open ground, a parade ground or common perhaps. On the other side of the open ground were brick barracks for laborers, and cottages with little gardens and privies, all of it neat and well-tended.

At the northern edge of the complex, seven brick houses and their wooden outbuildings formed an entirely different community. In this enclave was a general store, tavern, church, schoolhouse, and the workshops of mechanics and artisans. Acres of working farmland stretched beyond and then deep forest once again—wood being the most necessary ingredient for charcoal, the heart of the iron-making process.

The furnace chimney spat ash and sparks into a steel-gray sky as the freighter parked on the parade ground. Wolfe and Sam unyoked the oxen as the work day came to an end for the gangs operating the complex. For a few minutes, thirty or forty men and a great flock of sheep surged all around. Wolfe noted that a large number of the men were negro and they may have been slaves, although their clothing and demeanor did not pronounce it—yet they all retired to barracks at the same time.

As quickly as the complex filled it emptied, but for a handful of men who approached the freighter. Madam Roos intercepted them and had matters sorted by the time Wolfe and Sam were ready to pen the cattle.

Wolfe was washing up at a well when Madam appeared with articles of toilette and a towel. Waiting for him to finish, she said, "I believe this would be a good place to ask after your dead man. If you would know what passes in this part of the country, Pieter Renseleer is your man. He owns the plantation. If you've a mind to, you may escort me to his house this evening."

"That is very kind of you," Wolfe said. "What about guard duty?"

"We need no guard here. I'll say that much for Pieter."

"I shall be happy to escort you," Wolfe said.

He left the freighter to Madam when she returned from the well. When next they met, he'd greased his boots so they looked respectable and she'd donned Dutch petticoats of red, yellow and blue stripes. A cowled cape of bright blue transformed her stern aura but before Wolfe could fairly judge her merit in skirts, she took his arm and led him to the north end of the complex. Her destination was a three-story brick house with a tile roof and white windows. On the sheltered porch, whale-oil lamps blazed either side of a Dutch door.

The inside of the Renseleer home was as handsome as the outside, and clean and tidy as would be expected of a Dutch household. What was not expected was the large staff to accomplish it. Slaves or indentures, Wolfe couldn't say. Probably a mix as there were whites and blacks, but it suddenly pressed heavily upon him that there were more slaves in America than ever he remembered.

No wonder there is so much talk of liberty, he thought, *the blasphemy of slavery is everywhere.*

The big conceit of the house was a grand staircase; two floors of oak-paneled stairs with a stand of arms and a rack of cutlasses built into the wall of the first-floor landing. Renseleer was proud of his stairwell. Inspired by one he saw in Maryland, he said.

Somewhere north of sixty, Pieter Renseleer retained an erect and imposing carriage. Dry skin flaked his face but the blue eyes were quick and clear and his hair was yet long and thick enough to club, although the original straw color was now white. So too his eyebrows, which were long and apt to look crazy when he rubbed them, which he did often. Perhaps most impressive, Pieter Renseleer put on no airs despite his obvious success.

They retired to the parlor, a well-appointed salon with carpet, wainscoting, and heavy furniture in the German style. Wolfe was introduced to Madam Renseleer and two associates of her husband, and their wives. The younger associate, near Wolfe's age, looked to be a competent bumped up from the ranks. He and his prematurely old wife were not yet comfortable in polite society.

On the other hand, Madam Renseleer was a perfect hostess. Ten or fifteen years younger than her husband, she was beefy and lighthearted and obviously born to good society. She knew Madam van Roos and enjoyed her company.

Wolfe couldn't fault her for that. Out of her over-mountain furs, Wilhemina van Roos had the manners and grace of a duchess. With golden braids wound about her head like a Saxon queen, she knew what to say and how to say it in a way that charmed men and offered no offense to other ladies. For two rounds of brandy, she held the room enthralled with anecdotes about the little accouterments attached to the Dutch belt of her gown, such as scissors and a little magnifier and tweezers. Each article had a story that she related in a most charming manner.

Mevrouw Renseleer adored that Mevrouw van Roos was traditionally dressed. "The old fashions are more practical and gay than any currently in vogue," she remarked, and no one would disagree. Madam Roos' Dutch petticoats were shorter than the English style and offered titillating glimpses of pale blue stockings.

Wolfe gathered that the third couple were lucky relations, the husband indebted to Mr. Renseleer for his livelihood. The wife was a pretty enough thing. Much younger. Bored. An easy mark for a traveling man was Wolfe's impression.

When it was his turn to divert the table, Wolfe told the tale of a son in search of his father. He left it unstated that he was the son. The story sparked a shrewd look from Pieter Renseleer. Madam Roos was studying Wolfe too.

When their gazes met, she coolly turned to Madam Renseleer and inquired whether Wolfe's father had stopped at the plantation. Without batting an eye, Madam Renseleer said, "I should think so. Everyone does, you know."

After a light sup, the couples retired to the parlor for cards. Pieter and Madam Roos were paired against Wolfe and Madam Renseleer in whist. During the course of the game, Pieter made it clear that Captain Nick was known to him, and that Wolfe was on the right road. Whether or not that road led to Boston he didn't know, nor would he say if he did.

After midnight, Wolfe had to all but drag Madam back to the freighter. She was tipsy and in no hurry. "We'll pay for this tomorrow," Wolfe said. She snickered at him.

"The morrow is Epiphany. We'll not travel on the morrow."

"Is Twelfth Day different in the colonies than England?" Wolfe said. Madam laughed.

"It could not be. Could it?"

"Well today is the sixth of January," Wolfe said. "Yesterday I mean. 'Tis after midnight." Madam was more amused than upset.

"You're sure?"

"Quite sure," Wolfe said. "Isn't that why Renseleer invited you into his home?" Madam giggled.

"They always invite me." She spun, enjoying the twirl of her petticoats until she came to a stop facing him. "I feared 'twas my society drove you early away." She was flirting outrageously and Wolfe was not immune.

"You are delightful company," he said. "But you know that." She was flush with wine and stared back brazenly. Wolfe knew the look and tried to accommodate it by kissing her. She was not unresponsive but nuzzling and petting was what she was after—and grinding. Extensive grinding. When she had what she needed, she bade him wait. Eventually she returned in her beaver furs and handed him a flask—schnapps that went down like candy and exploded in the stomach like Greek fire.

As Madam accepted back the flask, she said, "Sam hasn't returned."

"Where did he go?" Wolfe said.

"He visits a man in Hartford when we're here. He dislikes to be around slaves." She kissed him lightly on both cheeks and fled up the ramp into the freighter.

Hours later Wolfe was rudely awakened in the dark. Shaken awake. Anxious exhaustion on Madam's face brought him instantly alert.

"Sam isn't back, she said. "Will you go find him?" As Wolfe pulled himself together, she said, "I would go but as a woman I should accomplish little if there are Puritans involved. If you aren't willing to help, tell me and I'll ask Pieter. If you say you will help, I hold you to it. Sam's life may hang in the balance." Wolfe put his hands firmly on her shoulders to calm her down.

"Who was he going to see last night?"

Madam's face sagged in relief as she realized he would take up the search. She told him who Sam visited, where to look, and above all, what she feared.

32

The sun was up when Wolfe reached the Hartford waterfront. Despite being a busy little seaport, finding Sam's friend, Cesar, took no time at all. The first person Wolfe met directed him to Cesar's shop. Rousing the old shoemaker from an alcoholic stupor was the difficult aspect.

When his befuddlement fell away, Cesar was as concerned as Madam. He'd left Sam at a pleasure house hours before. "Hartford an't a Negro's friend at the best of times," he said. He was older, maybe a slave once but his own man now, with a good broadcloth suit and respectable wig. He had a calm way about him, and shoes of fine leather set off with opulent brass buckles in a style popular before Wolfe was born.

"Have you checked the gaol?" Cesar said. "You must find if he been taken up."

"Taken up for what?" said Wolfe.

"Being negro and out o' doors past sunset," Cesar said facetiously. "This am Hartford. They don't need a reason." He gave Wolfe directions to the gaol and said he'd ask around while Wolfe was gone.

The gaol was a squat wooden building near the blockhouse that was the original Dutch fort when the town was founded. It was a full minute from the time Wolfe banged on the door until a square peephole slid open.

"What?!" a disgruntled voice growled.

"I need know if you hold my friend," said Wolfe. The door flew open a second later.

"Are you focking mad? You woke me for what?" The brawny young Turnkey was pissing mad and ready to brawl, until he saw the hard look in Wolfe's eyes and the donderbus on his shoulder.

"I'm looking for Sam Roos," Wolfe said. "Is he here?"

"Don't know who that is," the Turnkey said, swallowing most of his outrage. Wolfe described Sam and the Turnkey shook his head. "Only got one Negro. Pompey James. He's here most nights. Might be your friend's in worse trouble than you think. They was lookin' for another Negro last night. I shouldn't wonder if a trader is pressin' crew. Men allus disappear when the traders sail."

That was the scenario Madam feared. Merchant ships trading in the West Indies were notorious for waylaying negros to fill out their crew. Any negro, slave or not. They'd use them to work the voyage then sell them into slavery when they reached the islands. Plantations needing a constant supply of cheap labor didn't ask questions.

Wolfe apologized to the Turnkey for waking him and asked where he could find the sheriff. The Turnkey said not to bother. "It's well known he's paid to look t'other way."

"Are you a Liberty Man?" Wolfe said. The Turnkey was. "May I presume the Hartford Watch are Liberty Men?" The Turnkey affirmed that they were. "My friend is driving a freighter of supplies to the struggling people of Boston," Wolfe said. "Can you get word that a Son of Liberty may be in trouble?"

"I Can do that well enough," the Turnkey said. "Got a rattle."

"The very thing," said Wolfe. "I need get back to the docks and find out what ships are sailing. Can you ask the Watch to join me there?" As he retraced his steps to the dock, the obnoxious ratcheting of an alarm rattle satisfied him that the Hartford Watch would soon make an appearance. There was nothing the home guard liked better than an important mission.

There were other men at Cesar's when Wolfe returned. He told them what he'd learned and it jibed with what they'd discovered. There were a few negroes missing from around the waterfront. The signs pointed to a West Indiaman taking on water that very day. The difficulty was, searching a ship required a warrant from a sheriff or Justice of the Peace.

Or an act of piracy.

Wolfe reported what the Turnkey said about the sheriff. Cesar didn't doubt but that the Turnkey was right, and that worried him even more. "We don't got a Justice gonna trouble over disappearing negroes," Cesar said. Wolfe was unfazed.

"They'll act if they fear what happens if they don't. Where's the ship?"

"Bourke's wharf."

"So we might walk right up to it?" Cesar nodded. Wolfe clapped him on the shoulder. "Let's go have a word with them. Wait. Are any of the missing men slaves?" Cesar looked to other men for confirmation.

"Two, we think."

"Their masters would help," Wolfe mused. "Can someone take word?" A couple of men volunteered.

In the mysterious way that news of unfolding events spread, word raced ahead as Wolfe and Cesar walked to the ship. By the time they arrived at Bourke's wharf, nearly a score of people had fallen-in behind them.

The *Bristol Maiden* was a seventy-five-foot trading brig with the Cross of St. George snapping at her sternpost. Aboard ship, two officers were overseeing sailors rigging a net through a yardarm block and prying up the main hatch in preparation of taking on stores.

Wolfe hailed them and asked permission to come aboard and palaver. In a thick, west country English accent, the Officer of the Deck, a tough looking fellow in scruffy work rig, told Wolfe to speak his piece from the wharf.

"I'm wondering if you accidently misplaced a friend of mine," Wolfe called. "A negro named Sam. A teamster. And these other people . . ." Wolfe waved behind him. ". . . are wondering if you've misplaced some of their friends." The officer laughed, precisely the thing to enrage Americans on the pier.

"We've misplaced no one, your lordship," the Officer called derisively. "And throwing accusations around is as like to get you called out as anything else." Wolfe cocked his head.

"Do you really suppose to frighten me? Come, man. I have a mate missing.

If you've no stowaways, I'll trouble you no more and move on to the next ship." The officer turned to his colleague and gave an order. When he turned his attention back to Wolfe, his crew ceased pretending to work.

"By what authority do you presume to search this ship?" the Officer said.

"I presume nothing," said Wolfe. "I seek a friend who is missing. Here's a proposition. I'll buy you and your men a firkin of rum if the ship is clean. You can't say fairer than that." The rumble of people behind Wolfe agreed. The Officer laughed.

"My orders are that no one comes aboard without the captain says so, and I can't say fairer than that."

"Will he be here soon?" Wolfe said.

"Any minute, I expect."

Everyone stood by quietly and waited for the captain to appear, which he did, blustering at his officer in a loud whisper before turning his red-faced annoyance on Wolfe. In a voice meant to intimidate, he bawled, "Are you the blackguard thinks to board my ship?" Wolfe grinned up at him, the little wheel deck of the *Maiden* being the height of his head above the wharf.

"I'm looking for my friend," Wolfe said amiably. "Some of the people with me are looking for their friends. We want to be certain they're not aboard your ship." The Captain scowled.

"You step foot on this ship without my leave, I'll shoot you dead as I have every right! I do my duty to custom and Parliament, but by God I'll not answer to some snot-assed negro lover. I'll have your poxed ass thrown in jail!" There was a general hubbub as the Captain's words were received by the crowd. Wolfe waited for the noise to die down before speaking again.

"I wish to avoid bloodshed Captain, but I will know if my friend is aboard your ship. If he is, you best free him now. I give you fair warning." As he walked back to rejoin Cesar, a torrent of threats and curses from the Captain rained down on him.

"I must find a Judge or Justice of the Peace," Wolfe said to Cesar. The cordwainer assigned one of his friends to lead Wolfe to a two-story brick house in the better part of town. After waiting ten minutes, Wolfe was led around back by a liveried slave and ushered into a cluttered study.

Sitting at a desk behind a flickering oil lamp, Justice Jeffords Hamlin was a pasty, heavy-jowled provincial aristocrat. He'd donned a full-bottomed legal wig for the interview and was clearly annoyed.

Wolfe explained the situation and requested legal permission to search the ship. Hamlin sat back in his chair and regarded Wolfe incredulously. With a voice dripping condescension, he said, "On what grounds do you propose I issue a warrant? Your suspicion? Have you any evidence? Any at all? You're either a madman or a fool. Where is the sheriff?"

"From my understanding, the sheriff is bought off. Or so says everyone I've spoken to. As to evidence, I have the knowledge of everyone in town that men disappear when the traders sail. I also have the certainty that my friend Sam has met with foul play. He's driving a freighter of supplies to the suffering people of Boston and has disappeared in your town. That won't sit well with the Sons of Liberty. I'll see to it." Wolfe was betting that as a Crown official, Hamlin was anxious to avoid the ire of Liberty Men at all costs.

A dark look came over Hamlin's face but he reached into his desk and took out a sheet of paper. Dipping a fine goose quill into a silver inkwell, he said grudgingly, "This will deputize you in the name of the colony."

"Does that mean I can do whatever I must?" said Wolfe.

"Do whatever you want," Hamlin said flippantly. "But you are accountable. That I'll see to. What's your name?" Hamlin wrote Wolfe's name on the authorization. "Rest assured that if someone is hurt, 'twill go hard with you. Even if you're right you'll make no friends this day. The traders fund both camps."

"Just not this time," Wolfe said. He took the warrant and departed.

At Bourke's wharf, the situation had taken on a life of its own. Thirty or forty people were milling around, most of them armed. Five or six men had scarves hiding their faces. Wolfe hoped that the captain and crew of *Bristol Maiden* realized that when men didn't want to be recognized, they were most likely bent on mayhem.

The trader's full crew looked to be perhaps thirty men. Occasionally a few disappeared below together and return on deck separately. Wolfe surmised they were arming below. They hadn't yet rigged out swivel guns or boarding nets however, which made superior numbers the better hand, or so he calculated.

The Hartford Watch arrived, led by a square-headed, no-nonsense Dutchman named Thomas Haeckel. Wolfe explained the situation and showed him the warrant. Haeckel hushed the crowd and indicated that Wolfe should address them.

Waving the document over his head, Wolfe pronounced loudly, "This warrant deputizes me to search this vessel for illegal contraband, namely your neighbors and my friend."

The Captain of the *Maiden* roared belligerently, "I don't give a piss what that paper says. First man tries to board me is a dead man!" Wolfe ignored the Captain and addressed his crew.

"If you do not produce the men we seek, you will be boarded. If you resist you may pay with your lives. Being that I'm legally deputized, if you hurt any of us you will surely pay with your lives. You have half a glass to decide. I suggest you choose wisely." Wolfe hoped he was choosing wisely. Sam might not even be aboard the ship. *That would be embarrassing*, he thought, but it never occurred to him not to act.

At his suggestion, Haeckel dispatched one of his men with a group of volunteers. After they departed, Wolfe laid out a plan that Haeckel and Cesar were happy to adopt—the responsibility not being theirs.

Wolfe organized two parties to board the ship simultaneously, forward and aft. One party would be the Watch, led by Haeckel. The other party was made up of friends and colleagues of the disappeared men. "It must be an overwhelming dash," Wolfe impressed upon them. "The swifter we are, the fewer get hurt." He hoped. They outnumbered the sailors. It was possible.

A growing rumble announced the return of Haeckel's man and the volunteers. People scurried out of the way as four hogsheads of tobacco rolled down the wharf. Wolfe showed the men where to place the massive barrels to create bastions at two different locations barely ten yards from the ship. He stationed men with muskets behind the barrels.

"My gun is the signal," Wolfe said. "When I fire, you must fire also. We need keep their heads down so we can board before they shoot back." He was betting his life that the crew of the *Maiden* wasn't willing to die to enslave other men. A quick easy profit was one thing.

The word went around to take cover. The wharf, which had been a torrent of voices and anticipation, went silent. The sound of the *Maiden* creaking at moorings was distinct.

Wolfe walked out in front of the hogsheads near the stern of the ship. Holding the warrant up to the wheel deck, he said, "As a legally deputized representative of this colony, I am coming aboard to search your ship." He tucked the warrant into his coat next to the pardon for his father, and unslung the donderbus. He aimed the business end at the Captain. The command to resist would come from there.

The Captain darted looks at his crew, indecision etched on his face.

As Wolfe stepped on the gangplank—which for some reason had been left in place—a clatter erupted on the wharf behind him. Unwilling to take his eyes off the ship, Wolfe stood still and fought the urge to turn around.

The clatter resolved into a coach and four clomping to a fast stop. The door opening. An angry voice called, "What the devil have you done, Jonns?!" Captain Jonns of the *Bristol Maiden* went slack jawed and the tension of the last minutes exploded.

"What have I done?! What have I . . . I refuse to let your ship be boarded by puffed-up negro lovers is what I done! Do something, Livesen!"

"You command the ship," Livesen said.

"I'm set upon by a mob!" Jonns roared at him. Wolfe turned around.

Livesen would have looked right at home in London as the handsomely petite and successful gentleman that he was, with the coach and luxurious wardrobe to prove it. The cocked hat perched atop his white wig was trimmed in fine gold lace.

"I'm told you may have one of my slaves aboard," Livesen called to Captain Jonns—who was getting angrier by the second.

"Don't play me for a swab, Livesen! Call out the Watch, damn your eyes!"

"The Watch is here!" Livesen snapped. "And not for your protection!"

Wolfe stepped off the gangway and backed away from the ship. There was no doubt in his mind that Livesen was throwing Jonns to the dogs to protect himself. Wolfe retired behind a hogshead to see how things played out.

Standing alone on the wharf by the ship, Livesen berated Jonns. "That slave is my property, you greedy fool! Turn him out at once and any others or so help me you'll be on the beach ere sunset!" Captain Jonns was stunned speechless until Livesen bawled at him, "At once you lubber!" Livesen turned to the crowd.

"Neighbors! I had no knowledge of what this man was doing. You may be sure steps will be taken! Steps will be taken!" He went on but the appearance of five men, including Sam, stumbling up from the fore hatch of the Maiden, drew everyone's attention.

Livesen's slave was an adolescent boy. Gingerly stepping down the gangway, he nervously stopped in front of his master. "That'll teach you to go whoring," Livesen said to the boy. "Get ye home!" The slave ran off, grateful to have avoided the probable death sentence of being sold in the sugar islands.

"Where's the fellow started this?" Livesen bawled. Wolfe was pointed out. "You there!" Livesen strode up to Wolfe. "T'was you done this?" Wolfe braced for a confrontation but Livesen surprised him.

"Well done. You saved me a hundred pounds." Wolfe shook hands with the well-dressed man before telling him that his friend, Sam, had a stick when he was taken up—his drover's stick—and they still had a long way to go before delivering supplies to the suffering people of Boston.

As with Justice Hamlin, Wolfe's none too subtle point paid off. Livesen roared at Captain Jonns to return the drover's stick or he'd turn him and his crew over to the Sons of Liberty to find it.

The stick appeared.

Sam received it back without comment or visible emotion. He was hungover, his lip was split, and an egg-sized contusion bulging behind his right ear was green and purple with a clotted blood crater in the middle.

A melee erupted as one of the previously incarcerated men attacked one of the Maiden's crew. Livesen's composure crumbled. He rushed aboard the ship bellowing like a fishwife.

Wolfe and Sam slipped away in the turmoil.

Sam was morosely silent as they walked back to Renseleer's. Wolfe felt good about his morning's work. Alone with his thoughts, he recalled a similar incident he'd been involved with some years earlier on the Spanish side of the Pyrenees. He and two gentlemen resolved to rescue a young noblewoman abducted by banditti. Wolfe's party affected the woman's release in an intimately brutal affray costing three lives, including one of Wolfe's companions. Sadly, not long after delivering the girl to her family, she took her own life.

It mattered to Wolfe that Sam's rescue ended well.

33

Madam welcomed them back with hugs, but her barely suppressed tears drove Sam to refuse all attention and take himself off to check on the cattle. As he walked away, Madam sniffed, "In twenty years I've never seen him so ill used." Wiping her eyes, she commanded, "Come and tell me the tale."

Beneath the Dutch oven heater inside the freighter, Madam's apartment consisted of heavy furs draped over a tick mattress with a proper quilt and pillows. After producing a bottle and two cups, she sat cross-legged on her bed and bade Wolfe tell her what happened—as she unbraided her golden hair and brushed it languidly.

When Wolfe got to Livesen's arrival at the wharf, she said, "Jan Livesen?"

"I never heard his Christian name," Wolfe admitted.

"A small man," Madam said. "Handsome in his way."

"That were him," Wolfe said. "You are acquainted?" Madam wrinkled her nose.

"He is my husband's cousin."

"Then I know not if you'll think this good news or bad," said Wolfe, "but he had a riot on his hands when we left." The news brought a happy smile to Madam's face. A second later she sighed.

"Poor Sam." Putting the thought aside along with her brush, she leaned across the mattress. "You have earned a reward, Mister Wolfe. Bravery must always be rewarded. Have you ever been poxed?" Upon Wolfe's indignant denial of such, she laughed wickedly and started unbuttoning his breeks. "My brave boy shall have his reward," she panted. "He saved my Sam and the brave boy shall have his reward."

Other than the apparent need to think of her behavior as an honor-bound duty, Madam was a wonder. She smelled of leather and beaver musk but was clean in the way of the Dutch. Passionate, lush and strong, she was a bawdyhouse duchess who dearly took pleasure in the slap and tickle. They used each other well.

Many hours later, Wolfe woke in the dark to rain splattering the canopy of the freighter. Madam slept next to him snoring lightly. When next he woke, it was to the thrum of steady rain and the smell of breakfast.

Madam reported that Sam was sulking. "He'll starve himself a week in penance, just you watch." She was cooking bacon and onions under an awning rigged off the back of the wagon. There was also fresh gingerbread from the Renseleers, pepernoten as delicious as Wolfe remembered from the low countries in Europe.

They ate in the back of the freighter watching rain puddle on the parade ground. Madam had no intent of getting back on the road until the severity of the storm could be gauged.

"'Tis wondrous how lucky we've been," she said. "This is my third trip and the roads have never been so good nor the weather so kind. I fear for when it turns."

Wolfe wanted to start barking his stick but he couldn't find it. Madam suggested his attention would be better spent elsewhere and convinced him of it.

A Renseleer servant calling from outside interrupted them late in the day. Miserably huddled against the rain, he had a note to deliver. Madam—currently dressed in very little—stuck her arm out under the canopy and waved it around until the note was thrust in her hand. Scanning the sodden paper, she said, "We are invited to sup with the Renseleers. If you'd rather not, I'll beg off. Personally, I should like to get out."

At early candlelight they trudged through cold rain to the Renseleer house. Wolfe was gratified with a supper of different slaws, cheeses and fresh breads, but he was particularly thrilled with the pea soup. On the quiet, Madam told him that putting Indian corn in pea soup was a profanity. Wolfe didn't tell her that he thought the Indian corn a stroke of genius.

After dinner, with the ladies' permission, the men smoked pipes and Pieter asked Wolfe about the incident at the wharf. Wolfe related what happened, to Pieter's obvious enjoyment, and that made Madam proud. *Like a queen basking in the acclaim of her warrior*, Wolfe thought dryly.

It was sleeting out when they slogged back to the freighter. In their absence, the big wagon had been moved from the parade ground to the lee of a barn. "More private," Madam said.

In the morning, risen and dressed, she shook Wolfe awake. Her hair was loose and she looked more girl than widow. "Come outside and see!" she said excitedly. Wolfe groaned but made no effort to comply. "Come!" she insisted.

"Stay!" Wolfe grabbed her and tried to drag her back under the covers but she fought free and jumped out of reach.

"Get up!" she said. Her breath was thickly visible and Wolfe didn't move. With a sigh she turned to go, then turned back and ripped the covers off him. With little choice, he got up and put his breeks on—cold to the point of stiffness.

But he forgave her.

The world outside had been transformed. Frozen where it fell the night before, sleet shrouded the plantation in ice like the village of a Nordic god at the top of the world. The surrounding forest was crystalline trees rendered fantastical by bright sunshine in a cloudless, infinitely blue sky.

But sober reality could not be denied. The freighter wasn't going anywhere. Madam would never willingly expose the cattle to a slip that might break a leg, or even to the dangers of sharp ice. Bovine hooves were more tender than equine hooves and far more work to re-shoe, there being two shoes on each foot and cattle being unable to stand on three legs, and often requiring time to heal.

But the world looked too magical to worry about such things.

Madam and Wolfe joined dozens of others sliding around the parade ground, which was a sheet of ice rippled like water. They hooted, hollered, giggled and fell, although Madam was quite graceful. "We Dutch are great ones for the ice skates," she reminded Wolfe. Later they heated toddies in the freighter and kept each other warm.

The next morning dawned gray and significantly colder, so that the plantation took on a foreboding aspect, like the village of a Nordic god abandoned at the top of the world. Madam didn't hesitate when the Renseleers sent an invitation to stay in the house until weather-break, even though it meant an end to her dalliance with Wolfe.

The following day she announced that she was preparing dinner for her men. Wolfe's contribution was to make sure that Sam attended. They hadn't seen him for the better part of three days. Wolfe was glad for the commission. It bothered him that Sam might be angry he'd tumbled his boss, despite Madam's assurances that it was merely men's madness. "What you call pride," she said.

Sam was keeping an eye on two slaves mucking out the cattle barn when Wolfe entered. "Look what the cat drug in," Sam said.

"She's preparing a ham in your honor," Wolfe told him. "It would be cruel not to oblige her. She was scared when you didn't turn up." Sam's big head drooped.

"Think I don't know? I'm begad, Joethan. I nearly spoilt everything." His emotion was palpable. The oxen looked on sadly.

"You ruined nothing," said Wolfe. "Perhaps you should just be grateful you're not on your way to the Indies." Sam looked at him queerly.

"I am grateful. What you be talkin' 'bout?"

"Your absence. Are you angry because of her and me?" Sam found that idea preposterous and snorted.

"Don't got a mind to hear you two rut if that's what you're askin'. 'Sides, it's nice and warm in here. They keep a fire all night. Think you're the first to be rewarded?" When Wolfe didn't answer, Sam laughed. Then he was downcast again. "I done worse than let her down, Joethan. I let God down. I dallied with jezebel and I was punished."

Wolfe's jaw dropped. "You disappointed God? Who in bloody hell doesn't disappoint God? Flogging yourself because you're not perfect is topping it the nod, wouldn't you say?"

They watched the cattle in silence.

After a while, Sam said, "Ham?"

"And speculaas. Whatever that is."

"Spice cake," Sam said. "Speculaas is spice cake."

"You'll not want to miss that. I hear it's your favorite. Come dine with your friends. She'll name me failure if you don't and you might spare me that at least."

"I must shift clothes," said Sam. "She don't care for the smell of cattle at table."

"Women ..." Wolfe said.

Madam served her meal in the freighter, made warm and cozy by a second pot of embers. With the back ramp pulled up, a board with two legs could be slotted-in to make a table that she covered with navy-blue damask. Bed furs draped carefully over stacked supplies made for seating. The effect was pleasing and intimate.

Sam showed up in fresh clothes, and with a thank-you gift for his rescuer. "Barked, burned, oiled, and boned," he said, handing Wolfe's tree branch to him. But it was a branch no longer. Sam had turned it into a quarterstaff. "T'were a better stick than first I thought," he said.

Wolfe ran his hands over the polished hickory and examined every smoothed knot and nub while Sam described stripping the bark down to the reddish-brown heartwood, heating the stripped limb over a fire to draw out the surface sap, oiling it and heating it again, oiling it one more time so it wouldn't be brittle, and then rubbing the wood on a cow bone for a whole day to harden and shine.

"This is as fine a gift as ever I've received," Wolfe said. "Thank you, Sam."

Although they had not been long together, nor shared any great hardship, there was a camaraderie inside the freighter that Wolfe was happy to share, along with ham expertly cooked in brown sugar and wine, and potatoes. And pea soup that—Wolfe told Wilhemina—was better than Madam Renseleer's.

Although it really wasn't.

But the specula was as tasty as advertised.

34

Following the dinner, three days of unrelenting cold kept the freighter parked at Renseleer's. As the boredom grew, Wolfe's quarterstaff lessons in the barn with Sam went longer and harder and his skill with a stick improved accordingly. Now when he and Sam exchanged blows, the music of oak striking hickory was lively and melodic.

Wolfe thought of the delay as being becalmed, a nautical phenomenon but it suited. For all of his traveling, he'd never plodded point to point with a wagon train or caravan. He'd shared the road with many such outfits briefly but his world was ships, horses and coaches. Speed was paramount in his line. Escorting the freighter was altogether different and not unpleasant, but he couldn't surrender the inclination to make haste.

And he could not abide walking day after day in riding boots.

Pieter Renseleer proved to be the perfect host for an extended stay. Wolfe mentioned in passing that he'd have himself a good wash when the river thawed. Renseleer immediately arranged for him to have a hot bath at once. Madam was angry that slaves were put out to accommodate Wolfe's whim, and he wasn't happy about it either, but he refused to insult Pieter. He accepted Madam's scorn and bathed.

A similar thing happened when Pieter marveled that Wolfe was walking to Boston in riding boots. When Wolfe admitted that walking long distance had not been his intent when he left London, Pieter brought him to his cordwainer. Under the boss's watchful eye, the shoemaker fit Wolfe for a pair of buskins and oilskin leggings.

Renseleer devoted an entire day to showing Wolfe proudly around his plantation, an impressive modern facility even though the cold had brought all work to a stop. The sluices that drove the waterwheels were frozen solid. "I could have the men break up the ice and get the water moving," Pieter said, "but it might be the weather has caught us up. Usually we stop coaling in October. Winter is for harvesting trees."

Even at rest the plantation felt like a military manufactory, especially the foundry. Wolfe asked Pieter if he forged arms. Pieter told him it was more dire to make lead and iron as there wasn't enough of either in the colonies.

"Did you build all this anticipating rebellion?" Wolfe asked him. Pieter rubbed his eyebrows wilder and thought of how to answer the question.

"Rebellion is a strong word," he said at last. "Redress of grievances is what I would say. After all, I served in a red coat myself for five years." As older men will, when younger men listen, he told Wolfe of his career in the army during the French and Indian War, how his occupation as a smith landed him in the Pioneers, the advance corps of the British army—clearing the way through forest, city or fortress as required.

In the Pioneers, Pieter learned firsthand of the materiel required to wage war, from shovels and cook pots, to axes and swords. He left the army with a plan to supply those requirements, especially musket bullets, easiest to produce and most in demand. "And here am I twenty years later," he said. "If it come to it I'll make bayonet, sword and cannon, but for now it need be iron and lead."

"With all your success, I'm surprised you're not a King's man." Wolfe said.

"Government don't respect us here in America," Renseleer said. "They don't respect anyone if we're honest, but they will never respect Americans lest we make them. They conceive to govern these colonies from across the ocean with no say from we who actually live here. They could not show us more contempt did they spit on us."

Pieter's views struck Wolfe as the most cogent reason for insurrection that he'd heard, for he could not dispute it. In his experience, all Englishmen viewed Americans as lesser creatures and the British aristocracy's disdain for

Americans was the worst. By their lights, disturbances in far-flung colonies were to be expected and dealt with, quickly and decisively. The better sort of Britons had no more tolerance for rebellious Americans than they did for rebellious slaves in the Indies. The only thing that elevated the American colonies over any other was Benjamin Franklin, and he was in disgrace.

Israel Grange considered the occupants of the freighter heathens. He was a New Light and despite the evangelical movement's dip in popularity, he was a strict adherent to doctrine, as he made known to any who would listen. Renseleer provided him a bed in one of the barracks to ride out the cold. Grange spent most of his time there reading the Bible, and singing for the men if they but asked. On the fifth day of the freeze however, he stopped singing. On the fifth day, tree limbs succumbing to the weight and internal expansion of freezing water started cracking like musket shots all over the forest.

For Wolfe, the brightest moment during the ice doldrums was when he claimed his new buskins from the cordwainer. The short leather boots gave him back the freedom to move his ankles when he walked, a true miracle, not the kind Grange was wont to sing about.

With his new footwear and leggings, he joined Sam on a scout up the road north where there were trees down all over. The only vehicles they saw were horse-drawn sledges belonging to parties of slaves working to clear the road.

The Sabbath came and went under slate gray skies and despite Madam's fervent attendance at the Dutch church, the ice didn't melt, it only got dirtier. Fireplaces all over the plantation were belching smoke and ash around the clock. When the sun finally returned on the eighth day of the freeze, the temperature climbed and the ice runoff pooled black. Two warm days afterward combined ash and mud into a horrific sludge that made everything in the world filthy. It wasn't until the next day that it finally dawned cold enough for the ground to harden.

That morning, with the oxen clad in leather booties to protect their hooves, the freighter set off northeast to regain the Post Road

West of the Connecticut River on a ridgeline above ascending levels of alluvial plain, the freighter fetched Windsor at noon. Crossing the River

Tunxis on a bridge, they arrived before dusk at Enfield, a village of numerous mills built out along tributaries of the Connecticut River.

The most prominent feature of Enfield was a new meeting house near Kibbe's Tavern, their destination. No one noticed that Grange hadn't arrived at Kibbe's until a hundred pounds of potatoes and fifty of tobacco had been added to the freighter's load. It was then Wolfe took it upon himself to walk back and discover what became of the Puritan.

Grange's wagon was parked at a different meeting house, a much older and smaller building with peeling paint and sagging lintels. As Wolfe stood outside, Grange came out shining with the inner light that psalmody seemed to confer upon him.

"Something you require of me?" he said.

"Just making sure you weren't in trouble," Wolfe said, to which Grange laughed in a booming voice. Having never heard him laugh before, Wolfe grinned at the dour man's good humor. For once, Grange responded with an easy fellowship.

"There can be no trouble in this blessed house," he said, patting the wall of the building. "This is where Reverend Jonathan Edwards preached his sermon, *Sinners in the Hands of an Angry God* for the first time. Think of it! Thirty years ago, on this very spot, Reverend Edwards said that the key to salvation lies in our own hands. Not with the Church of England, nor even the King himself. For there is no other king but Jesus."

Wolfe knew the sermon Grange spoke of, a fire-and-brimstone fear-raiser that said acting ethically and in good faith with the Bible was not enough to keep one from being punished after death; by a rather vindictive and bad-tempered God, in Wolfe's opinion.

He had little use for Calvinist theology. In London he'd met Reverend Edwards's more famous and influential colleague, George Whitefield. Whitefield was an intelligent and supposedly moral man, first among evangelists for many years, but he was also an advocate of slavery, a morally incomprehensible theology in Wolfe's estimation. Wolfe spent hours arguing with The Doctor that as long as Whitefield advocated slavery, he could never be a man of God.

To Wolfe's great discomfort, Grange burst loudly into psalmody as they walked back to Kibbe's. His singing drew attention from everyone in earshot including people inside their houses. They opened their doors to see who was disturbing the twilight and even more surprising to Wolfe, most of them smiled and waved. Grange smiled and waved back with a lightheartedness Wolfe wouldn't have believed possible.

The Puritan's bonhomie lasted all the way to Kibbe's, and then he and Wolfe parted as if the previous minutes had never occurred.

35

Dawn found the wagons trundling north on a road bound by tobacco farms on both sides. Tobacco fields gave way to orchard at Stony River, and then to woods as they approached Suffield, the last town in Connecticut Colony.

And the weather remained clear, dry, and unseasonably warm.

Sitting atop bold bluffs overlooking the Connecticut River, Suffield made little impression other than the view it provided. With no easy access down to the water, Suffield was more way station than destination and the freighter rumbled right through. Later, when Sam pointed out the Feeding Hills to the west, Madam announced that they were in the Massachusetts Colony.

In the afternoon they turned off the road at the sign of a crudely painted boat nailed to a tree. The rutted path through the woods wasn't really wide enough for the freighter and Wolfe and Sam had to use their staffs to fend off branches tearing at the canopy.

All progress stopped at the top of a bluff leading down to the river. At the bottom of the bluff, the path to the ferry landing was surrounded by wetlands churned into a quagmire by previous vehicles. Inspection confirmed that the muck was too deep for the freighter to traverse with the weight they had on. There was also no possibility that they could turn the massive vehicle around.

As Wolfe unhappily contemplated unloading the freighter, Sam and Madam discussed their options. "We'd have to cut cross there and turn hard," Sam said, pointing to where the mud was thinner along the edge of the morass. The maneuver he suggested wouldn't be easy. The huge wagon would have to come down the bluff, turn hard left at the bottom, with speed enough to carry some mud, then turn sharp right to stay out of the tall wetlands, which were probably less passable than the mud.

Wolfe thought the plan ill advised, imagining the only thing worse than unloading the freighter would be unloading the freighter standing in muck up to his knees.

Sam walked back up the slope and took the booties off the cattle. After talking to them quietly, he stepped out of the way and gave a sharp, "Hup, cattle, hup!" The oxen responded by lurching off at their usual plod. A well-placed shot from Sam's staff, to the flank of the wheeler, got the team thundering down the bluff. Sprinting to catch up, Sam jumped on to the side of the freighter and hung on, just as the lead yoke of oxen mashed into the outer fringe of mud at the bottom of the slope.

"Haw! Haw!" Sam bellowed. The oxen turned left even as the front wheels of the freighter hit mud and started throwing off clots and pinwheels of thick brown glop.

"They're too fast!" Madam yelled. The lead yoke of oxen were already nearly in the reeds and sedges.

"Gee! Gee!" Sam bellowed for the beasts to turn right. The oxen responded with an agility Wolfe didn't know cattle possessed. Leaning hard into their yokes, the oxen's massive bodies heaved way out over legs scrambling to keep purchase in the mud.

The freighter careened into a tight right turn that lifted the two inside wheels high off the ground. For a few interminable seconds the mammoth vehicle teetered on the edge of gravity, before slamming back down with a heavy crash.

Madam and Wolfe whooped and clapped in appreciation. Sam looked back at them wide-eyed, a big smile splitting his mud-spattered face.

To Wolfe's surprise and respect, the freighter remained solidly intact after the episode.

Despite repeated warnings, Grange permitted his wagon to get deep enough into the morass to get stuck. An hour was wasted unhitching a yoke of oxen from Sam's team to help pull Grange's wagon out.

This side of the river, the ferry dock consisted of planks dug flush into the riverbank. The only other improvement was a piling with a massive block and tackle to handle a man-of-war–sized heavy hawser. The hawser terminated at a large capstan on the other side of the river at a landing serviced by a tavern.

The turbid river was running but not dauntingly so. Gesturing to a horn chained to the piling, Wolfe asked Sam what he was waiting for, but Sam just shook his head. And then he stopped Wolfe from blowing the horn. Wolfe was trying to understand why, when Madam stepped up and seized the instrument. After a couple of experimental toots, she planted her feet and let loose a blare that made her beam with satisfaction.

Sam looked over at Wolfe with a bemused smile.

Mevrouw van Roos loved to blow that horn.

The ferry started out from the other shore propelled by a sun-burned, barrel chested man using the hawser to pull himself across the river. When he was in earshot, he hailed, "Din't 'spect to see you 'til spring!"

"I'll be planting in spring," Madam called back.

The ferryboat was a flat-bottomed scow with low gunwales and extended decks that served as loading ramps. Not long enough to take the freighter and cattle in one trip, it departed with Sam and the cattle first.

As Wolfe and Madam waited for the ferry to return, she said, "I don't think you should ask after your father here." Wolfe said he hadn't intended to. Anyone who spent time on the road knew that crossroad inns and ferry houses were riddled with thieves and flimflam men.

"This goes beyond the usual rascals," Madam said. "Theotis, who runs the ferry, is a Liberty Man. What they call 'Whigs' in this part of the country. The family he leases the business from, the Worthingtons, have held the royal grant for more than a hundred years. I should be surprised did they favor insurrection."

"Whose men run the place?" Wolfe said. Madam looked at him shrewdly.

"I haven't an answer which is why we'll keep to ourselves."

When the ferry returned they rolled the freighter aboard. After chocking the wheels, the ferryman blew the horn. A man on the other side of the river spurred two oxen, and they turned the capstan. The heavy hawser tightened, the big block on the piling squealed ferociously, and the scow nosed away from the landing.

Beyond the protection of the riverbank, the current caught the flat-bottomed craft and lurched it downstream until the rope leads from the ferry to the capstan hawser were taut. As the boat slapped slowly and steadily across the current, Wolfe prepared to swim for it.

"He wouldn't take us across if t'was dangerous," Madam chided Wolfe. He looked at her in astonishment.

"The graveyards are full of people who didn't think t'was dangerous. One good swell and this pig boat goes under."

"Hush," Madam giggled, slapping his arm. "He'll hear you."

After rolling the freighter off on the other side, Wolfe went to grab a hot meal while Madam and Sam set up camp.

At dusk the taproom in the ferry house was busy and loud, the noise spilling raucously into the public room where Wolfe ate. Eventually one voice overwhelmed the others. In snatches, Wolfe heard the tale of two Tories who'd recently been tarred and feathered in Worcester. Evidently tar-scalded men who screamed as they were bounced on a rail—splitting them between anus and testicles—was hilarious. It must have been. Everyone in the tap room laughed uproariously.

Wolfe kept his mouth shut, ate and left. Releasing Sam and Madam to go eat, he took up his watch and built up the fire they'd started. When it was burning well, he walked beyond the firelight to restore his night vision and have a look around. It was a beautiful evening. The stars were already out in a pristine sky.

The freighter was parked on a small rise away from the ferry house. Grange's wagon lay thirty yards away downhill. Surreptitious movement from there drew Wolfe's attention. He knew at once that it wasn't the Puritan. Dropping into a crouch, he worked his way downhill.

Initially he thought an animal might be scrabbling to get under Grange's tarp, but the intruder resolved into a smallish man in a long dark coat. A man thoroughly engrossed in his business, which turned out to be starting a fire. Flint sparks were shooting into the bed of the wagon.

Wolfe strode forward, the intruder sensed him, spun around and unhesitatingly lunged with a large knife. Without thinking, Wolfe brought the front end of his staff down on the arm holding the knife, then he blasted the man across the neck with the other end of the staff. The man flew sideways and hit the ground hard, but then, in one motion, he rolled, bounced up and sprinted for the woods.

Caught flatfooted by the speed of the man's recovery, it was seconds before Wolfe gave chase. And then he stopped chasing. If there were accomplices they'd welcome his absence. The intruder disappeared into the woods long before Wolfe resumed breathing normally.

According to Grange's wagon, the intruder was an arsonist. He'd been trying to ignite a turpentine-drenched rag, one end of which disappeared into a firkin with a pried-loose stave.

Grange's entire load was made up of eight-gallon kegs identical in appearance. Salted meat or rum, Wolfe would have thought in a different circumstance. They were of that ilk and some were even marked as such, but Wolfe was the son of a smuggler. Upon examination, as he surmised, the kegs were filled with gunpowder.

He took the doused rag and moved back up the rise to the freighter where he could keep an eye on both wagons at once. When Sam returned and learned what happened, he went to talk to men he knew at the barn. Madam loaded her musketoon.

Wolfe intercepted Grange on his way back from the ferry house. The Puritan's face grew dark, even dangerous, when Wolfe told him what happened. Grange swore God's vengeance on anyone trying to interfere with his wagon but never once did he thank the man who protected it.

As Grange walked away, Wolfe thought, *that arrogant bastard fancies himself a paragon of Christian virtue, but he's just as unlikeable as the worst Anglican lord.*

Sam returned with a name. "Joseph Le Poisse. A Indian who quit Reverend Wheelock's school. They knowed him right off by the bear coat. They say he works for one of the River Gods."

"River Gods?" said Wolfe. Madam smiled thinly.

211

"It's what they call some of the big plantation families in these parts."

"These are Tory River Gods?" Wolfe said. Madam nodded. Wolfe cocked his head and asked, "Are we to avoid the domains of these Tory Gods?"

"We should but we won't," Sam grunted.

"We cannot," Madam said. "But they shan't trouble us."

"Shan't trouble us?" Wolfe said in disbelief. "They just tried to explode Grange's wagon. How did that Indian know about the powder? I didn't know. Did you know?" Madam and Sam said they didn't know. Wolfe laughed acerbically. "Well … as long as there's nothing to worry about."

He and Madam did not resume their trysts that night. Perhaps it was Madam's dislike of the beard he was growing to disguise himself when he got to Boston—or perhaps she feared for the freighter's reputation in sternly conservative Massachusetts—or perhaps it was that Wolfe made no effort to couple out of respect for Sam. Whatever the reason, by unspoken agreement they returned to the way things were ante-Renseleer. Madam's pressing concern was security. Miles of empty country lay ahead.

36

In a drear predawn, they struck out away from the river on a worn country track. Hours later they gained the great wagon road to Boston on the Springfield Plain, a vast stretch of scrub pine and sand that was all but uninhabited.

Eight miles on they were plodding out of the river valley up a long, steep grade that punished the cattle. Wolfe estimated that the freighter had on three tons by now. Watching the beasts labor, he wondered how they could manage the five or six tons the big wagon could allegedly haul. To Sam he said, "I suppose we'd need a larger team to pull five tons?" Sam's dark eyes narrowed.

"Yeah. A bigger team. That's right."

When they fetched the Chicopee River and a string of houses known as North Wilbraham, the freighter had covered less than average miles but the cattle were more tired than Wolfe had ever seen them. Thankfully his new footwear spared him the same fate.

The next morning, being a Sabbath day, they left Bliss's Tavern before sunup. Madam wanted to clear the town without notice, to avoid the complications that notice would bring. Ordinarily she tried to respect Congregational travel restrictions, but after the attack on Grange's wagon, she was determined to keep moving.

Little clouds of respiration billowed overhead as the cattle leaned into their yokes and stepped off. Hoar frost crunched underfoot. The destination was a glow of predawn sun etching a pale notch in the ridge ahead. And for the first time since New Haven, the Puritan wasn't in company. Grange was loath to travel on the Sabbath but if he did, it certainly wouldn't be until after he attended meeting.

The descent into the next valley was rutted and steep, causing the cold-shrunk timbers of the freighter to jolt and rattle the length of her keel. On particularly steep sections, Sam and Wolfe chain-braked the back wheels, or tied ropes to the wheels and used trees as capstans to control the downhill speed. It was faster that way but going down a steep hill was always laborious.

The town of Palmer sat near the confluence of three streams forming the Chicopee River. With Palmer in view, Wolfe was walking alongside Madam and heard her sigh loudly.

"You are troubled?" Wolfe said. Madam looked off as if the answer lay somewhere on the horizon.

"If you would know, I don't like Massachusetts. I find the men insufferable, especially when drunk, which is often. I particularly distrust the religious men who rule their little parishes as a king, and their parishioners who obey them as one. I dislike that unless I pray to their God, their way, no matter how many supplies I bring to Boston, I'll never be more than a heretic woman. In short, I dislike hypocrisy and in Massachusetts, hypocrisy is the coin of the realm." Wolfe nodded that he understood.

"But what are your true feelings?" It took a few moments for Madam to realize that he was teasing her. She chuckled sheepishly.

The stench of curing leather permeated everything as the freighter pulled into Walker's Tavern in Palmer. In keeping with Madam's stated intent, to avoid the locals as much as possible, and Sam not being white, Wolfe was designated to deal with the tavern keeper.

Walker was a slovenly man in a faded red waistcoat. Greasy brown hair hung clumped like string to his shoulders. From inside the cage around his bar, he greeted Wolfe with, "That the Dutch Widow's rig?" When Wolfe affirmed that it was, Walker sniggered. "That African yet with'er?"

"His name is Sam," Wolfe said. "And I'll thank you to remember he's my friend." Walker's eyes narrowed but he got the message. "If you know the Widow's rig," Wolfe said, "you know she freights to Boston. Have you heard of any trouble on the road to Worcester?" Walker smirked.

"Two Tories was tarred and feathered a few days ago. From what I hear 'twaren't no trouble at all."

"So 'tis possible, even probable, that the Tories in Worcester are up in arms?" Wolfe said.

"More prob'ly lying low," Walker said. He called over to a table of teamsters. "You heard of any alarms down Worcester way?" The teamsters glared at him.

"Those men tarred and feathered in Worcester wadn't Tories," a short fellow in boiled leather said. "You keep braggin' on what happened to 'em an' it might be you get the same." Walker waved his hand dismissively but he suddenly found work to do. The teamster addressed Wolfe.

"The Tories in Worcester is always up in arms, if only to protect theyselves."

"What about Redcoat deserters or highwaymen?" Wolfe said.

"An't heard of any this far west. Gangs are apt to be east o' Worcester where the woods are thick and the roads are busy."

"You've been most helpful," Wolfe said. "Thankee." The man raised his leather flagon in acknowledgment and resumed talking to his mates. Wolfe put a coin on the bar and instructed Walker to set the teamsters up. He asked if there was anything Walker wanted to send to Boston on the freighter.

"We don't need Dutch Yorkers movin' Massachusetts freight," the tavern keeper replied curtly.

The freighter rolled down into the Quaboag Valley and shadowed the Quaboag River east across the valley floor. Eight miles on they fetched the town of Western, stopping for the night at the first tavern they came to. Grange rolled in after dark.

Late that night, a drunk inside the tavern started railing loudly against Catholics. Eventually Madam stuck her head out of the freighter and asked Wolfe, "Will he go on all night, do you suppose?"

"Not if someone shoots him," Wolfe said, only half joking. "Tell me. Does your Netherlander religious tolerance include Catholics?" Madam was horrified.

"After what they did in France? No. Never. No Catholics."

At cold dawn, the freighter trundled east through winter meadows grazed by herds of sheep. At the western edge of Brookfield village, they pulled into a tavern yard crowded with horses and shays. During their brief stop, no less than eight men came outside to trade news and views, but really to gawk or glare in disapproval at the Dutch Widow—the woman dressed in man's clothes, doing a man's job. In Madam's presence they tittered and smirked like adolescent boys.

Wolfe thought some of them were slow in the head but he came to realize that they were merely awkward, small-minded and judgmental—like Grange, who was at home among them, who was one of them.

The road out of Brookfield wound over a series of bald hills offering a splendid view of neat white steeples poking above bare trees, and ponds reflecting the clouds in the sky. Having been in Europe for the entirety of his adult life, Wolfe was moved by the enormity of a landscape interrupted only sporadically by civilization.

Beyond the eastern boundary of Brookfield lay Spencer, a new and somewhat odd sort of place, sprung up in the midst of a wood. Most of the barns and stables were built on the other side of the road from the houses and businesses they belonged to, making the town seem bigger and more developed than it actually was.

At the bottom of a hill dividing Spencer into upper and lower villages, there was a tavern large enough to boast a dozen rooms on the upper floor, each with a window. A substantial barn and stable squatted alongside, to form a sheltered yard currently filled with vehicles, animals, and children.

A dozen young boys stampeded out of the yard when they spied the freighter. As they surrounded the big wagon and escorted it in, their excitement and curiosity were entertaining. By the time Wolfe and Sam were loading donated firewood, they'd become a nuisance.

In the background, a gaggle of little girls was mesmerized by Madam, who was quite aware of their pointing and whispering. As she passed by, she made sure to flounce very close to them. The girls shied back giggling, a couple even shrieking, to Madam's delight.

Inside the tavern in the public room, more than a score of women had taken over to gossip and trade news, along with commodities like wool and beeswax. The atmosphere was that of a midwinter fair. In actuality, Spencer was hosting militias from Leicester and Paxton for a training day. Squealing fifes and tattooing drums floated down from the upper village.

After parking the freighter in a field away from the hubbub of the hostelry, Sam led the cattle back to the barn and settled them for the night. Wolfe and Madam finished building a fire as Grange passed by with two firkins of gunpowder slung from a yoke across his shoulders. Curious to see American militia in action, Wolfe followed him up to the training ground.

Other than one imposing house, and one less-impressive domicile, Spencer's upper village consisted of a one-room schoolhouse and a simple meeting house next to the training ground. Wolfe joined a crowd of spectators around a bonfire by the meeting house.

The combined militias performed their drill bundled in wool coats, mechanic's jackets, hunting jackets, flop hats and wool stockings. Six men stood out as officers by virtue of a cocked hat, sash, or sword, but they all looked like farmers and tradesmen more than soldiers.

Grange's donation of powder was met with great approbation. Before the militias dismissed, they gave onlookers, and the newly esteemed Israel Grange, a show they rarely had powder to indulge. Upon command, three companies of militia simultaneously volley-fired their muskets. In this part of the world, seventy or eighty firelocks venting jets of flame into a brooding dusk sky was fine entertainment.

"Dreadfully stirring," Wolfe heard one young woman confide to a friend.

While unimpressed by the militia's maneuvers, Wolfe thought it significant that different militia companies had come together to drill in larger formations. Gage called them rabble but they were training just as the Redcoats in Boston were, and as Wolfe learned from one of the spectators, being trained by Americans with more experience in the last war with the French than most of his British counterparts.

After muster, the hostelry was taken over for dancing and imbibing. As Wolfe stood his watch over the freighter, he enjoyed a steady program of reels and jigs blaring from the tavern. It was a welcome break from the somber monotony of Grange's psalms.

Numerous people drifted in and out of the field where the freighter was camped—keeping company, relieving themselves, retching. It reminded Wolfe of countless country dances on the other side of the ocean, with one exception. It was entirely possible that some of the men dancing and drinking tonight would be struck down by an angry King before too long.

Yet Wolfe was moved by the scenes of community he witnessed. He felt the sentiment abroad in the country; women socializing happily as their children ran underfoot and their men prepared for war. War that would destroy their lives. War of their own making. For what? he wondered. Why would the country rise up? It was unsettling to him because he didn't understand it. He admitted as much to Sam.

"These people are middling sorts with homes and farms, better off than most in England," Wolfe said. "Why would they risk rebelling against the King? There aren't even any Redcoats out here to be cross with. I understand why a slave or indenture might rebel, but why these people?"

"Damned if I know," Sam said. "But there ain't no sucha thing as a little liberty. You either free or not, and folks know if they is o' they ain't."

Hours past sunset, the fellowship of the militiamen feting Grange hadn't waned, but the man himself did. He wove past the freighter on the way back to his wagon. It was parked in a field a furlong beyond the freighter, a distance insisted upon by Wolfe since the discovery of the gunpowder. Grange and Wolfe acknowledged each other but didn't speak.

It was a cold, clear night, and quite bright when the moon rose. The tavern emptied as people took advantage of the moonlight to travel home. When things were quiet again, Wolfe packed a pipe and moved into the lee of the freighter to light it. When he stepped back out into the open, seven mounted men with torches were streaming out of the woods on the far side of the field Grange was parked in, already closer to the Puritan than Wolfe was. The torch riders were so brazen that they didn't appear sinister, but Wolfe knew at once that they were and he didn't hesitate to sound alarm.

The roar of the donderbus shattered the quiet night and stopped the riders in their tracks. Wolfe ran for ammunition to reload, yelling "To arms! All hands topside! Beat to quarters! Madam! Sam! Grange!" He bellowed the last at Grange's wagon as loud as he could.

At first glimpse, Madam said, "They mean to burn him, sure."

Sam ran to alert the tavern and protect the cattle. By the time Wolfe finished reloading, three of the torch riders had altered course for the freighter.

Conspicuously armed with her musketoon and the horse pistol, Madam said, "They're fools if they think they can take us." She was scared but determined, her face not as pale as the moonlight would have it. Wolfe flashed her a confident smile.

"I believe their intent is to discourage us from aiding the Puritan." He was confident in his assessment because Madam was right. The riders would die if they tried to take on two well-armed people with a Pennsylvania freighter for protection.

Shielded by the big wagon, he and Madam watched the approaching riders slow to a walk and then abruptly extinguish their torches. Fifty yards out they set up a picket but gave no sign that they meant to attack.

In the far field it was a different story.

Wolfe heard the unmistakable bang of a musket followed by two pistol shots in quick succession, and then the riders converged on Grange's wagon. Moments later the wagon erupted in flames. A stream of sparks shot twenty feet high into the night sky and before the sparks died out, an indistinguishable rumble resolved into a monstrous explosion that sent an orange fireball roiling into the night sky.

The blast concussion rattled and swayed the freighter. Wolfe and Madam instinctively ducked as a flaming piece of wagon thumped down nearby in a shower of sparks. And then it was unnaturally still.

By the time the retinal imprint of the explosion faded, the horsemen were gone. Madam fretted that they were circling around to come for the freighter, but Wolfe didn't think so. "Supplies for innocents is one thing," he said. "Powder for insurrection another, and fair game I think it could be argued." Madam looked at him sharply.

"They murdered the Puritan."

"I believe t'was Grange shot first," Wolfe said. "They had no call to murder him. He wasn't singing." The morbid joke slipped out before he could censor himself but Madam didn't laugh.

A large crater with smoke lingering in the bottom, a few pieces of burning wood, and the overwhelming stench of exploded black powder was all that remained of Israel Grange's wagon. Of the man himself there was no sign. Daylight might reveal more, perhaps even enough to bury.

37

It may have been because Grange was a stranger but there was little fuss in the village over his demise. The loss of gunpowder was more keenly mourned. The attack was attributed to a River God yet to be identified. The locals promised that the culprits would be discovered and punished.

On the Boston Road the next day, with every available weapon primed and loaded, the freighter lumbered up a high ridge into Leicester, a simple collection of unadorned one-story houses and barns, every one of which boasted a lightning rod. The lightning rods made Wolfe think of The Doctor, and that made him grieve for his previous life.

He wondered if Pru received the letter he'd left with Captain Arnold in New Haven.

In Leicester there were no knobs on the doors. Wooden latches kept them closed, manipulated by a string threaded through a hole in the door. Wolfe imagined the quick work his less-reputable friends in London would make of such a situation.

The freighter stopped at a crude unpainted clapboard building that turned out to be the meeting house. With no belfry or porch even, it was distinguished only by stocks out front for miscreants, and two large blocks with steps, to assist ladies mounting and dismounting a horse.

Madam went inside and returned with a teenage boy. With him leading the way, they rumbled past the schoolhouse and training ground on a wagon road that disappeared into a wood. A quarter mile on they emerged from the wood on a rocky hill overlooking a large pond. After bouncing and banging their way down the hill on a well-worn field road, a dozen chickens scattered as they rolled into the barnyard of a farm at the end of the pond.

A man was waiting for them when they pulled in, a forty-year-old farmer by appearance, but Wolfe sensed that he was more than he presented.

"I'm Henshaw," the farmer announced. Madam took him aside in the usual way while Wolfe and Sam watered and fed the cattle. When they were finishing up, Madam tugged Wolfe's arm.

"Mister Henshaw bade us break our fast up at the house. Sam chooses to stay with the cattle."

The door to Henshaw's new house was opened by Mrs. Henshaw, a thick woman in a dingy cotton cap and faded blue Osnaburg dress. With an unlit pipe clenched in tobacco-stained teeth, she invited them to warm by the fire while she put together something to eat.

"I'd offer you a pipe," she said apologetically to Wolfe, "but I'm out of tobacco a week. My old man don't smoke so he don't care. I'm gettin' fidgety though, I can tell you that."

"I have tobacco," Wolfe said. "I'll get you some."

"It can wait 'til we've broken our fast," Madam said.

"I don't mind getting it now," said Wolfe.

Halfway down the hill between the house and barn, Wolfe was surprised to see Sam carrying a five-foot-long iron bar from the freighter into the barn, which made no sense, until Wolfe saw another four bars lying on the ground near the freighter. Alongside some of the wagon's floorboards.

The freighter had a false bottom.

Wolfe was stunned. His immediate thought was, no wonder the cattle have been laboring so hard. His next thought was that the iron bars must have been loaded the night of the ice storm at Renseleers.

Inside the barn, Henshaw was pointing Sam to stack the bar next to a six-pounder cannon. A bloody canon! Next to the gun were a dozen kegs of gunpowder marked with red X's. No doubt the iron was intended for cannonballs.

Sam froze when he saw Wolfe, wouldn't meet his eyes as he went outside for another bar. Wolfe kept his tongue too. Considering Sam's history with Madam, what was to be said?

But Wolfe was angry. He could accept that as a stranger he was untrusted. What he could not accept was that his life had been at risk without his knowledge. Just last night he'd said to Madam that the raiders wouldn't come for the freighter because they weren't transporting war supplies. And she'd let him babble on like a fool.

He was a bloody fool.

With his ire really starting to get up, Wolfe retrieved some tobacco and returned to the house. Mrs. Henshaw was exceedingly grateful but he barely heard her. His attention was fixed on Madam, who was immediately aware that her deception was discovered. She pretended everything was fine. Wolfe didn't know if Mrs. Henshaw was aware of the sudden chill in her parlor but he made no effort to hide it.

Madam and Wolfe departed the house quickly after a weak breakfast of suppon and day-old bread, but then breakfast had merely been an excuse to get Wolfe away from the barn. Like Sam, Madam wouldn't meet his gaze as they walked back. Staring straight ahead, she said, "I wish I could have told you but I was sworn to silence."

"If wishes were horses, beggars would ride," Wolfe said. She ignored him and eventually he stopped and let her walk away. When she realized he wasn't coming, she stopped and turned back defiantly.

"What would you have me say? I told you at the first. Decisions are mine. I'm in charge." When Wolfe didn't respond, she said, "It's done, Joethan. Let that be the end of it." As if that settled everything, she turned and walked down to the barn.

When they were once again on the Boston Road, Wolfe kept to himself. He no longer felt connected to the freighter and was uncertain what to do about it. His uncertainty only grew during the six-mile trip to Worcester.

They entered the town from the south, where a crowd was gathered on the common to watch another militia drill—but it wasn't just another militia. They wore homespun like the others, but by every other comparison they were a flash outfit.

Sixty or seventy well-armed and accoutered men trotted the perimeter of the common in platoons. At the command of a bosun's whistle, wielded by a strikingly fit officer, the platoons flowed together to form two companies. At another blast from the whistle they devolved back into platoons, all of it carried out smartly and smoothly.

Wolfe's view of the drill was eventually blocked by the Meeting House, an edifice with numerous windows topped by a tall spire. Across the street were two imposing mansions. Indeed, as the freighter made its way through town, Wolfe became amused by a phenomenon he dubbed, 'relative delusion.' Relative to other stops on the Boston Road, Worcester felt like a city; delusion because Worcester was not a city—not nearly—but it did have a courthouse and that made it a shire town, and that made a difference.

Ascending south to north along the main street, there were four or five taverns, two general stores, an apothecary, law offices, a blacksmith, and residences. There were coaches abroad and enough people wearing wigs, or their own hair powdered, to indicate a professional class in town.

The courthouse sat on the west side of the main street at the top of a hill, its cupola haloed by the sun. There was a gallows and a whipping post out front, and knots of men on the lawn conversing and passing around flasks and jugs.

Just past the driveway to the courthouse, the road forked. The freighter took the right fork but Wolfe lagged behind. One of the men at the courthouse insisted he stop for a wet and he saw no reason to decline.

The man, Richard, was a delegate to the Worcester County Convention—the insurgent governing body of Worcester County—scheduled to convene the next day at the courthouse. Richard was intrigued by the freighter and wanted to know more about it.

Twenty minutes passed before Wolfe sauntered into the yard of the Hancock Arms, a drab, two-story tavern. He found Sam and Madam filling the freighter's feed troughs. In greeting, Madam said, "If your intent is to not work today, Joethan, you might at least have the courage to say it."

In that moment, the questions Wolfe pondered on the walk from Leicester were answered. To Madam's amazement, he unslung the donderbus and handed it to her. "I'll take my leave now," he said. Without waiting for a response, he walked up into the freighter to collect his things.

When he came back out, Sam was gone. Madam remained but eyed him defiantly. Wolfe nodded to her. "Fare thee well, Mevrouw van Roos."

"And you," Madam said, with a nod of her own.

38

Wolfe walked back to the main street. In front of a blacksmith shop across from the courthouse, he came face-to-face with the fit officer who'd been blowing the whistle on the common. A captain as it turned out. He was handing his coat and hat to a deferential black man in a singed leather apron, an officer's valet or slave, if they weren't the same.

"And who might you be?" the officer said to Wolfe. His tone was friendly but he expected an answer. Wolfe named himself and the captain said, "You came in with the freighter." A statement, not a question. Wolfe allowed that he had.

"And you command the militia," Wolfe said. The captain nodded.

"Timothy Bigelow. Can I steer you somewhere?" Wolfe grinned.

"Nicely put. And perhaps you can steer me somewhere. 'Twill take a little time, but."

Bigelow sent the black man off and led Wolfe inside the smithy. Pumping up the heat of the stone forge with a large overhead bellows, he said, "It'll be warm in a minute." When the coals were giving off a splendid amount of heat, he tossed Wolfe a bowl, took one for himself and filled it from a keg propped under the eaves. Wolfe followed his example and enjoyed cider perfectly mulled by careful proximity to the forge.

Wolfe was warm inside and out when he commenced talking about Pap, although Bigelow stopped him almost at once. "You're aware you sound like a Britoner, right?"

"Never heard that before," Wolfe said. Bigelow allowed the trace of a smile to bow his top lip delicately, which was incongruous with his strong, weathered face. His nose was more wide than long, his brown eyes large and alert. Although there were traces of gray in his clubbed hair, it was mostly shiny black. Perhaps ten years older than Wolfe and of a height, he was broader in the chest and thicker, a physically imposing man entirely. As soon as he caught the gist of Wolfe's story, he interrupted again.

"No true Liberty Man will tell you the whereabouts of another and that includes me. The web you seek is spun at the sign of the Green Dragon in Boston. 'Tis there you'll be reunited or hung as your case warrants." Wolfe laughed at the implied threat. To Wolfe's good opinion, Bigelow's reserve cracked and he chuckled too, but his point was well taken and appreciated. It was a relief to hear someone say plain what others only hinted at.

Wolfe asked if Dr. Warren carried weight at the Green Dragon. "Is Warren known to you?" said Bigelow.

"Acquainted," said Wolfe. By Bigelow's reaction, Warren's name carried weight. "Whom else might I need see?" Wolfe asked. Bigelow shrugged.

"My own self, I'd start at the top. That's Hancock and Adams. In your case, I'd say Adams or Revere. Revere an't in charge but he knows everything. That's who I'd see was I you. If I didn't know Warren, I mean. I'd see him first."

Hours later it seemed that no time had passed. Joeth and Tim—as they bade each call the other—were old friends. The slave, Hector, brought meat and bread which piqued a sad irony in Wolfe's heart.

Tim had just proudly paraphrased a resolve passed in Worcester the previous fall, ". . . the people are entitled to life, liberty, and the means of sustenance by the Grace of God and without leave of the King." In Wolfe's estimation, the appearance of a slave immediately after rendered the words hollow. Tim saw it on Wolfe's face and said, "Hector would be free if he desired." Wolfe was skeptical.

"What man would wish to be a slave?"

"That's what I used to think," said Tim. "Then I inherited Hector and tried to free him. He begged me not to. I'll call him back and you can ask him yourself if you don't believe me." Wolfe shook his head, but he also looked Tim in the eye to see if he was putting one over. Wolfe didn't think he was.

"I'll take your word for it," Wolfe said. "And beg leave for doubting. But damn if I don't find it queer." And he did. He found it shocking enough to change the subject.

"When do you think the war will start?"

"Six months ago," Tim said. His answer required elaboration. "In Boston they think everything starts and ends with them, but it an't so," Tim said. "Whenever government declared our elected judges would be replaced by appointees, we drove every King's Man out o' office. I don't think anyone would deny we're at war." Wolfe doubted that Tim took anything lightly, yet he seemed supremely confident.

"You don't fear the consequences of a war with Government?" Wolfe said. Tim's eyes sparkled.

"No. And I'll tell you why. Last autumn an alarm went out that the Redcoats were attacking Cambridge. Within hours nigh on ten thousand of us were marching to fight 'em. If the Provincial Congress hadn't stepped in to say the alarm were false, Redcoat blood would have run in the streets. Gage needs ten times the number of men he has to contest this country."

"You can't wait for the fighting to start, can you?" Wolfe said. Tim did him the honor of not pretending otherwise. He backed his ardor with a concise argument based on the English Constitution and especially the Massachusetts Colony Charter, but in the end, Tim wanted to fight.

At Wolfe's request, Tim recounted the start of the war back in the fall, how in the face of threats against royally appointed officials, Gage promised to send troops to protect the court when it sat in September. Prepared to fight if they had to, five thousand Sons of Liberty turned out but no Redcoats showed up. Gage lost his bluff, and with it any chance of stemming the tide of democratic despotism.

Lining both sides of Worcester's main street, Liberty Men forced Royal Officials—of which there were many—to walk a gauntlet of humiliation and physical intimidation from the courthouse to the common. Many of the men being rousted weren't young. Some even fought the French alongside the men degrading them.

On the common, Royal Officials were forced to resign and apologize to the satisfaction of everyone. Men with particular grievances against an official weren't shy to take advantage either. Many officials were demeaned out of proportion to their crimes, but Tim didn't mourn for them, even those he once called friends. Of greater concern was what to do about men selling liquor without a license.

Tim owned a tavern and illegal liquor sales were killing business, along with the business of every other licensee. There was no longer a sheriff, or Court of General Sessions of the Peace, or any authority at all, other than a few committees and the mob, and they weren't brave enough to restrict the sale of liquor.

Near midnight, Tim bade Wolfe make comfortable in the forge, and removed to his home, one of the handsome domiciles above the courthouse. Under glowering skies, the next day, Wolfe took Tim to breakfast at his favorite spot. It was a kitchen favored by friends of Government, although in the case of The King's Arms an allowance was made by both factions. Mary Sternes was acknowledged to lay the best breakfast in town.

After parting from Tim, Wolfe went to a general store and rigged himself out with a couple of blankets and a thin rope. He wrapped his riding boots up in the blankets, twisted and lashed the blankets tight with the rope, and carried the whole strapped across one shoulder. His haversack slung over the other. He was eager to get to Boston now, confident he'd figure out a way to contact Warren.

39

He set out in misting rain but by noon it was pouring. Lowering his head, he lengthened his stride and hoped he'd find a tavern sooner than later. By the time he stood in front of the fireplace at Farrar's in Shrewsbury, he was drenched and spattered with mud, but satisfied too. He'd kept a fast pace the entire way. The walk from New Haven had done him some good. He was more fit by far than he'd been in a year.

Drying out by the fire in Farrar's taproom, he had a bowl of cider and listened to the chatter. For once it wasn't purely political. The freighter had driven through earlier in the day. "Stopped down the road at Baldwin's on the drilling ground," it was said.

Sordid innuendos were bandied about. Madam was laughed at as "Mevrouw Massa," and "Mevrouw Negro." Sam was referred to as "The little black Dutch boy" and "the Dutch widow's boy." The slander was barely worth the name, and for originality there was none, yet Wolfe resented it.

He paid Farrar's girl a few coppers to brush out his coat and grease his boots and leggings. Due to the weather, the beds were all spoken for. Wolfe wrapped up in his blankets and slept by the fire in the public room.

It was cold and clear at dawn. He paused on his way out to drink a cup of coffee and watch a turkey drover coax his flock down from the trees with handfuls of seed.

He set a fast pace when he departed Farrar's. If Massachusetts was already at war, as Tim said, Wolfe was resolved to be no less fit than any militiaman or Redcoat.

He covered the ten miles to Marlborough on road starting to churn up with the passage of carts and drays. Loping and walking in turn, he declined offers to ride with passing vehicles, instead using them to pace himself, as he did men on horseback.

He'd asked about buying a horse but Tim said he'd pay at least thirty dollars hard money for a mediocre animal. That was a good chunk of purse and Wolfe had no idea how long he might need lurk around Boston, or if bribes might be involved. Besides, he was unimpressed with the horses in New England. He was aware that many folk were apt to coddle their good animals in winter but even so, all the horses he'd seen were more suited to pulling plows than carrying someone.

He rested briefly at Williams Tavern in Marlborough, then did another seven or eight miles to the sign of the Red Horse in Sudbury, which looked more like a picturesque estate than a tavern or ordinary. An ordinary with rather extra, Wolfe thought. More of an extra-ordinary. It was a hideous pun, which of course was the art of it. Dr. Franklin's pain at such a gibe would've been profound. His admonishment hilarious.

It cost a dollar for a private room at the Red Horse, a gouge Wolfe grudgingly paid. The public room was loud with talk of war and politics, as it was everywhere, and he was weary of it. The thoughtful discussions on the rights of man, the inane discussions on the rights of Englishmen, the swaggering boasts of the ignorant. All of it.

In the morning he was well away before the teamsters hitched up. Fifteen miles to Watertown. The route through Sudbury village was near a mile long, exiting via a causeway along the swampy banks of the Sudbury River to a bridge. On the other side of the river, he shed his greatcoat and began composing in his head, the letter he'd write to Joseph Warren that evening.

Four miles on, in the town of Weston, it seemed that every house doubled as a business. He drank a pitcher of cider at the sign of the Golden Ball and learned that it was a Tory house. Weston was where the roads from Vermont and eastern Connecticut joined the Boston Road. There was a meeting house in Weston and a couple of mills built out along the river, a pottery, a tannery that stank—as did they all—but mostly Weston was a crossroads.

The temperature rose giving the road a topcoat of slick mud. Traffic was steady, mostly locals draying between villages. In the afternoon, a rig coming up from behind got Wolfe's attention. A stubby covered wagon was bouncing and slithering behind two heavy draft horses running full out.

The rig was going too fast and as it drew closer, Wolfe was obliged to vacate the road so as to not be trampled. He started to curse out in anger but the curse died on his lips. The postilion—the man riding the wheel horse—was not controlling the team so much as trying not to fall off the horse. Bug-eyed with fear, the inept bastard would be lucky if he didn't break his neck. The thought mitigated Wolfe's anger somewhat.

As the wagon thundered past, he had a brief view of a frightened woman in the back. When she was gone, Wolfe amused himself by imagining what her story might be.

Waltham was bigger and busier than Weston. The streets bustled with vehicles, animals, and people, many of them dressed as they would be in a respectable London neighborhood, and accompanied by armed servants as they would also be in London.

A clutch of well-dressed children openly gaped and whispered when Wolfe walked by. He knew he cut a strange figure away from the context of the freighter, but from the children's reaction, he didn't appreciate how strange.

He did not invite intercourse with the people of Waltham, by demeanor or stride, and so passed through quickly. He was over the Beaver Brook bridge and on the road to Watertown before his presence as a stranger could invite scrutiny.

Between Waltham and Watertown, two riders overtook him, driving their mounts hard—plow horses really. Muskets lay across the men's saddles in front.

They reined up with the smell of liquor effusing like perfume. One of the men had shaggy blond hair and wore a black cocked hat. The other had brown hair and wore a flop hat, but his harelip was what drew one's attention. Both appeared to be in their twenties and wore tattered homespun that needed retirement a year ago.

"Have you seen a campaign wagon?" Cocked Hat demanded. Wolfe didn't care for his tone.

"Have I seen a wagon?" he repeated dully, putting a hand to his chin to think about it.

"You can't hardly miss a campaign wagon!" Cocked Hat said. "There's Tories aboard! We're militia, you dolt!"

"He want to be paid!" Harelip said, misconstruing entirely.

"Not at 'all," Wolfe said, somewhat insulted—and in what he thought was a pretty good American accent. "Just wonderin' what's so 'portant 'bout that wagon."

"I told ya! They's Tories runnin' for Boston!" Cocked Hat unslung a canteen from his saddle and guzzled some of its contents.

"I saw a campaign wagon stopped in Waltham," Wolfe said.

"Ballocks!" Cocked Hat slammed the cork into his canteen and prodded his horse to bowl Wolfe over. Wolfe easily sidestepped the clumsy beast and gave it a shot on the haunch with his staff. The horse hopped away, almost unseating Cocked Hat. When the militiaman got himself straightened out, he made it clear by look and attitude that he meant to have it on with Wolfe—who was happy to oblige. Cocked Hat was a ha'penny tuff who needed to be taught a lesson.

Seeing the coming storm, Harelip said to his partner, "We an't got time for this." His words struck home. Cocked Hat glared in frustration at Wolfe and spit pointedly.

"You best hope I never lay eyes on you again!" Wrenching his dobbin's head around, he pummeled the horse's ribs with his heels to convince it to lumber off east. Harelip's tired mount followed at a slow trot. Wolfe felt sorry for the horses but he was glad he'd given the woman in the wagon more time to get away. Harelip and Cocked Hat might be militia, but Wolfe knew enough criminals in London to recognize their brethren. He was sorry Harelip butted in. He would have enjoyed knocking Cocked Hat off his high horse.

Continuing east, the road wound through plains of winter grass that gave way to numerous ponds and elegant mansions, the country seats of rich Bostonians. Some of them were small forts from back when the Pequot

Indians were massacring Englishmen and Worcester was the frontier.

Watertown was abuzz when Wolfe strode into town. The Massachusetts Provincial Congress—the Faction's shadow government—was to meet in Cambridge the following day. All the major actors among the Massachusetts rebels were expected to attend. Wolfe took it as great news. It was entirely possible that he could orchestrate a meeting with Warren without going into Boston. The bad news was that many of the attendees were staying in Watertown and there were no beds to be had for any price.

Although Watertown was a shire town, and larger and more refined than Worcester, refinement faded at the Charles River. A waterfall at the head of the tidewater powered two large mills. The waterfall also provided commercial fishing in the form of weirs built on stilts in the river to catch alewife and shad. The area around the falls was the neighborhood of unskilled laborers and fisher folk.

Ordinarily Wolfe would shun the poor part of a strange town, if only to avoid bugs and stink, but he'd been pointed to a private home where he might rent a bed for the night. At the door of a dilapidated two-story house, John Pliney answered Wolfe's knock.

Pliney was a slight man with a whiny voice, and red-rimmed eyes that were remarked upon by everyone he met. His wife Sal was taller, stouter, and coarser, with a noticeable mustache. It was she who set the room price at a ridiculous two shillings and would not be swayed. Wolfe got her to throw in a meal of watery stew and accepted the gouge.

Despite the bed being an old tick mattress only a little softer than the floor, Wolfe fell quickly and deeply asleep … until he dreamed of a woman screaming. Groggily he become aware that he wasn't dreaming, he was disoriented. With only one small window, the strange room was impenetrably dark and he'd been in so many strange rooms for months.

A woman was screaming—outside—screaming bloody murder—until suddenly she wasn't. Wolfe was half out of bed before ten years of road experience came to the fore. Flopping back down, he swore, "Sod off, you bastards."

The 'Screaming Woman' was a con so out of fashion he'd nearly forgotten it, a flimflam particularly effective on officers and gentlemen of the better sort. Men who could be counted on to race to a woman's rescue while her accomplices robbed their effects.

Wolfe supposed the ruse tonight was for the provincial congressmen in the crowded town and he was inclined to ignore the episode entirely. But he couldn't. He'd stayed in plenty of places where they'd kill a stranger in his sleep for much less than a greatcoat.

In a disgruntled frame of mind, he got out of bed, grabbed his staff, and loudly thumped down the stairs. He opened and closed the front door but remained inside and waited. Almost at once, footsteps overhead moved to his room. Whether Pliney was seizing an opportunity or the scam was his own, Wolfe didn't know. Nor did he care.

He padded upstairs, stopping on the upper landing when another scream came from outside, but fainter. The screaming woman was luring her marks farther afield.

By the light of a tin lantern, Pliney was going through Wolfe's things like a professional. Absorbed in his thieving, the first notion he had of being discovered was a bash from Wolfe's staff that sent him flying over the bed. On the floor on the other side, Pliney curled up in the fetal position and covered his head with his arms, expecting to be beaten. As he'd no doubt been beaten before.

Wolfe didn't disappoint. He bashed the thief again and had the satisfaction of knowing it hurt, but also knowing it wasn't as painful as Pliney's anguished cry would have it.

"With no sheriff, I'll see to my own justice," Wolfe said. He was about to administer more justice when a swinish grunt announced Sal Pliney. She burst through the door brandishing a meat cleaver that she swung from overhead like a tomahawk. Wolfe barely avoided decapitation by throwing himself back into the wall.

Pliney sprang up from the floor with a wicked-looking knife in hand. Sal cocked her cleaver again, but before she could swing it, Wolfe hit her flush under the chin with the flat bottom of his hickory stick. The impact was loud and hollow, followed by the supremely unsettling sound of two eyes popping out of their sockets.

In the dim flicker of the tin lantern on the floor, Sal's eyes bounced and dangled by nerves and blood vessels on her cheeks. Blood, like black tears, began to ooze from her empty eye sockets.

Pliney froze in horror as his hideously maimed wife babbled something unintelligible, keeled over backward and hit the floor head-first with a sickening thud. For interminable seconds, Pliney and Wolfe stared in stupefaction at the eyeballs gruesomely dangling on either side of Sal's nose.

Pliney sobbed and came for Wolfe with his knife. Before he took two steps, Wolfe's stick hit him viciously across the side of the head. The red-eyed man dropped like a marionette with its strings cut.

Breathing heavily, Wolfe stared down at the unmoving bodies in disbelief. They looked to be dead. He was apt to stand trial for murder. It was bloody madness.

The bed erupted in flames, the oil from the fallen lamp having ignited the tick mattress. Wolfe tried to grab his blanket off to smother the fire but it was too late. Flames were already running up the wall and arching across the exposed beams of the ceiling.

Voices outside demanded attention. Down on the street, men were returning from their fruitless quest for the screaming woman. Soon they'd discover they'd been robbed and all hell would break loose.

Wolfe didn't want to be the stranger among two possibly dead locals when all hell broke loose.

He snatched up his things and fled downstairs. By the time he put his boots on, the house was thick with smoke. By the time he was a block away and dogs started to bark alarm, the Pliney house was well aflame.

Suddenly Watertown had more to worry about than a screaming woman.

40

Wolfe could see his breath in the darkness as he labored through hilly woods. He was shadowing the main road to Cambridge as fast as he could, cursing as he tripped over unseen obstructions. Anger over the mayhem he'd been forced to commit had given way to bitter recriminations against himself for the very idea of blundering around America looking for his father.

But now he need focus on the task at hand. His thought had been to skirt Cambridge and enter the town from the other side, as if he came from Charlestown, but that no longer seemed feasible. The sun would be up soon.

After four or five miles, the Charles River reappeared on his right, having disappeared just outside Watertown. As the sun broached the horizon, he encountered dank marshland too mucky to contend with and crossed the road. There were orchards on the other side and it was hilly.

At the top of a hill he was provided a vista of the surrounding country, handsome country with scores of well-established acres. The reason lay up ahead. A half-dozen great houses proudly lined the north side of the road into Cambridge.

The discharge of a musket startled him to his belly. Another shot followed and then five or six almost at once on the other side of the road. Through his pocket glass, he saw men aimlessly discharging their muskets into the ground.

Wolfe swore at himself. He'd been so concerned with pursuit he hadn't given thought to what might lie ahead. Militia were guarding the town, clearing their muskets as they were relieved and went off duty.

And why wouldn't they be guarding the town? he thought. If the Redcoats decided to put an end to the illegal Congress, the war everyone was waiting for might well start today. He decided that sneaking around was probably not the best plan and made his way down to the road.

Close up, the mansions he'd seen from the hill were impressive—three stories, dormers, interior chimney stacks and many windows. All of the houses faced south toward the road and the Charles River, that the trees in front might shade the dooryard on hot summer days. Each dooryard was contained by a fence, and each fence was handsomely distinct from the neighbor's.

"Dreadfully charming," Lydia Grieves would have said sarcastically.

Lydia Grieves. The punch line of a joke played at Wolfe's expense; who never spoke to him again after he was stabbed in a fight over her. Lydia Grieves, who'd stolen from him the likelihood of ever trusting another woman. Madam van Roos reinforced that notion, but Lydia Grieves was the devil.

What did that make Pru?

As he walked past the mansions he felt watched, the feeling rendered eerie by the absence of activity. There wasn't man nor beast to be seen around the houses, or across the road all the way down to the river. If it wasn't for smoke wafting from a couple of chimneys, he might have thought the estates deserted.

They must be Tory houses, Wolfe thought, the occupants making themselves scarce with the Faction in town.

He was welcomed to Cambridge by the familiar smell of burning peat, a common source of fuel in Europe. He surmised that the price of wood around Boston must now be beyond the means of any but the wealthy.

Militia manned a guardhouse on the outskirts of town. Wolfe was stopped and questioned until someone the guards knew rode up and they lost interest in the stranger. The first Cambridge inhabitants he saw were matrons in lappet caps and heavy capes, grimly trudging in line, each carrying a spinning wheel.

The main road led to a square at the bottom of a treeless, hardscrabble common. On the right of the square were two houses as fine as those on the

Watertown Road. Across the road from those houses was a church, and beyond the church was the courthouse, and the brick buildings of Harvard College, austere and new compared to Oxford in England.

Near the Harvard buildings a score of horses and vehicles were drawn up in front of the Cambridge Meeting House, a churchlike structure with a bell tower.

Wolfe found a tavern and broke his fast at a table by himself in the public room. The establishment soon filled up as men poured into town. Without being asked, he abandoned the table and took a chair on the periphery where he could eavesdrop.

Amid the din of the crowded room, one conversation he overheard was between yeomen supposing that Gage would send troops to put an end to the Provincial Congress. "Lobsters," they called the British soldiers, pronounced "Lobstahs," which Wolfe found amusing. If the Lobstahs did come out, the yeomen had every intent of shooting at them, or so they said.

A different dialogue regarded tax collection. Two mechanics argued over what military ordinance ought to be bought with tax monies being collected. Wolfe gleaned that people in the country were still paying taxes, only now they were paying them to the Provincial Congress instead of the King, which further confused his grasp of what was motivating the insurrection.

Yet it was other talk that drew his particular interest. A half-dozen teamsters came in boisterously cracking jokes about a fire in Watertown. "T'were lucky there 'as no wind," one said, "or them Plineys a' had the satisfaction of taking the whole town to hell with 'em!" The teamsters were laughing uproariously as they called for food and drink.

Wolfe dared relax a little. Perhaps there wouldn't be as many questions asked about the Plineys as he feared. A most bizarre episode even by his standards. He tried to summon remorse for his actions but he had no intent of harming anyone when he overpaid for the room.

Late in the afternoon he joined a crowd outside the meeting house. To his surprise, when the Provincial Congress adjourned, the members proved to be men of the better sort mostly. There were yeomen and mechanics to be sure, but many appeared to be gentlemen. More than a few wore wigs or their own hair powdered, or curled at the temple in earlocks like Warren's. They were men who might not be from families that traditionally ran things in the colony, but they looked to be their peers. They certainly didn't appear as the rabble portrayed by word and cartoon in the London press.

Warren was last to emerge from the meeting house, with another man, and a surprise. Tim Bigelow was with them. Wolfe tried to remember if he'd said anything that might get him tangled but the problem was rendered moot. After bidding farewell to some associates, Tim caught sight of Wolfe and called him over. As Wolfe approached, he heard Tim say to Warren, "The very man I spoke of."

Wolfe shook Tim's hand. Warren—as fastidiously neat in his black doctor garb as the first time they met—looked at Wolfe quizzically. "Captain Bigelow says you know me?"

"I said we were acquainted," Wolfe corrected him. "We shared a conversation in Commodore Loring's study not two months ago." Warren looked past Wolfe's beard and shook his head.

"You're either rash to the point of madness or a very brave fellow. If discovered 'twill go hard with you." Tim was bursting to ask a question and perhaps the other man was too, but Warren cut them off.

"Come, gentlemen. It won't do to discuss matters here. Let's to food and fire. I'm cold in my bones and hungry as a new-woke bear." He hooked Wolfe's arm with his own and led the way.

Wolfe exchanged nods with the man named to him as the eminent physician, Dr. Benjamin Church—about forty, thin, with a complexion more sallow than a cold February dusk could account for. Like Warren, Church's garb was the requisite black of the physician, but where Warren was stylish and fastidiously neat, Church was rumpled and old fashioned. Unlike Warren, Church wore a powdered wig.

Warren's destination was one of the great houses across the road from the Anglican Church. As they entered the bricked dooryard, Wolfe noted that some of the second story windows were boarded up. Warren followed his gaze and explained, "Last fall General Brattle saw fit to remove himself to Boston. As he swore everything he did was in the best interest of the colony, we're confident he'd want us to use his home." Church and Bigelow found Warren's remark very droll. Wolfe doubted that General Brattle would.

It was a fine house even by the light of only two candles. On the ground floor, a center hallway and stairs to the upper floors were flanked by two large rooms. The Congressmen had taken over one of the ground floor parlors for a dormitory. Despite Warren's outwardly cavalier attitude, the squatters were not abusing the place. To minimize their intrusion, most of the furniture had been put aside and covered. Cots had been brought in.

The congressmen crowded in front of the fireplace without removing their coats. "T'were so blasted cold in that meeting house I couldn't take notes," Warren laughed.

"You're too tender," Tim Bigelow said. Before Warren could remonstrate, a slight, middle-aged man wearing a white wig and Brattle livery came in.

Setting down a pewter service of pitcher and cups, the servant said morosely, "Supper directly." Warren introduced the man to Wolfe as Cuthbert, the house steward, stayed on with his wife Melody to care for the place in their master's absence.

The Congressmen drank heartily and took off their coats. Wolfe ceded proximity to the fire and kept his coat on. Determined to keep his wits about him, he did not refill his glass with the others. Applejack was more potent than cider.

After supping together on cold partridge, bread and beans, the men took out their pipes and ritually passed around a pouch of tobacco. When they were lit up, Warren closed the two doors to the room.

"Now, gentlemen, it's time for Mister Wolfe to explain why a Tory hero has seen fit to don a disguise and enter the lion's den, as it were."

"I wear no disguise," Wolfe said. "I've spent the last month escorting a freighter of supplies to Boston."

"That's true," Tim said to the others. "He were with the Dutch widow when I met him."

"The woman with the Pennsylvania wagon?" Warren said. Tim nodded.

"I din't know he were a Tory hero, but."

"Hardly," Wolfe said. "I aided an old man accosted in the street by rascals.

I didn't know he was Commodore Loring 'til after." Tim looked to Warren for confirmation. Warren shrugged. Doctor Church laughed, a rich and resonant sound incompatible with his cadaverous appearance.

"So you're that fellow! Delighted to make your acquaintance Mister Wolfe."

Warren said, "Mister Wolfe was warned out of Boston publicly. If discovered he'll be tarred and feathered at the least. Then I should have to answer to Benjamin Franklin at some future date as it seems they're bosom friends."

Church said to Wolfe, "You present as one of the roaming poor, speak like a gentleman and call Franklin a friend. Tell me sir, are you a spy?" Wolfe sighed wearily.

"Since landing on these shores, gentlemen, all I've sought to do is locate my father. I sincerely wish that you and everyone else would believe me."

"I might if I knew your story and could judge for myself," Church said. "T'would be a welcome diversion after a day of the most tedious drivel imaginable." The last was said with a glare toward Warren, as if the fault lay there. Warren assumed the patient demeanor he'd used with the Commodore when Wolfe first met him.

"Everything legal and proper, Doctor Church. We voted."

"Oh ho! We voted, all right," Church said. He turned to Wolfe. "Do you know what great resolution the Provincial Congress voted on today?" Bigelow snickered. Warren waved a dismissive hand. Church said, "We voted to allow ourselves to keep our hats on in session!"

"Be glad the resolution passed," Warren shot back. He explained to Wolfe, "There's no fireplace in the blasted meeting house."

Wolfe complied with Church's request and told his tale, omitting a few things and shading a few others, but largely keeping to the truth. When he finished, Church said, "What is your political leaning, Mister Wolfe?" Wolfe took a moment to collect his thoughts, and then he spoke carefully.

"A good many men I respect believe that this colony, by right and by law, ought be brought to heel. Yet a small cadre of men I also respect, insist you are being treated unfairly. Personally, I don't count myself qualified to judge who is right. I will say however, for all the lamentation I've heard and read about trampled English rights here in America, the most egregious trampling I've witnessed is by your Faction. Meanwhile Government affords you the liberty to form a movement with the goal of independence. I don't see that you can be granted more liberty than that." Warren shook his head as if Wolfe just didn't get it.

"In the first instance," Warren said, "no man may grant another his liberty, not even the King. In the second instance, we seek no independency." Wolfe gave Warren a bemused smile.

"No man may grant another his liberty is a noble sentiment Doctor Warren. But whether you admit it or not, 'tis wholly untrue in factuality. As to whether you seek independence or not, the only successful conclusion to your movement must be independence. But you know that. One of your refrains is liberty or death, is it not? Be assured the ministers in London take you at your word, and eventually they're going to make you prove it. When they do, you'll either tear free of Mother England or 'twill be the Forty-Five all over again. I can tell you firsthand Doctor, the Scottish Highlands have yet to recover from the rebellion thirty years ago." His thought complete, Wolfe put a hand across his heart and bowed his head—as Warren had done the first time they met. When he spoke again, he assumed a different mien.

"Now that I've answered your questions gentlemen, perhaps you'll do me the courtesy of answering one of mine. Where do I find Nicholas Wolferd?"

Warren's mouth gaped open. "Your father's name is Wolferd?"

"Aye," Wolfe said. "My name was changed when I was sent to England as a boy." Warren shook his head in disbelief.

"Had I known at Loring's we might have walked across town and you would have been reunited." Wolfe was dumbstruck.

"Can it be true?" Tim said. Warren nodded.

"The very day I met Mister Wolfe his father was at the Dragon. Of course, I didn't know the connection at the time."

Recovering his composure, Wolfe said, "You know Nicholas Wolferd?"

"Captain Sedition they call him. And more of a troublemaker than you are."

"How's that?" said Church. Warren chuckled silently until his shoulders jiggled.

"Remember that donnybrook three weeks ago between the Dogberries and the Welch Fusiliers?" Church nodded. Warren pointed his pipe at Wolfe. "His father started it." For Church and Bigelow it was as good as watching a play. Church even clapped.

"In the event," Warren continued, "Mister Wolferd was asked to leave Boston same as his son, albeit not so publicly. 'Twill take inquiries to discover his whereabouts now." He looked at Wolfe. "For obvious reasons, few men know the comings and goings of others."

Church offered to assist in locating Wolfe's father but Warren waved him off. "That won't be necessary. I believe Mister Wolfe has no interest in our affairs. My one regret is I won't be there when he tells his father that. The old man is quite a fire breather. In the interim, what are we to do with the son?"

41

With the weather turned pissy and an offer from Warren to stay on until he determined Pap's whereabouts, Wolfe decided a holiday was in order. He slept in front of the fireplace with down pillows for a mattress, drank prodigious amounts of Brattle cider, ate prodigious amounts of Brattle cheese, and made use of the Brattle library.

Doctor Church turned out to be an affable, witty and learned man. He'd studied medicine in London and shared Wolfe's affection for the city. He was also interested in everything about Doctor Franklin. The thing Wolfe most admired about Church however, was despite being one of the most important men of the Faction, he, like the Reverend Tallmadge, was not a wild eyed radical. He was a conservative in the Faction. He spoke rationally about ways to solve the differences tearing the colony apart with a fervent desire that tensions not erupt in bloodshed.

On the third night of his stay, Wolfe got into a deep political discussion with Warren, wherein Warren justified any and all measures against the Crown as the rights of free Englishmen. The next morning when he went off to the Congress, Warren left behind a political tract for Wolfe to read, an oration he'd delivered at the first commemoration of the Bloody Massacre of 1770, when a platoon of Redcoats, in fear of their lives, fired on a Boston mob.

Warren's oration was a good rabble-rouser of a speech although Wolfe found the logic thin in places. He responded by selecting a pamphlet from

Brattle's collection for Warren to read. A piece by Samuel Johnson of dictionary fame.

Johnson's tract asserted that a colony accepting protection in blood and treasure from a mother country, is by definition a dominion of the mother country. As such, the colony is by all measures subject to the laws and taxes imposed by the mother state.

Warren left a note the next day saying that he was familiar with Johnson's tract, but by suggesting that the King arm slaves and Indians to ravage Americans—so Americans might better appreciate the true cost of blood and treasure—Johnson blackguarded his own argument.

Warren's response didn't make the dominion argument less powerful in Wolfe's estimation, but he could see where Americans might be touchy about Johnson's cheeky illustration of his point. But that was Sam Johnson as Wolfe knew him. The man lived to gibe, much like Dr. Franklin, whom he detested, and whom detested him. In Wolfe's opinion, they were too alike to ever be friends. Each needed to be top dog. It was too bad too, because if they were ever to sit and trade witticisms and observations together, Wolfe expected it would be one of the great entertainments of the age.

With the Provincial Congress in session, Cambridge was crawling with Liberty Men. Fearful of being recognized, Wolfe kept mostly indoors and out of sight, but he did spend the better part of one day outside. He was determined to have a proper wash.

He located a beat up old tun in one of the barns, drew water the from the well, heated it in the kitchen house and bathed right there. The doctors heard about it that evening and cautioned him not to bathe too often. Warren nodded agreement when Church said, "Removing the natural oils on your skin that protect you from disease is dangerous."

"I don't know if my body's oils will protect me from disease," Wolfe said. "But I do know, and Doctor Franklin will concur, women of the better sort prefer a cleanly man."

Church and Warren had no reply.

Wolfe came to understand that the Provincial Congress was actively organizing for war. They were coordinating resistance with other colonies and endeavoring to gather munitions and supplies. All of this he gleaned without trying, yet of Pap he learned nothing.

When he'd been in the house a week, cabin fever hit hard. He almost began to hope that the Lobstahs would come out, just for the excitement, but they didn't and wouldn't according to Warren's intelligence, which, Wolfe gathered, was perfectly accurate. Gage hadn't been far wrong when he said the Faction knew his orders before the Redcoats on Cobb's Hill did.

Much to the consternation of the Faction however, it turned out that Gage knew everything taking place in the Provincial Congress just as well. Wolfe's hosts were usually closed-mouthed when they returned after a long day, convivial but careful not to discuss anything important in front of him. At the start of his second week in the house that changed. That day they learned that Gage all but had the minutes of one of their committee meetings. That night they overlooked Wolfe's presence. They took it hard that there was a spy amongst them.

Church happened to chair the committee that had been compromised. It was he who conducted the lengthy discussion of who the spy might be, although, as he readily admitted, among eight committeemen, five were all but strangers.

Warren said, "What does the Cleanly Man think?" They'd taken to referring to Wolfe as the 'Cleanly Man.' Whether in fondness or disparagement, Wolfe wasn't sure. "Tell us," said Warren, "how does one recognize a spy?"

"I should start by assuming there was more than one," Wolfe said. To his amusement, his observation sparked an entirely new round of worry and analysis.

Ten days after Wolfe arrived in Cambridge, Warren produced a letter and said, "This is an introduction to Colonel Pickering in Salem. There you will find Nicholas Wolferd. I give it to you on one condition. I need your word you shan't speak of anything you see in Salem. Even if it might be what is considered common knowledge." Wolfe grinned. Warren remembered their first meeting well enough.

"Will you so swear?" Warren said.

Wolfe addressed the men, his friends by now, as one. "Across the ocean where I make my way as a private courier, I have many worthies for clients, among them Doctor Franklin, as you know. Upon my honor, I shall exercise the utmost discretion in your affairs at all times."

Warren handed Wolfe the letter. "The Committee of Safety authorizes Colonel Pickering of the Salem Militia to direct you to the whereabouts of Nicholas Wolferd." Wolfe looked over the letter and dared believe it might be the endgame.

"What will you do when you find him?" Warren said. It was a question Wolfe had asked himself many times of late.

"That depends on my father," said Wolfe. "But when I find him, I will have fulfilled my duty. My life will once again be my own. That is the main chance." Warren handed him a small piece of parchment.

"This pass authorizes you to traverse the road between Cambridge and Salem. It may come useful. If you're found on another road it won't answer, nor would Tories be apt to take it lightly. It might make your journey easier however." Wolfe took the pass a little dubiously. Tim clapped him on the back.

"The Provincial Congress has agreed to lease you one of General Brattle's horses. You must return it hence, mind." Wolfe was supremely grateful until Church said the rental would cost two guineas. He justified the outrageous amount by saying it was for the cause, and after all, Wolfe had been entertained by Congress for some days.

Wolfe thought, *Devil burn thee for thievery, Benjamin Church*, but he laughed and raised his glass. "To happy reunions of every stripe!"

The others raised their glasses and echoed him.

42

Part of the following morning was lost to the logistics of hiring a horse being more or less stolen. Church bullied the Brattle stable master, Mr. Leonard, until the beat-up old Scotsman grudgingly accepted that Wolfe was going to use one of the Brattle horses, or he, Leonard, was going to be looking for a new place to live.

The Brattle horses were broken to saddle but would be happier pulling a cart or a plow. Wolfe assumed the good animals went to Boston with the family when they fled. He chose a chestnut mare whose winter fat was less egregious than her stable mates. He accepted Leonard's choice of saddle, but rejected the suggestion of a curb bit whether the horse was used to it or not.

Essie, as the horse was called, took the single snaffle well enough but she was grown fat and content over an inactive winter. Horse and rider had an uncomfortable time until Essie grasped that she wasn't returning to the barn anytime soon. Not long after, she showed Wolfe her best gait, which was a slow canter.

It was a chilly morning but exertion soon had Wolfe sweating comfortably. It felt good to be wearing his riding boots again for the purpose they were intended. Even aboard a poor mount, it was glorious not to be on foot.

As hoped, he encountered no one on the road. By now he was familiar enough with Massachusetts culture to know that a rider abroad on the Sabbath would not go unchecked if observed, and indeed he did not.

In Medford, a scattered village amid farmland and rolling hills along the Mystic River, roads from the northeast converged and split off prior to Boston. There were some stout and handsome structures in Medford, courtesy of a brickworks on the waterfront.

Wolfe was stopped at a bridge crossing by a man whose job it was to keep an eye out for Sabbath breakers. Perhaps out of boredom more than anything else, the guard stretched the encounter interminably before allowing Wolfe to continue on his way, after paying the Sabbath fine, of course.

He was stopped again in Lynn by a squad of militia. He sat quietly as they debated whether communications of the Provincial Congress took precedence over Sabbath law. Eventually he was allowed to proceed.

The chill added damp as he neared the coast. On the outskirts of Salem, a town framed by a forest of masts from shipping in the harbor, and smothered by the miasmic odor of the sea, he heard bells clanging what sounded like alarm, and drums beating what sounded like a call to arms.

He entered a town in turmoil; fearful people streaming down the road lugging their precious possessions by any means available. A tandem of horses pulling an empty wagon careened out of a side alley in front of him, scattering everyone in its path.

Wolfe followed the human tide past midcentury mansions set back from the street by dooryards and gardens, and dark gabled houses perched on the edge of the road since the days of the witches. Beyond the shops and warehouses leading to the river, the throng was converging on a drawbridge.

The bells in Salem stopped ringing and the alarm drums ceased beating. In the relative silence that followed, not-so-distant fifes and drums could be heard. Judging from the activity, Wolfe supposed they had to be Redcoat fifes and drums, and they were getting closer.

A hundred yards beyond the chaos at the drawbridge, hauling vehicles were drawn up around a low rambling structure, a forge if the chimney was an indication. As Wolfe watched, two wagons broke from the cluster and rumbled away west, a scene evoking long-dormant memories. As a boy he'd helped move enough contraband to recognize the routine.

He dismounted to lead Essie across the bridge. Almost immediately he was identified as a stranger and surrounded. Holding up Warren's letter, he said, "I have a communication for Colonel Pickering from the Provincial Congress."

"No doubt to warn that ministerial troops be on the way. Which I already know." Colonel Pickering—looking no different than any other man at the bridge— held out his hand for the letter. Roughly the same age as Wolfe, the slanted thrust of his nose and chin lent him an air of permanent determination. Receding brown hair and thick glasses did not. Colonel Pickering exuded indecision.

"The business is not urgent," Wolfe said. Pickering read the letter anyway.

The sound of fifes and drums became loud and clear as if an obstruction between listener and sound was removed. And then a British column came into view, marching under the King's colors and the regimental flag of His Majesty's 64th of Foot. They stomped precisely down the bridge road to the fife shrill of *Yankee Doodle,* a tune the ministerial troops considered highly derisive of provincials. The sound of their drums echoing off the buildings on either side of road was an ominous thunder.

"This'll wait," Pickering said. He tucked the letter into his gray broadcloth coat and ordered three militiamen to take Wolfe across the river and keep him there.

The men objected.

While they debated, Wolfe watched the 64th come on. They were an old-fashioned-looking regiment, perhaps two-hundred-fifty men in red coats with black facings, black gaiters cinched above the knee, and black cocked hats with a single strip of white lace. Someone in the crowd said they were stationed at Castle William in Boston Harbor.

By the time Pickering came to an accommodation with his men, the commotion around the drawbridge had dissipated. The assigned militiamen escorted Wolfe over the bridge to join the crowd gathered on the other side.

But not everyone fled Salem. A small mob of local men and boys marched alongside the Redcoats, taunting and insulting them. When the 64th halted at the bridge, along with the reek of dead fish and seaweed, the smell of trouble was in the air.

A diminutive British colonel detached himself from the troop and walked out onto the bridge to the draw, which was being raised by Americans on the other side. "I am Colonel Leslie," the officer called cordially to the men hauling up the draw. "As duly commissioned by the governor of this colony, I order you to lower the draw in the name of the King." A long second after he gave his order, the bridge squeaked to the apex of its opening and was tied off, as inaccessible as ever it could be, which was not lost on Colonel Leslie. His friendly egg-shaped face went as crimson as his uniform. "How dare you obstruct the King's Highway!" he barked indignantly.

"This ain't no King's Highway!" one of the bridge keepers called back. "This road and bridge was built by them own lots this side o' the river."

"Lower the leaf by God or I'll fire on you!" Colonel Leslie swore.

Someone in the crowd around Wolfe yelled, "You're dead men if you shoot! Every damn one of you!" It wasn't an idle threat. Elevated slightly on the north side of the river, Wolfe could see a steady stream of armed provincials coming in from the west.

Two young men sitting atop the draw with their legs dangled over, began hurling invectives at the British Colonel. They were immediately chastised by their countrymen to shut up and get down, which they did.

Colonel Leslie calmed down and examined the situation. Moored at a pier alongside of the bridge pilings were two flat-bottomed cargo barges. Gundalows the locals called them. Glorified rafts is what they were—thirty to forty feet long with no freeboard to speak of. They might be efficient at moving cargo up and down a river, but the river best be calm. Some gundalows had a removable mast rigged for a lateen sail, but the propulsion of choice was sweeps or poles.

Predictably the gundalows caught Colonel Leslie's eye and he gave orders to seize them. The mob of Americans on the Salem side of the river had anticipated such an order, and prepared for it. Seven Americans with axes and mauls sprinted for the pier. A burly Redcoat Sergeant had his men fix bayonets before double-timing it in pursuit, a race in plain view for all to see.

The first roar from the onlookers was provincial as their men reached the gundalows and started bashing in hull strakes. The excitement grew as the

Redcoats—cheered on by their comrades—lumbered down the gangway to the pier.

It didn't take much to sink a gundalow. Another American cheer went up as the gundalow closest to shore lurched and began to settle. The men who'd done for her clambered up the pilings of the bridge.

A roar went up from the 64th as their men reached the second gundalow. One of the last two Americans aboard went scrambling up a piling just in time but his mate was caught. With a wide smirk, he threw his ax overboard, tore open his shirt and dramatically proclaimed, "Go ahead, if you dare!" The British Sergeant dared with the point of his halberd. He gave the cocky provincial a professionally managed poke in the chest that made the man cry out and collapse in a spurt of blood. As the 64th roared their approval, the Sergeant's men unceremoniously tossed the wounded man onto the pier.

But the second gundalow was settling and had to be abandoned.

Leslie called his men back. He was mad but not as angry as the people of Salem. The chant, "Bloody murder!" grew louder and more threatening until Leslie barked an order and his men happily fixed bayonets. The mob got quiet then but the anger, tension and fear on both sides was palpable.

On the Salem side of the bridge, a heavyset man in a long black coat and wide-brimmed black hat held a conference with the British Colonel. Wolfe's escorts named him the Reverend Barnard, an Anglican minister. Barnard and Colonel Leslie were soon joined by a militia captain named Felt. Wolfe was too far away to know what was said, but the Redcoats didn't have good options as far as he could see. And it would be dark soon.

After ten minutes of parlay, Felt walked out onto the bridge. Pickering climbed a ladder to the top of the draw and peered over to hear his report.

"It is proposed that the ministerial troops be allowed to march to the forge in the name of the King's honor," Felt said. "Should they find nothing there, they shall return to their ship at Marblehead. Colonel Leslie gives his word. What say you?"

"Do you trust him?" said Pickering. Felt shrugged.

"I expect his word is good. He's the third Earl of Buggershire or some such." The men around Wolfe snickered and guffawed at the word

Buggershire, but at least one man objected.

"Make them cross! Let'em try!" Many of his comrades agreed. Pickering held up a hand for silence.

"If we fight now they might could burn the town. In an hour we'll be five hundred more."

Felt backed Pickering. "Colonel Leslie says if we don't let 'em cross, he'll turn West's store into a barracks and stay 'til he does. Says he won't leave with the King dishonored." Pickering nodded and gestured for Felt to wait. Climbing down off the draw, Pickering conferred with his militia again. After ten minutes of discussion, he climbed back up and told Felt to accept terms.

As the draw squealed and lowered, Wolfe thought about Debins, in New Haven, and the absurdities he'd pointed out. Leslie's march across the bridge was such a one. When the draw was down, the drums and fifes of the 64th started up and with all the pompous pride they could muster, the regiment paraded across the bridge and up the road to the forge.

After a less than perfunctory search, Colonel Leslie not being simple enough to believe that the contraband was still there—cannon, Wolfe learned—the 64th came ready about. To fifes squealing, *The World Turned Upside Down*, the Redcoats marched back over the bridge the way they came. The last Wolfe saw of His Majesty's 64th of Foot, they were being ignominiously escorted out of Salem by crowing, strutting locals.

43

"The man you seek is gone," Pickering said. The best the Salem Captain of Militia could do was point Wolfe to Concord with a note added to the bottom of the original letter.

Wolfe had trouble sleeping at the Black Horse Tavern that night, and it wasn't the rumble of excited men in the taproom that kept him awake. His brain would not disengage. He was desperately tired of having no control over his life and no sign of a resolution in sight. Warren's question was his own. What did he expect to happen when he found his father? If he found his father.

The knowledge that Pap was alive should be enough, but it wasn't. Pru and Qua would be vastly disappointed if he gave up now, that he knew. He had no idea why their opinions should suddenly matter. Up until some weeks ago he hadn't thought of either of them in years. But their opinions did matter now and that was that.

He retraced his route through Lynn back to Medford in the morning, but instead of taking the road south to Cambridge, he kept on west, much to Essie's disappointment. She fussed and balked all the way to the Lexington Road, which crossed their road south of the village of Menotomy.

At the crossroads he stopped at Cooper's Tavern to water Essie and quench his own thirst. He was questioned closely by locals there. They didn't ask to see his pass but he let them know he had one.

On the road to Concord from Menotomy there were houses much of the way and occasional hamlets of three or four houses in proximity. Wolfe didn't stop or respond to the few men who tried to challenge or engage him as he rode through.

Lexington was a village scattered around a triangular green. The bottom point of the triangle was anchored by a three-story meeting house and detached belfry. The right, and longest side of the triangle, was fronted by a large tavern and stable. The shorter side of the triangle fronted the road to Concord. From Cambridge, the road at the bottom of Lexington Green forked. The right fork went to Bedford. The left fork bent to Concord.

Along the Concord Road were low rolling hills of woods and farms, and a couple of taverns. In the outer precincts of the town of Lincoln the road turned rugged, rising and dipping between deep declivities formed by a series of ridges. Beyond the ridges was pastureland separated from the road by fences constructed of cairns of large stones. Tree trunks stripped of branches laid across the top of the cairns served as rails. In this stretch Wolfe made good time until he was stopped by militia.

He produced his pass, showed them Warren's letter and named the recipient as Colonel Barrett, the name Pickering provided. To his annoyance, and at the loss of a great deal of time, Barrett's name sparked a lengthy discussion. Colonel Barrett was attending the Provincial Congress in Cambridge. If Wolfe bore a letter from them, why didn't he, and they, know that?

Wolfe explained the circumstance again. The militiamen fell to conferring and he waited, imagining what would happen when they fought the Redcoats and decisions had to be taken instantly. He managed to keep a good outlook and eventually was cleared to see Major Buttrick, Barrett's in-charge subordinate. A young militiaman, Jonas Ledward, was dispatched to show him the way.

Unconcerned swine rooted under fruit and nut trees either side of the road as Jonas jogged comfortably alongside Wolfe and Essie. Trees gave way to tired brown pasture as they neared the town, and tired pasture gave way to the shops required to sustain modern civilization. Cooper, blacksmith, cordwainer, and a half-dozen others, one after another, each with its own yard, outbuildings and equipment.

They passed a millpond and the burying ground, and a dozen unescorted milk cows wandering down the street. Concord Center was a tavern, blacksmith, meeting house and homes around a green, upon which sat three, six-pounder cannon in open view.

Eyeing the cannon, Wolfe said, "Don't you worry Gage may pay a visit?"

"More worried he won't," Jonas said carelessly.

Concord was a handsome town but with an aura of sober austerity that Wolfe found unsettling. Or perhaps it was the people out and about, every one of whom scrutinized him closely as Jonas led the way through town.

Away from the green, to the left of the road, was the Concord River. Also west of the road, was an impressive clapboard-sided manse marking the approach to Concord's north bridge—a railed, humpbacked span supported by six sets of oak pilings, anchored on either bank by stone piers.

The west side of the river had been cleared of trees years ago. The bottomland was now tillage and hay fields evolving to hardscrabble pasture as it rose up to a knoll. The road from the west end of the bridge went south for a few hundred yards—parallel to the river—before forking. The left-hand fork continued along the river briefly before curving inland and disappearing around the knoll near a red farmhouse.

Jonas took the right-hand fork up to a low ridge and an ideally situated two-story clapboard house. From this seat, Major Buttrick had a sweeping vista of the surrounding country. A mile away, Concord center was clearly visible.

The Major was a well-off farmer in his forties; solid, weathered, and sober. His face was round and open, his hair tied back nonchalantly. A leather apron hung below the bottom of his worn woolen coat. After reading Warren's letter and the postscript added by Pickering, the Major sent Jonas off to find someone.

Chatting amiably as they waited for Jonas to return, Buttrick offered Wolfe a bed for the night in exchange for a public report on the incident at Salem. Wolfe accepted if the major would see Essie watered and fed. Buttrick agreed, spit in his hand and proffered it to seal the bargain. Wolfe reluctantly spit in his own hand and shook.

Jonas returned to say that Nicholas Wolferd was not in Concord and no one knew of his whereabouts. No one had ever heard of him actually, by any of the monikers Wolfe provided.

With the futility of his search slapping him in the face again, what little optimism Wolfe clung to dissipated. A light supper with Major Buttrick and his wife was numbingly dull and it wasn't due to the blandness of rough brown bread and potato gruel, or even the major's wife, a stern soul who uttered not a word more than required by the most basic manners.

By first candle the house had filled with men eager to hear an eye witness account of what they called, the Salem alarm. Mrs. Buttrick was the only female present. She lurked in the background to make sure her furniture wasn't harmed—heavy, uncomfortable, Puritan furniture that couldn't have been harmed with a hammer.

Man after man lit a pipe, and Buttrick's great room became shrouded in smoke. By the time Wolfe related the incident, the audience was almost invisible, but they listened carefully to every word. At the conclusion of his narrative, disembodied questions came flying out of the pall. The interrogation lasted two hours and more, but after belaboring a trivial detail for the third time, Wolfe begged off. Buttrick was satisfied enough to dismiss the house.

Wolfe was wrapping himself in blankets to lie down in front of Buttrick's fireplace when there was a sharp rap at the door. The Major wearily answered the knock and welcomed in the Reverend William Emerson. Billy, as Buttrick called him, was a fiery fellow not much older than Wolfe. His face was an earnest one, drawn sharp by thin lips and a narrow nose. Although not physically large, under his cloak the Reverend was made ample by the armor of the New England cleric, being a black suit with white preaching bands.

After removing a bowl-crowned, black beaver-skin hat, Emmerson pulled off his mittens, put them inside the hat and handed the lot to Buttrick. Stepping over Wolfe to stand by the fire, he said, "You are the man from Salem?"

"I am," Wolfe said, looking up at the Reverend in annoyance. "And anxious to sleep."

"The time to sleep is when the day's work is done," Emerson said. "You and I have not finished our work."

The Reverend questioned Buttrick about Wolfe's mission as if he was Buttrick's superior and Wolfe wasn't there—and Buttrick took it. At one point, Buttrick urged Wolfe to show Emerson his pass and Warren's letter. Emerson wasn't impressed.

"You must needs get new orders from the Committee of Safety," he told Wolfe. "Letters are easily forged and this one begins to take on the appearance of a diary. I will say plain, sir. This is no good time for unknown men to roam the countryside."

"I am but unknown to you," Wolfe said. Emerson's thin lips got impossibly thinner.

"In this parish that is enough," he said grimly. He stepped over Wolfe to retrieve his things and address Major Buttrick.

"The decision is yours of course," he said to the Major, "but my counsel is send him back to the Committee of Safety. One name in the wrong hands is the end of us all."

When Emerson departed, Buttrick said to Wolfe, "What is so important about this man you seek?"

"He's my father," Wolfe said. "Of no great import with a war coming but I should like to see him again. For a time I thought him dead." Buttrick shook his head sympathetically.

"Get yourself papers for Worcester. If they don't know where he is, he prob'ly holed up 'twixt there and here. I'll keep an eye open myself. Like as not he'll turn up. Is there something you would have me say?"

"If you were to tell him he might reach his son through Doctor Warren, Doctor Church, or Captain Bigelow in Worcester, I should be grateful." The names impressed and Buttrick said if the opportunity presented, he would pass the word.

44

Wolfe left Concord in light snow flurries shortly after dawn. By the time he came trotting out of the ravines in Lincoln, the flurries had evolved to a gale. Occasionally a stand of trees along the road provided respite from the wind but inexorably the wind-driven snow all but blinded him.

He trusted Essie to keep the road and she did, until the open expanse of Lexington Green confused her. Peering through the flying snow, glimpses of a red door and the flicker of a candle in a window—the country signs for bed and board—led Wolfe to the tavern he'd passed the day before. He tipped the stable boy thruppence to help him get Essie stabled.

At midmorning in a snowstorm there were a half-dozen men in Buckman's Tavern—militia—and all of them suspicious of Wolfe. He produced his pass, held it up for all to see, and said what it was. Afterward they didn't trust him any more than they did before, but they were hungry for news and the Salem alarm was just the thing. By the time Wolfe finished relating what happened, men were buying him drinks and celebrating. Except those who viewed the event the way he did, as a black stain on British arms that would require cleansing, and soon.

The tavern owner, John Buckman, said Wolfe was welcome to pull up a piece of floor in front of his fire overnight but that was as much as he could offer. The day was to have been a training day which meant his rooms would be full. Wolfe was dubious because of the weather but Buckman knew his trade.

A score of men straggled in and Wolfe came to understand why. The Lexington Training Band was a men's club. Twice a week, in these, the dreary days of winter, the local males had an escape from the daily monotony of being trapped indoors at home, and especially—if they were being truthful—the company of females.

When one of Wolfe's drinking companions raised his glass and offered, "A health to the Lexington Train Band. Willing to walk miles in a snowstorm to do their duty," Wolfe thought, *In a pig's eye.* The Lexington men wanted out of the house like every other married man in the history of the world.

That night, in front of Buckman's seven-foot-wide fireplace, Wolfe lay down on a floor reeking of every drink ever spilled on it. Despite being closed in on all sides by snoring, belching, farting men, he fell instantly asleep.

Buckman didn't charge Wolfe for his stay, or his drinks, or his food. He'd poured a prodigious amount of spirits thanks to Wolfe and being a godly man, he was not lost to avarice. He even included a warm breakfast in the morning. His travel advice was free also.

"Lately there been mounted Redcoats as far north as Menotomy," he said. "With your pass from the committee you best keep an eye out. Wouldn't do to be found with such a thing."

Regardless of gray clouds that remained low and threatening, yesterday's snow was melting by the time Wolfe set out. Thankfully Essie knew she was riding home and gave no trouble.

They cantered into Cambridge before mid-day and something had changed. Even allowing for weather, the town bore little resemblance to the place Wolfe left just a few days before. If it wasn't for the smell of burning peat and sparks from chimneys, he might have thought the town deserted. He became aware of people, but nothing like the numbers before he left.

A one-horse shay was parked in front of Brattle House. Wolfe rode around to the stable and found Mr. Leonard. The old Scotsman was grumpy but glad to have Essie back. When Wolfe asked him what was acting, Leonard spit in disgust.

"Congress run off like rabbits when they heard the Regulars was marchin' out."

"Everyone's gone?" said Wolfe. Leonard grunted.

"Doctor Church inside. Stealin' the silver, most likely."

Wolfe found Church in the study on the second floor. The good doctor was tying up a folio of papers and perhaps Leonard wasn't far off when he suggested that Church was stealing the silver. Something was amiss when Wolfe entered the room. Nothing to hang a hat on, but something wasn't right.

"I brought the horse back," Wolfe said. "What's acting?"

"Walk with me." Church led the way downstairs and explained that there'd been word that Gage was marching out to put an end to the impertinence of a Provincial Congress. "'Tis just as well," Church said. "Factionalism has rendered us incapable of resolving anything. The herd in the country want us to evacuate Boston. So as to attack the town, if you can believe it."

"Because if Gage marches out 'tis their homes that burn," Wolfe said. Church grinned.

"Some men have no patriotic spirit." He stashed the folio in the shay next to other items wrapped in a blanket. When he was up in the rig, he said, "Well come on, man. Grab your kit and get in. You can board with me 'til you get sorted. I gather you didn't find your father?" Wolfe shook his head.

"And I shan't go to Boston, thank you very much. I have no desire to be tarred and feathered. I need a pass for Worcester." Church frowned.

"Regretfully I cannot give you such a one. The committee requires two signatures on an official pass. What if you stay here?"

"I doubt Cuthbert will invite me," Wolfe said. Church climbed down from the shay.

"To hell with Cuthbert. Tory rascal ought be grateful to have a roof over his own head." He went into the house and came back a minute later. "I told him you'll be staying on and if there's any trouble, I'll withdraw the protection of the Committee. You'll be comfortable enough."

When he was back up in the shay, Church said, "I'll send a pass for Worcester in a few days. Have faith Joethan. 'Tis the currency of the age." With a cavalier salute of his whip, Church drove off.

Cuthbert had watched the exchange from the front door. When Wolfe approached him, he drew back and Wolfe realized that the older man was fearful of him. The revelation came as a surprise because Wolfe never thought of himself as being a person who induced fear, but when he considered himself from Cuthbert's point of view; as a significantly younger and stronger man with a ragged beard and mismatched clothes, a stranger who might as easily be a religious zealot as a madman, or an insurrectionist son of a bitch, perhaps Cuthbert had a right to be afraid.

Wolfe swept off his wool cap and bowed elegantly. "If there's anything I might do to make my stay less of a burden Mister Cuthbert, you may name it." Cuthbert started to reply but thought better of it. At Wolfe's insistence, the house steward grudgingly said that the congressmen had used up a great deal of wood. With the slaves gone off for weeks at a time and Wolfe moving in, he didn't see how . . .

Wolfe said he'd make it right.

Cuthbert lodged Wolfe in an upstairs bedroom, the nicest room Wolfe had occupied since leaving London. In thanks, and to make things right, he split wood for two days. Cuthbert and his wife Melody were grateful enough to invite him to sup on the second night. They were genteel people and took pains to maintain their civility, come what may.

With no word yet from Church, and enough wood split to endure a blizzard, Wolfe offered to exercise Leonard's stable. The old man was grateful to accept. His days of working horses were in the past and he had the gimp and arthritis to prove it. He was only stable master because the true stable master took himself off when the Brattle family fled the previous fall. Leonard was a retired groomsman and had been for years.

While exercising the horses, Wolfe discovered that when he rented Essie, Leonard hadn't shown him the finest animal in the Brattle stable; a stallion that was in no way to be confused with a draft animal. The beast looked like a mixture of Friesian and Spanish Andalusian. A specimen, to be sure.

"But What is he?" Wolfe said. Leonard chuckled.

"He's a rare great beastie is what he is. Five-year-old get of a stallion from Florida and Gen'ral Brattle's favorite mare. The sire never took to the cold and died so you'll nae see another like him."

Wolfe believed the old Scotsman. Despite needing grooming months ago, the horse was striking. In general, he was a handsome chestnut color but his mane and tail were a lush black. A feather of black hair long enough to curl cascaded in a ribbon down the back of his legs, puffed at the fetlocks and shagged over the top of his hooves. When he moved, hair flowed around him dramatically, or would if he was groomed. Wolfe wondered if the animal could even see through the tangled mess that was his forelock, and he was pretty sure the stallion's mane would whip a rider's face raw at the gallop.

As he led the big horse out of his stall, Leonard warned him repeatedly to be careful. "He ain't been rode since last summer. I don't usually handle him at all. He ain't mean but he do hae spirit, if you know the difference." Wolfe did know the difference and Leonard was right. When Wolfe put a halter on the brute, it was obvious that he hadn't spent time around men recently. He was skittish, distrustful, and ready to explode with pent-up energy. That made him aggressive but he wasn't overly obnoxious. Wolfe had certainly seen and dealt with worse. At sixteen hands, the stallion was just more horse than a beat-up old groomsman wanted to deal with.

"What do you call him?" Wolfe said.

"Gus," said Leonard. Wolfe was unsure if he'd heard right.

"Gus?"

"The official name is some Don gibberish," the old Scotsman explained. "His sire was Augustus. He's plain old Gus."

Gus tested Wolfe at once, but Wolfe refused to be bullied. Calmly and confidently, he worked the horse around the paddock on a lead, talking to him and establishing dominance by position and demeanor. Gradually shortening the lead, he was eventually able to stroke the stallion's muzzle and feed him an apple.

Looking on from the paddock fence, Leonard said, "He look right handsome when he groomed."

Wolfe wanted to see it for himself. He tied Gus to the fence and brushed him until he shone. And the legs beneath the curls of hair were strong and long, and the withers and quarters were powerful and athletic in proportion to a deep chest.

Gus was a rare great beastie indeed.

After a few tantrums, Gus became playful. He liked being groomed and was unabashed by the terrible knots in his mane and tail that Wolfe tried to brush out, until he bid Leonard fetch his shears. The old man brought them quickly, embarrassed by Gus' appearance. He blamed it on absent slaves, advancing age and Gus' own cussed streak.

When Wolfe finished grooming Gus, the tail and mane were thinner and shorter. The beehive-sized puffs of hair around the fetlocks were reduced to bracelets. "He don't look like a hauler nae more," Leonard laughed. Indeed Gus did not. He looked like a warhorse to carry a knight into battle as at least one of his ancestors had been bred to do.

When Wolfe turned Gus out to play with his stable mates, he parked himself next to Leonard on a fence rail to admire the stallion. As if to mock him, Gus bobbed and weaved around his stodgy draft-horse pals trying to get them to play. Gus was a more showy horse than Wolfe would ever seek out, but then he wasn't seeking out anything but his father.

The next day, after working in the paddock with Gus for hours and tiring him out, Wolfe put a bridle on him. The stallion reacted to that well enough. He hopped around a little when Wolfe flapped a blanket on and off his back, but he stayed calm enough for Wolfe to saddle him without undue trouble.

Gus balked at the bit—snapped a few times—but Wolfe had ridden many well-trained horses that behaved worse. Eventually he was able to balance one foot in the stirrup and put his weight on and off a few times without Gus getting too mad. When he sensed it was time, Wolfe hauled into the saddle and waited to see what happened.

Leonard's stated expectation, that Gus would break Wolfe's neck, did not take into account Wolfe's skill as a horseman. Gus bucked and hopped to dislodge Wolfe but the big stallion's heart wasn't in it. Soon enough he sought expression in stubborn defiance, but that quickly grew tiresome as well. By the time Wolfe dismounted, took the saddle off, brushed Gus down and turned him out, they'd come to an accommodation. By then Leonard had formed an abiding respect for Wolfe's horsemanship.

Three days later, Wolfe had a horse crush of the first order on Gus. He'd never known an animal so eager to learn and anxious to please. It was as if Gus had been waiting for Wolfe to come along. Much the same as it had been with Gascon, once upon a time.

Thinking of Gascon made Wolfe feel guilty about Gus, like he was cheating on Gascon. In truth it wasn't far from that. But having Gus in his life right now was a joyous thing.

There was still no word from Church a week later, and Wolfe began to consider alternate plans(as hard as it would be to leave Gus. In the afternoon of the seventh day, an overcast, blowy day, a courier clattered into the dooryard of Brattle House and delivered a letter to Wolfe. The cover was brief. *Good luck. Church.*

Wolfe found Leonard in his apartment over the stable, a cramped space that looked as if the old Scot had lived there forever. "Do you think General Brattle would sell Gus?" Wolfe said. Leonard's eyebrows raised archly.

"The Gen'ral gave everything to his son when he removed to Boston. Gus belong to Major Brattle now."

"Do you think the Major will sell?" said Wolfe. Leonard scrunched up his face.

"The Major be in England wi' more on his mind than a horse. I hae' nae doubt but that hard money to the Major's Man will see Gus sold."

"I would you tell the Major's Man I wish to buy Gus," Wolfe said. "And that you think he should sell."

"Oh I do, do I?" Leonard said. Wolfe thought the Scotsman was fishing for a bribe.

"Or say nothing to no one and name a price. Think on it. First thing they snap up in a war is horses. Especially a brute like Gus. You'll lose him to one side or the other and sooner than later." Leonard didn't dispute it. "Meanwhile," said Wolfe, "I should like to hire him to go to Worcester." They settled on three shillings, horse and tack, a pittance compared to what Church charged.

At midnight, the stillness around the house was disturbed by the approach of horsemen. Being completely unexpected, the clatter of many hooves in the dooryard was menacing. Wolfe joined Cuthbert assessing the visitors discreetly from behind a curtain.

The horsemen wore dark cloaks, scarves, and cocked hats broad enough to shadow their faces. One man stayed with the horses, three came up the steps. One knocked.

"Do you know them?" Wolfe said. Cuthbert shook his head.

"Who knocks?" he said through the door.

"His Excellency the Governor of Massachusetts. Open up in the name of the King."

They were British soldiers. Not exactly hiding the fact but definitely not advertising it. When they were inside, the Captain said, "You're Cuthbert?" At Cuthbert's nod he said, "Find us a couple of bottles for the ride back if you please." Cuthbert was happy to disappear.

"And you must be Wolfe," said the Captain. "I have orders from General Gage to bring you to Boston."

"And if I choose not to go?" Wolfe said. The Captain shrugged.

"My orders are to bring you to Boston." Wolfe sighed loudly and petulantly in disbelief. The captain grinned. "Just so. If you'd be so good as to collect your things, we'll be off. As soon as Cuthbert returns that is. Cuthbert!"

Cuthbert turned up with two bottles that he handed over. Shortly after, Wolfe rode into the night on a horse brought for the purpose by the Redcoats.

45

After brashly thundering over the Charles River bridge, it was seven miles to Boston. They rode through villages and hamlets shrouded in a cold mist occasionally pierced by the glow of a candle through a window. With each step closer to the big town, the air grew rank and damp with the smell of wetlands, sewage, and rotting tidal refuse.

It was low tide when they reached Boston Neck. The exposed mud on either side reeked. On a road well paved with tight gravel, they trotted past two log redoubts—to be manned in case of a landward attack on the town—and approached the fort.

Spanning the entire width of the narrow and barren isthmus, the curtain wall of the fort was a ten-foot height of earth-and-stone-packed logs with cutouts and angles for cannon. Loaded canister, the big guns could sweep the neck like a donderbus. Along the base of the curtain wall was a wide moat that filled with sea water twice daily. By the light of torches, gallows threw grim shadows outside the east wall.

The captain leading Wolfe's party opened his cloak so guards on the wall could see his regimentals. They opened the smaller of two gates blocking the road and the riders ducked through.

The inside of the fortification was function itself: barracks, powder bunker, latrine, a small stable for horses, and a shed for vehicles. Wolfe's party rode through the fort and right out the back to cross a narrow causeway connecting the neck to Boston Town.

Passing through another gate on the town side of the causeway, they rode up Orange Street and made their way to British Headquarters. At Province House, Wolfe was handed over to one of General Gage's aides and ordered to wait in the anteroom of the General's office. Wolfe didn't know if the Grenadier on guard was for Gage's office or for him.

It took an hour for Gage to show up but he wasted no time when he did. "Come," he said to Wolfe as he walked through. "You too," he said to the Grenadier. Inside he ordered the Grenadier, "Search him." The Redcoat found the pardon and the letter from Church in Wolfe's coat. Upon turning them over to Gage, he was dismissed and the General turned his attention to Wolfe.

"Is that you under all that hair, Mister Wolfe?"

"Aye, sir. It's me," Wolfe said, unconsciously combing his beard with his fingers.

"You've been a busy fellow since last we met."

"You have no idea," said Wolfe.

"Actually, I do." Gage held up Wolfe's documents. He barely glanced at the pass and the letter, but the pardon interested him. He untied the ferret and examined it, musing, "The power of life and death scratched out in a few lines of ink. A rather wondrous thing a pardon, wouldn't you agree?" Wolfe smiled wryly.

"Once upon a time I would have. I have since discovered that a pardon is no more wondrous than any other commodity one purchases. Except, if my own experience be a guide, more subject to abuse by unscrupulous sellers. Sir, how did you know where to find me?"

"I'll keep my confidential channels confidential, if it's all the same." Gage rolled up the pardon and retied the ferret. When he was done he looked at Wolfe squarely. "Your King has need of you, Mister Wolfe." Wolfe let out a long sigh.

"Me, sir?"

"I need send a scout to Worcester and you're just the man to guide them. Having been there recently, I mean. And in possession of this." Gage held up Church's pass. "A pass from the Faction's Committee of Safety might prove useful on a scout. Don't you agree?" Wolfe wondered how Gage knew perfectly what papers were to be found on his person.

Wolfe said, "You were right not to send troops to Worcester last fall, General. Five thousand men were waiting for you and they're not all rabble as you suppose."

"I'll have that judgment from professionals, if you don't mind."

"What do you offer as enticement?" said Wolfe. Gage frowned.

"In addition to the honor of serving your King?"

"Yes. In addition to that."

"I'll pay you twenty dollars as I pay my best guides."

"My life is worth more to me than twenty dollars," Wolfe said. Gage nodded.

"All right, then. If you help me, I'll return this pardon to you." He held it up, lest there be any question which pardon he meant. Wolfe was going to Worcester in any event.

"I need remain free to look for my father."

"I have no objection. What else?"

"Are you acquainted with Major Brattle? I want to buy a horse from him."

"I'll press the damn beast and give it to you," Gage said impatiently.

"I'm willing to pay," Wolfe said. "But however you manage it, Gus is my price. In writing. I shan't go to Worcester until, for fear of losing him." Gage shook his head.

"Does for King and country mean naught these days?"

Wolfe didn't laugh but he wanted to. "With all respect, sir. You're asking me to risk my life on an unnecessary scout. You can't march on Worcester. It's too far, the provincials are too many, and they're too eager to have it on."

"If I get you the horse, will you go?" Gage said.

Wolfe sighed deeply.

Gage smiled.

46

It took two days for Gage to produce a signed, stamped and sealed document transferring ownership of Gus. And then he locked it in his desk along with the pardon. Gus wouldn't cost Wolfe a penny, but there was a price to be paid.

The soldiers Wolfe was to accompany to Worcester were brought in the same day. Henry De Berniere, 10th Regiment of Foot, was an ensign barely in his twenties, but already a mapmaker of some note in the army. Henry was a fine-boned, handsome young man with alert dark eyes and a white wig clubbed to regulation. He came off as more thoughtful than the usual young British officer.

The other officer was Captain William Brown of the 52nd Regiment of Foot.

Wolfe's first inclination was to give up the pardon rather than share a road with Brown, but he held his tongue. Brown held his too. They greeted each other as strangers.

The meeting commenced with Gage explaining to his scouts that Wolfe, having recently been in Worcester, would act as guide and counsel on their expedition. He told the officers that Wolfe had private business in Worcester but would show them the road and help negotiate the more confusing local customs. But, Gage told them, Wolfe would not be bound by the officer's decisions and he would not act as a spy, stipulations Wolfe insisted on.

Confident in his own abilities, Brown suggested dismissing Wolfe entirely, which was fine with Wolfe, but Gage wouldn't have it. He made it clear that Wolfe was going and Brown had better listen to him.

"What will your story be?" Wolfe asked the officers.

"Our story?" said Brown.

"What are you to give out as the reason you're abroad on the road? You'll be asked by everyone you meet."

"I'll tell them to tend their own damn business," Brown growled.

"Which you'd soon regret, I assure you." Wolfe said. Brown would have answered tartly but Gage cut him off.

"If you aren't up to it Captain, I'll find someone else."

Brown hastily assured the general that he was his man.

In spite of Wolfe's discouragement, the officers decided that they would pose as surveyors taking notes on the roads. Wolfe would be what he was, a man who knew the way.

After the officers left, Wolfe told Gage that he thought Brown an unlikely man to lead such a mission. The General was annoyed that Wolfe questioned his judgment, but good breeding outweighed his pique. "Captain Brown has a mind for the military arts," the General said patiently. "At times he's positively scientific. Employs equations, if you can imagine it." Gage said the last as if the use of equations trumped any argument against Brown's fitness. The look on Wolfe's face said it did not. Gage sighed.

"I grant that Captain Brown is arrogant to his detriment, but poorly connected officers often are. As I'm sure you know, they must make their name to advance as the captain is determined to. The chip on his shoulder makes him hungry and dogged, qualities I need in a scout. Captain Brown wasn't selected at random or by favor, I assure you. Those officers are the envy of the army. 'Tis imagined there are laurels to be had, what with war coming."

"In the middle of a snowstorm," Wolfe said, "I watched Captain Brown bivouac his men in tents next to a barn offered for the very purpose." Wolfe's tone implied that the irrationality of such an act trumped any argument for Brown's military genius. Gage just laughed.

"That's the Prussian method. It works well enough for Frederick the Great."

Wolfe was unconvinced. "Brown's men had to find their tents the next morning after they blew away in the night, which they spent huddled in the barn. While Captain Brown slept comfortably in the house, I might add."

"Which is why I want you along," Gage said, ending the discussion.

Wolfe met with Brown and De Berniere briefly the next day to review the map they'd be working from. The officers had duty in the afternoon and the session was cut short. Everyone at headquarters had duty. A soldier caught trying to desert for the second time was to be flogged on Boston Common. Five hundred lashes. Liberty or death.

Of greater concern to headquarters was the mood of Bostonians. Congregationalists were offended by any whipping of more than thirty-nine lashes, the number prescribed by the Bible. Five hundred lashes was a death sentence sure to attract protests from the devout and opportunities for the mob.

Province House emptied from midmorning to late afternoon. A lieutenant on the skeleton staff invited Wolfe up to the cupola to watch the proceedings. Wolfe had no interest in observing a man's military penance, but not having had a chance to traverse Boston, an opportunity to acquaint himself with the layout of the town was appealing.

The cupola contained a fine telescope on a tripod that afforded a good view of the action on the common. The deserter was trussed to sheaved halberds as the cat was laid on, with most of the British garrison—more than two thousand men—drawn up on three sides to witness punishment. Being a cold day, many of the Redcoats were shivering, if it wasn't the horror of watching a man's back flayed off.

Ringing the drawn-up soldiers, knots of Bostonians gaped, prayed, and read from the Bible. Some men drank and were entertained. Dozens of boys scrambled from vantage point to vantage point seeking a better view. A number of bystanders joined together in psalmody, cued by bells all over Boston that tolled simultaneously for a minute in protest.

Scores of gawkers came to witness the spectacle despite the resentment of a Redcoat Light-Infantry company on perimeter duty, struggling to suppress the urge to crack civilian heads as one of their own was whipped to death.

Gage commuted the sentence at two hundred lashes. It was said the man might live. It was not unknown to survive two hundred.

The night after the whipping, General Gage was somber. He'd given his officers written orders. His final verbal orders were a reiteration. Sketch the roads, passes, bridges and places most likely for ambuscade. They were to note the farms where fodder and forage might be had, good encampments with access to water, and particularly, the location of rebel stores. Wolfe had nothing to contribute until Gage advised the officers to take the tenor of the country, then he spoke up.

"In Worcester they consider themselves at war with government," Wolfe said to Brown and De Berniere. "If you're identified as soldiers out of uniform, I believe they'll hang you for spies. That is the tenor of the country." He could tell by the look on the officers' faces that they thought him high strung, if not downright craven. Their thoughts were of naught but glory. The realization was a cold knot in Wolfe's stomach.

They set out from the North End of Boston the next morning and were nearly undone before they started. In a disheartening lapse of planning, Brown's company was guarding the ferry landing and their Captain was hard to miss.

Dressed in homespun as any country fellow might be, Brown carried himself unnaturally erect. Provincial clothes look glaringly false on him. Even the ubiquitous red neckerchief and flop hat worn by men in the country looked unnatural, and without a wig, his short hair was obvious. Like De Berniere he carried his necessaries in a bindle—a balled blanket tied to a slim tree branch such as many country folk used on the road—unfortunately Brown carried his bindle like a musket. The captain's appearance would have been in all ways laughable if Wolfe wasn't traveling with him.

A Redcoat on duty at the dock recognized his superior officer right off, and went over to one of his mates to laugh about it. Brown was oblivious. De Berniere caught on when Wolfe nodded at the conferring soldiers and then at Brown. Wolfe briefly considered that this was his chance to rid himself of the officers, but Gage had delivered Gus. Wolfe would not be the one to dishonor their agreement.

He approached the Redcoats on guard and in his haughtiest London voice, said quietly, "You have done your duty and observed what there is to observe. Now is the time for discretion and not putting your officer in danger. What do you think will happen if I tell him what it is you whisper about?" The threat troubled the guards, as it ought. "Eyes open and mouth shut," Wolfe said. With a nod he followed De Berniere and Brown onto the ferry.

The trip across the Charles River took no time. On the other side, Charlestown was a warren of houses and businesses crammed around the waterfront. Behind the town, acres of meadow and pasture stretched inland up a pair of hills.

At Cambridge, Wolfe told the officers he had business to attend and would leave them for a time. It was agreed they would rendezvous in Weston at the sign of the Golden Ball, a place Wolfe knew to stand with Government. As he set the officers on the Watertown Road, he said, "Don't stop in Watertown or Waltham and talk to as few people as possible. But don't be rude. Be men who need to get somewhere, but unremarkable men." The officers impatiently said that they'd see Wolfe in Weston.

Wolfe went and found Leonard when he got to Brattle's, told him he had paper for Gus. The old Scotsman didn't even blink. "Got a note saying Gus were sold and the owner would make arrangements," Leonard said. "Thought it might be you. How much?"

Wolfe shrugged. "I have to risk my life in His Majesty's service for a sennight. I need leave Gus here while I do, if you don't mind." Leonard didn't mind. "Will you see he eats well?" Wolfe said. Leonard said he'd see Gus well, as he had every night of Gus's life before Wolfe ever laid eyes on him!

Wolfe went to the house to take care of another piece of business. For days he'd wondered who disclosed his whereabouts to Gage and why. Cuthbert was the only person he'd come up with. He found the house steward sweeping out the fireplace. Cuthbert started to greet him warmly but perceived that something was wrong. Perhaps it was Wolfe's smile, a frozen canine grimace.

"Whom did you tell I was staying here?" Wolfe said curtly. He did not raise his voice but Cuthbert's expression morphed from warm greeting to dread.

"I told no one," the steward said. "We were sorry to see you leave. Ask my wife. We felt safe with you here." His words struck Wolfe as oddly honest and it shattered his conviction. Besides which, Cuthbert seemed genuinely glad to see him when he first came in.

"Perhaps the man who brought the letter told someone," Cuthbert said. Wolfe hadn't considered that. He always read his commissions, why wouldn't another courier? He cursed himself for an idiot and apologized.

"I imagine it's difficult to be abducted," Cuthbert said graciously. Unsure if he was being made jest of, Wolfe apologized again and took himself off to Weston.

47

In Watertown, the Pliney place was charred rubble.

Those bloody eyes, Wolfe thought. The unintended double entendre made him inwardly chuckle but the chuckle died in his throat. What kind of twisted murderer laughs at such things?

As he left Watertown and entered the precincts of Waltham, a mechanic wearing a gray wool coat over a leather apron caught his eye. The man was thoroughly engrossed with something in the window of Brewer's Tavern. As Wolfe approached, the man tore his attention away and lit out across the street, last to be seen disappearing down a path through the woods.

Wolfe made a point of looking in the window. To his horror, Brown and De Berniere were the only people in the place, dining in style. They never so much as glanced over when Wolfe went in. The bloody fools weren't paying the least bit of attention to their surroundings.

A negro wench manned the tap. Wolfe talked her up for a few minutes using his American accent, rather good now he fancied. Mary was a cute thing, brown as nutmeg, early twenties, a twinkle in her eye.

When he and she were friends and he had a New England in hand, the rum and molasses staple of the working man in the country, Wolfe said, "Who are they?" meaning the Officers.

In a whisper that brought her close, Mary said, "They say they's surveyors but they Redcoats sure." She smelled of wood fire. Her skin was smooth as velvet. "The tall one's a Officer," she said. "He threatened me an' my friends in Boston once. I'll never forget his face."

"What's he doing here?" said Wolfe.

"Scouting the country, I 'spect." She drew in again. "The younger one were drawing on a map. He kinda pretty but if he go up the country he shan't remain so. I gave the alarm."

"Smart girl," said Wolfe. "Won't be long 'til they're swinging from a rope."

Mary blanched. "You think they'll hang?"

"Don't you?" said Wolfe. Misgiving clouded the girl's eyes and she gazed over at Brown and De Berniere. When she looked back, she bent across the counter to give Wolfe a good look down the scoop of her loose blouse, a well-practiced exercise but no less charming.

"A certain body who ain't me could tell the pretty one not to go up the country," she said. Wolfe could have kissed her, but not for the splendid view.

"The Bible says we are our brothers' keepers," Wolfe said. "I suppose it shall have to be me." With a heavy sigh, he got up and walked over to the Officers' table.

"You are discovered," he quietly. "Pay the bill and leave. I'll be outside." Without waiting for a response, he went back to his seat.

Brown called loudly for the bill. When Mary ran to settle with him, Wolfe left a few coins and departed. He was leaning on a corner of the building when the officers came out. Brown was irate but Wolfe spoke first. "They know what you're about!" Brown started to argue but Wolfe talked over him. Chided him. "You had maps out in front of her. Bloody hell! Even if you were surveyors she'd think you spies. You need get to Boston before you're taken up."

"If we march out this way, I'll kill that bitch," Brown said.

A rider came in view down the road and Wolfe pulled the Officers around the side of the building. "You'll find the road to Boston neck at the bridge you passed in Watertown. You can make the fort before dark if you hurry."

"I'm not going back," Brown said firmly. De Berniere agreed.

"We'd be the laughingstock of the army. I'd rather hang."

"That's a distinct possibility," Wolfe said. "I saw a man running to raise alarm."

"You can turn back," said Brown. "Whatever comes, I'll say you warned us. You're a civilian after all."

"I'll do the same," said De Berniere. "You've made us aware of the danger."

"I'm going to Worcester with or without you," Wolfe said. "I always was."

The officers were just as resolute on going with or without him.

Against Wolfe's better judgment, they set off in company for Weston. It wasn't long though, before Brown bade De Berniere stop and make some sketches. In exasperation, Wolfe left them behind. They were still lingering in the road when he walked back fifteen minutes later.

"Are you mad?" Wolfe said to Brown. "In all probability there are men tracking us this very instant."

"Mapping is the only damn reason we're out here," Brown said. Wolfe stared at the ground and swallowed fifty wisecracks.

Eventually, calmly, he said, "Here's a thought. When you want something mapped, one of us goes out front, the other lags behind and we keep lookout while the ensign draws. If someone comes we alert him. So he doesn't look like a bloody spy when they meet."

"That's why the pretense of surveyors!" Brown said hotly. "A surveyor would be drawing!"

"And people would assume he was a spy, not a surveyor," Wolfe said. Brown's eyes widened in understanding.

"Ohhh. I see what you mean. By pretending to be surveyors, we'll be suspected of being spies pretending to be surveyors." De Berniere grinned. Wolfe shook his head in disbelief.

"When a provincial comes along and sees the ensign sketching," he said to Brown, "he doesn't think, oh there's a surveyor, or there's a spy pretending to be a surveyor. What he thinks is, here's a stranger making a map of the country. I'd better tell someone."

Wolfe was never sure if Brown took his meaning but the captain agreed to his suggestion. From then on, when he wanted De Berniere to draw something, he and Wolfe took station ahead and behind. When someone came in sight, they signaled and the ensign hid his incriminating tools.

Late in the day they were overtaken by two men leading a team of oxen.

De Berniere hissed at Wolfe that the man keeping the drover company was a Redcoat deserter. Wolfe told the ensign to lag back with Brown and say nothing.

In the way of the country, the strangers fell in step with Wolfe's party. When the officers lagged back, it was Wolfe the locals peppered with questions. Going to Worcester? Them too. Share the road?

"Course," said Wolfe. "But I'm stopping at the next tavern I come to."

"That's the Golden Ball," the drover said. "You can't stop there. That's a Tory house."

Which Wolfe knew, but he said, "I don't care if 'tis Buckingham Palace. Long as I can have a wet and don't have to wipe my arse with the bark of a tree, I'm stopping." The explanation seemed to satisfy the men and before long, Wolfe realized that they assumed that Brown and De Berniere were British deserters. He encouraged the misconception. In the course of things, it was made known to him that "men seeking work" would be better off at a tavern down the road from the Golden Ball, a good Whig house where men might find the work they sought.

Outside the Golden Ball, when the drovers had disappeared in the gathering dusk, Wolfe told De Berniere and Brown what he'd learned. He suggested that the officers would be better off posing as deserters, that being the only acceptable explanation for British soldiers disguised in the countryside.

"I will not stain my honor pretending to be a deserter," Brown said unequivocally. De Berniere was just as adamant.

"Well at least remember that you are men seeking work," Wolfe said. "That is the signal for deserters requesting succor. It could save your lives."

48

They entered the Golden Ball together and for a time were the only customers. Jones, the proprietor, poked up the fire and bade them sit. By offering coffee and tea he made it known that he was a King's man. It was also clear, to Wolfe, at least, that Jones knew precisely who his guests were. Without prompting, Jones told them to be careful what they said and to whom they said it. He also let it be known that they would find few Tory havens on the road to Worcester.

"And if Gage expects friends of Government in the country to rise up," Jones said, "he damn well better bring firelocks when he marches out. Most of those loyal to the King have surrendered their arms as the price to stay in their home." When Wolfe wondered how Jones was able to defy the Faction and survive, the tavern keeper laughed sardonically. "I have five grown sons. Anyone do for me, my boys'll come for them and they know it."

After a worthy dinner featuring mutton, and the entertaining company of Jones, who was a hostler in the finest tradition, the scouts shared a room for the night. The officers shared the bed. Wolfe slept on the floor rolled up in blankets.

It was alternating rain and sleet the next day. Following instructions from Jones, the scout left the Post Road for the Framingham Road. They passed through country dotted with ponds, swamp, and stubble fields broken up by stands of bramble wood and trees, all of it wet.

There was tillage land toward Framingham, and more ponds and small rivers with versions of the weirs in Watertown, which made Wolfe think that they were still catching alewife and shad this far inland. But it was a miserable trek and they met no one else foolish enough to be traveling on such a day.

At Buckminster's Tavern on the Framingham green—recommended by Jones—they dried out in front of the fire. They were not offered tea, but Buckminster, a hard-looking fellow, let it be known that he didn't care what political sentiments they held. "But if you're a Tory, prob'ly best to keep your mouth shut." To make his point, he held up a fist as big as a child's head, connected to an arm that belonged on a blacksmith.

When Buckminster stepped away, Wolfe said, "He almost makes it feel like home." Brown laughed. De Berniere even managed a smile. He was all in from the walk and the weather, his youth was as nothing.

"Tell me, Captain Brown," Wolfe said. "Have you seen our friends the Lorings?"

"I have not," said Brown. "When I saw them last, however, I saw them well." De Berniere was nonplussed.

"You two are acquainted?"

"We are," said Brown.

"Which brings to mind," said Wolfe. "Did you ever stand your men drinks with the purse you owed me?"

"You left me little choice," Brown said sourly. Wolfe smiled.

"That was my intent."

That night Wolfe unloaded and reloaded his pocket pistols before retiring. He suggested the officers do the same. De Berniere took the advice and reloaded the pistol he had tucked into the belt under his shirt. Brown scowled and said, "I'll resign the army the day I take advice on weapons from a provincial civilian."

The next morning was clear and bright after the previous day's storm. The country being somewhat flat and open, there wasn't much mapping to be done and they made good time, although they got lost in Southborough. They asked a hog reeve for directions. From atop a three-rail fence where he was keeping an eye on thirty or forty pigs, he said to backtrack to a lesser road, which was the road they wanted, and take it.

They rejoined the Post Road in Shrewsbury, some four miles from Worcester. There they stopped for De Berniere to sketch a pass through the hills that Wolfe remembered well. The first time he'd walked it, he thought it prime for ambuscade. In the company of Redcoats, he thought it prime for massacre.

As De Berniere drew, Wolfe asked Brown, "Do you really need sketch it?" They were standing together at the apex of the pass, able to see quite a distance in both directions. "Don't you already know that marching out here would be a dreadful mistake?"

"Only if the objective isn't dear enough," Brown said firmly. "Might be we could finish them at one stroke."

"Or they you," Wolfe said.

"I'll take any wager you wish to make that if it comes to blows, the provincial rabble will run for the hills." Brown was as sure as Tim Bigelow.

One of them is wrong, Wolfe thought.

On the other side of the pass, rolling hills of trees barely noticed where a farm had been carved out here and there. A steeple way far off glowed in the late-February sun. The smell of wood fire wafted now and again on the breeze. It was hard to imagine rebellion festering in such an Eden.

In Worcester, nearing sunset on Saturday, the beginning of the Sabbath, the main street was all but deserted. The scouts found the tavern that Jones in Weston recommended, another sign of the Golden Ball, run by another man named Jones.

Before they went inside, De Berniere and Brown stopped to gape at three, four-pounder cannon parked on the nearby green. A platoon of militia was on guard, building up fires for their evening watch.

Brown pointed out the powder horns slung off the barrels of their sheaved muskets. "We'll outshoot them two volleys in a minute and it won't matter how many they are," he declared.

Despite an empty tavern, Isaac Jones was not happy to welcome them— and him a supposed Tory. Wolfe could only surmise that he recognized the officers for who they were and was nervous to host them. Not the best of portents, but with sundown fast approaching, Wolfe didn't have time to worry about it.

Hector was locking up Tim's smithy when Wolfe got there. The slave directed him to Tim's house, just above the Courthouse.

Tim answered Wolfe's knock and called to an unseen child within, "Tell Mother I'll return in time for first prayer." Slipping outside, Tim led Wolfe behind a bush that screened them from the house and the road. A worn patch said it wasn't the first time he'd held a meeting there.

"Can't be seen palaverin' on the Sabbath," Tim said. "And my wife will throw a fit if I ask you in. Din't find your da, did you?" Wolfe shook his head and told him what Buttrick said in Concord. "Sounds 'bout right," Tim said. "I must return to my hearth but I'll talk to some men at meeting tomorrow. Be at my forge when the sun's a hour high Monday."

The Officers were in their room at the tavern when Wolfe got back, poring over sketches and notes. After letting him in, Brown returned to a partially drawn map opened up on the bed. "We're organizing to survey the town tomorrow," he said.

"I suppose you could try," said Wolfe, "but tomorrow is Sunday. The men whose job it is to see that the Sabbath is kept, patrol . . . religiously." He was unable to suppress the pun. It flew by Brown but De Berniere snickered. Wolfe said, "If you're abroad in town before sunset tomorrow, you'll be stopped and questioned." For once Brown didn't challenge him. Wolfe retired to his own room shortly after.

In the morning, Jones said that they might have anything they wanted for breakfast including tea, so whatever troubled him seemed to have subsided. This Isaac Jones was a pale imitation of his blood cousin of the same name in Weston, but an imitation nonetheless. He lived scared was the difference.

Not enough sons, Wolfe supposed.

Jones told the officers that he knew who they were and that they could rest easy at his place. The officers vehemently denied that they were anything but surveyors taking a preliminary view of the roads. Jones paid them the respect of not laughing in their faces.

Just after sunset, the Redcoats headed out to scout the town, briefed on the highways and byways by Jones. He played along with the farce that they were surveyors working in the dark.

They returned hours later, clomping up the stairs like a yoke of oxen. When Jones knocked on Brown's door ten minutes later, Wolfe got up and cracked his door to hear what he could.

Jones said that two men followed the officers down from the courthouse and wished to have a word. When Brown declined, Jones said, "You have nothing to fear. I know these men to be ardent friends of Government." Brown refused and sent the tavernkeeper away.

Wolfe shut his door quietly and wondered if he was missing something. Why would Brown not want to meet with men that Jones vouched for? Men with local intelligence. It was sure that Jones knew Brown was a British officer. For all Brown knew, the men may have come with a warning. Wolfe slept lightly that night with his boots on.

Tim was bellowing up his forge when Wolfe arrived an hour after sunrise on Monday. To Wolfe's surprise, he was greeted brusquely.

"Where are you staying?" Tim said curtly.

"The Golden Ball," said Wolfe.

"I hear there's a couple other men there," Tim said. Wolfe hoped his grin wasn't as nervous as it felt.

"You speak of the British soldiers?" he said. Tim nodded, perhaps a little surprised that Wolfe came right out with it. "I walked some miles in company with them," Wolfe said. "They claim to be surveyors."

"They'll soon find out we're not so stupid as they think," Tim snorted.

"But why not let them think you stupid?"

"Let them think us stupid?" Tim didn't understand what Wolfe was getting at.

"Let them report the roads passable and a battery of canon guarded by farmers. That should prompt Gage to act." Wolfe hoped he sounded more convincing than he felt. Tim looked at him in disbelief.

"You're sincere?"

"If you want Gage to march out I am. He won't without intelligence."

"And how do you know that?" Tim said. Wolfe laughed as if it were obvious.

"Because he hasn't and here are two soldiers probably on a scout." Tim grudgingly saw the logic.

"Don't seem right to just let 'em go, but."

"Do as you will," said Wolfe. "What news of my father?" He wasn't surprised or disappointed when Tim shook his head.

"No one has heard of him."

"Thanks for asking," Wolfe said. Tim nodded.

"What will you do now?"

"I'm going back to Cambridge and buy a horse. I'm tired of traveling shank's mare."

"Where should I send word?"

"Brattle's," Wolfe said. Tim's eyes narrowed and Wolfe shrugged. "'T'was Church's idea." The look on Tim's face said he didn't think it was a good one.

"Have a care for the company you keep, Joethan."

49

The route back to Boston on the Post Road was through Marlborough. At the split where the Post Road continued east to Marlborough, and the Framingham Road dipped to the south, Brown—watching out behind—whistled someone's approach. De Berniere had his things put away and was walking on by the time a cloaked rider in a cocked hat came in view.

The horseman drew up to De Berniere and walked alongside for many long seconds before urging his mount to a trot and riding on.

Out in front, Wolfe kept walking but the hand in his pocket eased the throat-hole safety off a pistol.

As the horse fell in step with Wolfe, Tim Bigelow said, "Now I know what they mean by country clowns." Wolfe chuckled and reset the safety on his pistol.

"What brings you out?" Wolfe said. Tim looked down at him as if he'd just heard the stupidest question in the world. "Are you going to take them?" Wolfe said. Tim looked frustrated.

"I should have to take you with and I'd hate to see you hang before finding your da."

"As would I," Wolfe said.

"I'm taking the Marlborough Road, Joethan. If they take it, I suggest you do not." Tim spurred his horse and rode off. When he was out of sight, the officers sprinted up.

"Who was he?" Brown said.

"A provincial scout looking for us," Wolfe said. "As he took the Marlborough road, I shall return through Framingham."

De Berniere looked to Brown.

"We'll take the Framingham Road too," Brown said.

Militia was training on Framingham green when they arrived at Buckminster's. They took a table at a window with a view of the drill, and Wolfe insisted that the officers forgo their usual Holland gin and join him in ordering a New England. They complied reluctantly, considering the drink swill, but they complied. He also insisted that they eat whatever was in the pot as any country fellow might.

Tim had made Wolfe nervous.

They watched the militia for almost an hour. At the end of the drill, the militia marched over and formed up directly in front of the tavern as if to put on a show for patrons—or arrest a party of spies. For a time the officers thought themselves discovered and nervously discussed what to do.

The Militia Captain began loudly addressing his men. He spoke of bravery being no more than patience and coolness under fire, which Wolfe thought eloquent. He told his men that they would always conquer if they didn't break, which was also true, if not obvious. And he spoke at length of the great victory over the French at Louisburg in the last war, and how the British would not have taken the fortress but for Americans. It was a good harangue and after a general huzzay, the troop dismissed—fully half of whom retired to the tavern.

De Berniere and Brown were disquieted all over again. After observing the militia lay into their spirits, Wolfe thought they needn't worry. "If we to bed before they grow bored, they'll pay us no mind."

And so it happened.

The next day was mild but to Wolfe's relief they met no one on the road carefree enough to do more than exchange pleasantries.

At the Golden Ball in Weston, Jones gave them a warm homecoming, saying, "I half expected you'd be taken up and hung." To which Brown questioned why surveyors abroad in the country were liable to be hung. Jones made a placating remark and moved on to other subjects.

After they'd supped, the officers questioned Jones about the Post Road to Marlborough. Two of Jones's sons and their wives were present, all of whom implored Brown not to go back into the country. They said there were reports of British spies on the road and innocent surveyors could easily be mistaken for British spies. Brown thanked them for their concern but said that he and his colleague had taken on a job and would see it through.

When Wolfe retired, the Officers were in the room whispering.

"Would you prefer I leave?" Wolfe said.

"We have a proposition," Brown said. "We mean to explore the Post Road west to Marlborough. I wish to send our notes to Boston in case we're taken up."

"What if I'm taken?" Wolfe said. De Berniere frowned.

"You would be as guilty as if they found the documents on me and we were taken together." Wolfe stared at the ensign in surprise and grinned.

"You're right, of course. Except if the documents were on you and we were taken, I'd say I was merely sharing the road."

"And I'd say you were lying," Brown said.

"No doubt," said Wolfe. "All right. I'll do as you ask." Brown smiled as if he'd won something.

"I'll write you a pass to clear the fort on the neck," he said. Wolfe caught himself rolling his eyes.

"That won't be necessary." The last thing Wolfe wanted on his person, in addition to maps and sketches, was a pass confirming that he carried them for Government. If Brown wasn't trying to get Wolfe hung, then he was merely an imbecile. Either way, the sooner Wolfe was away from Captain Brown, the happier he'd be. But he still felt an obligation to the agreement he had with Gage.

"I ask one thing," Wolfe said. "I would have a chit that says I urged you not to go to Marlborough." Brown laughed.

"We are soldiers, Mister Wolfe. We don't run from danger."

"As you will," Wolfe shrugged. "But I would have a note that I counseled against it. I don't want General Gage to think I was complicit in your decision."

"Yes, yes," Brown said impatiently." "I'll absolve you of responsibility. You may rest your head tonight with a clear conscious."

The morning promised snow and the Officers decided a large breakfast would fortify. Wolfe wanted to beat the weather to Boston. Jones used a piece of charred wood from the fireplace to draw a map on the hearth and point out a road that would allow Wolfe to avoid Watertown center.

In wind-driven sleet like needles of ice, Wolfe found Jones's road and crossed the bridge over the Charles River.

A mile on, going up a long grade, he overtook two raggedy youngsters trying to keep up with their mother. She was twenty yards ahead, doggedly pushing a heavy barrow made more difficult by the wheel which was disintegrating around the axle. The woman's red cape was little more than a tattered rag. Her leather shoes were falling apart. By her fixed stare and the way she put one foot in front of the other, Wolfe could see that she was on her last oats.

"Let me help!" he yelled, coming up on her. She shied away almost upsetting the barrow. "Let me push it for you!" Wolfe yelled over the escalating storm. The woman looked at him with bitter, haunted eyes, as if one more terrible thing was about to happen. Wolfe made as if pushing the barrow but she didn't react. Gently he undid her death grip on the barrow handles and took her place. Leaning in to her, he said, "Let's find a fire." The woman just stood there. Wolfe waved the kids over and told them to bring their mum.

The kids grasped their mother's hands and all but dragged her up the road following Wolfe. After trudging for a mile, he saw a candle in the window of a house set back from the road.

Gratefully he parked the barrow under an open shed on the side of the house and rotated his arms to work the burn out of his shoulders. His muscles were screaming. He couldn't imagine the amount of torment the woman had endured.

He opened the door of the tavern for the woman and children but she wouldn't go in.

"Close the damn door!" a voice yelled from inside. Wolfe shut the door.

"'Tis warm inside," he said to the raggedy woman.

"They'll throw us out," she croaked.

"The hell they will. Come." But the woman wouldn't move. Wolfe wondered if she was mad. "At least let me take the children in. They look half dead."

"I haven't money," the woman croaked. "I don't want trouble. The Lord will see to us."

Wolfe didn't say what he thought about that; instead he opened the door and guided the woman forcibly inside by the elbow. The children followed, stood and dripped by the door, until Wolfe nudged them toward the fire. That was all the encouragement they needed.

A big woman in a dirty white cap, faded Caraco jacket and brown skirt hustled to intercept them.

"I told you," the ragged woman croaked at Wolfe.

"My friends and I require food," Wolfe said loudly. The big woman changed direction and came directly for him. She was intimidating. Her shoulders were almost as broad as his.

"Let's see the color of your money," she said, with a guttural twang. Wolfe handed her a shilling that she bit with blackened teeth. Satisfied the coin was good, her eyes narrowed.

"Them's roamin' poor. They'll eat my larder empty and the little ones got the itch most like. I'll have to clean up good after the bastards."

"They do not have the itch!" the ragged woman croaked fiercely. "And orphans are not bastards." Wolfe held up another sixpence.

"No more blatherskite or I take my coins up the road." The suddenly contrite woman introduced herself as Mrs. Lowry. She bade her guests make comfortable.

Mrs. Lowry's place was not a proper tavern. It was a home willing to serve a meal and pour a dram, or put a stranger up for a night or two. There was no proper tap room or dining area but the house was warm, and the smells emanating from the fireplace were alluring. The woman and her children huddled as close as they could to the flames without getting in Mrs. Lowry's way.

The family was a pitiful sight. Providing them with a roof, fire, and a meal, was the least Wolfe could do. He sat quietly in the corner watching them reclaim a semblance of humanity as they ate shad, potatoes, and barley soup.

The children touched him deeply. As difficult as their own circumstance was, their energy was focused on trying to coax their mother back from the mental precipice she clearly teetered on.

The warm ambiance disintegrated when the door was thrown open and two men with muskets stepped inside. Backlit by flying snow, they looked like faceless villains in a shadow play. The family reacted as if they were. The little girl shrieked. Her mother started shaking uncontrollably.

Mrs. Lowry intercepted the men before they got far into the room. "How's 'bout something to take away the chill boys?"

"There's the bitch!" One of the men pushed Mrs. Lowry out of the way and made a beeline for the family. The young boy stepped in the way to protect his mother but was roughly knocked to the floor—by Cocked Hat, the Tory-chaser Wolfe almost tangled with on the Watertown road.

In outrage and with a terrible anger, Wolfe rose up out of the shadows and delivered a blow with his staff that Cocked Hat never saw coming. The road agent was unconscious before he crashed sideways over a chair and hit the ground like a rock.

And Wolfe was already going for his partner.

Harelip fumbled his musket up, cocked the dog leg and pulled the trigger but the flint didn't even spark. Wolfe speared him end-on in the stomach with his staff and doubled Harelip over, then he struck him across the back of the head, driving him to his knees. Dropping his musket Harelip raised an arm to ward off another blow or surrender.

"Please, Mister ... I'm sorry ... please ..."

Not wanting the children to see him deal with the scoundrel, Wolfe grabbed Harelip by the collar and dragged him outside. As the snow whipped around them, Wolfe hauled the cowering thug to his feet and shoved him toward the road. "Run before I change my mind," he snarled. "If I see you again, I'll kill you." For encouragement he laid a wicked shot across Harelip's back with his stick, staggering the bully forward, then a whipping blow across the calves. Howling in pain, Harelip awkwardly stumbled off into the pelting snow.

Inside the tavern, Cocked Hat was conscious but groggy. Wolfe sat him against a post and lashed his arms behind it with a rope that Mrs. Lowry provided. "I don't know what to do with him," Wolfe said.

"I've dealt with a might worse," Mrs. Lowry said. "Leave him to me." She was bigger than Cocked Hat and looked at least as tough. Wolfe let it be.

The ragged woman had summoned survival strength and was doing her best to get the children organized to flee. "Finish eating and rest," Wolfe said gently. "When the weather lets up I'll see you safe to Boston." The woman looked over at Cocked Hat tied to the post and nodded. Suddenly overcome, she would have collapsed if Wolfe didn't catch her and ease her into a chair. There she sat mute and immovable, a picture of complete and utter exhaustion.

Hours later, when wind and snow had ceased, he roused the family and set the journey in motion. As they were leaving, the raggedy woman stopped in front of Cocked Hat. He was still dazed, his head lolling on his chest. Looking down at him, the woman croaked, "Devil greet thee when you pass, John Patterson, and may the Lord grant your mother, who is a decent woman, peace from the torment of the monster she spawned in you."

50

Wolfe led the little family to Boston perched atop Harelip and Cocked Hat's horses. Their worldly possessions from the barrow rode in makeshift panniers he'd constructed with more rope from Mrs. Lowry. The excursion unfolded in a lovely quietude, the world a-hush with a blanket of fresh snow and the comforting rhythm of muffled hooves.

After passing through the fort on the neck, the little caravan ambled up Orange Street to Province House. The children were thrilled by the hurly-burly of the headquarters stable yard. Their mother was intimidated. Notwithstanding the gray hair poking from under her cap, she was younger than Wolfe. Her ragged clothes were also deceiving. They'd been well-made imports at the start of their career.

Wolfe told the woman to stand by and he'd return soon. Thirty minutes later he handed her a purse with a satisfying chink to it. "The army has purchased the horses from you," he said.

"Praise be to Jehovah," the woman said in wonderment.

"Yes. Praise Jehovah," Wolfe agreed, unsure if he was bemused or insulted.

Leaving the family, he went to report to General Gage. A lieutenant said that the General was presently unavailable.

"General Gage is engaged?" Wolfe said. The lieutenant was not amused.

When he was finally summoned into Gage's presence, the General examined the materials Wolfe brought back with a professional eye and calm demeanor, although Wolfe thought the calm practiced. A blue vein at the

General's temple throbbed.

After receiving a verbal report of what transpired on the mission, Gage thanked Wolfe and asked if he thought the officers would make it back safely on their own.

"They're courageous and determined," Wolfe said, "but they're blind to the antipathy of the country and how obvious they are. I don't know what will become of them." Gage looked at him unhappily.

"If they're harmed, the war is thrust upon me. T'was a miracle no one was hurt aboard *Halifax* when they wrecked her."

"*Halifax* was wrecked? The packet?" Wolfe said. Gage nodded wearily.

"Up north. A local pilot purposely steered her aground. Fortunately, none of the crew was hurt or I'd have to send men that I cannot spare." In a different tone, one of resignation, Gage said, "They mean to have war, Mister Wolfe. A civil war that will scar this country for generations. It breaks my heart."

Gage is a decent man, Wolfe thought, *with the worst job in the world*. His opinion remained unchanged even when the General wouldn't return his pardon. Gage maintained that their arrangement wasn't settled until the officers returned. Wolfe would continue on at Province House until they did.

The next morning, Gage went off to inspect the fort on the neck. With nothing to do, Wolfe made his way up to the cupola. Free to study Boston through the telescope, the first thing he examined was an estate perched on the almost treeless Beacon Hill above the Boston Common. Dozens of children were taking advantage of the snowfall to do a little sledding on the hill. It had been a bad year for sledding. Every time it snowed, it melted right after.

The mansion on the hill was three stories of hewn stone with gardens laid out in the yard. There was a stable, a barn and a coach house on the grounds, but the house was the imposing thing. Four chimneys anchored the corners of a sloped roof with three dormers large enough to stand in. The roof was flat at the peak for a spacious widow's walk railed by white latticework. On the second floor, double French doors opened onto a balcony that was the roof of the front door portico. It was an estate in all ways worthy of a lord.

The last time Wolfe was in the cupola, the lieutenant told him it was John Hancock's place. The Faction's money man.

The sound of volley fire drew Wolfe's attention to the waterfront. At the end of a wharf next to the Long Wharf, two companies of Redcoats were shooting at barrels anchored at different distances out in the water. Unlike militias drilling in the countryside, the ministerial soldiers could afford to burn powder.

Around noon he spied Gage and his party riding back from the fort on the neck. To his relief, De Berniere and Brown were in company. Sometime later they were reunited in Gage's office.

The officers looked awful, or better actually, now that their clothes were dirty and wet-dried by fire like any provincial on the road. They'd had a rough go of it, but.

De Berniere related that the day Wolfe left them, he and Captain Brown made Marlborough at sunset, in snow over their ankles, the storm being stronger away from the coast. They walked to the tavern Jones recommended and along the way, every person on the main street came out of doors to stare at them as they passed.

Twenty minutes after arriving at the tavern, a mob started collecting outside and they were forced to flee to a house on the outskirts of town. Three hours after that they were forced to flee again by blundering through a wood in the dark. They finally found the Post Road and got back to Weston at ten-thirty that night.

Glad I missed that, Wolfe thought.

The officers expressed relief that their earlier intelligence arrived safely. De Berniere even had the quality to thank the courier. Wolfe participated in two bumpers toasting the success of the mission then offered his regrets that he must retire.

"Something about a horse," Gage said jovially. The return of the scout was the best news he'd had had in months, and said much about how desperate he was for good news.

Gage retrieved Wolfe's pardon from a locked drawer in his desk along with twenty dollars and the paper ceding Gus's ownership. Handing each of them to Wolfe, he said, "Perhaps I'll ride out one day and take a look at your animal."

"Bring your best miler and a bag of coin," Wolfe said. Gage's eyes sparkled at the prospect.

"You know the Faction banned wagering?" Gage said. Wolfe nodded. Gage shook his head. "That's the work of the Black Brigade, that is." Wolfe didn't know the expression and Gage had to explain. "The Black Brigade are country ministers who preach sedition every Sabbath along with the wrath of God. I shouldn't like to live in their world and I suspect you wouldn't either, but the rebel herd follow them like sheep." Wolfe nodded that he understood and drew himself up.

"I hope you'll forgive me sir," he said quietly, so only Gage would hear, "but you've been honorable with me so I shall not be less with you. Despite what Brown's equations say, I believe that marching to Worcester would be a very bad idea." Gage didn't reply and Wolfe took his leave.

At the Brattle stable, Gus nickered and pawed the ground in happiness when Wolfe returned. Wolfe was happy too, although he was unsure why he'd gone to such lengths to obtain a horse he wouldn't risk transporting back to London. It felt right, was the only thing he came up with. It felt like Gus was supposed to be with him. It was as simple as that. But he also had to concede that under the circumstances it made no sense. He resolved to make a present of the big stallion to Pru before he left for London. She'd appreciate and take care of him the right way.

Less demonstratively, Cuthbert was also glad to see him. He was busy pouring candles from the wax of used nubs and mixing them with grease to cheat the quantity up when Wolfe came in. Melody fixed toast and beans and the couple were happy to oblige when Wolfe asked if he might stay on a while longer.

He shaved that night. The officers might be safe back in Boston, but it was sure that men in the country would keep an eye out for the bearded man who'd been seen with the British spies.

Wolfe's life soon fell into a routine. In the morning he'd greet Gus with a treat and they'd ride. After that he'd breakfast, usually prepared by Melody, then he'd help Leonard around the stable before spending the rest of the day working with Gus unless needed elsewhere.

Occasionally Wolfe went to market with Melody. They were shunned by some folks but met with no open hostility. Indeed, many welcomed them. The Brattle larders offered treasures in bottles and sacks that were not to be had with the Faction's embargo.

Once as they walked home, Melody commented, "The people of this town are pious hypocrites. The lot of them. General Brattle did more for the people of this town, for this colony, than any man, and they repaid him with ashes." She was a slight woman with lively brown eyes and a thin-lipped, somewhat fearful smile, as if she used to smile all the time but was afraid to now. "I wish you could have seen Cambridge before the Faction ruined it," she said. "Society was so gay and genteel. People had respect for one another, from the meanest to the better sort."

The days flew by pleasantly and Gus grew stronger and smarter. He came to understand the subtle pressures of Wolfe's knees and hands, and Wolfe came to understand the nuances of Gus's ears and muscle twitches. With the help of an iron kettle and a horseshoe, Gus got used to sudden loud noises. The sound of gunfire was similarly dealt with. The stallion also learned not to be afraid of torches and bonfires, and to come when Wolfe whistled or waved although he was apt to do that anyway.

As March slipped by and men began to plow the fields, Wolfe and Gus became a familiar sight flying about the countryside. Once they rode by Loring's place in Roxbury, an impressive farm with a large and well-kept house. From the railed widow's walk on the roof, the Commodore could see Castle William and the shipping in and out of Boston. Wolfe came away from Loring's farm with a greater appreciation for how much the Commodore was sacrificing to stand with his King.

Another day, on the main road from Boston neck to Cambridge, Wolfe and Gus had to make way for the 23rd Regiment. They were tramping along to fifes and drums, getting used to marches in the countryside, getting the people used to seeing them marching in the countryside. It roused Wolfe's suspicion that Gage was getting ready to march on Worcester.

Toward the end of March, on a breezy day when clouds played hide-and-seek with the sun, Doctor Church took a holiday from the Provincial Congress—reconvened in Watertown—and drove to Cambridge in his shay to visit Wolfe. Church was sorry to hear that Wolfe hadn't found his father but he wasn't surprised. There were so many men coming and going that it was all but impossible to know where anyone was at a given time.

Over cider and Melody's tea cakes, Church told Wolfe about the most recent Boston occurrence setting the country abuzz. According to him, the commemoration of the fifth anniversary of the Bloody Massacre almost ended in a pitched battle worse than the original.

The incident took place at the Old South Meeting House, across the street from Province House. Adams and Hancock were there along with most of the Faction elite. Dozens of bored British Officers attended also. In fact, the meeting house was so crowded, the aisles so packed, Warren—who was to deliver the keynote—had to climb a ladder in a toga, his costume for the speech, and enter through a back window.

From the pulpit—shrouded in black for the occasion—in a toga, Warren delivered a polemic on the origins of American liberty going back to Roman times. The mixed audience was mostly respectful but at one point, one of the Redcoats in the front row held up a handful of bullets with the implication that they were intended for Warren and his colleagues. Without interrupting his oration, Warren came down from the pulpit and gracefully dropped a handkerchief over the offending ammunition.

"No man in attendance could but appreciate the poise Warren exhibited in that moment," Church said. "When his speech concluded, the audience rose to its feet in acclamation. Except for the Redcoats, of course. They were yelling, 'Fie! Fie!' in opposition. Alas, 'Fie' in our Boston dialect is apt to mean 'fire' and the meeting broke up in panic. Some men threw themselves out the windows!" Wolfe's laughter was only slightly less raucous than Church's.

"Wait," Church said, "it gets better. Just as the doors of the meeting house were thrown open to escape the supposed fire, the fifes and drums of the 47th Regiment started up in front of Province House across the street. Someone in our crowd yelled, 'The Lobstahs mean to attack!' and in the blink of an eye, every liberty man thought the Redcoats were coming for him!" Church shook his head. "You cannot imagine the quantity of weapons that can be concealed on a man's person, Joethan. By the time the 47th marched up, most of our crowd was armed and resolved to sell his life dearly." Church paused for effect.

"And there we stood, twenty-five feet apart; a regiment of Redcoats and every important Liberty Man in Boston. Finally, after some minutes, a British Officer walks up and says, 'Are you jolly well going to block the street all day or will you let us pass?'" Church roared with delight to remember it. "We stepped aside and the soldiers went on their way." When his laughter died away, Church was somber.

"T'were terrifying, Joethan. One little spark would have set the town aflame and neither side intending it would have made a bit of difference."

Before Church departed, Wolfe told him to beware the loyalty of the courier he'd sent with the pass for Worcester. He didn't elaborate but Church took his meaning well enough.

March rolled into April, planting began, and Cambridge came astir at the story of two spies recently chased out of Concord. The ineptitude of the spies—as Wolfe heard it—made him believe it was De Berniere and Brown. That they managed to elude capture only lowered his opinion of the provincials chasing them.

A ship landed at Salem with a rumor that orders were on the way for Gage to act against the Massachusetts rebels, particularly the ringleaders. Wolfe presumed the rumor true because within days there was an exodus of high Liberty Men from Boston. Dozens of frightened families passed through Cambridge, riding or traipsing in company with carts and drays crammed with their worldly belongings. Wolfe heard that Warren was one of the few provincial leaders to remain in town.

The tension in Cambridge grew palpable. Despite the mildest winter anyone could remember, a naturally gloomy populace was even more grim. Or maybe the men were just angry because their diversions were banned and there was no mutton to be had.

Midway through April, mounted Redcoat Patrols increased. Wolfe saw them north of Watertown, and soon after at night on the other side of the river. Gus heard them first, quivering and tilting his ears to alert Wolfe that something was acting. Seconds later, Wolfe heard the dull rumble of hooves and steered Gus into the shadow of some trees.

Up ahead, four riders, perhaps the very men Wolfe rode to Boston with, burst from a wood and pounded across an open hillside. Backlit by a three-quarter moon, their billowing cloaks made shadow wraiths that flew across the hill in their wake.

Gus whined, snorted and reared up, torn between obeying Wolfe or following his primal urge to lead the racing herd. Wolfe couldn't deny that the horsemen struck a stirring sight, although for stealth they'd made a poor choice of route. In bright moonlight they could be seen for miles.

"Perhaps they want to be seen in such light," he said to Gus, but Gus didn't get it.

Wolfe found himself missing Doctor Franklin.

51

At Brattle House they began standing watches through the night, and usually a teenaged slave named Devin patrolled the grounds, if he wanted to eat. And almost everyone went armed.

When Wolfe first suggested keeping watch, he asked if there were any weapons on the premises. By way of answer, Cuthbert showed him to a pantry in the basement. Reaching above one section of the paneled cupboard, he activated an unseen latch that released the panel to hinge open. In the empty space behind, a dozen new fusils—slightly shorter and lighter muskets carried by officers—leaned against the wall. There were also a dozen pistols of the same bore. All of the arms were British Government issue and bore the Crown stamp of the Tower of London Armory.

"General Brattle bought them for the officers of the Cambridge Militia," Cuthbert said. "Ere they were presented, he was forced to resign."

Wolfe took two pistols. Leonard took a fusil for himself and one for Devin. Cuthbert declined to go armed, saying he was more apt to hurt himself than anyone else.

A week after they started keeping watch, Wolfe was shaken awake after midnight.

"Something's afoot," Cuthbert said. He'd heard someone ride hard over the bridge from Boston and gallop right through town.

Wolfe went outside with him. After a day of on-and-off showers of fine rain, the night was clear and cold. It was also bright. The moon was all but full and full risen, but sitting oddly low on the horizon.

Leonard was outside. He reported the horses nervous. Something was in the air.

They walked out toward the common. There were others walking out too and Leonard wasn't wrong about something in the air. Every now and then when the breeze was right, they heard a bell tolling. And then they distinctly heard gunshots to the north.

Wolfe went directly to the stable and saddled Gus by the light of a lantern. He was filling a sack with feed when Leonard came in. "What's got into you?" the Scotsman said.

Cinching the feedbag to the saddle, Wolfe said, "If my father hears an alarm announcing the start of the war, I believe he'll attend. It may be my chance to find him."

The bell at the Cambridge meeting house began to ring.

Devin ran into the stable and breathlessly announced, "The Regulars is marching on Concord!"

Cuthbert and Melody drifted in, nervous and worried. Wolfe encouraged them to go to Boston but they didn't want to be abroad if the Faction was running amok. When Melody heard what Wolfe was about, she went back to the house and returned with a sack of food and a bottle of wine for his journey. She fussed over him and adjusted his neck cloth. With a final pat to his chest, she said, "God speed, Joethan. And may He that watches over us all keep thee safe."

After settling his pocket pistols in their customary places inside his coat, Wolfe thought he might have to leave the Brattle pistols behind. Leonard solved the problem by presenting him with an old pair of sheepskin-lined saddle holsters. "Don't reckon General Brattle will need these auld things nae more," he said.

After rigging the holsters and adding Brattle's pistols, Wolfe was ready to bid his friends farewell. *We've become a little family*, he thought, *like Pru's orphans*. The parting felt important. There were no tears, only the communal realization that they would all remember this night. Where they were and who they were with. Gus sensed it too, but more in the way of being anxious to get on with it.

Wolfe rode Gus over to the common where a striking scene was playing out. The Cambridge Militia was mustering under the bright moon. Women were handing out food, filling canteens from jugs, making plans where to meet if the village had to be abandoned. There were no great displays of emotion, just a pragmatic and simple faith that whatever the day wrought was in God's hands.

As Wolfe and Gus left them behind, Wolfe wished he had his Denmark back. It felt like a night for a proper hat.

They started encountering refugees a mile south of Menotomy—women lugging heavy sacks of precious belongings and fearfully shielding their children at the approach of a rider. They said Gage had sent an army. Two thousand men at least.

Menotomy village was a chaos of bobbing lanterns throwing shadows of people packing every available conveyance to flee. A few misguided souls were fortifying their houses and yards as if to fight. A Minister comforted women and children in the dooryard of his manse. As Wolfe rode by, he called, "How far ahead are the Regulars?"

Nigh on an hour.

Despite his generally positive regard for Government, Wolfe had no intent of going anywhere near the Redcoats marching out. Not dressed in civilian clothes. Not tonight. To avoid them he aimed Gus cross-country, keeping the road to his left. In the moonlight, Gus daintily picked his way through bogs, pastures and fields planted with early crops bordered by thickets and stone walls.

They overtook the Redcoats miles on, heard them marching off to the left, like a giant millipede. It was impossible to say how many they were, the narrow road forced them into a very long column, but it took the better part of an hour to keep to the shadows, ford a brook, and navigate through orchards and fields to get around and out in front of them.

Wolfe wanted to be in Concord as the militias came in from other towns.

Scattered shots were heard now and again from different directions but they weren't fighting shots. They were more in the way of alarm.

A bell came to life up ahead. Wolfe hoped that the steady clanging was from the stand-alone belfry by the meeting house in Lexington, because he used it as a guide. Off the road he had no reference points. It wasn't until Gus forded a brook downstream from a mill that Wolfe placed himself not far south of Lexington green. He made for a hill up ahead. It would be first light soon and he wanted to see what was acting on the Concord Road before he took it.

At the bottom of the hill, in thin woods, a woman jumped out brandishing a pitchfork. In addition to scaring the hell out of Wolfe, Gus shied so hard that Wolfe almost went flying off. Bent far over, he reined Gus in the direction he shied and jabbed him with his heel to keep him turning. He ducked so that his head wasn't taken off by the branch of a tree.

"I'm not a bloody soldier!" he yelled at the woman. "I mean you no harm!"

"You sound like a Britoner!" she screeched.

"Well I'm not!" Wolfe roared.

Gus started bucking in protest at being spun. Wolfe broke off the turn and steered him away. When he calmed, Wolfe dismounted and led him up the hill. They were followed by a gaggle of women and children who'd hidden at their approach.

They summited as sunlight glowed the horizon. A few hundred yards away across open country, Lexington Green manifested as a thin triangle.

The alarm bell near the meeting house ceased ringing and was replaced by a drummer beating a call to arms. In the dim dew of false dawn, militia turned out of the surrounding houses, especially Buckman's Tavern.

The provincials formed up in two lines toward the end of the green, on Wolfe's right. In front of him, the Bedford Road ran along one side of the green. On that side, civilians were milling between the back of Buckman's Tavern and his stable. People were starting to congregate along the Concord Road as well.

And a little south of the Meeting House, where the Concord and Bedford Roads merged to become the road to Boston, was an advance party of Redcoats, perhaps two hundred men. Closer to Wolfe, a Redcoat flank party was working their way across the field that he and Gus had recently traversed.

But the Concord Road above Lexington was clear.

The Redcoats in the road had fallen out and Wolfe presumed they were waiting for the main column to come up, which should leave him time to get out in front and beat them to Concord. Snapping his pocket glass closed, he mounted Gus and bade a woman standing nearby, "Good luck."

"God's will be done," the woman said.

Or Joseph Warren's, Wolfe thought, as he plunged Gus down the hill.

The ground below the hill was boggy and the going was slow. Gus was still twenty yards from the Bedford Road when three Redcoat Officers on horseback cantered around the Lexington Meeting House, closely followed by three companies of Redcoats at the quick march.

Evidently they hadn't been waiting for the main column to come up.

Wolfe brought Gus up hard.

One Redcoat company took position near the meeting house. Two companies hustled straight at the Lexington Militia on the green. According to their shorter, more practical campaign jackets and black leather caps, the Redcoats were light company men. With a start Wolfe realized that their yellow turnbacks marked them 10th Regiment. De Berniere's outfit.

In easy musket range of the militia—perhaps a hundred feet—the Redcoats deployed by company into two firing lines and began chanting the war cry of the British infantry.

"Huuzzay! Huuzzay! Huuzzay!"

In the face of the intimidating red horde, the Lexington Militia—sixty or seventy strong in two lines—began to confer. A British officer on a white horse waved a pistol and yelled at them across the intervening space. The only words Wolfe made out over the chanting infantry were, "Villains! Rebels!" but some of the militia began to retire, some toward the stone wall along the Bedford Road in front of Wolfe.

A shot went off, a pistol or small-bore fowling piece, but not a musket. A moment later another shot came from behind Buckman's Tavern.

Some coward starting trouble, Wolfe thought.

A handful of Redcoats reacted to the random shots with shots of their own, but to no effect, except to prompt some of the militia to return fire in earnest, but their accuracy was as poor as the Redcoats.

And then one of the British companies unleashed a proper volley.

That's done it, Wolfe thought.

The Redcoat volley tore into the Lexington Militia. Spectators screamed and ran for their lives, as did the Militiamen that yet could. But Redcoat bloodlust wasn't slaked. These were Betsy Loring Redcoats. The pent-up anger and hatred of their long and contentious Boston posting exploded on Lexington Green. They shot indiscriminately at every provincial they saw until the common was engulfed in roiling clouds of thick gray powder smoke. When they could no longer see, the Redcoats broke ranks and went after the fleeing provincials with bayonets, stabbing those they could catch and any that couldn't run.

And then they came for the men who'd taken up behind the stone wall.

As bullets started flying in his direction, Wolfe got Gus galloping for their lives. The big stallion thundered over the boggy ground like a mudder, splattering them both with black goo. Where the stone wall ended, they joined the road and raced toward Bedford.

Behind them on Lexington Common, a British drum started beating *Assemble.*

A quarter-mile on, Wolfe encountered three militiamen slogging out of the woods. As he pulled Gus up, a thunderous roar erupted in Lexington, what must have been every British musket firing simultaneously.

"To celebrate their great victory," the eldest of the militiamen spat. Three distinct 'Huzzays!' on the morning breeze seemed to confirm his calculation. He spit again and said to Wolfe, "You need get thee to Concord and tell what happened." Wondering if he was making a big mistake, Wolfe had him point a way that would avoid Redcoats.

The sun was barely starting to burn off the dew when he found the white stones marking a narrow path at the edge of the woods. He followed the path to a rocky lane that he took west.

Under a bright sky with few clouds, through a landscape well in bud, he rode in view of men walking alone and in groups. He saw a company of militia marching across the top of a hill miles away, and before long, from a different hill, he saw a long red snake on the road from Lexington.

Concord was a magnet drawing everyone into its thrall.

He made for a hill a mile east of the town, occupied by Minutemen it turned out, including Jonas Ledward, the young man who escorted Wolfe to Major Buttrick's house.

Maybe it was Wolfe's imagination, but as he dismounted, he sensed a crazy ambience in the air. An energy that seemed to heighten his senses as if the world was electrified.

After relating what he'd witnessed in Lexington, Jonas's captain asked Wolfe to ride into town and repeat his news to Colonel Barrett, their Commander. Wolfe agreed because he wanted to be where the rank and file militia was collecting.

As he was leaving the hill, the British column came in sight to the east, an intimidating chain of red that continued to grow until even the high-spirited Minutemen were sobered.

Wolfe wished them luck and rode out.

52

Concord was a poked beehive. Dozens of people milled about the green, meanwhile the militia was preparing to fight from a low ridge running behind the town, where the liberty pole was. Wolfe found sixty-five-year-old Colonel Barrett of the Middlesex Regiment there. He was in counsel with his subordinates including Major Buttrick.

"Reckon your father will show today?" Buttrick said in friendly greeting.

"That's why I'm here," said Wolfe.

The Concord Commanders had heard there'd been shooting in Lexington. They were anxious to know if the regulars were shooting ball. Wolfe told them that men were dead in Lexington. The Concord men were not unmoved by the news but outward expression was not their way. When Wolfe finished his report, they returned to discussing whether to stand or retreat.

Wolfe watered Gus and washed the worst of the mud off both of them. Despite all the excitement, Gus was enjoying himself. For all the miles they'd ridden he gave no appearance of being tired or winded. He'd been a hero at Lexington too, hadn't flinched at the gunfire, even the balls whistling by. They'd troubled Wolfe well enough, especially as it was his misjudgment that got them shot at.

He loaded Brattle's pistols and checked the priming in his pocket pistols.

The town felt almost deserted by the time he and Gus finished their business. The people milling on the green were gone and the main body of militia had withdrawn farther up the ridge.

Suddenly ravenously hungry, Wolfe broke out the food Melody packed. As he ate, fifes and drums announced the approach of the Minutemen he'd met earlier.

The minutemen came marching in faster than the tempo of the music would have it, but it was understandable. The van of the British column was in sight behind them, pouring relentlessly over a hill in the road, three abreast, their white cross-belts heaving like storm caps on a red wave. The swelling tattoo of their drums was as the roar of an approaching flood.

Wolfe mounted up and rode for Concord's north bridge just as the militia on the ridge decided to get out of town too. As Wolf rode by the large manse, the Reverend Billy Emerson was trying to calm a score of panicked parishioners in his yard.

Wolfe and Gus beat the retreating militia across the bridge, but not Colonel Barrett. The Middlesex Regimental Commander, in an old coat and flop hat, was already over the river and riding hard to the west when Wolfe and Gus clumped over the humpbacked wooden bridge.

Wolfe waited on the west side of the river for the Concord Militia to cross. They were led by Major Buttrick. The Major nodded to Wolfe as he paraded his men past. Assuming that incoming militias would form on those already in the field, Wolfe fell in behind.

He followed them to a hill not far past Buttrick's farm. Punkatasset, the locals called the hill, affording a clear view of Concord Town as the British column marched in unopposed.

The squealing fifes and thundering drums of the Lobstahs ceased with a flourish and the sudden silence was startling. Wolfe watched the Redcoats occupy the green, and the ridge behind the town recently inhabited by the Militia, in distant silence. The first thing the Redcoats did was cut down the liberty pole and use it to make a bonfire.

A Redcoat Light Company could be seen securing Concord's south bridge, even as seven Light Companies—perhaps two hundred men—marched the half mile from the green to the north bridge. Led by two officers, in what must have been a commandeered shay, one Redcoat Company secured the bridge, two Companies secured the upper and lower roads on the west side of the bridge, and four Companies trudged behind the shay heading west.

"If we was allowed to wager," a Militiaman called to no one in particular, "I'd wager they's goin' to Colonel Barrett's house!"

"If they find anything, someone gonna get whipped!" a man called back. The men in earshot laughed. Wolfe gleaned that Colonel Barrett hadn't been running away earlier. His farm was the hiding place for insurgent cannon.

Militiamen continued to come in from the surrounding country and Wolfe continued to lead Gus over and ask if they'd seen Nicholas Wolferd. Inevitably the answer was "Never heard of him," but Wolfe kept on asking.

There were three types of militia on the hill. Minutemen were picked men, like British Light Companies; ordinary militia were the rest of the active-age men. Alarm-listers were old men and boy auxiliaries. Women, children and dogs had come to the hill too, in ridiculous numbers. The dogs in particular were a nuisance. A few men finally took the situation in hand and led the women and children away, and as many dogs as they could wrangle.

In Concord, the Redcoats were methodically searching for military supplies. Eventually the militia got itchy watching them. After Buttrick consulted his captains, they marched in formation toward the little knoll west of Concord bridge, currently occupied by one of the British Companies guarding the road west.

Heavily outnumbered, the thirty-odd Redcoats on the knoll withdrew back to the bridge. Without the company on the knoll to protect their flank, the Redcoats guarding the lower road had no choice but to withdraw too, but they remained on the west side of the bridge in plain view.

Colonel Barrett reappeared on the upper road and rejoined his commanders. A few minutes later, the militia—numbering four or five hundred now, seemingly none of whom had ever heard of Nicholas Wolford—formed a line facing the bridge and the town beyond it.

And the commanders fell to conferring. Again.

The provincials can't take a piss without talking about it, Wolfe thought.

As he gazed on the scene, he was struck by a relative delusion. Despite not wearing uniforms, the militia drawn up on the hill looked remarkably uniform. Their everyday garb was a uniform; leather shoes, heavy gray or black stockings, the same for the color of their knee breeks. Most had flop hats and the same style homespun coats and jackets in muted colors. Shirts were mostly homespun. Waistcoats provided the only splash of color, and every man was clean shaved. Most wore their hair queued or straight, although a few of the professional men sported earlocks like Warren.

The combatants would have no trouble identifying each other.

Smoke wafted over Concord as the Redcoats started burning whatever military stores they were finding. In the provincial line, men started questioning whether the Lobstahs were going to be allowed to burn down the town—to which many other men asserted that they were not, and let their opinions be known. Loudly. In the face of growing outrage, Barrett had no choice but to order the men to charge their firelocks.

Most of the provincials were double-shotting their guns or using heavy swan shot, which by Wolfe's reckoning was the best choice under the circumstance. Many of the militia guns were not large bore military weapons and most men carried horns for powder, meaning a slower rate of fire against Redcoat cartridge. Against a better armed adversary, a light gun with swan shot or a double-shotted musket was apt to do more damage in a volley. But volleying against Redcoats was a bad plan, a lesson that had been taught all over the world.

The Concord meeting house roof caught fire. As smoke darkened the sky, militiamen on the hill became increasingly agitated. Finally, the latest conference ended and Buttrick led the men down the hill in a double file. As the militia advanced, the Redcoats lingering on the west side of the river retreated across the bridge, tossing the planks of the bridge into the river behind them.

In the first display of emotion that Wolfe saw out of Buttrick, the Major angrily waved his arms and yelled at the Redcoats to leave the planks alone or they'd be damned sorry! Wolfe found it extremely funny and wondered how Buttrick would react when the Redcoats shot at him.

At the bottom of the hill, Buttrick led the militia along the causeway toward the west end of the bridge. To contest the provincials from crossing the bridge, two companies of Redcoats clumsily formed a street-firing formation in the road on the east end of the bridge. Half the Redcoats knelt while the other half lined up behind them to fire in volleys. Another Company of Redcoats deployed along the riverbank on either side of the bridge.

As the front of the provincial line neared the west end of the bridge, the Redcoats flanked out along the river fired a few shots, and then a ragged volley. Some men in the fore of the provincial column went down, but not Major Buttrick. He called for the militia to shoot back.

Buttrick's order took three or four beats to pass down the provincial column, and then a ferocious and sustained volley thundered out. Hundreds of flat explosions almost as one.

The Redcoat street formation visibly shuddered under the storm of bullets. A moment later they broke ranks and fled in disorder toward Concord center. Their wounded comrades—those that could—hobbled after them. Some men were carried. Some lay where they fell.

Wolfe was astonished that the Regulars broke and ran so quickly. The militia was equally surprised. They stood around wondering what to do, except for one man. He ran along the side beam of the bridge all the way across, to bash in the head of a wounded Redcoat with his hatchet.

The handful of Militia casualties were reverently carried up to Buttrick's house.

Men gathered the planks of the bridge from the river to restore them while the Militia Commanders conferred. When they finished, Colonel Barrett led what was left of the militia and alarm-listers back up to the knoll. Major Buttrick took two hundred Minutemen across the bridge and followed the Redcoats toward Concord. Ultimately, they took position behind a stone wall atop a rise commanding the bridge road.

The Reverend Emerson had more distraught parishioners in the yard of his manse. The brief fight at the bridge had all but been in his yard.

Not long after, a Redcoat relief force marched from Concord Center to retake the bridge. They paused just out of range of Buttrick's Minutemen so the Redcoat commander—a fat fellow—could study Buttrick's position and consider his options. As he pondered the matter, a solitary man meandered through the open ground between the two forces.

In Wolfe's pocket glass, the fellow appeared to be mad. He talked to himself and gesticulated wildly, occasionally skipping like a child. More insane was what Wolfe witnessed ten minutes later, when the Redcoat relief force declined to test Buttrick's resolve. They retired, leaving four companies of comrades cut off on the other side of the river.

After a brief lull in activity, drums thundered to life back on the knoll, calling the resting militia and alarm-listers to form up again. The cut-off Redcoats were coming back.

The British Light Companies coming in from the west faltered when they saw farmers drawn up like soldiers where they expected to see Redcoats. And the farmers outnumbered them, and the road to the bridge took them within easy gunshot. One well-aimed volley could be devastating, which, for all they knew, was what happened to their messmates.

The Redcoat Officers reacted swiftly and ordered the quick march. Trailing arms, the light companies came on at a fast trot, one eye glued on the militia, one on their sergeant, waiting for the slightest sign from either.

Wolfe spotted De Berniere near the fore of the Redcoat column. At the closest point between the road and the militia on the knoll, the ensign removed himself from the column and took position to watch his men pass under the militia's guns.

The ensign didn't lack for courage, Wolfe thought.

Beyond the immediate proximity of the knoll, the Redcoat quick march became a ramble and then a sprint. They fled across the bridge as an undisciplined throng, past the Redcoat who'd had his head stove in, and two more dead comrades. A little farther on they ran right past Buttrick's Minutemen, who made no attempt to maul them—which they could have— nor did the Redcoats demonstrate toward the Minutemen.

There seemed to be an unspoken truce in effect, as if, perhaps, events were not yet irreconcilable.

53

At noon, in advance of the march back to Boston, Redcoat Flank Companies started sweeping the ridge behind the town. By then Wolfe and Gus were behind the ridge, loosely following militia units as they streamed across, what the locals called, The Great Meadows.

East of Concord, near a small bridge crossing a stream that cut the Concord Road, a man named Merriam had a farm. Merriam's Corner was crawling with militia when Wolfe got there. He looked unsuccessfully for his father among men from Chelmsford, Reading, Billerica and Framingham, formed by company in the fields either side of the Merriam house.

He was questioning militia in the woods across the road from the Merriam farm when two advance companies of Grenadiers swept down off the ridge onto the Concord Road. A few provincials peppered them from long range but their shots were ineffectual. As the Redcoats drew closer however, bullets began to find targets. Tired of taking fire, the Grenadiers stopped near the little bridge to deliver a volley at the provincials drawn up in Merriam's fields. Seventy or eighty British muskets flamed in precise anger but no Americans were hit.

The militia officers around Wolfe admonished their men to aim low. The advice paid off. Redcoats up and down the column crumpled and screamed as provincial muskets roared out from the fields, woods and buildings of Merriam's farm.

The provincials paused their shooting as a parade of vehicles passed by.

Anything with wheels in Concord had been commandeered and stacked with blankets and pillows to serve as ambulances for wounded Redcoats. Many of the injured wore the true scarlet coats that could only be achieved with the dye of cochineal beetle shells, the dye only an officer could afford. The militia was targeting officers. At Merriam's farm they had to make room in the vehicles for more casualties.

The firing resumed when the ambulances passed but not as committed as before. Provincials were already working their way ahead to find another spot to shoot from.

To avoid the fighting, Wolfe steered Gus in a wide loop through cultivated acres divided by orchards, field roads, and irrigation ditches.

And all around him, the landscape was alive with militia on the move.

A quarter mile ahead of the most advanced Redcoats, Wolfe steered Gus up a hill south of the road. Hundreds of Americans were gathered in a wood at the top of the hill. He went from company to company but the men from Framingham and Sudbury had no knowledge of Pap.

Wolfe and Gus rejoined the road near Brooks Tavern. A company of Bedford Militia was deployed around the yard. After establishing that they'd never heard of his father, he set off east—just as musket fire erupted from the hill he'd just left.

The van of the Redcoat column was plunging up the hill taking heavy fire as they fought the incline and the militias. The distraction was helping the main column go largely unmolested from that side of the road, but at Brooks Tavern it was a different story.

The Bedford men did good execution on the front of the British column in the road, unfortunately a Redcoat flank company charged largely unseen from the woods alongside the road and were on the Bedford men before they knew it. The tavern became the scene of desperate hand to hand combat although the outcome was never in doubt. Redcoat bayonets were simply too formidable at close quarters.

Wolfe couldn't watch the slaughter.

The road ahead dipped and curved through ravines perfect for ambuscade. Not wanting to be the victim of an accident, he steered Gus onto a field road that led to a thin wood which was to be the site of an ambush. Hundreds of provincials were lying in wait on the south side of the road. There were fewer men on the north side but more were coming in by the minute.

De Bernier's 10th of Foot led the way into the ravines and they paid for it. They were caught in a crossfire and the provincials had enough steep cover—young trees and boulders—to be obstinate when the flankers came to root them out. The one saving grace for Redcoats was that it took time for provincials to reload—using horns for powder—but that advantage was fading in the face of sheer numbers.

Wolfe estimated that Gage sent a thousand men to Concord, and they were already outnumbered. And the disparity was only growing. And it was another twelve or thirteen miles to Boston. And everywhere one looked, on both sides of the road, the country was lousy with militia. It occurred to Wolfe that if provincial numbers continued to swell, and they had enough ammunition, the Redcoats were doomed.

I'd be scared as hell if I was wearing a red coat, Wolfe thought. He wondered what Gage would think of Brown's military equations tomorrow.

Beyond the ravines, the road was bordered by rocky pasture broken by the occasional copse of trees, irrigation ditch, or stone wall. On a field road north of the main road, he traveled among new companies of militia from Bedford, Woburn and Billerica, taking positions around a farmstead. None of them had ever heard of Nicholas Wolferd.

He was two hundred yards east of the farmstead when the militia opened up on the front of the British column. Coming on at the quick march, the Redcoat formation stumbled as men in the front ranks went down and tripped up those behind. The column had outpaced their flankers and they suffered for it. The Flank Company however, coming late out of the ravine, appeared unexpectedly and once again exacted a brutal retribution on the militiamen around the farmstead.

And on it went.

On a rocky hill north of the road, another militia band waited behind granite boulders—remnants of the Lexington Company and as many more who hadn't mustered for the morning skirmish. The Lexington band exacted some measure of revenge by leaving the hillside mottled with red uniforms before they fell back, but Wolfe saw at least a few homespun bodies down too. Lexington paid twice.

And yet another hill north of the road, and south of the road a steeper, taller hill, both crawling with militia. As Royal Marines trudged into withering fire on the big hill, Wolfe thought the Redcoats couldn't have much left. It was a clear, crisp day but they'd been marching since before midnight. He didn't see how men could take much more.

They couldn't. The British column began to disintegrate. Those who could, started running. Others collapsed. Some just sat down. Men clung to the hospital vehicles or the tail of a horse, desperate not to be left behind but too exhausted to trust their own will. And all the while, from every side, provincials shot at them.

It was painful and terrible to watch, and to Wolfe's mind would soon have to end in surrender or annihilation. Either way, he was deeply shaken. Every expectation he held, as to what would happen if the regulars and provincials fought, was turned on its head.

He rode on, unsure of what to do. The prospect of finding Pap in the mayhem was laughable. The scope of the fight was far beyond anything he'd imagined. He'd been hopelessly naive.

At Lexington, the Concord Road bent southeast toward Boston—and everything changed. Beyond Lexington Green there were Redcoats blocking the road, their lines stretching all the way up to the hill Wolfe occupied at sunrise. And they had cannon.

Gage had sent a relief force.

Or more Redcoats to their death.

54

Cannon fire paused the provincial pursuit at Lexington. The British set fire to three houses that offered protection to marksman and took up positions east of Lexington Green. Then they watched in stunned disbelief as their beleaguered comrades stumbled through the lines and collapsed in exhaustion.

The provincials rested too. Under smoke-polluted blue sky, they rearmed and ate from supply wagons sent out by their respective towns, or boys come from home with sacks of food and ammunition.

Wolfe was riding from militia to militia looking for Pap when the Redcoats quit Lexington around three in the afternoon. Their column was considerably longer now. There were twice as many men including bluecoats of the Royal Artillery, and more Royal Marines.

Instead of an endless column, the relief commander, Lord Percy, reordered his line of march into three divisions to better react to diverse threats. Percy also abandoned the quick march so that his flank companies might not expend all their energy trying to stay ahead of the column.

Leaving Lexington, Wolfe paced the middle Redcoat division from a boulder strewn field. A mile below Lexington, he ran headlong into Joseph Warren. Warren was with another man, who rode off to collect militia when Warren and Wolfe came together.

"I cannot call you the cleanly man anymore," Warren said by way of greeting. Wolfe could not protest. Despite washing off in Concord, he and Gus were plenty road dirty.

"I'm glad I see you safe," Wolfe said. "Have you perchance seen my father?"

"I'm sorry to say I have not," Warren replied. "If I do, I shall bid him seek you out." Beneath an expensive cocked hat, Warren's eyes shone with fighting madness, and he too exhibited the dirt and dust of miles in the saddle. Sweat rivulets etched dirty lines on his face. It was the first time Wolfe had seen him appear anything less than neat and clean.

"Tim Bigelow will hate that he's not here," Warren said, relishing the thought. Wolfe laughed because Warren was perfectly correct.

In a voice that cut across the field, Warren called to a knot of militia, "Form upon General Heath!" He pointed to the man he rode in with, a chubby fellow who gave the appearance of anything but a soldier, let alone a General. Warren saw that assessment in Wolfe's eyes and said, "Don't let looks deceive you, Joethan. Heath's made a study of tactics. It's his plan we follow. Disperse but adhere, he calls it. We're forming a great moving noose around them."

"You mean to harry them all the way to Boston?" Wolfe said. Warren smiled with a lot of teeth.

"We don't have to. The bridge to Boston is torn up by now. They'll either lay down their arms when they can't cross the river or be destroyed."

"But either way you've got your war. Yeah?"

"That's quite a horse you've got there," Warren said, as if seeing Gus for the first time. Before Wolfe could respond, Warren had to go. They shook hands and wished each other luck. Warren rode to join General Heath. Wolfe rode to stay ahead of the fighting.

In the country between Lexington and Menotomy, small bands of mounted militia entered the fray. They rode ahead of the Redcoats as Wolfe was doing, but they dismounted to take shots at the ministerial troops whenever the opportunity presented.

Approaching Menotomy from Lexington, a wooded ridge ran along the right side of the road. On that side there were fewer houses until the ridge ended at the far end of Menotomy village.

The other side of the road was flatter, with houses continuously to

Menotomy Village and beyond. Many of the houses were occupied by provincials. An advance party of Redcoats, perhaps fifty men, were detailed to clear them out. After killing anyone defending a house, and looting what they could, they fired the house so it couldn't be used again by marksmen.

Smoke marked the Redcoat retreat.

Wolfe decided to settle at a location and let the battle pass him by, although battle was a misnomer. The fight was more of an unrelenting skirmish.

Provincials were taking position all over Menotomy when he rode through, all the way past the Medford Road, almost to Cooper's Tavern. Wolfe couldn't believe that a few die-hards were actually still drinking at Coopers. It was quiet this far ahead of the fighting but wouldn't be for long. Furious shooting was already erupting at the other end of the village.

Beyond Coopers Tavern there was swampy meadow and a pond on the right side of the road. Wolfe and Gus rode into a wood on the other side, to a spring they'd refreshed at before. As Gus drank at the spring, the crackle of musketry in Menotomy Village became constant and ferocious, seemingly incapable of rising in pitch or intensity until cannon started adding their distinctive percussion.

Free of Wolfe's settling presence on his back, Gus got a little anxious at the cacophony of noise. Wolfe took him by the halter and spoke quietly to him, face-to-face. Stroking Gus' muzzle calmed the big stallion and Wolfe was about to give him back his head, when a thrum in the air announced a cannonball had overshot its mark. Putting his forehead against Gus's, Wolfe said, "Easy my friend," but he flinched a little himself as a ball waffled overhead and blasted a small tree into splinters.

Gus shrieked and jerked his head up, bashing Wolfe's head like a forge hammer. Seconds later, Wolfe was on the ground only dimly aware that Gus was galloping away as only a terror-stricken horse can gallop—stirrups banging, reins flying. Wolfe's pistols, his stick. The pardon.

Gus.

Wolfe cursed and got unsteadily to his feet, blood dripping down his face. With a loud buzz in his ears, he stumbled to the spring and thrust his face in the water, trying to reclaim his wits. The cold water helped and eventually he untied his neck cloth and used it to staunch the blood running from his nose and inside his mouth. He was still unsteady when he set off to find Gus.

The trail was easy to follow and he dared hope to find Gus trapped in a thicket calmly grazing. It was not to be. The big stallion had crashed his own path through the woods out to the road. Wet hoofprints led toward Menotomy. When he settled the terror in his stomach, over the danger Gus was in, Wolfe muttered every curse he knew and set off in pursuit.

On the edge of the village, a band of horse militia was taking position. They hadn't seen Gus but they'd just arrived. Wolfe took a moment to check his pocket pistols, and then he warily skulked his way to the edge of the village proper.

The van of the British column was fighting its way through Menotomy. Impossibly, the unceasing roar of musket fire was growing more intense. Between burning houses and spent gunpowder, Menotomy was a deadly netherworld of thick churning smoke regularly slashed by coordinated jets of sparks as Redcoat volleys crashed out.

Regulars rampaged past the bodies of slain comrades laying grotesquely in the street and dooryards, risking death to loot anything they could, and slaying every living thing they came upon, animal or human.

Behind one house, Wolfe primed himself to risk life and limb to assault a squad of Redcoats viciously bayoneting a screaming horse. The savagery against a dumb animal was more jolting to Wolfe than the violence against men, especially until he was sure it wasn't Gus being hideously stabbed to death by British steel.

Two provincials darted from behind a house and shot at the British column from thirty paces away. A moment later they were both shot dead in their tracks. Wolfe wondered if they were drunk or just hated redcoats that much. Probably both.

Many of the yards on the flat side of the road had fences that would discourage a horse, even a frightened one. Wolfe couldn't imagine Gus—or any horse—running into the wall of smoke in the road, so he made for the other side.

The yards behind the first two houses were open but evolved up to the wooded ridge after few flat acres. In an orchard, a company of militia lay in wait behind a breastwork they'd built out of rocks and scrap wood. Wolfe snuck behind a barn, a stable, and a privy, to make his way over and ask if they'd seen Gus. Before he got there, Redcoats were suddenly everywhere in the orchard.

He watched in horror as the British Soldiers shot, bludgeoned and bayoneted the provincials in the orchard to death. He saw four militiamen threw down their muskets and surrender only to scream like dying rabbits as the redcoats stabbed them to pieces with bayonets. Wolfe distinctly saw one militiaman look down and dissolve in horror as his entrails came spilling out of his belly.

The raw savagery, so unlike the relatively benign murder of a single combat duel, shook Wolfe. He was aware of gaping open-mouthed, until a Redcoat saw him peering around a privy and yelled to his friends.

Wolfe ran like hell for the wooded ridge. Bullets buzzed past his head as he ran up into a copse of young trees and tangled underbrush, and tripped. Was tripped. By a provincial. Before he could rise, curse or fight back, a man was on top of him breathing into his ear with liquored breath. "Shut your gob or you'll get us both kilt."

Wolfe went still. The burly man rolled off and scrambled quietly up the hill to take cover behind a boulder surrounded by bushes. Wolfe followed him.

The man had long gray hair restrained by a sweat rag, and red-rimmed eyes blazing out of a face blackened with powder soot. He put a 'be quiet' finger to his stained lips and pointed down the ridge.

Redcoats were coming up into the woods.

As Wolfe took out his pocket pistols, he marked it extraordinary that amid the deafening musket fire just down the hill, he could clearly hear the footfalls of the approaching Redcoats.

He eased toward the end of the boulder to line up a shot but a hand on his shoulder stopped him. His new friend gestured to wait.

The Redcoats were twenty feet from the boulder when four or five muskets opened up from another part of the little wood. Wolfe heard lead cutting through branches, the distinct *whoomph-splat* as a ball found flesh—a grunt—a body spinning and crashing to the ground—the curses of scared men scrambling away down the ridge.

Wolfe sat back against the boulder and breathed deeply. "My thanks," he said. The man nodded. Wolfe asked him of he'd seen a horse, and described Gus. The man shook his head.

"Ain't seen one like that. C'mon. Won't do to stay here. Wait." He crabbed over and retrieved the musket and cartridge box from the fallen Redcoat. Handing them to Wolfe, he said, "Without a gun, might as well get you gone."

"I have proper pistols on my horse," Wolfe said.

"You have to be close to kill with a pistol," the man commented.

"I wasn't planning on killing anyone," Wolfe said. "I'm looking for someone. Don't suppose you know Nicholas Wolferd?"

"As it turns out I do," the man said. "What do you want with him?"

"I'm his son," Wolfe said. The man's jaw dropped.

"You're Joethan?"

55

Hearing his name from the stranger's lips was unreal to Wolfe. It was odd to the man as well. He shook his head with disbelief and stuck out his hand. "Selah Dushay." Wolfe was about to shake when shots exploded from up the ridge. Bullets ripped through the branches and foliage around them.

Redcoats were pouring down through the woods.

Dushay and Wolfe bolted down the hill together. Before reaching the bottom, they were joined by half-a-dozen other provincials who materialized out of the brush. Eight of them sprinted across the Waltham Road into meadow on the other side. The Redcoats in pursuit, perhaps forty men, crossed the road behind them and fanned out.

The closest cover near the meadow was a grove of trees. Wolfe and the fleeing militiamen ducked into it and discovered a dozen provincials were already there taking refuge, in a degree of confusion as it turned out.

On the far side of the grove, a Redcoat advance company was clearing a house. The main British column was coming down the Road, and the Flankers in the meadow were closing. Surrounded by Redcoats, the men in the grove were nervously looking for a way out, but no one was in command and there was no good option.

With a vision of the butchery he'd just witnessed in the orchard, and the knowledge that provincials couldn't take a piss without discussing it, Wolfe moved approximately to the middle of the grove and yelled, "Form a firing line at the edge of the trees!" Men looked at him askance, unsure what was happening. He pointed and bellowed, "Form a firing line at the edge of the trees!" This time the men scrambled to do as bid, grateful that someone was taking charge.

Dushay looked at Wolfe. "What now, General?"

"Two platoons," Wolfe directed. "Men to my right are number ones." He pointed. "Men to my left are number twos." He pointed the other way. "We fire one platoon at a time. Yeah?!" The men assented.

Dushay pointed behind them toward the Redcoats besieging the house on the other side of the grove. "I'll keep a weather eye on them others." Wolfe nodded but he was focused on the Redcoats eighty yards away in the meadow.

"Number ones," Wolfe yelled. "Make it count. Fire as you will!" The men to Wolfe's right all shot within five seconds of each other—to good effect. Four or five redcoats were hit including an officer.

"Number twos take aim and shoot!" Wolfe fired along with the men on his left. He had no desire to kill Redcoats but he had less desire to be shot or bayoneted. He put one of the Redcoats out of the fight. And then he was tearing off the end of a cartridge with his teeth, spitting the bitter powder residue from dry lips, opening the frizzen, powder in the pan, close the frizzen, rest of the powder down the barrel. Stuff the cartridge paper with the ball down the barrel and ram it home.

He was about to call for another volley when it was suddenly perfectly clear to him. His side would get off but one more round before the Redcoats were on them. Even if every provincial hit a target, the Redcoats would have numbers enough to kill every man in the grove with bayonets.

"Don't shoot!" Wolfe yelled. "Hold your fire! We can't stop them this way. Follow me." Not knowing if men would follow, he went to find Dushay on the other side of the grove.

The men followed.

At the edge of the trees, Dushay pointed out at Redcoats besieging a house thirty yards away. "They's only a half company and don't know we're here," he told Wolfe.

As a prelude to their bayonet charge, the flanking party in the meadow unloaded a volley into the grove. The man next to Wolfe jerked, spattering warm blood across Wolfe's face and neck. The man sank to the ground with a long sigh and moved no more.

Wolfe wiped the gore off with his sleeve and stared at it, until the reality of what would happen when the Redcoats reached the grove inserted itself into his thoughts above all others.

"We must get out of these trees or we're dead!" he yelled to the men around him. "Straight at them! Straight through them! Follow me!" He burst from the grove and ran at the Redcoats besieging the house. He wasn't happy about it, but he knew if he was caught in the trees by Redcoats with bayonets, he'd die there. The men around him must have believed the same thing because they ran with him.

The Redcoats assaulting the house goggled in surprise and fear as a score of screaming provincials suddenly appeared behind them. They turned and ran like hell for the road. Wolfe ignored them and trampled through a plot of new vegetables on his way around the back of the house. He was making for a covert at the far end of the property beyond the barn.

He reached the barn at the exact moment a half-company of Redcoats came trotting around the other side; to stand stock still twenty feet away as surprised as he was. Stomach-churning fear ignited the pain, frustration and anger that was the last year of Wolfe's life. Cursing the unfairness of it all, he threw himself into the teeth of a disorganized and panicked Redcoat volley in a crazed rage.

As the world around him exploded in primal savagery, Wolfe saw everything clearly, especially the surprise and terror on the faces of two Redcoats directly in front of him. He knocked their discharged muskets aside with his musket and launched his body sideways at them. They went down together but Wolfe was on top and rolled clear.

One of the Redcoats scrambled away. The other grabbed for Wolfe but caught the vicious impact of Wolfe's musket butt in the face instead. The man was whimpering as Wolfe came to his knees.

Dushay was grappling with a Redcoat, holding the soldier's musket off with his left arm while his right stabbed the man repeatedly under the ribs with a dirk. Wolfe almost vomited. He knew exactly how that felt.

Ten feet away, one of the men following Wolfe out of the grove was on his back, his hands grasped around a Redcoat bayonet as he desperately struggled to keep it from piercing his chest, bug-eyed with certainty that he was about to die.

Wolfe blew the Redcoat sideways with the bullet in his musket.

In his periphery, a British officer slashed down with a sword. Wolfe barely got the musket up in time to block the stroke meant to kill him—delivered by none other than Captain William Brown. Fate, or some twisted cosmic joke, had run Wolfe smack into the 52nd. Not many months ago, some of these men put their lives at risk to protect him from the Boston mob.

Brown's sword slashed down again.

A musket was heavier and more awkward than a staff, but not fatally so. Wolfe intercepted Brown's blade with his musket held crosswise, rose to his feet and savagely shoved Brown away from him. Their eyes met and in that moment, Wolfe saw Brown realize who his adversary was.

Brown's recognition was replaced at once by a murderous snarl. He stepped back, drew a pistol from the bucket holster slung over his shoulder and without hesitation, cocked the pistol with his sword hand, aimed and pulled the trigger.

The flint sparked but the pistol hung fire … a heartbeat after a sharp *spark*, *boom*! exploded from Wolfe's pocket pistol. As Wolfe's bullet struck home, Brown lurched with an audible oomph and blood started spewing promiscuously from his mouth. The captain looked at Wolfe reproachfully for a second, and then his eyes went dull and he collapsed.

"C'mon!" Dushay shoved Wolfe toward the covert. Together they grabbed the arms of the man Wolfe saved from being bayoneted—still laying where he'd almost died—and dragged him.

They ran to the culvert and slid into a long ravine behind the brush, gasping like blown horses. The men they'd charged with were doing the same. Being a good piece of natural cover, there were other provincials there too.

"We must reload," Wolfe said to Dushay. He called down the line of men, "Reload! Pass the word to reload."

The man they dragged rolled over. His blouse and hands were bloody, his face scorched by the muzzle flash of a musket, but Wolfe recognized Harelip at once; the man he'd beaten up with Cocked-Hat. Wolfe shook his head in disbelief. Harelip was uneasy too. His "Thankee" was almost a whisper.

"If I knew 'twas you," said Wolfe, "I would have let that Redcoat kill you." Dushay looked on curiously but said nothing. Wolfe felt around his own face and realized that the rank smell of burned hair was his own.

Warren came crabbing down the ravine in high excitement. "I saw that!" he bubbled at Wolfe. "T'was the maddest thing!" He gave Harelip a clap on the shoulder and jerked a thumb at Wolfe. "He saved your life." Harelip nodded. Warren turned to Wolfe and grasped his chin, angled it up to the sunlight to see more clearly.

"You've got powder burns on your face. And blood. Were you hit?" Wolfe shook his head. "You're fortunate not to be blind," Warren said. "Your eyebrows are half gone but I dare say they'll grow back. The dermis isn't blistered or raw, that's good. Wash your face carefully. Diluted vinegar will sting but if you can find some use it. I fear you have powder lodged in your cheek. Just there." He touched Wolfe's left cheek. "I doubt it harm you other than cosmetic." Warren straightened Wolfe's chin so they were face-to-face and he was looking Wolfe in the eye.

"You recognize that you've declared yourself, right?"

"I've declared myself?" Wolfe said. Warren was dead serious.

"If the Crown lays hands on you, Joethan, you'll hang. The penalty for killing a Redcoat is death. You killed an officer in plain view. You can't flit from camp to camp anymore and you can't go back to London. Not if you value your life."

Bile rose in Wolfe's throat. He swallowed sour to keep it down. Warren was right. Killing a Redcoat was a death sentence. What in bloody hell had he done? What was he thinking?

He wasn't thinking. He was trying to stay alive. He was trying to find Gus.

Bullets spattered the covert. One knocked out the pin holding one of Warren's earlocks. A roll of blond hair uncurled and drooped down the side of his face. Barely caring, Wolfe said, "There's a flank party chasing us." Warren nodded but he was preoccupied with the dead earlock. If the bullet had been a fraction closer, he'd be dead.

"Perhaps we ought withdraw," Warren said soberly.

Nearly three dozen provincials followed Warren to where he'd left his horse. As he mounted, he turned to Wolfe and said, "Where is your horse?" Wolfe's disgusted look elicited a big laugh. "So now you seek your father and your horse? And you shot a Redcoat Captain in full view of all to see." He shook his head. "This really hasn't been your day, Joethan."

"Pay him no mind," Dushay growled. "If you're alive when the sun sets, it been your day." In substance Wolfe agreed with him, but with Gus missing and Pap as yet unfound, Wolfe could not resent Warren for smirking. He took it good naturedly and bid Warren luck, then he and Dushay set off back toward Menotomy.

Caught up in the terrible reality that he'd ruined his life, it was a while before Wolfe noticed Harelip trailing behind. When he did notice, itching to focus his anger on something tangible, he seized upon Harelip.

"What in bloody hell do you want?!" he snarled. Harelip backed away.

"I an't attached to a company. Don't know where to go." He was younger than Wolfe thought, probably still in his teens.

"What's your name?" Wolfe said.

"Billy Chalke. William Chalke, sir."

Dushay said, "You best find a gun, William Chalke."

"Not if he's anywhere near me," Wolfe said. Dushay squinted at him.

"Whatever's between you, man got a right to defend himself."

"That's precisely what I'm doing," Wolfe said. Dushay put his hand on Wolfe's shoulder.

"His face is powder flashed same as you"

Wolfe sighed loudly. Selah Dushay had a bit of Doctor Franklin in him.

After avoiding the third wave of Redcoat Flankers by looping around them, they arrived on the outskirts of Menotomy in time to watch the tail end of the last British Column depart the village. Royal Marines had the rearguard now, with militia pressing them hard on three sides. The Marines were hopscotching lines backward while delivering regular, concentrated volley fire, precisely executing the maneuver and reloading under an unrelenting hail of lead.

"That's professional soldiering," Dushay said in admiration.

When the Marines were gone, Wolfe and Dushay walked out onto the road. Chalke followed behind, gaping in amazement. Wolfe couldn't fault him for that. They were passing through a scene of unimaginable destruction.

Flames from burning houses pierced the thick layer of smoke smothering the village. The air was sodden with burning wood, burnt gunpowder and blood. The stench of blood overpowered everything. Bodies were awkwardly strewn across the landscape like discarded dolls—Redcoat, provincial, animal. Mercifully Gus was not among the mutilated horses that Wolfe saw.

Dushay found a canteen. After slaking his thirst, he passed it over. Wolfe was savoring cider as good as any he could remember when Chalke showed up with a musket and cartridge box. "T'ain't charged," he said timidly, opening the frizzen for Wolfe to see. Wolfe grudgingly handed him the canteen.

On the Lexington Road beyond Menotomy, Dushay spotted a man he knew sitting on the side of the road with other wounded men, including Redcoats. With a gait that proclaimed him a sailorman, Dushay ran to his friend and cried, "What happened Tom?"

"I'm glad I see you alive," his friend said. "We feared you was dead."

"What happened?" Dushay said. Tom looked down at the blood-soaked rag wrapped around his wounded calf.

"Caught a bullet. Now I'm gonna lose my damn leg," he half sobbed. Dushay looked closely at the location of his friend's wound.

"Did it hit bone?"

"Don't know but it took a big bite."

I reckon you won't be running soon," Dushay said. "But you might not lose the leg. Where are the others?"

"Last I saw'em was at a farm down the road." Tom described a location a mile on toward Lexington. They talked for a few more minutes before Dushay promised to send a cart if he saw one, and handed Tom a flask. The last they saw of Tom, he was sharing Dushay's flask with a Redcoat sitting next to him.

Not far down the road, they came upon two wagons collecting wounded. Dushay urged them to get to Menotomy as fast as can.

Two dead Redcoats lay next to a well in the front yard of the farmhouse they were looking for. On the side of the house, half-a-dozen men clustered around a spreading oak. A grievously wounded man was sitting propped up with his back against the trunk of the tree. Blood and mucus oozed from his mouth.

Dushay's face went pale. Handing Wolfe his gun, he went to the wounded man, took his hand and spoke privately to him until he passed, which was not long. Muttering sorrow and regret, the little troop came together and prayed.

Wolfe paid his respects from the periphery. He could be no part of the fight these men shared. This moment was theirs only, just as he and Dushay would always be bound by the fight they shared.

After praying, the men surrounded Dushay, relieved to see him. They'd been separated shortly after joining the fight and feared the worst.

When eyes turned to Wolfe, Dushay said, "This here's a new friend o' miun." He nudged the man next to him. "Says he knows you. He goes by the name Joethan."

Wolfe's mouth gaped open as he realized he was looking at his father.

56

Pap was shockingly older. His once brown hair was gray on its way to white. The face, desiccated and polished by salt and sun, was a weathered caricature of the face Wolfe remembered. But under the shabby clothes and three-day stubble, he still had the smile with the black tooth on the bottom, and the green eyes and dimpled chin he'd bequeathed to his son.

After many long moments staring at Wolfe in disbelief, Nicholas Wolferd's first words were, "What in bloody hell are you doing here?"

"Delighted to see you too," Wolfe said. "I've been searching for you is what I'm doing. All over bloody New England. Where in bloody hell have you been?"

"Medford," Pap said. He was confused when Wolfe laughed out of all proportion to any humor that might have been conveyed, which there wasn't any. Pap couldn't have known that his son was laughing at the absurdity of his own life.

Pap had been five miles away.

Father and son walked south with the other men—Boston sailors beached by the port closure, Wolfe learned—itching to get back in the fight. All the action they'd experienced was defending the house where their friend died.

"I'll ask again," Pap said. "What are you doing here?" Wolfe thrust out his chin.

"I got a letter said you'd been taken up."

"And you meant to save me?" Pap snorted as if the thought was ridiculous. Wolfe bristled.

"As a matter of fact, I did. I've sought you for months." His father grimaced in a way that Wolfe remembered clearly.

"Well you found me," Pap said. "Now what?" To Wolfe's disgust and embarrassment, he had no answer. In truth, the entire purpose of his trip was moot and had been for some time. Pap was free and in no danger other than that of his own making. Besides which, Wolfe didn't even have the pardon. It was in his coat which was rolled up on the back of the saddle on Gus's back. Gus who was missing.

Thinking of Gus gutted the elation Wolfe felt at finding his father.

Menotomy Village was coming back to life as they walked through. Noncombatants were reappearing, and with fresh militias from the far reaches of the countryside, forming bucket brigades to fight the fires.

At Cooper's Tavern a terrible scene was unfolding. The horribly maimed bodies of civilians were being carried outside. Innocent victims of Redcoat rage it was said. Wolfe presumed the victims were the same men drinking at the tavern earlier. He did a double take when he realized that one of them was Patterson—Cocked Hat. Wolfe hadn't recognized the road agent at once because he was drenched in blood, his body having been obscenely mutilated by bayonets.

Chalke stared at the corpse of his recent partner for a few seconds, met Wolfe's interested gaze, shifted his musket and walked on.

On the outskirts of Cambridge they heard that the Redcoats had turned away from the bridge over the Charles River and were making for Charlestown. In view of the news, Pap and his friends agreed there was no sense trying to catch up to the fight. It would be dark before too long.

"We best find moorings for tonight," Dushay said.

"I know a place." Wolfe led the way through the bedlam and pandemonium on Cambridge Common, now a staging ground and field hospital. Although he'd left Brattle House less than twenty-four hours ago, the world had turned upside down in his absence.

Certainly his world had.

Militia yet to blacken their faces with powder were all over Brattle House, except for the stable. Around the stable they were hunkered down. The

Captain of the unblooded militia reported that there was an old man with a gun. Wolfe told the Captain to wait, and walked into the stable yard.

"Mr. Leonard!" Wolfe called. "'Tis Wolfe. Do you require assistance?"

"What do ye think!" Leonard squawked from inside. Wolfe turned and addressed the Militia Captain.

"This is Mister Leonard's domain. On this day of all days, you have no more right to violate his home than Redcoats have to violate yours. If that isn't reason enough to leave off, know you that I and my friends will defend him." It was not lost on the Militia Captain that Wolfe's friends were a hard looking lot who'd obviously been fighting already.

"He got horses in there," the Captain said. "We 'as told to find horses."

"And if strangers came to take your horses, you'd just hand them over?" Wolfe said. The Captain didn't answer. "If horses are needed arrangements can be made," Wolfe said. "But done proper with a warrant and a receipt. Elsewise a horse thief is a horse thief. Yeah?" The Captain conceded the point and withdrew his men.

Wolfe called Leonard outside but it was Devin who swung the door open. "I want to see what actin'," he said, and sprinted off. Leonard limped out behind him looking exhausted.

"When Gus come in, I figured was you alive you'd tarn up. But we 'as runnin' outta time, so we was." Wolfe didn't hear a word after Gus.

The stallion whinnied loudly and nuzzled Wolfe like a puppy when they were reunited. "I feared the worst," Wolfe said when Leonard joined them. "'T'was like to break my heart."

"Came in hours ago with this stickin' out his flank." Leonard handed Wolfe a ten-inch shard of splintered wood. "He bled a wee bit but he all right."

Wolfe examined the injury for himself and had to agree. The wound wasn't bad but it was no great mystery why Gus bolted. He told Leonard how it happened as he brushed Gus down.

Eventually he noticed his kit in a corner of the stall—coat, pistols, tumpline, even his stick. It was hard to accept that he'd been lucky, but he had been. In his present circumstance, having Gus well and his few possessions intact was no small thing.

In truth, it was everything.

Pap and his friends lit a fire in the stable yard. Leonard broke out a hank of mutton. The smell of it cooking put a smile on Wolfe's face. Finally, an act of rebellion he could agree with.

When the burble of humans on Cambridge Common was as the drone of cicadas, yet still blessedly quiet compared to the noise of the day, he left Gus and joined the others around the fire. As he sat down, he dropped the pardon in his father's lap.

"What's this?" Pap said.

"See for yourself."

Pap untied the ferret, rolled out the parchment, and angled it to the fire. After reading but a moment, he scowled. "I need no pardon from the damn King!" He would have tossed the parchment in the fire but Wolfe stayed his wrist with the iron grip of a swordsman.

"After what I've been through to hand that to you, I'll break your bloody arm before I see you burn it." They glared at each other but Pap didn't test Wolfe's resolve. Instead he laid the pardon aside to take a long pull from a jug being passed.

"I require no pardon to live as a free man," he croaked.

"Were you always an ungrateful bastard?" Wolfe said. His father laughed and Wolfe's green eyes flashed in anger. "That pardon would've rescued you from slavery in the Islands. I'll leave you rot next time." His father handed him the jug.

"Calm yourself boy. I don't care about your pardon but 'tis damned glad I am to see you. To tell true, I thought you'd come home years ago."

"You told me not to come back if I didn't finish school," Wolfe said. Pap stared at him in disbelief.

"Of the few times in your life you chose to obey me, that's one? Good god boy, I half expected when you got to England you'd come about and sail straight home to America. Then I'd have kept my word and you'd have been where you belong. That what I'd 'a done."

"So 'tis my fault," Wolfe said. "I should've known." The silence that followed spoke eloquently of the time and tides separating them.

Eventually Pap picked up the pardon and examined it. "This must 'a set you back a cargo or two."

"Most of eight years savings." Wolfe's tone was bitter enough that Pap tossed the pardon at him.

"I didn't ask you for it. Keep it. Might be you can recover some of your investment. There'll be plenty men looking to purchase insurance against the future after today. Can't do better than a King's pardon."

Wolfe was tempted to imagine that the pardon could be as wondrous as General Gage had said. *But for the killer of a King's Officer, that might be a stretch,* he thought. He was proud of the pun but unable to enjoy it. It hit a little too close to home.

"With that pardon you can go back home to Setauket and no man can say a word against," he told Pap. "Qua's getting old. He's lonely. Though that might be over with. I left a boy with him." Pap's face lit up.

"You was in Setauket?" He made Wolfe tell him everything.

A pouch was passed around. Pipes were filled.

Chalke said, "What happens now?"

"Damned if I know," Dushay said.

Leonard told Wolfe that Cuthbert and Melody went to Boston. Wolfe was glad of it. Cambridge was no place for Tories now.

After they ate, thunder, lightning and cold rain tore the skies apart and drove them into the stable. By the time the storm passed, Wolfe was the only one awake.

Reliving what he'd seen and what he'd done.

He went out into a chilly, clear night. The water in the rain barrel was shockingly cold but felt good on the scorched skin of his face.

When he lay down again he was physically, mentally, and emotionally spent. But his brain would not rest. His life had profoundly and irrevocably changed in the course of the afternoon.

The Doctor would be glad for the way things turned. So would Pru, but damn, fourteen years on and he was back where he started.

Only worse.

Bloody hell.

Notes

The Redcoats completed their march to Charlestown at sunset. Wounded and exhausted, their evacuation across the Charles River to Boston went long into the night. It would be hard to imagine men enduring a more punishing mental and physical challenge than the Regulars did on the Lexington Road. The words "post-traumatic stress" come immediately to mind. Just two months later, some of the same men would be asked to endure even worse.

There were ninety-four American casualties along the battle road. The British listed two hundred seventy-two killed, wounded and missing—more than one-sixth of their combined force, and a great number of them officers. It might have been worse but for Lord Percy. Percy was a general at age thirty-two. On the retreat from Lexington he proved that he deserved to be.

Those versed in pre-Revolution American history will note that two of the historical events portrayed in Captain Sedition do not occur on the precise dates that they actually took place. For that I beg indulgence. I've sought to be as accurate to the historical timeline as possible but in the end, Captain Sedition is a tale and my aim was to tell it in the context of some less widely known incidents on the eve of the war.

Had Colonel Leslie been as arrogant as many of his British colleagues, the war would have started in Salem. If Gage had marched to Worcester to protect the court when it sat, the shooting would have started in 1774. For the sake of the tale I manipulated the date of the incident at Salem bridge and the dates of the recon scout to Worcester—not by much, but I'm honor bound to say so.

Dr. William Hewson died in May 1774 of septicemia, perhaps contracted from one of his dissections. I chose to keep the good doctor alive for another year.

Probably the most egregious liberty I've taken is with the Brattle house, especially in my invention of the people to staff it.

One of Joseph Warren's hairpins was shot out during the British retreat to Boston.

Commodore Loring was forced from his Roxbury farm prior to the outbreak of violence, but in actuality he moved to Castle William, not Boston. His son's family—Betsy's family—moved to Boston right after Lexington and Concord. Betsy was, and is, fated to become an infamous woman of consequence. Indeed, Elizabeth Loring will prove to be one of the two most intriguing women of the American Revolution.

Captain William Brown did perish on the road to Boston but how is unknown to me. If my fictional explanation gives offense, I humbly apologize to him, his descendants, and to His Majesty's 52nd of Foot. I mean no disrespect—but by Ensign De Berniere's own report, the British officers were as oblivious as I portrayed. Details such as the officers being identified by a tavern girl at the first place they stopped, or traipsing off to "map" Worcester at night come right from De Berniere.

The liberty I took with De Berniere and Brown's adventure was substituting Wolfe for the enlisted man / valet who actually accompanied them. According to De Berniere, this batman—officer's valet—was the most capable man on the scout to Worcester.

John the batman was the inspiration for Wolfe, whose saga will continue in, *A Relative Delusion.*

Acknowledgements

First and foremost, I have to thank my wife Joan for everything but especially her daily inspiration and wisdom. She was also among those who slogged through early drafts of this manuscript despite the grammatical obstacles placed in her path. Thank you honey.

I deeply thank the aforementioned wife of gold, and my sisters, Jody and Randy, and Bill Brown, Steve Kluger, Peter Crabbe and Elaine Smith, for the generous gift of their time and input. Thank you all. I hope that you recognize your feedback in the finished pages, but even if you do not, I assure you it's there.

Thanks to the Three Village Historical Society in East Setauket, New York. Archivist Karen Martin was generous and thoughtful, providing an early map that I didn't know existed, as well as pointing me to other resources. Thank you, Karen.

Three Village Historical Society docent, Mary Leming, on short notice, provided a wonderful tour of the Sherwood Jayne farm that was immensely helpful and appreciated. Thank you, Mary.

Thank you, Carolyn Haley, for your equine expertise.
And thank you for reading Captain Sedition.
I'm always grateful for a brief review or rating on Amazon.

Cheers,
K C

The Author

K. C. stands for Kerry Christopher. Some time ago my career as a singer-songwriter morphed into writing fiction. My first novel, The Expedition, was released in 2009. Since then—evidently in need of an adventure—my wife and I moved from the west coast of the U.S. to the east coast.

The rebellion that founded the United States has been of compelling interest to me since boyhood. In fact, the more I learn about the first American civil war, the less surprised I am at how crazy American politics are today. For me, the true miracle of these United States is that it still works at all.

For more information and some images of places and people referenced in this story, please visit *kerryfusaro.net*

48499898R00195